Evil Never Dies

S. M. HARDY

Allison & Busby Limited
11 Wardour Mews
London W1F 8AN
allisonandbusby.com

First published in Great Britain by Allison & Busby in 2020.

A CIP catalogue record for this book is available from the British Library.

First Edition

ISBN 978-0-7490-2565-6

Typeset in 11/16 pt Sabon LT Pro by
Allison & Busby Ltd

The paper used for this Allison & Busby publication
has been produced from trees that have been legally sourced
from well-managed and credibly certified forests.

Printed and bound by
CPI Group (UK) Ltd, Croydon, CR0 4YY

To the big guy
my cousin Tony

CHAPTER ONE

Emma found me in the conservatory nursing a glass of good malt and contemplating the intricacies of life. Looking out over the brightly coloured and sweet-smelling flower beds, watching the birds and other wildlife scampering across the freshly mown lawns revitalised my soul. It was a haven of peace and calm and, given half the chance, this bright and airy room would be where I'd spend the majority of my time. For one thing it was a place where the dead appeared to keep their distance.

'Ah, there you are,' she said, stooping to press a soft kiss against my cheek. She smelt so damn good; I could breathe in her scent all day long and then some. She looked pretty fantastic too. She had let her blonde hair grow a little longer than she used to wear it; still cut in soft layers it now curled down below the collar of her cream jacket.

'How was the committee meeting?'

She pulled a face. 'Tedious, as usual.' I gave a non-committal grunt; she knew what I thought about her committee meetings. 'I was going to ask if you wanted a drink, but I see you already have one.'

I folded the letter I'd been pondering and stuffed it back inside its envelope.

'Bad news?' she asked.

'Hmm. Couldn't get much worse, I suppose.'

I ignored her expectant look and took a gulp of whisky as she sank down into the chair opposite me. When I wasn't forthcoming she raised an eyebrow.

'Are you going to elaborate?'

'It's from an old friend. He wants us to go and visit him.'

Seeing my no doubt glum expression she laid her hand on mine. I wrapped my fingers around hers, instantly feeling a lot better than I had a right to.

'We should go. It would do you good to meet up with one of your old friends.'

'I'm not so sure it would; not at the moment.'

She leant forward. 'Why?'

My hand went to my beard, a nervous habit of mine, then, realising what I was doing, I let it drop back into my lap. 'His brother has just died.' I kept my eyes on my drink.

'That's sad. Had he been ill?'

I grasped the glass a little tighter. 'No, not as far as I'm aware.'

'Oh dear. It was sudden?'

I took a quick peek at her face and knew I couldn't put off telling her without being subjected to the third degree. 'Yes – he was murdered.'

She blinked and stared at me for a moment, as if making her mind up whether I was joking or not. 'Really?'

I shrugged and went back to my drink.

'Jed Cummings, you can't drop something like that into a conversation and not explain it,' she said, pulling her hand from mine.

'I can't tell you something I don't know,' I said, I thought quite reasonably.

She made a huffing sound. 'Then tell me what you do know.' With a sigh of defeat, I pushed the letter my old friend Simon had sent me across the table. She turned the ivory envelope over in her fingers. 'Nice stationery,' she commented, running her forefinger over the embossed coat of arms on the flap, before flicking it open to slip out the letter.

She carefully unfolded the two sheets of paper and spread them out on the table before delving into her jacket pocket for her glasses. Once perched on her nose she began to read.

Leaning back in my seat I watched her face. By the time she'd reached the second page her expression was full of sympathy.

'How terrible,' she said, returning the letter into the envelope and sliding it back across the table to me. 'Did you know his brother Oliver?'

I shoved the letter in my pocket. 'I met him on a couple of occasions. I stayed at Kingsmead several times when Simon and I were home on leave together.'

'So you were good friends with Simon?'

I nodded, feeling a little guilty. We'd been best mates at one time; him, me and Reggie. If I dropped this last bit of information into the pot, I knew exactly what would happen: if Emma had any idea her late husband was one of the three amigos, our bags would be packed by the morning.

'We sort of lost touch once we left the forces,' I told her. There was more to it, but it had been many years ago and best forgotten.

'Perhaps this would be a good opportunity to reacquaint yourselves.'

I doubted it would. Then I started to think about all the good times we'd had, and we did have a lot of them. We were young, we were reckless and we thought we could rule the world. Maybe Emms was right. He had offered an olive branch and perhaps I should accept it.

'It would do you good. It would do us both good to get away,' she pushed.

I gave a morose laugh. 'To visit a crime scene? You really think?'

'You'd be helping out a friend in need.'

Knocking back the last of my drink I said, 'I don't do that sort of thing any more.'

'And you miss it.'

I slowly shook my head. 'No, I don't.'

She very sensibly kept any thoughts she might have on the subject to herself, instead asking, 'Do you want another?'

I contemplated my empty glass. 'Maybe just the one,' I replied.

With a smile she took my glass into the next room and, while I waited for her to return, I thought about Simon and how fond he'd been of Oliver. They had grown close when they'd lost their elder brother, Edward. From memory Oliver had been a couple of years younger, but there had been a full ten years or more between him and Simon. He hadn't talked about it much, but from what I remembered Edward had died in a freak accident and the family had never been the same afterwards. On one occasion, when Simon was in his cups, he'd told me that after Edward's death it had been like living in a mausoleum – hence Simon joining the forces as soon as he could.

'Well?' Emma asked, when she returned with the drinks.

'What?'

'Are you going to call your friend and say we'll be coming?'

I thought about it a moment longer. We wouldn't be meeting again under the happiest of circumstances, but if we were ever to make amends, now was probably the time, neither of us were getting any younger. 'All right,' I said.

'Really?' she said, with a surprised smile.

'Yes, really. Just for a few days.'

She didn't argue. She'd won the battle. She'd concentrate on winning her never-ending war to get me to go away on a proper holiday upon our return. I didn't mind; she kept me on my toes.

Simon had been uncharacteristically grateful when I called to tell him we'd be on our way for the weekend and it brought me up short. Had he changed so much? Had I also changed into a man he would barely recognise? Maybe this *was* a mistake.

Emma brushed aside my concerns. 'The poor man is probably still reeling from the shock of losing his brother,' she said as she packed my suitcase. 'Besides you *both* will have changed. How long ago was it since you last saw him?'

I sat down on the bed beside the suitcase. 'Do we really need all this for two or three days?'

'Yes,' she said, slapping my hand away when I reached into the case to check what she'd packed for me.

I knew when to give in and went back to trying to remember when Simon and I had parted company. 'It must have been twenty-five years or more,' I said.

She gave me a sideways look. 'Did he and Reggie know each other?'

'Hmm,' I said and decided now we were going to Kingsmead I might as well tell her – it was bound to come out over the course of the next few days, anyway. 'They did, but towards the end they didn't get on.'

'Really?' she said with a frown. 'Why ever not?'

'You know what toffs are like.'

'Reggie was not a toff.'

That made me laugh. 'Yes, he bloody was. Simon and him were both old school tie. Why Reggie ever chose to be friends with me I have no idea.'

She stopped what she was doing to look at me. 'Because you were both good men, perhaps?' Emma's smile had returned. I knew she would always love Reggie, but I didn't mind as long as there was a little bit left for me. 'And if I recall rightly, you spent your formative years at a rather good boarding school.'

'Huh, it was no Eton or Gordonstoun.'

'Still . . .'

Grabbing her hand, I pulled her towards me. Standing above me, her knees touching the bed between my legs, she began to laugh before leaning forward and, cupping my cheek, planted a kiss on my lips.

'I am not, and never will be, a member of the "Old Boys' Club",' I grumbled.

'And I wouldn't want you to be any different to the man you are.' She stroked my cheek, her eyes sparkling, and any concerns I had about our forthcoming trip melted away. There would be time enough to worry in the morning.

CHAPTER TWO

'Good Lord,' Emma muttered as the Jaguar rumbled to a halt outside the six-foot-high electric gates blocking our entry into Kingsmead. 'They certainly take their security seriously.'

'Not seriously enough, judging by recent events,' I said, winding down my window to announce our arrival into the intercom at the side of the gate. A disinterested voice took my name and the gates began to slowly swing open.

'Was it like this when you were here last?' she asked.

Gazing up at the razor wire strung out across the top of the ten-foot-high brick walls I gave a grunt. 'More or less. I seem to recall Simon saying sometime, way back when, one of the Pomeroys was a politician and we all know how popular they are. I believe they used to have Dobermanns running around the grounds at night.'

'Not now?' Emma said, peering through the gates.

Emma loved dogs, I'm surprised she never had one, but even she would draw the line at a pack of Dobes. Or perhaps not – knowing her I wouldn't be surprised if she had them rolling over to have their tummies tickled within five minutes of meeting them.

'Fortunately not.' As I guessed, her expression was slightly disappointed.

I put the Jaguar into gear and rolled forward through the still-opening gates and onto the drive, the gravel crunching beneath the tyres as we rumbled along.

'When you said Kingsmead was a country estate, I didn't for one minute think it would be so huge.'

'It's smaller than Reggie's family pile.'

Emma shifted in her seat, leaning back and folding her arms. 'I only went there once and it was dark.'

I glanced her way and could have bitten my tongue. Her lips were pressed into a thin line, and I'm sure if I could have looked more closely her eyes would have been sparkling with unshed tears.

Reggie's family, for some incomprehensible reason, had disapproved of his choice of wife and, when they told him to choose between them and her, he chose Emma. Out of all his siblings he was the only one to have had a happy marriage, and this alone should have vindicated his decision, but his family never forgave him and not one of them attended his funeral. This had hurt Emma more than anything they might have ever said about her.

We carried on along the tree-flanked drive, meandering through vast expanses of manicured lawns. I had left the window open and the scent of freshly mown grass filled the car. Last time I'd been here there'd been a team of gardeners keeping the grounds in check. I doubted this had changed much throughout the years, though the motorised lawnmowers had probably become more efficient.

Then we reached the brow of the gentle upward slope and there, spread out below us, was Kingsmead Manor. I drew the Jag to a halt so Emma could get the full effect.

She actually gasped. 'My God, it's massive.'

It was impressive. I had forgotten how huge the H-shaped building was, and the woodland beyond the fields behind it, a mass of relentless green disappearing into the distance for as far as the eye could see.

We started down the slope. It was too late to turn back now, and I had a moment of stomach-fluttering disquiet. We hadn't even reached the building and I was already experiencing the tingling sensation at the back of my neck I usually get when someone from beyond the veil wants to make themselves known. I hunched my shoulders, ignoring it, and concentrated on the driveway ahead.

Out front of the house I swung the Jag in next to a blue Mercedes convertible parked close to a low, ornate stone pillar wall separating the drive from more lush lawns as smooth and green as any snooker table.

'Well,' I said, 'we're here.'

'Do you think they dress for dinner?' Emma asked, peering out at the steps leading to the front door.

I frowned at her. 'What?'

'I packed you a suit, but—'

'Emms, he's just lost his brother – the last thing he'll be thinking of is dinner parties.'

She took a deep breath. 'I suppose you're right.'

I took her hand in mine. 'Emma, you have wined and dined dukes and duchesses and heads of state, why are you getting in a panic over this?'

16

She exhaled – slowly. 'I know I'm being stupid.'

'Err, yes. If anyone's going to muck up it'll be me, so stop stressing.' She laughed and leant in to kiss me on the cheek. 'Come on,' I said, 'let's get this over with.'

I slid out of the car and, by the time I'd crunched my way across the gravel to open the passenger door, Emma was already pushing it closed behind her. I hefted the cases from the boot and, as I slammed down the lid, a blonde, floppy-haired young man, in white shirt and black trousers, came hurrying down the steps to take them from me. His smile was a little tentative and nervous. I guessed he hadn't worked here long and, judging from his fading acne, was probably not a lot older than seventeen. He gestured we go first and followed us up the marble steps to the front entrance.

A tall, grey-haired woman stood in the doorway waiting. Dressed in a black, calf-length dress with a bunch of keys hanging from her belt she was the epitome of the country estate housekeeper.

'Mr and Mrs Cummings,' she said, greeting us with a convivial smile. 'How nice to meet you. Please come in. I'm Sarah Walters and if I can help you with anything during your visit please don't hesitate to ask.' She stepped back. 'This way, if you please. I'm afraid Mr Simon has been caught up on the phone.'

She led us through the spacious entrance hall, the echo of Emma's heels clicking on the white, grey and black veined marble tiles making it as welcoming as a mausoleum and I had to hold in a shudder. I remembered it as being carpeted, and fragranced by vase upon vase of colourful, scented flowers sitting upon small tables around the periphery of the hallway. No flowers today, only the aroma of lavender furniture polish. Looking around there was plenty of wood to be kept shiny; the small tables remained, and huge chestnut-coloured banisters swept from the centre of the hall to the first floor. It was weird and almost as though the hall had been drained of any colour or life in the twenty-five or so years since I'd last crossed the threshold. It *was* a house in mourning, though I somehow doubted it had been any different in the years prior to Oliver's death.

This place was full of ghosts. Always had been and it hadn't got any better. I had an inkling it had probably got a lot worse. The first time I'd visited I'd hardly slept the first couple of nights, there had been so many of them vying for my attention. By the last time I'd been invited to stay I'd apparently become boring. By the tickle at the top of my spine I guessed their interest had been renewed.

Mrs Walters showed us into a room I remembered as being the study. My memory wasn't failing me and the room had changed hardly at all; it was still a clutter of old books, hunting memorabilia and sagging leather chairs. The same couldn't be said for my old friend. I hoped the shock didn't show in my expression. I forced a smile onto my face as he ended his phone call and hurried around the desk, a candle-wax-hued hand outstretched to greet me.

'Jed,' he said. 'It's so good to see you again.' He pumped my hand, his fingers icy in mine, and unexpectedly pulled me into a hug. After a second's hesitation I wrapped my arms around him and had I not been concerned about his health before I certainly was after his bony frame pressed against mine. Beneath his jacket he was all sharp, jutting angles with hardly any flesh cushioning his body. He pulled away from me. 'You've hardly changed at all.'

I managed a laugh. 'I know that's not true,' I told him.

His attention turned to Emma. His smile was genuine and bright. 'And you must be Emma,' he said and took her hand, raising it to his lips to kiss it. '*Enchanté*.'

'It's lovely to meet you, Simon,' Emma said, 'and I'm only sorry it's not under better circumstances.'

He grimaced, deep lines etching his forehead and, with his sallow and waxy complexion, I could have been looking at the death mask of a man decades older. 'Yes, it hasn't been easy.' Then he snapped into host mode. 'Come, I'll show you to your room. It'll give you the chance to settle in before dinner.' He glanced at his watch. 'Shall we meet for pre-dinner drinks at say, seven? Jed, you remember where the sitting room is?'

Our bedroom was on the first floor and at the back of the house, giving us a panoramic view of the gardens, fields and the forest of trees behind them. As soon as we were alone, Emma made straight for the French windows and the balcony outside.

'This is beautiful.'

I stood in the centre of the room taking it all in. 'I prefer The Grange.'

She glanced back at me over her shoulder and laughed. 'Only because there's less lawn to mow.'

'Hmm.' I slowly turned full circle. There was a large fireplace with a pile of logs stacked decoratively to one side and I could imagine, with a fire roaring away in the winter months, it would make the room warm and cosy. On a bright, spring day the room was dreary and a bit like the master bedrooms on show to the public in the many stately homes scattered around the countryside. I was surprised there wasn't a protective plastic sheet over the Persian carpet.

Vellum yellow wallpaper, decorated with blue and green birds interspersed with twisted vines, no doubt created by one of the masters of design in the Arts and Crafts period, covered the walls. All credit to whoever put it up, it must have been a bugger to hang and get the pattern aligned. Antique furnishings littered the room and I made a mental note of where anything vaguely breakable was located, so when I stumbled around half-asleep in the morning I knew where to avoid.

The bed was a four-poster and very nice too – if you were five foot five or so. The frame *was* beautifully carved and swathed with colourful tapestries. Some might find it romantic – to me it was just an impractical dust trap. But if anyone had ever died in this room they had moved on – and for this reason alone I'd put up with a cramped night's sleep.

'A four-poster bed,' Emma said, coming over to link her arm through mine. 'How lovely.' Then she began to laugh. I made a humphing sound, which made her laugh even more. 'It's only for a few nights.'

'Just as well.'

'We'll have to snuggle,' she said, with a naughty grin.

I sucked in air through my teeth and followed it with a dramatic sigh. 'I guess it'll be a sacrifice, but to help an old friend . . .' She thumped me on the shoulder and then she was in my arms and the cramped bed instantly became a lot more inviting.

*   *   *

Dinner was excellent and surprisingly the conversation flowed. So much so it could have been only a few months since Simon and I last broke bread together. It was as it had been before and I wished we hadn't left it so long, mainly because I was pretty sure Simon was dying. It wasn't only how he looked. There was what I can only describe as an aura around him: a dark grey, writhing mist gradually deepening to black at the extremities. If nothing else this made me determined to help him if I could. A man shouldn't die without knowing who had killed a loved one and why.

It wasn't until we had finished dinner and retired to the living room for after-dinner drinks that he got to the point of our visit.

'I am really grateful to you for coming,' he said, handing me a glass of good whisky.

I settled into the corner of the leather Chesterfield settee, slightly at an angle so my knee was practically touching Emma's. 'What happened?' I asked him. 'You said Oliver had been murdered, but not much else.'

He slumped back in his matching high-backed chair, his expression pained, his eyes wet and rheumy. I hadn't noticed before, I'd been so shocked by his fragility, but his once-cornflower-blue eyes had faded to a clouded opaque.

'It was nearly a month ago and, as I said in my letter, the police are getting nowhere and . . . I just need to know. I need to understand why.' His voice broke and he turned his head away for a moment while he fought to control his emotions.

Emma gave me a helpless glance. I wasn't much better; I didn't know what to do either.

'I'm sorry,' he said.

'Don't worry,' Emma replied, her voice gentle and tinged with sympathy. 'It's quite understandable. His death is still raw.'

He nodded, raising the crystal tumbler to his lips. His hand was trembling.

'Where did it happen?' I asked.

Simon swallowed and, cradling the glass on his knee, sagged into his chair. 'Here. Here on the estate.'

'Not in the house,' I said, and it wasn't a question. Many things had happened in Kingsmead, I sensed terrible things, but not this.

'No,' he agreed. 'Not in the house. In the woodland at the back.' He pushed himself out of his chair. 'I'll only be a moment.'

Emma leant forward. 'Can you feel anything?' she whispered.

'No, not anything connected to Oliver's death, anyhow.'

'This house has its own vibe,' she said and shivered.

'You feel it?' I asked. Emma was by no means as psychic as I am, but she did sometimes sense things, sometimes things I didn't.

She took a sip of her drink and gave an abrupt bob of the head.

'Are you OK?' I asked.

She gave me a shaky smile. 'I think so. It's just . . .' She didn't get to finish what she was about to say as Simon returned, bringing with him a Manila file.

'Here,' he said, handing it to me. 'Don't read it now; it'll give you nightmares. The morning will be soon enough.'

I held the file on my lap for a moment and rested my

22

hand on the cover. The unease I'd felt as we approached the house swept over me. I was sure he was right; the contents of the file were the stuff of bad dreams and night chills. I dropped it on the settee between Emma and me. I would read it by the light of day.

'Why did you fall out?' Emma asked as she took off her earrings and dropped them into a small crystal dish on the bedside table.

I pulled off my shirt and padded towards the bathroom. 'Water under the bridge, Emms. It was such a long time ago.'

'It must have been serious.'

I grunted in reply and shut the bathroom door, hoping she'd take the hint. It was something I didn't want to talk about. I was here now, when he needed me. It'd have to be enough.

She was sitting in bed, a pillow plumped behind her, when I came back out, glasses perched on the end of her nose as she pored over her latest read. I stripped off and slipped beneath the sheets beside her.

'I packed pyjamas,' she said, not looking away from the page.

'I can see,' I said, running a finger down the sleeve of the silky, lilac pyjama jacket she was wearing and I had never seen before.

'What if there's a fire?'

'I would do the same as I would back at home – run from the house stark bollock naked.'

She gave me a sideways look. 'I really believe you would.'

I grinned at her. 'It would give the fire brigade a laugh if nothing else.'

She dumped the book on the bedside table and folded her glasses, dropping them on top. 'You are the limit,' she said with a laugh and flicked off her light. 'Goodnight, Jed.'

I clicked off mine and snuggled down under the covers to give her a kiss on the forehead. 'Goodnight, sweetheart,' I whispered and wrapped my arms around her.

CHAPTER THREE

We had agreed to meet with Simon for breakfast at eight-thirty. We made it by a whisker, having overslept. I felt a bit guilty, as I hadn't had a chance to look at the file he'd given me, but was let off the hook when during breakfast he received a phone call, which had him apologising and saying he had an unexpected meeting with his solicitor.

'Make yourselves at home,' he said, wiping his lips with his snow-white napkin. 'It's a nice day – go for a walk around the grounds or use the swimming pool. Jed, you know where everything is.'

'Swimming pool?' I said. 'I don't remember a swimming pool.'

He dropped the napkin on the table. 'Of course not – I was forgetting. Oliver had it put in about fifteen years ago. It's in a conservatory off the west wing.' He got to his feet. 'I'll see you later. If not before, lunch is at one.'

'Great,' I said and, with a smile, he was gone.

'A swimming pool,' Emma said. 'I wish I'd brought a costume.'

'I'm sure your underwear will do.'

'Hmm. I don't s'pose there'll be anyone else around.'

'We could always skinny-dip.'

She raised an eyebrow at me. 'Typical man.'

'Just a suggestion.'

'Come on, shall we take a look?' she said.

I threw down my napkin. 'Why not? Maybe there's somewhere local where we can go and get you a costume if you fancy a dip.'

We found the poolroom without too much trouble. You could hardly miss it, it was bloody enormous. When Simon had said a conservatory, I was expecting a glass and white UPVC lean-to tucked on the corner of the building. In reality, it stretched across the whole end of the wing and was a glass and dark green wrought iron, decorative structure, which wouldn't have been out of place in Kew Gardens.

The inside, I imagined, would hold its own against the mightiest of hotel poolrooms. It had somehow been integrated into the back of the original building rather than being added on. Consequently the grey-and-black-veined white marble flooring, covering the whole ground floor of the house, continued into the room to surround the pool and the line of changing rooms stretched along the inner back wall, together with an open showering area for a quick washdown before and after your dip. There was even a fully stocked bar.

Several white wrought iron tables and chairs were

scattered around the pool area together with white-painted wicker sunloungers and matching drinks tables.

'My goodness,' Emma said when we reached the edge of the pool. 'This is stunning.'

It wasn't the expression I would have used; once again a feeling of disquiet flowed over me. The interior of the pool had been tiled completely in a very dark blue, which gave no perspective at all of its depth and, for anyone brave enough to try diving into it, would give the impression of throwing oneself into a bottomless void. I shivered. Nothing on earth would get me into the pool.

'A very unusual choice of colour,' Emma said.

'Hmm. Shall we take a walk around the gardens?' I said, wanting to get away from the place as soon as possible. There was something unwholesome about the room and it had set my nerves a-jangling. And when I looked into the pool, a growing sense of dread rose from the pit of my stomach. I could sense something was there – just below the surface – watching me.

Emma linked her arm through mine as we left and it was on the tip of my tongue to say something about the pool but, as she hadn't a costume with her, I thought why bother? I did make a mental note to scupper any mention of the possibility of a visit to town to get her one. I didn't want her going anywhere near the pool, especially on her own.

About three-quarters of an hour before lunch we went back to our bedroom to freshen up. I also wanted to spend some time looking at the file Simon had given me – after all, its contents included details of Oliver's death and this was the reason we were here.

While Emma washed and changed and did all those time-consuming things women do, I sat out on the balcony in the sunshine with the file. With a dyspeptic feeling in my gut I flicked it open. I wasn't sure what I expected to find inside, but it certainly wasn't a copy of the police report. I quickly riffled through the pages and yes, it was a copy of an official police file.

'Typical bloody Simon,' I muttered under my breath.

By the time I'd worked my way through and reached the end, the disquiet I'd been feeling, from almost as soon as we'd arrived, had grown into full-blown anxiety. I should never have brought Emma here.

She appeared through the door on a waft of Chanel to sit beside me. 'Interesting?' she asked.

'Horrifying, more like,' I muttered.

She put her hand on my wrist. 'What's the matter?'

Shutting the file, I tapped the front cover. 'This is a copy of the official police report, forensics, photos, witness statements, the lot.'

She frowned at me. 'Is it usual for the victim's family to have a copy?'

'Nooo. It could cause all sorts of problems should someone be charged and it go to court.'

'How do you think Simon got hold of it?'

I stared down at the file. 'I have no idea,' I said. I was lying – I had a very good idea how Simon had got his hands on it and I could feel all the old resentment creeping back. He hadn't changed. I'd been a fool to believe he had.

'Can I take a look?'

'Better you don't,' I said with a grimace. 'There're some very gruesome pictures. In fact, it's all pretty grisly stuff.'

'Then tell me.'

I slumped back in my chair and she took hold of my hand. 'Oliver was quite literally slaughtered. There's no other word for it.' I needed a drink and I really hoped there'd be some with lunch. 'He was so badly disfigured by his wounds he was identified by his signet ring and a tattoo he had on his left shoulder.'

'That's terrible.'

'The pathologist said he had never before in all his years seen such a vicious and sustained attack.' I squeezed her hand. 'I'm beginning to think maybe I should do what Simon wants and then we should get ourselves away from here.'

She put her palm against my cheek. 'Jed, you never run away from anything. Never have and never will.'

'That's where you're wrong. If I'm putting us in danger by being here, I will run as far away as it takes to make us safe again.'

'No, darling. You're not thinking about "us", you're worrying about me.'

I gave a sort of half-shrug. The woman could read me like a book. 'If something happened to you . . .'

She stroked my cheek. 'Nothing is going to happen to me.'

'You don't know that. Who would have thought— ?' I stopped mid sentence, I didn't need to go on, she knew exactly what I was talking about.

'*That* is all in the past and I know I'm perfectly safe if you have anything to do with it. Now, let's go down and have a nice lunch with Simon and see if we can help him with his problem,' she said, getting to her feet.

I grabbed her as she went to go inside and wrapped my arms around her. 'I love you,' I murmured against her hair. It was funny, she meant so much to me, but I still had trouble spitting out the words.

'I know,' she whispered.

Simon wasn't alone in the sitting room. 'Jed, Emma,' he said upon seeing us come in, 'let me introduce you to Brandon Fredericks, my old friend and the family legal advisor.'

The solicitor must have been well past retirement age. A big, rotund man who, judging by his ruddy cheeks and bulbous nose, clearly enjoyed the better things in life. He was dressed for business, in navy suit and waistcoat, white shirt and navy tie; he even had a gold fob watch and chain stretched across his ample belly. For all that, he had a genuinely friendly smile and a twinkle in his eye, making it easy to take an instant liking to him.

'How nice to meet you at last,' he said, pumping my hand. 'Simon has told me so much about you.'

'Jed and I go back a long way,' Simon chirped in. 'Can I get you both a drink?'

While Simon sorted out a VAT for Emma and a whisky for me, we made small talk for a few minutes; about the usual sort of thing, where are you from, how long have you lived there?

'Simon told me you're some sort of clairvoyant,' Brandon said.

Emma cast me a worried look. I didn't take offence, Brandon's expression was interested, not disparaging.

'Yes,' I said.

30

'I went to a spiritualist once,' he said. 'What she said . . . Well, in retrospect, it was probably what she told all bereaved clients.'

I smiled sympathetically; there were a lot of frauds out there preying upon the vulnerable and I despised them. What they did was mercenary and cruel. 'Sadly, that's most likely true. Unfortunately, it's not always easy to know who's the real deal or who's a fake. I tell people true psychics shouldn't charge, other than for expenses if, say, they have to travel to see a client and so forth. If they ask for money – well, I'd avoid them like the plague.'

'You don't charge a fee?' he was surprised.

'Nope. It would be immoral. What I have is a gift. Whether it comes from a higher being or not' – I shrugged – 'I couldn't tell you, but I don't believe I should profit from it.'

Simon handed us our drinks. 'Did you have a good morning?'

'Yes, thank you,' Emma said. 'We took a walk around your lovely gardens and had a look at the swimming pool; it's beautiful.'

'It is rather spectacular,' he said, 'though not for the faint-hearted. There's no shallow end and it's over six feet deep all the way across.'

'That's a bit unusual, isn't it?' she asked.

Simon laughed. 'That was Oliver for you. He never did things the way other people did.' He paused, his smile all but disappearing. 'Maybe it's what got him killed.'

'It was most strange,' Brandon said. 'It was almost as though he knew his time was limited.'

'How do you mean?' I asked.

'A week before he died he changed his will, and was adamant it was done immediately.'

'A coincidence, surely?' Simon said. 'He must have been meaning to do it for ages. He'd been split from that dreadful woman for at least five years.' He glanced my way. 'Oliver married a totally unsuitable young woman about ten years or so ago,' he explained. 'It didn't last very long and they eventually separated. Of course, he never got around to divorcing her or changing his will. You know what it's like, we all think we're going to live for ever.'

'He must have had a premonition, then,' Brandon said, 'and a good thing too – if he hadn't, she would have inherited the lot.'

'What? All this?' Emma said.

Brandon nodded sagely. 'His stocks, his shares, this estate, everything.'

It made me wonder: men had been murdered for less. 'Could she contest it?' I asked.

Brandon's smile was wolfish. 'She could try, but Oliver had me tie it up so tight she'd never see a penny, even if she took it to the highest court in the land.'

'Brandon has tried tracing her, just to let her know about Ollie,' Simon said.

'It's a waste of time, really,' Brandon said. 'Oliver told me the last he'd heard of Carla she'd joined some weird cult and was living in a commune in Texas.'

I was surprised, not so much that she'd debunked to a commune, but that she couldn't be found. Simon could find anyone he wanted if he put his mind to it, I was quite sure. I didn't get the chance to voice this opinion as we were called in for lunch.

Brandon was good company and a witty raconteur, having us all in stitches throughout the meal. Simon was enjoying himself; he had even gained a little colour to his cheeks and it was good to see.

When Brandon was leaving he drew me slightly away from the others. 'I'm glad you and Simon have put aside your differences,' he said. 'I can hardly believe the change in him. You being here has worked wonders.'

'I'm not sure why.'

He beamed at me. 'We all need friends, Jed, and I think at the moment Simon needs you,' and with that he went off to say his goodbyes to Emma and Simon and was on his way.

'Did you read the file?' Simon asked. We had adjourned to the courtyard at the back of the house outside the poolroom, to finish our drinks in the sunshine.

'Yes,' I said and hesitated, wondering quite how I could ask the obvious.

Emma had no such hang-ups. 'How did you get a copy of the police report?'

Simon shifted in his chair a mite uncomfortably. 'I have a contact,' he said, after a pause long enough to make me think he knew what my reaction would be. I passed no comment, just gave him a long, hard stare. He grew a little flustered. 'I had to do something, damn it. The police weren't telling me what was going on, or even doing anything, as far as I could see. I have to know why it happened, Jed. I have to know who killed my brother.'

I took a swig of my drink. I did understand, but it didn't mean I had to like it.

'Will you try and contact him?' Simon asked, a plea for help if ever I heard one and making it difficult to refuse, despite my promise to myself never to deliberately seek out the dead again.

I thought about it for a bit. If I did as he asked I couldn't do it in the house: holding a seance in Kingsmead would open the floodgates to a whole load of trouble.

'Can you take me to where he died?'

Simon gave a short, sharp bob of the head. I took a deep breath; this was probably a mistake, but it was what I was here for. 'All right.' I glanced at my watch. 'Give me half an hour to change.'

'Us,' Emma said. 'Give *us* half an hour.'

I was about to argue, but one look at her told me I'd be wasting my breath. 'Give us half an hour.'

'You'll need sturdy shoes or boots,' he said. 'It's a bit of a walk.'

We agreed to meet in the courtyard. Emma and I arrived first, dressed for a five-mile hike. Fortunately, she had brought our walking gear with us on the off-chance we might go exploring across the estate. Emma likes her walks and since we married had coerced me into joining her whenever she set off on one of her jaunts. Consequently, I was the fittest I'd been for years.

We stood there, her arm through mine, looking out across the gardens and fields to the woods beyond. The sky was blue with hardly a cloud in the sky, and it was already the warmest spring we'd had for many a year. Of course, the fanatics were screaming global warming. It was probably just as well they hadn't been about in the summer

34

of '76: I'd hate to think what they'd have made of the four or so months of no rain and constant sunshine.

'It's quite a trek to make to murder someone,' Emma said, her hand shading her eyes as she peered into the distance. It was, and she had a point. 'He was battered to death?'

Following her gaze, I squinted against the sun. 'It was worse than that, Emms. After the beating he'd been stabbed multiple times and possibly with multiple, but identical, weapons.'

Her head whipped around so she was facing me. 'You mean it could be he was killed by more than one person?'

I blew out through pursed lips. 'The forensic pathology report was inconclusive; there were so many wounds, but it said there were a couple that could have been made by a left-handed assailant.'

'So possibly two people? Or more?'

'Possibly.'

Emma hung onto my arm and moved a little closer. 'That's horrible.'

I looked back at the forest of trees. It *was* a long walk to commit murder. Why not kill him in the gardens or fields? Unless they wanted his body to remain hidden, though if this was the case it hadn't worked. The report reckoned he hadn't been dead more than twelve hours when he'd been found.

There was a thud of boots on stone behind us and when I glanced around Simon was hurrying towards us with a tall, mousey-haired chap walking along beside him in long, easy strides. Dressed in an olive tweed jacket, beige trousers, shirt, brown boots and cheese-cutter cap I guessed he was the estate manager or gamekeeper. He was about my age and looked vaguely familiar. I supposed it was possible he'd been a stable hand when I last visited and had worked his way upwards. It was usually the way of such things in these country estates.

'Jed, Emma, this is Donald Walters, he manages the grounds.'

'Nice to meet you, Mr and Mrs Cummings.'

'It was Donald who found Oliver.'

'How terrible, it must have been dreadful for you,' Emma said.

The groundskeeper grimaced. 'It was pretty grim,' he agreed.

I glanced at Simon. 'Are you sure you want to come? It's a long walk.'

He hesitated long enough for me to know he was thinking the same thing.

'I could take us in the Land Rover, Mr Pomeroy,' Donald suggested.

'Maybe it would be for the best,' Simon said. 'I haven't been in the best of health recently.'

Donald gave a bob of the head. 'I won't be a tick,' he said and headed off towards the stables and garages.

'Do you still keep horses?' I asked.

Simon tore his eyes away from Donald's back. 'Oh yes, though only three now. Ollie sold the others last year. It was a shame, but they weren't getting ridden as much as they should and it was taking a lot of Donald's time exercising them. If you fancy going for a trot, feel free. Donald will be happy for another chore being taken off his hands.'

'I haven't ridden for years,' Emma said, her tone wistful. 'I used to go with Reggie, but when he took sick . . .'

'I was sorry to hear about Reggie,' Simon said, but I knew he was only being polite. The last time the two of them had spoken, their final words to each other had been beyond vitriolic and I'd had to step between them. Less than two years later Simon and I had parted on similar terms, so I suppose this must say something. I pushed it from my mind – there was no point going over old scores, they would only make me angry and neither of us needed it right now.

After a few minutes, with the growl of an engine and the rumble of tyres, a battered khaki-coloured Land Rover swung into the courtyard with Donald at the wheel. He ground to a halt directly in front of us and hopped out to open the front passenger door for Simon and the back doors for Emma and me.

It was a typical working country estate vehicle. The inside smelling of diesel and straw and the back seats scuffed and sagging. We all bundled in and, as soon as we'd settled, Donald stuck his foot down and we roared out of the yard and along a track leading past the gardens and lawn and onto the fields.

It was a bumpy ride. A couple of weeks with very little rain had turned the ground rock-solid and it was pretty unforgiving on the spine as we bounced along. Several times my head brushed the inside of the roof as we were thrown up and down and from side to side while Donald expertly manoeuvred the vehicle along the rutted and cratered track. He did have to stop a couple of times to negotiate gates, which I jumped out to open and close for him, otherwise it was full pelt ahead and only when the track entered the treeline did he slow to a more leisurely pace. I think it was then we all lost our smiles – I certainly did.

Inside the woodland the temperature plummeted and it grew dark and, to my mind, foreboding. I felt Emma shiver against me, and I wondered whether she was experiencing the same sense of unease. The back of my neck began to tingle and I was aware of a presence on the periphery of my psyche.

The Land Rover slowed and rolled to a halt. 'We'll have to go the rest of the way on foot, I'm afraid,' Donald said, glancing at us over his shoulder.

We all piled out of the car into the small clearing. Although the track continued on through the trees it had narrowed to a path, which was just about wide enough for us to walk two abreast. Simon and Donald went ahead, with us following behind and Emma clinging onto my arm.

We exchanged a look and she whispered, 'I don't like it here.'

I would have said it was because she knew something terrible had happened in this place; I knew differently – we could both feel the prevalent evil. And it was quiet, too damned quiet, the only sound being the crunch of leaf litter beneath our feet and the creak of the occasional branch above us. There was no birdsong, no sound of creatures scampering away from us through the vegetation, nothing. It was like we were in a bubble, cocooned from the outside world.

After about ten minutes, during which I found myself

getting edgier and edgier, we walked into a large, circular clearing, so round it made me wonder whether it had been deliberately cleared of trees and vegetation at some time in the past. I didn't need telling this was the place. Donald's grim expression and the presence waiting on the edge of my consciousness conveyed the message quite eloquently – and the fluttering remnants of blue and white police crime scene tape strung out between the trees.

'It was here,' Donald said, pointing to a spot slap bang in the middle of the clearing.

I walked to the centre, turned full circle taking in the other narrow paths leading off in various directions and the tall pines surrounding us, then stopped and closed my eyes.

Sometimes I have to ask for the dead to speak to me. On this occasion I didn't get the chance; he hit me like a sledgehammer. I think I gasped. I heard Emma ask if I was all right and then in my head I was running – running for my life.

My heart pounded, my chest wheezed and I could taste blood. My nose was broken and one eye was swollen shut, making it hard to see. From behind me I could hear whooping and jeering as my shoes skidded and slipped on the rain-soaked grass.

Desperation flooded through me. Then straight ahead the woodland loomed against the night sky, the trees towering, gaunt grey ghosts in the moonlight. If I could make it through and out the other side I might stand a chance.

The shouting behind me was getting ever closer as I stumbled on; slipping, sliding, falling then dragging myself to my feet. I could feel the rain against my face. I could feel the mud beneath my feet.

I staggered into the forest and behind me there was a roar of frustration. They were close, but not close enough. I thrashed through the vegetation, brambles tearing at my flesh, my clothes, my hair. Panic drove me on. My chest was on fire and my side burned with pain.

Then I was in a clearing. And I fell to my knees as the realisation hit me that they had me where they had wanted me all along. I couldn't afford for them to find me here. I struggled to stand.

A light flared. I could hardly see through the rain and my blood and tears. Cloudy, ghostly figures closed in around me, their blurred faces obliterated by masks. Hands grabbed me, holding me tight. Fingers gripped my chin, forcing my head back as another pinched my nose. A knife rose and fell, a blast of terrible pain and I was choking. Then I was surrounded and more blades rained down on me, slashing and hacking and turning my body on fire. As I slipped to the ground a face loomed over me. Ruby-red lips smiling and laughing as she reached towards my face, fingers splayed, thumbs pointing inwards towards my eyes. Then everything blurred and turned to blood as the real agony began and I couldn't even beg, I couldn't even scream, I could only hope I would die and die soon. It was a blessed relief when my pounding heart finally slowed and then stuttered to a standstill, my life slipped away and everything went black, as I descended into oblivion.

'Jed, Jed. Are you all right?' As the mist spiralled away the voice grew louder and clearer.

'Emma?'

'Thank God,' and then I was being held.

I opened my eyes and I was kneeling with both Simon and Donald crouched down in front of me, anxious expressions clouding their faces while Emma hugged me so tight I thought my ribs might break.

'Emms,' I managed to gasp, 'I think you can let go of me now.'

CHAPTER FOUR

Emma wanted us to go back with Simon and Donald in the Land Rover, but I needed to clear my head – and think about what I had seen. I had never had an experience like it before and my mind was reeling with all the images and emotions whirling around inside it.

'You go back,' I told Simon.

'What did you see? Did Ollie speak to you?' he asked.

I closed my eyes for a moment. The presence was still there – it was almost like he was waiting for something, but I wasn't sure what.

'I need to get my thoughts in order. I'll speak with you when we get back,' and I gave a sideways glance at Donald. Simon took the hint. It wasn't something we should be discussing in front of the groundskeeper. 'You go with Donald. Emms and I will make the most of this glorious afternoon and walk back.'

He gave me a tight-lipped nod and started off along the track to the Land Rover.

'I can come back for you a bit later if you want,' Donald said quietly to me.

'Thank you, but I really could do with a walk.'

With a smile, he tipped his cap to me, then Emma, and followed after Simon. We stood there watching them until they were out of sight and I relaxed a mite.

'So?' Emma said. 'What happened?'

I shook my head. 'I have no bloody idea. I've never had an experience like it before. In fact, I've never heard of anything like it happening to anyone, other than—' I stopped, not wanting to go there.

Emma stroked my cheek with her knuckles. 'Are you all right?'

I took her fingers in mine and kissed the back of her hand.

'I'm fine.' She didn't appear convinced, but didn't push it. 'Come on,' she said. 'Shall we start heading back?'

'Uh-uh – I want to take a look around here first.'

Her brow crinkled into a frown. 'What for?'

'I haven't the foggiest. But Oliver was killed here for a reason. He was deliberately herded to this place.'

Her frown grew deeper. 'Herded? By whom?'

'I don't know; all I can tell you is there was a pack of them.'

'You *are* joking? You said there might have been more than one – but a pack?'

I grimaced. 'I wouldn't joke about something like this,' I told her. 'It was like I was seeing it through Oliver's eyes and living it through his body. He was hunted down, like an animal.'

'And you've never had anything like this happen before?' she said, biting her lip.

'There's no need to worry,' I told her.

She sniffed. 'Of course not, why would there be? You tell me you experienced something similar to a friend of ours before he . . .' She took a deep breath. 'I don't even want to think about it'

'I saw a vision, Emms. Not dead people walking around like he did.' She dipped her head. 'Emma,' I said and wrapped my arms around her, pulling her to me. She kept her chin down. 'Look at me.' She gave a little shake of her head. I put my fingers under her chin and raised her head so I could see her face. Her eyes were full of tears. This was not my rock-steady, strong Emma. 'Hey, what are these for?' I asked, wiping a teardrop away with the pad of my thumb.

She gave a sniff and lowered her eyes away from mine. 'Most people aren't lucky enough to find one good man, let alone two. I don't want to lose you as well.'

'You're not going to lose me. I'm not going anywhere – at least not without you.' She managed a weak smile, though I could tell she wasn't convinced. 'Let's take a look around and see if we can find anything the police might have missed.' She nodded and I gave her a quick peck on the cheek before letting her go. 'You start here and I'll start over there,' I said, pointing across to the other side of the clearing, 'and we can meet in the middle.'

I began to scuff the leaves away with the edge of my boot. It had been pouring with rain in my vision so the area would have been a whole mess of footprints, though if there had been a mention of this in the report I'd seen, I'd missed it. I supposed if it had continued

44

raining like it had been for the whole twelve hours after
Oliver had died it could have washed most of them
away, or made it difficult to tell whether the footprints
were new or old.

Beneath the leaf litter the mud was still thick and
sticky in places. It was a churned mess and there was no
real evidence of anything other than the ground having
been trampled at some point when it had been very wet.
I carried on scraping, gradually working around my side
of the perimeter and towards the centre. Occasionally
I would glance Emma's way to see how she was doing.
She was taking playing detective very seriously, an
expression of determined concentration etched upon
her lovely face. I watched her for a minute – even
scrabbling amongst leaves and mud she managed to
appear graceful – and for the millionth time I wondered
what she saw in me.

She hesitated a moment, frowning, and crouched
down at the far edge of the clearing where the earth was
less disturbed.

'Found something?'

'I'm . . . No, not really. Just some strange prints.' I
wandered over and dropped down beside her. 'Look,' she
said, pointing. 'What are they, do you think?'

I peered at the imprints in the soil. 'Some kind of hoofed
animal,' I said.

'They're pretty big.'

'Well, they're cloven, so not a horse. A cow, perhaps?'

'How would a cow get in here? I haven't seen any cattle
on the estate, have you?'

She was right. Unless things had changed a lot over

the years the Pomeroys had never been into farming. Maybe a hundred years or so ago, but not recently. 'A neighbour's maybe?' I said, standing before my knees seized up. 'Interesting, but not evidence left by a possible murder suspect.' I took her hand, pulling her to her feet.

'No,' she said, with a shaky smile. 'I suppose not.'

'What's the matter?'

She gave a little shiver. 'I'm not sure,' she hesitated, looking down at the hoof prints. 'It's nothing. I just felt a little' – she wriggled her shoulders – 'I don't know. I had the strangest feeling.' She forced a smile. 'It's this place. It's giving me the heebie-jeebies.'

'Do you want to go back?'

She shook her head. 'Don't be silly. Let's finish what we've started.'

'If you're sure.'

'Of course. It's what we're here for.'

After about forty minutes of searching we'd found nothing else. I couldn't help but be disappointed. I'd been so sure there would be some sort of clue, albeit a small one. I closed my eyes. He was still there hovering on the edge of my consciousness, but if he had something to tell me he was keeping it to himself.

Kicking at the earth as I went, I wandered over to Emma. 'Come on,' I said, 'let's start back.'

'Are you sure?'

'There's nothing for us here.' I slung my arm around her shoulders. 'Perhaps what I saw will mean something to Simon,' I said, though I doubted it.

When we arrived back at the house Simon was on

the phone, so we didn't get a chance to speak until we met for pre-dinner drinks. Despite my reservations, as we were about to eat, I told him about the chase across the lawns and fields and how Oliver had been hunted down by masked figures. His reaction wasn't what I'd expected. His eyes had narrowed and sparked with anger, but he didn't question what I said I'd seen. In fact, he didn't even appear shocked or surprised, but maybe his ministerial post had left him jaded to the horrors of the world.

His questioning of me carried on throughout the meal and, consequently, as the subject matter wasn't particularly conducive to eating, we ate very little and drank far too much, which was why, against my better judgement, I agreed we would stay a few more days.

This necessitated yet another drink in celebration and, tongues loosened by the wine and a few too many nightcaps, I asked one of those questions, which one really shouldn't in polite society and to which one would usually obtain no reply.

'So, I suppose this all belongs to you now?' I said and received a nudge in the ribs from Emma for my trouble. 'What?' I asked and she gave me a look my eyes were too bleary to appreciate.

Simon didn't notice; he was more sloshed than me. 'Now, that's where you'd be wrong,' he said, and I put his flushed cheeks down to the drink. 'I don't get a thing, zilch, nada.'

Emma and I stared at him, flabbergasted. 'You're joking?' I eventually said.

He leant back in his seat and shook his head. 'Nope.'

'Then who . . . ?'

'Everything goes to his long-lost granddaughter.'

'Granddaughter? What granddaughter?' I asked.

He laughed at my no doubt confused expression. 'Laura, the daughter of Oliver's son William, by his first wife, Constance.'

'I didn't know he had been married before.'

'Ah well, there was a reason for that. Oliver married Constance when they were both very young and little William turned up about six months after the wedding.'

'Oh,' I said.

'Hmm. It didn't go down at all well with the family, as you can imagine. Constance was a really nice girl, though; I liked her a lot. Then when William was three or four she fell pregnant again.' His shoulders sagged and his expression grew pained. 'She was almost full term when she had a nasty fall on the stairs. Neither she nor the baby survived it.'

'How dreadful,' Emma said.

'It was a terrible time. Ollie, as you can imagine, was distraught. Then only a matter of weeks later Edward died. It was then things got really bad in the house. Mother was like a wraith and Father started drinking heavily and spending a lot of time away. If it wasn't for Ollie and William it would've been unbearable.'

'So what happened between Oliver and his son? If you don't mind me asking,' Emma said.

Simon ran a hand through his thinning hair and sighed. 'It was like history repeating itself. William suddenly announced he was getting married to some girl he'd met. I don't know what Ollie's objection was – he'd been roughly the same age when he'd married – anyway he and Ollie had a terrible row and next thing I knew William was gone and Ollie refused to have his name mentioned in his hearing ever again. Of course, Mother and Father had both passed away by this point, so there was no one to reason with him and he certainly wouldn't listen to me.'

'And yet he's left his estate to his estranged son's daughter?' Emma said.

'As Brandon told you, Ollie changed his will only days before he died.'

'It must have been quite a shock to you,' she said.

Simon shrugged. 'It would have gone to William in the normal course of events and I sort of always thought when it came to it, it would.'

'What do you think William makes of it all?' I asked and wondered whether this was possibly causing a family rift of its own.

'Well,' Simon said, and paused for a moment staring into his drink, 'here's the thing. I had no idea until a few days ago, but William's dead.' He took a swig of his drink and looked up. 'He and his wife were murdered.'

I was suddenly feeling an awful lot more sober than I'd been a few minutes before. 'They were murdered?'

Simon nodded. 'Nearly sixteen years ago and,' he hesitated, his expression strained, 'there are apparently some similarities to how Oliver was killed.'

Emma and I shared a look. I didn't like this one little bit. 'I don't suppose your "contact" will be getting you a copy of the police report for their murders as well?'

Simon studied the bottom of his glass. When he raised

his eyes to mine his expression was a calculated neutral, which reminded me of why we'd fallen out all those years ago. He was lying to me. I wasn't sure what about, but he was definitely lying. 'It's on its way.'

CHAPTER FIVE

'Fancy going for a ride this morning?' Emma asked as I came out of the bathroom. 'It would be a good way to see the rest of the estate.'

I sat on the edge of the bed towelling dry my hair and wondering whether the dull ache at the front of my forehead would go away if I had a little fresh air. 'I'd quite like to go back to where Donald Walters found Oliver's body,' I said.

Emma glanced over at me, lipstick poised, hovering millimetres from her lips. 'Why? What do you expect to find today that we didn't find yesterday?'

'I'm not sure.' I opened my mouth to say more, then shut it again. I couldn't explain why I needed to go back there – I just did. After Simon's revelation about Oliver's son and daughter-in-law I felt like there might be something else I could learn from being there.

She ran the lipstick over her lips then studied herself critically in the dressing-table mirror before rummaging in her make-up bag for another of the mysterious lotions, potions or salves women keep in the damned things. 'Do you think Donald Walters is the housekeeper's husband? They have the same surname.'

'It wouldn't surprise me,' I said.

'He seems like a nice man.'

I gave a distracted nod, masked figures swarming through my head like a pack of jackals intent on bringing down their prey. There was something I hadn't mentioned to Emma. I had told her he had been badly beaten, so badly I was surprised he could walk let alone run, and how he had then been stabbed to death. What I hadn't told her was about the awful injuries they had inflicted upon the man once he had lost his race for life. They had cut out his tongue and, as if this wasn't enough, they had finished him off by gouging out his eyes.

Why had they done such a terrible and brutal thing? And why had they made him run? Was it to give him some hope, although in truth there was none? It was vicious and cruel in the extreme and it made me wonder – was it a punishment for some crime? And if so, what about William and his wife? Were they also murdered in some act of retribution?

'Penny for them,' Emma said.

I gave a little start. 'Oh, just mulling things over.'

'Oliver's murder or his son's?'

'Both, really. Such terrible things happening to one member of a family is bad enough – but three, if you include William's wife? There must be a connection.'

'Sixteen years apart?' Emma said, looking doubtful. 'That's an awfully long time.'

In normal circumstances I would tend to agree, but people who would mutilate a man after hunting him down were most likely capable of anything. What I said was, 'Let's go for that ride this morning,' I said. 'We can kill two birds with one stone.'

Simon was already at the table when we went down for breakfast. He greeted us with an excited smile, dabbing at his lips with his napkin. 'I have some news,' he said. 'Laura will be joining us tomorrow afternoon.'

'Really?' Emma said, glancing my way with a concerned frown. 'Is this really a good time with Oliver's murder unresolved?'

'It made sense for her to come now,' he replied. 'It means I can show her around and answer any questions she might have before I leave. Anyway, I would like to meet the girl. I was quite fond of William.'

'Where are you going?' Emma asked.

'Back home to Sussex. I haven't lived at Kingsmead for years now, since I left the forces, in fact.'

'Oh,' Emma said, pouring us both a cup of coffee from a very old, antique silver coffee pot. 'I didn't realise. I thought Kingsmead was your home.'

He helped himself to some toast. 'No, when I came back it wasn't the same. Ollie wasn't the same.' He paused while buttering his toast, his expression thoughtful, and whatever he was remembering, from the gentle curl of his lips, I surmised it was bitter-sweet. Then it was almost like he had slammed the door on those memories. His face hardened and he attacked the slice of toast with the slender butter knife. 'Anyway, I'd made a place for myself in the City. I'd bagged a good job and commuting from the West Country wasn't an option.' He glanced my way and his nostrils flared. 'It was the best thing I ever did.'

I ignored the dig and passed no comment. It was about this time when the friendship between the three of us began to unravel. His new job changed him. He had moved up the chain of command and become one of the mandarins we had all so hated when we'd been in service. One of those faceless men who made decisions, which could cost a man his life, and not worry about the consequences. In my naivety I thought he would change the system. He had once served on the ground; he knew what it was like; he would be on the side of the troops. Reggie had known differently, he had known it would be Simon who would change and not for the better. I hadn't believed Reggie, my best friend in the world, and we'd had words about it, eventually agreeing to differ. And this is what had hurt me most, Simon's betrayal of my trust when he had proved me wrong.

'We thought we'd go for a ride this morning,' I said, changing the subject before it became contentious. Simon knew exactly what I thought about his job and how he did it. I forced my expression to remain neutral. 'Do you mind?'

'No, of course not. I'll probably be tied up most of the morning, anyway. I have some work to get on with and also there are a few things that need doing in preparation for Laura's arrival. You go ahead.' He knocked back the last of his coffee, dabbed his lips again with his napkin, threw it down on the table and got to his feet. 'If you'll excuse me, I'll see you at lunch.'

'See you later,' I said and he was gone.

Emma waited until the sound of his footsteps disappeared into the distance. 'Did I notice a sudden chill descend between the two of you?'

I gave a grunt and helped myself to some eggs and bacon, waving away the hovering maid.

'Jed?'

'I told you, Emms. It's all water under the bridge.'

'Hmm.' She cradled her coffee cup in her hands and took a sip. 'It didn't look that way just then. The temperature dropped so low, I thought we were in for a heavy frost.'

'I wonder what this Laura's like,' I said, not wanting to continue with Emma's line of conversation, especially as the maid hadn't taken the hint and was still hanging around, probably hoping we'd hurry up and leave so she could get on with clearing the table. 'She must have had a pretty sad upbringing losing both parents at such a young age, and this place will be a bit of a shock to her, I would have thought.'

Emma regarded me over her cup. 'We'll no doubt find out tomorrow. That is, if we're still staying.'

The maid cleared Simon's plate and disappeared out the door.

My eyes met Emma's. 'I think I have to stay now,' I said, keeping my voice low, 'though it might not be such a bad idea if you went home.'

She gave a short, sharp laugh. 'No way.'

'It might be safer.'

'For whom?'

I put down my knife and fork. 'We're talking about three people having been murdered . . .'

She rested a fingertip against my lips. 'If you're staying,

55

so am I. Anyway, two heads are better than one.' She wrapped her other hand around mine. 'Now, if you've finished filling your face, shall we go for that ride?'

The old Land Rover was parked in the stable yard, next to a battered motorbike I doubted was road legal. As we drew closer to the stable block music drifted out of the open door. Inside it was pretty empty now most of the horses had gone, though there was one chap at work cleaning out the stalls. He looked away from what he was doing as we strolled over and straightened with a slow, easy smile.

'Hallo there,' he drawled, putting down his shovel and wiping his hands on the back of his jeans. 'Can I help you with anything?' He had a slight Irish lilt to his voice and the black curls and deep blue eyes to go with it. He was as tall as me and with his bad-boy good looks I reckoned he'd broken many a young woman's heart.

'Mr Pomeroy said we could take a couple of the horses for a ride,' Emma said.

He smiled at Emma and I might as well have not been there. He was a ladies' man, that was for sure. 'I think we can sort you a couple out,' he said. 'I'm Dan Crouchley, by the way.'

'I'm Emma and this is my husband, Jed.'

He gave me a nod, before his attention returned to Emma. 'Are you up for Horse of the Year or would you prefer a more gentle ride?'

'Slow and steady,' Emma told him. 'I haven't ridden for years.'

'Never fear,' he said with a laugh. 'We have just the girl.'

He gestured we follow him along the line of stalls and

stopped halfway down. 'This is Angel, so named for her gentle nature. She'll give you no trouble.' A white and tan head stretched over the door and nuzzled at Dan's shoulder. He reached out to pet her muzzle.

'She's beautiful,' Emma said.

'You're a lovely girl, aren't you, sweetheart,' he said, stroking the filly's head. He turned to me. 'And how about sir?'

I shifted uncomfortably. 'Jed, call me Jed.' The master–servant thing had never sat well with me and I was too old to get used to the idea now.

His smile broadened, showing very white teeth. 'Well, Jed, we have Jericho, who is a steady lad, or Satan, who isn't as bad as his name would have you believe, though he can be a little lively if he doesn't have a firm hand.'

'Can I take a look?' I asked.

Dan moved on to the next stall. 'This is Jericho,' he said.

Jericho was a beautiful creature, his coat a glossy chestnut and with eyes the darkest of browns. He whinnied softly and trotted over for some attention. I scratched his forehead and he stretched his neck, pushing against my hand.

When I'd finished petting the creature I wandered along to the next stall. I didn't need an explanation as to why the magnificent beast inside had been given the name Satan. He was absolutely massive, as black as coal, and I wouldn't have been surprised if, when he looked up, his eyes had glowed red. Seeing me he flicked his tail and shook his huge head, snorting.

Dan murmured his name and the beast came over, ducking his head for a stroke, and allowed me to give him a scratch.

'He's a big brute,' I said.

Dan reached in and handed him a sugar cube on the palm of his hand, which Satan took with a kiss of his big, velvety lips. 'Deep down he's a big softy,' he said, with a laugh.

'Maybe I'll give him a try tomorrow.'

'You're staying on for a bit, then?'

I nodded, still looking at the massive horse. 'Just for a few days.'

'Right,' Dan said. 'I'll get them saddled up for you.'

'I'll give you a hand,' I offered.

Despite saying she hadn't been on a horse for years, Emma appeared immediately at home on the aptly named Angel, who was as placid as Dan had promised. As for me, well, I hadn't ridden for a good few years either, but when I had I'd ridden hard, especially when I'd been here on leave with Simon. We'd either been sleeping, drinking or riding and, sitting on Jericho trotting along the bridle path towards the forest, I felt like I'd never been away.

The sun was shining, the birds were singing, and the air smelt fresh and clean with the ever-present, overriding aroma of cut grass and vegetation. With Emma riding along beside me I felt on top of the world and it was seriously tempting to say to her, 'You know what? Let's give the clearing in the forest a miss.' It was definitely going to bring our moods down. Once again I had to remind myself it was one of the reasons I was here, in fact, the only reason: to see if I could help my old friend find out what had happened to his brother. I had told him the how, now I had to try and find out the who and why.

The clearing hadn't changed any since our last visit. It was still dark and gloomy, overly quiet and had an atmosphere that instantly put me on edge. We both dropped down off our steeds and Emma held onto Jericho's reins while I took another slow walk around the perimeter of the circle, and it *was* a circle, an almost perfect circle. It brought to mind my previous notion that this area had deliberately been left devoid of trees when the woodland had been planted or had subsequently been cleared.

I walked into the middle and closed my eyes. *Oliver, speak to me. Tell me why this happened to you.*

I stood there waiting and boom – once again I am seeing the world through Oliver's eyes and feeling it with his senses. *I am in a darkened room, maybe some kind of vault or mausoleum. I am not alone. People surround me. It's cold. Damp stone chills my sandalled feet and mould-streaked walls enclose me and the others, mildew scenting the air. Lamps flicker, giving off a yellow, oily light enveloping us in shifting shadows.*

The faces of the men and women surrounding me are covered with the same masks of black leather I saw in my previous vision, though I sense it's mainly for effect, Oliver knows his companions, I am positive of it. As I look around I try to gain some clue from the congregation. The figure next to me turns slightly and I catch a glimpse of a slender white neck, a woman's neck, and around it hangs a string of jet beads upon a silver chain that glints and shimmers in the lamplight. There's something wrong with this picture. She reaches out and presses a dagger into my hand and . . .

I am in a child's room. Painted wooden mobiles of the moon and stars hang above the empty bed. And there are feathers – feathers everywhere. Floating in the air like snowflakes, coating my face and sticking to my lips. More feathers litter the carpet. I feel like a child again. Smiling, I turn and walk from the room, the words I am not a monster reverberating through my head. And, with a wrenching sensation inside my mind, he was gone, leaving me slightly light-headed and unsteady on my feet.

I forced the feeling aside; I had to think. He had been showing me these visions for a reason – but why didn't he speak to me? Though something was now very clear – Oliver had known his killers. Why, then, didn't he tell me who these people were? Surely he no longer felt any loyalty to them? As for the feather-filled bedroom – what was that all about? Whatever he was trying to impart to me I didn't get it.

'I'm sorry,' I whispered.

Emma walked to my side, the horses both trailing along behind her. 'Anything?'

'Yes, but . . .' I gave a frustrated shake of my head. 'Come on, let's go.'

I threw my arm around Emma's shoulders and we started off along the track out of the woodland, letting the horses trot along behind us. As we walked, I told her what I'd seen, venting my frustration at being given such tiny titbits of knowledge.

'So you think Oliver was involved with some sort of cult?' she asked.

'I don't know.' I kicked at the dirt beneath my feet, remembering what one of my old training instructors used to say, *If, laddie, it looks like shit and smells like shit, it is, more than likely just that – shit.* 'They were all wearing masks – what else could it be?'

She frowned at me for a moment and her expression grew doubtful. 'In this day and age? Really?'

'Unless you can think of an alternative?'

I walked along beside her in a bit of a daze. If it hadn't been for what I'd seen I wouldn't have believed it either. It was 2020, for God's sake, not 1720. But for all that – it didn't really matter what I believed or thought. If these people were members of some sort of weird cult or playing at being devil worshippers, or were just plain bat-shit crazy, they had still killed one man and possibly his son and daughter-in-law. So where did this leave William's daughter, who, within twenty-four hours, would be arriving at Kingsmead? Was she on their hit list too? Crazy people did crazy things, I knew this only too well.

'Do you think Laura is in danger?' Emma asked, and her putting into words what I was already thinking didn't help ease my growing anxiety.

For some reason the feather-filled room floated through my head. I was missing something. 'I would be very interested to see the police report of her parents' death,' I said.

'You think Simon will get one?'

I laughed, although I was in no way amused. 'I have no doubt he will. Simon is a very important man.'

She stopped walking. 'What aren't you telling me?'

I rubbed my beard, which I saw from her expression hadn't gone unnoticed. 'Simon works in a government department,' which was a bit of an understatement, he was head of a government department; a covert government department. Emma wasn't stupid, she got the picture.

'Ah-ha, so that's how he got hold of the police report on Oliver's death.'

61

'Undoubtedly,' and, despite knowing if it was my family member who had been murdered I'd do exactly the same thing had I been in his position, it still made me angry, unreasonably so. I guess because I knew Simon always did whatever it took to get his own way, even if it meant abusing his position. It was the kind of man he'd become – or maybe it was how he had always been only I hadn't realised. Reggie was the more perceptive of the two of us. In retrospect I could see it now. He had never really liked Simon as much as I had; he only hung out with us because of me; *I* was his friend, not Simon. I was a stupid young man and now I was a silly old fool and I was beginning to seriously wish I'd torn up his letter and hadn't let Emma talk me into coming.

We carried on with our ride, but the sunshine seemed a little less bright and the scenery a little less vibrant; the dark clouds of reality had taken the joy out of the morning. Consequently we were back at the manor, showered, changed and ready for lunch earlier than planned.

As soon as we walked into the living room I knew something was wrong and my simmering anger instantly drained away. Simon was pacing the floor, shoulders hunched with an expression so grim anxiety fluttered in my chest.

'At last,' he said upon seeing us.

I glanced at my watch; by my reckoning we were over ten minutes early. 'What's the matter?'

He strode towards me thrusting out his hand, his cheeks flushed and expression angry, frightened, agitated, possibly all of them. 'This,' he said. 'This.'

I glanced from his face to his outstretched fingers; in them was a greetings card. I hesitated and, with a curt gesture of his head indicating he wanted me to take it, he pushed it into my hand. It *was* a greetings card. Emblazoned on the front in gold lettering were the words 'Happy Birthday' beneath which was a pastel drawing of an iced cake with a single burning striped candle. I frowned at him, confused by his reaction.

'Open it,' he snapped.

I flipped the card open and was aware of Emma moving in close to see. Inside, written in blue ink with a flourish were the words: *Dearest Edward, wishing you a very happy birthday, from all your friends at Goldsmere House. Hoping you have a wonderful day with your family.* My stomach gave a lurch – Goldsmere House? If I'd never heard of the place again it would've still been too soon. Unfortunately, I could never completely wipe it from my life; it was always hovering there at the back of my mind.

I had to swallow a couple of times before I could bring myself to speak. 'Goldsmere House?'

A look of irritation flickered briefly across Simon's face before my own reaction registered with him. 'You've heard of it?'

I nodded, reading the words again. 'This was addressed to your brother Edward?'

'I received it this morning. Had he lived it would have been Ed's seventieth birthday today.'

Emma took the card from my limp fingers and turned it over, studying the front, back and inside before handing it back to Simon.

'And you've never heard of Goldsmere House?' she asked.

'No,' he said, looking from Emma to me. 'Where is it? What is it?'

I didn't think there was any way of sugaring this pill. 'Goldsmere House is an exclusive care home,' I said, trying my best to be tactful.

His eyes narrowed. 'There's more to it than that,' he said, again looking from me to Emma. 'I can tell by your faces.'

A memory floated through my head. A flash of lightning and the dark silhouette of Goldsmere House looming up ahead of me, as I drove through the torrential rain lashing against the windscreen of the Jag.

'I think I could use a drink,' I said.

CHAPTER SIX

'So this Goldsmere House is some sort of upper-class asylum?' Simon said, passing me a large whisky.

'More or less,' Emma said.

I took a swig of my drink. 'It's a place where rich people hide their dirty little secrets,' I said, not bothering with diplomacy.

'Dear God,' Simon said.

'Maybe there's been some sort of mistake,' Emma quickly said, as ever trying to calm the waters.

To my way of thinking it was going to take a lot more than a few words. If what we surmised was true, the much-loved brother, who Simon thought had died almost forty years ago, had actually been alive and living in a mental institution for all those years. It didn't bear thinking about. The big question, however, was why had Goldsmere sent a birthday card to his home address?

'You have to phone them,' I said.

He gave a curt nod, his expression grim.

Emma found him the phone number and we all sat clustered together as he made the call and put it on speaker. The phone was answered on the third ring by a slightly officious-sounding woman. 'Goldsmere House, how can I help you?'

Simon cleared his throat. 'Hello, is it possible to speak to whoever is in charge?'

'To whom am I speaking?'

'Simon Pomeroy.'

'Oh,' she said, clearly knowing the name. 'Please hold the line for one moment.' There was a faint click and orchestral music began to play. I vaguely recognised the tune. It was quietly gentle, but uplifting, comforting music chosen to put anxious families of patients at their ease. It wasn't having the desired effect: after a minute Simon began impatiently tapping his fingers on the arm of the chair.

There was another click and the music abruptly ceased. 'So sorry to keep you, Mr Pomeroy,' a pleasant female voice said. 'I am Alice Barnard, the manager here. What can I help you with today?'

'Ah, yes,' Simon said, sounding, for him, nervous and tentative, reminding me of how he hated being the one who wasn't controlling the situation. 'Ah, I received a card from you today addressed to Edward in celebration of his birthday.'

'Oh good, we wanted him to know we were thinking of him. Is he well?'

Simon pulled a face at me.

'Ask her why they sent it here,' I whispered.

66

'It was very kind of you, Ms Barnard, but I'm rather at a loss as to why you should send it here – and now.'

It went very quiet on the other end of the phone. 'Ms Barnard?'

'I was under the impression from your brother that Edward was going to live with the family during his twilight years.'

'Really?'

Another moment's silence. 'Mr Pomeroy, I think perhaps you should be having this conversation with your brother Oliver,' she said, with that practised sympathetic voice medical professionals use when they're delivering bad news.

'My brother Oliver is dead, Ms Barnard.'

There was a sharp intake of breath. 'Dead?'

'Yes, dead, and I have not seen hide nor hair of Edward. In fact, until we started having this conversation, I believed Edward to have died some forty-odd years ago.'

'Oh dear,' the woman said. There was something in her tone of voice that worried me and, had she not been talking to a patient's family member, I think it more than likely the expletive would have been stronger.

'I'd better pay you a visit,' Simon said.

There was a soft sigh from the other end of the phone. 'I agree,' she said, 'and it's probably best we have a conversation sooner rather than later,' and with that Simon arranged to call on her that afternoon. When he hung up, he appeared drained.

'What on earth is going on?' he asked no one in particular.

As much as I didn't want to go anywhere near Goldsmere House, there was only one thing I could say. 'Do you want us to come with you?'

Emma drove as Simon and I had both knocked back large whiskies. I wished I'd had more. The journey passed in an anxiety-fuelled blur, the beautiful countryside unseen, vanquished by my darker memories.

As we pulled into the lane leading to Goldsmere I had a feeling of déjà vu. I had visited this place once before and I had hoped never to visit it again.

Although a high-security unit, the buildings were surrounded by lovely gardens, but the electronic gates, high walls strung with razor wire and the inner palisade steel security fencing told the story: they didn't want anyone getting out without their say-so. Although last time I'd visited it had been dark, and I hadn't exactly been compos mentis through loss of blood, it looked to me like the security had recently been upgraded.

From the front of the building one could be forgiven for thinking you were about to enter a rather posh hotel, even inside it had the air of an expensive establishment's lobby and reception area. The only giveaway was the number of staff wandering around with clipboards, dressed in hospital whites.

Upon our arrival we were required to sign in and give our names and addresses before being ushered into an office by the softly spoken receptionist. The room was more like a gentleman's study, the high walls lined with shelf upon shelf of leather-bound tomes. This was completely at odds with the slim, middle-aged woman who hurried from behind a huge desk stacked with files and pieces of paperwork, to greet us, hand outstretched. Dressed in a pink tweed skirt with matching pink cardigan and a double string of pearls she looked more like a kindly headmistress than the manager of a mental institution. She introduced herself as Alice Barnard and her expression was so serious it didn't take psychic abilities to know we were about to get some very bad news.

'Firstly, I would like to offer my sincere condolences for your sad loss. Your brother Oliver was such a lovely man,' she said to Simon.

'You knew him?' Simon said.

She summoned a tight smile. 'Oh yes, he visited every few weeks or so and usually took dear Edward home for a couple of days once a month.'

She gestured that we sit in a more informal area furnished with a sofa and chairs surrounding a long coffee table and I guessed this alternative was intended to make any visitors feel more comfortable. I had news for her – it didn't. We all sat, perched uneasily on the edges of our seats.

'And how long had this been going on?' Simon asked.

'I couldn't say for certain, but for at least as long as I've been here, so over ten years.'

'You said on the phone that when Oliver collected Edward last time it was for good?' Simon said.

'Yes, he said he was taking Edward home,' she replied and was interrupted by a knock on the door and an orderly appearing with a tray of tea, coffee and biscuits. Not another word was spoken, other than a whispered thank you from the manager, until he left. 'Are you aware of what we do here?'

'Yes,' I said, and it came out as a curter response than I'd meant.

There was a moment's embarrassed silence before Ms Barnard continued. 'Then you know Goldsmere is a very private and exclusive home for the mentally disabled, whether it be by some kind of head trauma or psychological disorder, like debilitating dementia, for instance,' she said.

'How "mentally disabled"?' Simon asked.

Ms Barnard gave a sigh. 'In quite a few cases very,' she replied. 'Obviously there are several levels of care we offer, but all our patients are residential and most of them are very unlikely to return to normal society.'

'They're not here to be cured?' I asked.

'No,' she shook her head emphatically. 'No, they're incurable.' Ms Barnard had apparently found her groove. As uncomfortable as it was for us, she was now talking about a subject she knew and knew well. 'Sadly, our patients' families usually can no longer cope. In fact, they would be irresponsible to try in most cases, but on the whole our patients are unlikely ever to return back into the family circle.'

'Then why was Edward allowed home?' Simon asked.

'We don't make the decisions – we provide a service. However, we take our patients' and their families' needs very seriously. Edward was terminally ill. He had only a few months to live at most. Your brother wanted him to spend his last days at the family home.' She smiled sympathetically. 'Myself and Dr Gilbert, our senior consultant, did try and dissuade your brother, but he gave his assurance he would personally ensure Edward received his medication as prescribed. We had no reason to doubt him, as your brother knew very well how Edward behaved if unmedicated.'

'And how did he behave?' I asked.

She didn't even hesitate. 'Like a man possessed, Mr Cummings. Like a man possessed.'

The shock must have shown on our faces. Her face softened and she leant forward towards us, no doubt like she would have to a patient who needed her reassurance.

'Edward is the sweetest man alive when he's medicated, but if not he is . . .' She sighed. 'I don't want to offend or upset you, Mr Pomeroy, but he's a danger to everyone around him.'

Simon and I glanced at each other. I could tell by his expression that he was just as surprised as me.

'A danger?' I repeated.

'I'm afraid there isn't a textbook name or explanation for Edward's condition. Something happened to him when he was a teenager, as far as we can make out. We don't know what, but whatever it was drove him over the edge. I understand he spent years in various institutions more or less in isolation until an experimental course of treatment worked for him and gave him a semblance of a normal life.'

'That's terrible,' Emma said.

'I know,' Ms Barnard said. 'It's sad because once he started taking the right cocktail of meds he became a different man. A gentle soul. A real sweetie, in fact.'

'Without the drugs, would he be able to function like a normal person?' I asked.

'That's the scary part,' Ms Barnard said, and I must admit I could see fear in her eyes. 'If unmedicated, I doubt you would have any idea until it was too late.'

'What do you mean?' I asked, not at all thinking I would want to know the answer.

'Let me put it this way,' she said, fiddling with the pearls around her neck. 'Edward when medicated is Dr Jekyll. When not, he is far, far worse than Mr Hyde.'

'He's schizophrenic?' Simon asked.

She shook her head. 'No, no. As I told you, his condition is undiagnosed.'

'He's violent?' I said.

She nodded. 'This is why I'm so worried. If he's no longer with your brother, where is he? Without his medication there's no telling what he would be capable of.'

Simon leant back in his chair lost in thought, a frown wrinkling his forehead. We had been prepared for most things but not this.

'Ms Barnard,' Simon said, breaking the silence. 'You said Edward could be violent – what exactly did you mean? Can you give us an example?'

'Oh dear,' she said and began to worry her pearls with such intensity I was sure they would end up scattered across the floor before long. 'I can only tell you what I've heard,' she said. 'There has never been an incident here. Never.'

She waited as if expecting something from us.

Emma gave her an encouraging smile and it apparently eased her dilemma, as her hand dropped from the pearls to her lap where she grasped it tightly with her other.

'Edward came here a very long time ago. Well before I took up my position. I think Goldsmere was the last resort before the poor man ended up in a secure public facility.'

'Like an asylum?' I asked.

She shuddered. 'I do hate that word, but yes. Edward

would have been destined to living in a drugged stupor and, in the circumstances, probably in solitary confinement. He came here after an incident at the previous facility.' She glanced up from the papers. 'Apparently Edward had charmed a member of the female staff at his last care home, and believe me he can be very charming.'

'A real "sweetie",' I said.

'Quite so. He was so charming the girl got careless. She didn't check he was swallowing his meds.' She consulted the papers on her lap. 'They found about three days' worth hidden in his room. Why he didn't wash them down the sink was a mystery, but anyway, after three days he was back to his normal self, which to say the least was dangerous.'

'What happened?' I hardly dared to ask.

'I suppose no one will ever know what he was planning as on the fourth day the girl called in sick, so it was a male orderly who was sent to give Edward his final meds of the day. Edward flew into a rage and if it hadn't been for another nurse and a doctor being just along the corridor when it happened the orderly wouldn't have got out of the room alive.'

'He was seriously hurt?' Emma asked.

'Yes, Mrs Cummings, very seriously.'

I wasn't about to let her off the hook, we needed to know. 'How seriously?'

Her hand went to her pearls. 'His injuries were life-changing.'

I gave her a look. 'Life-changing?'

She went to pick up her coffee cup and then thought better of it, her hand was shaking so badly. 'By the time they reached him, Edward had torn out the man's tongue and gouged out one eye.'

I wasn't sure if it was the light, but when I glanced at Emma and Simon they both had a sickly green pallor.

'I'm surprised he was allowed a transfer to another private facility after such an incident,' I said.

She pursed her lips, giving me a direct look. 'I understand the orderly involved was very comfortably looked after by Edward's family.'

I sank back in my chair. It figured – Oliver obviously hadn't been a lot different to his younger brother when it came to getting his own way. Simon used his power and connections, while Oliver threw money at his problems.

We sat there for a bit sipping our tea; eventually Simon stood. 'You've been very kind,' he said to Ms Barnard. 'Thank you.'

'But what about Edward?' the poor woman asked. I could tell she was anxious because she was hanging onto her pearls as though her life depended on it.

'He's not your responsibility any more. You handed him over to his family in good faith and you've alerted us to how dangerous he can be. I don't think anyone can blame you or Goldsmere House for his actions since he left your care,' Simon said.

To say she looked relieved would be an understatement.

She saw us out into the reception, talking quietly to Simon as we went. I wasn't listening; in fact, I was finding it hard to think straight. As we had waited to be shown into Ms Barnard's office I had managed, for the most part, to block out the chorus of voices infiltrating my head and, once inside her room, it was almost as though a barricade had been thrown up between me and them. Outside in the reception I was again subjected to a barrage of cries, screams and the incessant ramblings of the one-time occupants of the building surrounding me. And there were images. Images so deranged I was finding it hard to focus on the real world and I could feel reality slipping away from me.

I must have staggered, as Emma's arm abruptly linked through mine and, walking at speed, she almost hauled me towards the entrance and outside.

'Are you all right?' she asked as the doors slid shut behind us.

I winced. 'Let's get in the car,' I managed to say, though I could barely hear my own voice.

She marched me to the Jag as fast as she could, but by the time we reached it she was sagging under my weight as my legs began to crumple beneath me. As she unlocked the car, I slumped against the passenger door, pressing my hands over my ears and screwing my eyes tight shut. It made no difference – now they had found me they weren't about to let me be.

'Jed?' I heard a voice say.

'Help me get him inside the car.'

Somehow between the two of them, Emma and Simon manoeuvred me into the front passenger seat and then with a solid clunk the door shut behind me. The voices didn't stop. Instead they became more frantic, some begging me to help them, others just wanting me to share their pain.

I felt rather than heard the Jag roar into life and then we were pulling away and, for a few terrible moments as we headed along the drive to the exit, I thought the late inmates of Goldsmere House were going to come with me. Then with howls of impotent rage we drove out through the gates and they faded away and were gone.

I slumped back in my seat, massaging my temples.

'Jed, are you OK?' Emma asked.

I opened my eyes and let out a shaky breath. 'Don't ever let me go back in there again,' was all I said.

CHAPTER SEVEN

The car journey was rather sober. With Simon listening I didn't say a lot. I didn't want to. The inside of my head felt like it had been shaken very hard with a handful of loose stones inside it. I was surprised I didn't have blood coming out of my eyes, ears and nose. He was easily satisfied as he had other things on his mind, like a psychotic brother on the loose. Emma didn't say a thing, though I knew once we were alone she would want a blow-by-blow account of what had happened to me.

As Emma drove, Simon leant forward between the two front seats from where he was perched in the back. 'Where do you think Edward can be?' he asked. 'I mean, I can hardly believe it – he's been alive all this time and Ollie knew, but never told me.'

I sat there quietly until my brain slipped back into gear and, while the pounding in my head faded away, my thoughts became coherent again. And with clarity returning,

I pondered on what we had learnt from Ms Barnard.

Simon wasn't stupid, far from it, and it occurred to me that he must surely be wondering along the same lines as me. Both Oliver and the orderly had similar injuries; could Edward have been one of Oliver's assailants? I still hadn't mentioned these injuries to Emma; even so, it was she who broached the subject before I had worked out how to.

'Simon, I hate to even ask,' she hesitated, glancing at him in the rear-view mirror, 'but do you think Edward could have had something to do with Oliver's death? It was a particularly violent way he died.'

It went very quiet and, as Simon didn't immediately refute the possibility, it made me think he had been considering it.

'I have to tell the police,' he said eventually. 'Then at least they'll be on the lookout for Edward. If he's as bad as they're saying . . .'

'I suspect Ms Barnard will notify them,' I said. 'You might have said it was all down to the family, but she's going to want to cover herself and Goldsmere.'

'You're right,' he said, 'and it's probably for the best if I report it sooner rather than later.'

For the next ten minutes or so he was on his mobile; first to the detective in charge of the murder investigation, he apparently would be calling to speak to Simon in the morning, and then some nameless person, who listened a lot and spoke very little judging from what I could hear. I had the impression it could possibly be a member of his staff at the ministry. I wouldn't be surprised: if the shit did hit the fan Simon would want to make sure none of the stinky stuff came his way.

* * *

When we arrived back at Kingsmead House Simon disappeared after saying he would see us for pre-dinner drinks at seven and left us to our own devices. It was a relief. I was in no mood for small talk and I could tell Emma was itching to hear about what had happened to me at Goldsmere.

She managed to hold out until the door to our room closed behind us. 'Are you feeling better now?'

I sank down onto the bed. Even thinking about it made me tense and agitated. She sat down next to me and took my hand. 'What is it, Jed?'

'That place,' I said, thoroughly miserable. 'I've never been in a place that has had as many lost souls. It was dreadful.'

'What happened, love?'

So, I told her – everything. At least everything I could bear to talk about. There were some things she didn't need to know. It was bad enough one of us not being able to sleep at night. 'What makes it worse is there isn't a thing I can do for them. They're lost and afraid, tortured spirits and even in death their madness and isolation goes on and on. I want to help them, but there's nothing I can do to save them.'

Emma squeezed my hand 'Even you can't save the world, Jed – no one man can.'

I had to take a shower. I needed to wash away the disturbed feelings of the tormented and insane, which not only filled my head, but had somehow wrapped themselves around me. I cranked the thermostat to as hot as it would go and let the water pound down upon me until my skin was lobster pink and I couldn't see for the steam. I wasn't sure it was helping.

I turned the temperature down to a more bearable level and leant forward, my hands flat against the wall, closing my eyes and allowing the water to spray down upon the back of my head. My mind turned to Oliver and Edward. What on earth had Oliver been playing at? Bringing home a psychopath was never going to end well. And the way he had died – had Edward wanted to punish the brother who, in his mind, had been having him held prisoner at Goldsmere? And who were the others? Yet another mystery. There had been masked figures running Oliver down.

Oliver was not a fool, I knew that much about him, and yet he had ignored the professionals' advice and brought home a brother everyone believed dead. If it was such a big family secret, with even Simon not knowing Edward was alive, the man being terminally sick surely wouldn't be a good enough reason to bring it out into the open. It made no sense at all.

Simon was barking at someone on the phone when we went down for drinks. He was clearly not happy, though this was hardly surprising in view of all we'd learnt at Goldsmere House.

By the time he'd finished the call his cheekbones were flushed red, which made his waxy complexion even more obvious. He dropped his mobile into his jacket pocket with an irritated twist of his lips and, upon seeing us, gave a rueful smile.

'Sorry,' he said. 'Just sorting some things out at the office. I've been away longer than I was expecting and as usual everything has gone to pot.'

'Are you never going to retire?' I asked.

He laughed. 'No, they'll have to carry me out in a box. Now, what can I get you to drink?'

We gave our orders and waited until he had poured them into heavy crystal glasses before broaching the inevitable topic.

'Do you think it might be a good idea to put off Laura for a few days?' Emma asked.

He gave a sniff. 'How can I? This is all hers now.'

'I suppose so,' Emma said, giving me a look.

'If she knew she could possibly be in danger . . . ?' I said.

'Why should she be? She didn't know Ollie or Ed.'

It might have sounded logical to Simon, to me it was irresponsible. 'Simon, we are talking about someone who has more or less absconded from a mental institution.'

He gave an irritable flap of his hand. 'He didn't abscond, he was released to Ollie.'

'Who is now dead? Possibly killed by his own brother.'

He took a swig of his drink. 'It is a bit of a mess,' he admitted.

We sat without speaking for a few minutes, each of us lost in our own thoughts. 'Why do you think Oliver never told you Edward was still alive?'

Simon slowly shook his head. 'I have no idea. None of it makes any sense.'

We lapsed into silence. It was a conundrum. Then something else occurred to me. 'Alice Barnard said Oliver used to take Edward out of Goldsmere once a month. Could he really have brought him here, do you think? Surely the police would have considered him a suspect if he had.'

Simon glanced across at me. 'No – at least, if he did,

the servants didn't know anything about it. I spoke to Mrs Walters earlier and she was quite shocked when I told her Edward had been alive all along.'

I leant back in my chair unconvinced. Servants were good at keeping secrets; they had to be if they wanted to keep their jobs. Simon had been the one to tell me this. 'A servant's job is to serve, and part of that service is to know when to be discreet and hold one's tongue.' Oliver must have taken Edward somewhere and, I'd bet my Jag on it, Edward had been here.

All through dinner we batted the subject of Edward and his 'death' back and forth, falling silent whenever a member of staff appeared. It might have been my imagination, but they were unusually attentive. One maid in particular didn't appear to want to leave us unattended for more than a few minutes.

'That will be all, Maddy,' Simon eventually said, clearly frustrated by her constant ministrations. 'I'll ring when we've finished.'

She bobbed something halfway between a bow and a curtsy and trotted off out of the room, though she didn't look very happy about it.

'So, what are you going to tell Laura about all this when she arrives?' Emma asked.

Simon sat back in his seat. 'I suppose I'm going to have to tell her some of it, but it isn't exactly the best introduction to her long-lost family. Lovely to meet you, Laura. Oh, and by the way, your criminally insane granduncle, who we all thought dead, is on the loose. And, would you believe, your grandfather, who knew he was alive all this time, was the one who had him let out of the secure facility where he'd been locked up for the past forty years?' His lips curled in distaste. 'God alone knows what she'll think of us.'

'Maybe this is a good enough reason to put her off for a week or so,' I said. 'Until this is all sorted out.'

Simon took a swig of his wine. 'And there lies another problem.'

Emma and I exchanged a glance. 'What sort of problem is worth possibly risking her life?' I asked.

'I told you, there's no risk to her life,' Simon said with an irritable flap of his hand. 'But there is a risk to her inheritance.'

I rubbed the bridge of my nose. This was giving me a headache. 'How?' I asked, Simon wasn't the only one who was feeling a little irritable.

'Brandon gave me the impression that Laura was going to be an extremely rich young lady even after death duties, provided *she fulfils* the terms of the will.'

My ears pricked up. 'Terms of the will?'

He dropped his knife and fork onto his plate with a clatter, the majority of his meal untouched. 'Brandon said there's nothing too onerous. But she does have to move into Kingsmead by the end of this month and live here for at least two years. And, as the end of the month is fast approaching, she has no choice. She either moves in within the next few days or forfeits her fortune. I, for one, am not going to let her forgo what is rightfully hers without a very good reason.'

I watched his face and his expression was determined and, as far as I could tell, with not a shred of jealousy or rancour considering a huge fortune was completely bypassing him and going to someone he had never met. True, I had never known him to be particularly materialistic, but then he'd always had everything given to him on a plate. He was a typical rich boy despite the traumas in his life. One of those traumas being the death of his eldest brother. Now this having turned out to be a lie was perhaps more upsetting than the loss of the family home. But all those millions? Perhaps he was resigned to it; he'd had time to get used to the idea: after all, as far as he was concerned William had still been alive.

'Have you finished, Mr Pomeroy?' the maid Maddy asked, appearing by his side. The girl certainly was quiet on her feet; I hadn't even realised she'd returned to the room. He gave an abrupt nod of the head and she began to clear the dishes.

Simon stood. 'Shall we adjourn to the living room?'

CHAPTER EIGHT

I woke with a start, my heart thumping. I hadn't been dreaming, but something had caused me to erupt out of sleep. I turned onto my side to read the bedside travel clock. It was a little after two, about an hour and a half after we had retired to bed.

Rolling onto my back, I glanced to the other pillow. Emma was lying facing me, her breathing slow and even. She was dead to the world. I lay there listening for any indication of what might have woken me. It was all quiet – then the distant hoot of an owl, followed by more silence.

I pumped my pillow. I was wide awake and was destined for a few hours of tossing and turning. There was also the matter of the growing pressure on my bladder. It was no good, I'd have to go.

I slid out of bed, hoping I wouldn't wake Emma, and crept across the room. The bathroom was too dark to do without any light and, as I didn't want to end up pissing on my feet, I pulled on the light cord, blinding myself for a couple of seconds. I took my time. I was in no hurry to return to my restless sojourn. When I could delay it no more, I skulked back to bed. Sitting on the edge for a moment, I rubbed at my face and yawned; there was nothing worse than feeling knackered and being unable to sleep.

With a sigh I stood to pull back the covers and icy fingers traced their way across the back of my scalp. I stopped stock-still, all my senses screaming danger. I'd had this feeling several times before and I'd never worked out whether they were warnings from some kind of ghostly guardian angel or I had a sixth sense for bad things happening to me or my friends. Whatever the case it had saved us from harm on a number of occasions and I treated it with upmost respect.

I crossed the room to where I knew Emma had left me a dressing gown should a fire really occur. I couldn't help thinking her fear was more for the sanity of the attending fire crew than my modesty, still it was appreciated now. I could hardly wander about the house stark naked.

Tugging the dressing gown on, I pulled it tight around my waist, still listening. My scalp icy cold, like the feeling you get on the back of your skull when you've been swimming in the sea, then – *bang* – a loud thump came from somewhere along the corridor. I padded to the door and pressed my ear against the wood.

There was another thud and I yanked open the door. There was hardly any light at all, only one of the night lights that usually lined the hallway was burning, which was weird in itself; they'd all been alight when we'd retired for the evening.

'Who's there?' I called and was rewarded by the scrabbling of feet and a shadow appearing out of a room along the corridor. 'Who's there?' I called again and a slight figure clad in black made off along the hallway and disappeared into the darkness, gone except for the diminishing thud of feet on the staircase.

'Jed?' Emma called from the bedroom.

'Lock the door and don't open it until I come back.'

'Jed?'

'Just do as I say,' I snapped, immediately regretting it, but not having time to apologise. I shut the door behind me and hurried along the hall to an open doorway.

The room was pitch-dark. It was like peering into a black hole of emptiness. I hesitated on the threshold, for all I knew the person who'd run for it could have been a distraction and someone else could be lurking inside waiting to poleaxe me. The aching chill to my cranium was slowly dissipating. I took this as a good sign and reached inside the door groping for the light switch and, with a click, the room was flooded with light.

The bedroom was very similar to the one I was sharing with Emma, cluttered with old, dark antique furniture. It had a masculine feel to it and, even as I glanced around the room taking in the wanton devastation, I wondered whether this could have possibly been where Oliver used to lay his head or perhaps even Edward.

Some unknown person had been through it like a whirlwind. Wardrobe doors hung open, with suits and jackets thrown into a pile upon the bed. Drawers had been pulled out, the contents strewn where they had fallen. A suitcase, lining ripped apart, lay abandoned where it had been dragged from beneath the bed. Clothing and papers were strewn haphazardly across the carpet. A briefcase and jewellery box had been prised open and tossed upon the mattress where broken-spined books also lay scattered. A couple had bounced onto the floor, missing the carpet. Had this been what I'd heard, books hitting the polished floorboards?

Barefooted, I padded inside surveying the mess. Whoever I had seen run from the room had been searching for something, that was for sure, but who? And for what? As much as I didn't want to wake Simon I had to. The police needed to be called.

I turned to leave and froze. Half-hidden by the open door, Simon lay sprawled on his side, blood trickling from his hairline just above the temple.

I dropped down onto my knees beside him, though I doubted there was much I could do. His complexion had been the colour of candle wax before, now it was the shade of skimmed milk and his lips had taken on the lilac blue tinge of death. I tentatively put two fingers to his throat, expecting it to only confirm what I was thinking. His skin was icy to the touch and I wondered how long he'd been lying here. Had his assailant callously searched the room after assaulting him, leaving him collapsed on the floor while he could have been dying?

There was a faint flicker beneath my fingertips; I'd found a pulse. It was weak and irregular, but it *was* a pulse. I grabbed a discarded coat from the bed and covered him over before running back down the corridor to our room.

'Emma, it's me,' I called. 'Open up.'

There was the rattle of a key in the lock and the door swung open, Emma appearing in the doorway. 'What is it?'

'Call an ambulance,' I told her. 'It's Simon – he's been attacked.'

'Oh my,' she said, her hand flying to her throat.

Not waiting to see if she was going to do as I said, I hurried back to kneel next to Simon. He looked so terrible I checked his pulse again. It was still there, faint, but there. I heard Emma speaking and then she was crouching down beside me, mobile phone pressed to her ear.

'Did you move him at all?' she asked me.

'No. All I did was check his pulse and then cover him with the coat.'

Emma dutifully repeated this into the phone. 'Yes,' she said. 'I can see blood on his forehead.' She leant over him getting a little closer. 'There's a lot of blood in his hair.' Then there were more questions.

I tapped Emma's arm to get her attention. 'I'd better rouse someone to tell security to let in the ambulance,' I said.

She gave a small nod and I padded back to our room to ring the extension annotated as night service. A young man answered after three rings. 'There's been an accident,' I said deciding to be a little circumspect with the truth. 'An ambulance will be coming. Can you make sure security opens the gate when they arrive?' Assured that this would be arranged I returned to where Emma was still on the phone, crouching beside Simon.

With a final 'thank you' she finished the call. 'They're on their way,' she said to me.

'Good. Should we phone the police?'

'All done. The operator put a call through to them as soon as she had alerted the paramedics.' I knelt down beside her. 'What made you get up?' she asked.

'Something woke me. Then I heard some thumps, probably whoever it was throwing books about and opening drawers.' I realised my hand was on my beard and let it drop to my side. 'I saw him, Emms. He did a runner when I called out.'

'Just as well you didn't chase after him.'

'I wasn't exactly dressed for it. Anyway, I didn't realise how serious it was.'

'Good job too. It could have ended with you both being taken off to hospital. What do you think they wanted?'

I glanced around the room. 'I have no idea. It's yet another of the mysteries of Kingsmead Manor.'

Emma crossed her arms, hugging herself. 'I fear for Laura coming here as things are.'

'You and me both,' I said and, as the chill at the base of my skull hadn't completely gone, it didn't fill me with optimism that this was in any way over.

Donald and Sarah Walters appeared about five minutes before the paramedics, apparently alerted by the guy on night duty as soon as he'd come off the phone to me. Donald had dressed in a hurry, in faded jeans and elbow-patched jumper. Mrs Walters, like Emma, was in her nightclothes covered by a full-length, navy dressing gown, making me feel considerably underdressed, my own dressing gown only just reaching my knees and showing off my naked legs.

'Oh my goodness,' Mrs Walters said upon seeing Simon lying on the floor. 'How could this have happened?' I explained about the unknown assailant while the couple listened stony-faced. 'This is dreadful,' Mrs Walters said. 'We have all this security and yet for the second time we've had such a terrible incident.'

I didn't voice an opinion, though it was something I'd been dwelling on. 'Whose room is this?' I asked.

'Mr Edward's,' Mrs Walters replied without any hesitation. 'Mr Oliver sometimes used it for storage when he was married. You know – for old clothes and books, things his wife might think were surplus to requirements.' She wrinkled her nose.

'You didn't like Mrs Pomeroy?' I asked.

Her expression said it all, she could have been chewing on a wasp. 'It's not my place to like or dislike any member of the family.' She glanced down at Simon, her face pinched. 'Is there nothing we can do for him?' she asked. 'I hate seeing him lying there like this.'

'They said not to move him,' Emma said. 'We could do more harm than good.' At this point I excused myself to pull on a pair of trousers and a shirt. I really didn't want to have to deal with medical staff and the police while half-naked, and Emma's constant urging for me to wear pyjamas while we were away wasn't quite so funny any more.

By the time we had finished with the paramedics and then speaking to the police there wasn't a lot of point going back to bed. The soft flush of dawn was colouring the horizon by the time I saw the police officers out and the nice WPC warned me the detective investigating Oliver's death would be calling to speak to us later in the morning.

I returned to the living room to join Emma, Donald and Sarah Walters drinking the tea and coffee the housekeeper had very kindly provided, when it looked as though we'd be spending the rest of the night answering questions.

'Mr Cummings,' Mrs Walters said, as I flopped back down next to Emma on the couch, 'I was asking your wife what you both thought we should do about Miss Laura? She's due to be arriving here sometime later today.'

'It was something we'd discussed with Simon,' I said. 'He was of the opinion he could hardly put her off now this is all hers, but this happening . . . I don't know, I guess it should be her decision.'

'I suppose,' she said, biting her lip. 'It's just we, Mr Walters and I, are a bit concerned, what with all that's been going on. I mean poor Mr Oliver's' – her eyes flickered shut for a moment – 'murder and now this. We're both worried for her.'

'I suppose we *could* contact her and tell her what's happened,' Emma said. 'What do you think, Jed?'

My heart began to sink. I didn't sign up for this. Helping an old friend get closure was one thing, but this was beginning to all get out of hand. Then I thought of how the poor girl was coming to Kingsmead, probably all excited at meeting her new-found family and inheriting a fortune, only to find herself walking into a major crime scene.

'Have you her number?' I asked.

Both the Walters stood in unison, duty done. 'I'll get it for you,' Mrs Walters said.

It wasn't exactly an easy phone call. Laura Simmons, as she was now known, came across as a nice young woman. She was horrified by what had happened to Simon, obviously, but saw no real reason why she shouldn't take residence at the estate as planned. After all, she had to move in by the fast-approaching month's end. Had I been a cynical old whatnot I would have said it was the vast fortune she was about to inherit or possibly lose that swayed her decision. Had it been me, I couldn't with hand on heart say I would have been any different. When you're young you don't have a real sense of your own mortality. It's only when you get older and have come face-to-face with death, whether it be natural or malicious, that this begins to change and every moment becomes precious.

I had faced both. I had watched my best friend in the world slowly succumb to cancer and I had killed rather than be killed while doing my job. I didn't need my sixth sense for danger to tell me there was something evil at work in Kingsmead. I could feel it closing in around us and it made me worry for the blissfully unaware young woman who was soon to arrive.

'So, she's still coming,' Mrs Walters said when she had Maddy bring us mid-morning coffee.

'Yes,' I said.

'And what will you be doing, Mr and Mrs Cummings?'

I glanced at Emma and she cocked her head slightly, her expression questioning. 'Well, obviously we'll stay until we know Simon's out of the woods. Then I suppose it's Miss Simmons's decision. She doesn't know us from Adam, and this *is* her house now.'

'The hospital said Simon was comfortable and stable,' Emma added.

'So, we'll just have to wait and see how he is this afternoon.'

Mrs Walters managed a smile. 'You will keep us informed?'

93

'Of course.'

'Then, if that will be all?'

'Yes, yes, thank you,' I replied and, with a bob of the head, she left, gesturing to Maddy to follow on behind her.

I sipped on my coffee, waiting until they were out of earshot. 'Do you mind staying on a bit longer?'

'I'd rather that than leave this poor young woman alone with only the servants to keep an eye on her. They haven't exactly been doing a good job of keeping the family safe so far.'

'I don't suppose they signed on for bodyguard duties, Emms.'

She gave a sniff. 'What about the security guards? What are they being paid for?'

She had a point. 'It does make you wonder how the intruder got into the house. I can understand it must be difficult to keep anyone from getting into the grounds, the boundary must be massive. The house, though . . .'

'I thought it was alarmed,' Emma said.

'So did I.'

'So how did this mystery man you saw get in?'

I shook my head and wondered whether perhaps he hadn't needed to.

CHAPTER NINE

Detective Inspector Brogan turned up with his sidekick after lunch. Despite the seriousness of Simon's assault, and the news that there was apparently a dangerous psychopath on the loose, they certainly didn't appear to be in any hurry, and I was already irritated with the bloke before I'd even met him. They both went upstairs to take a look around before talking briefly to Donald and Sarah Walters, then asking to speak to us.

Brogan was a big man, about my size, and had the air of carrying the weight of the world upon his shoulders. His grey suit had a crumpled, worn look, its creases matching those on his face. The rest of his clothing was equally unprepossessing. His once-white shirt was an overwashed grey and his navy tie, although clean, had the evidence of having seen many a hurried meal, eaten behind the steering wheel. Even with my lack of sleep, compared to him I looked as fresh as a daisy. He'd cut himself shaving and judging by the remaining patchy stubble had given up immediately afterwards.

Sergeant Peters was as different as chalk is to cheese. He was young, enthusiastic and, I guessed, newly promoted. His dark grey suit was pressed to perfection as was his light grey shirt and maroon tie. His black shoes were polished to a patent shine and I hate to think what they must have looked like after having to traipse through the woodland to Oliver's murder scene. Perhaps in rural settings they kept wellingtons in the car boot.

The detective inspector introduced himself and Peters in a gruff, perfunctory manner before telling us they hadn't been able to question Simon as of yet as, although comfortable, he was presently under sedation and wouldn't be allowed visitors until the following afternoon. In the circumstances, he continued, any information we could give them would be most helpful.

Their questions were much the same as the officers who had taken our statements in the early hours of the morning.

The detective inspector came to the end of what I thought were his questions and went to stand before changing his mind and sinking back onto his seat. 'So, you're an old friend of the family?'

I had an icy tickle at the back of my head. 'Not really. I'd met Oliver Pomeroy a couple of times, but Simon was my friend.'

Brogan lifted his red-rimmed eyes to mine, his bloodhound expression getting longer. 'How did you meet?'

I shifted in my chair. It was something I didn't like speaking about; in fact, the majority of it I couldn't speak about. 'We served together.'

'In the forces?' the sidekick asked, glancing away from his notebook, his pencil hovering above the page.

'Yep,' I said.

'What were you in?'

I met him eye to eye and I don't think he liked what he saw. His Adam's apple bobbed, but he didn't look away. I leant back in my seat. 'And the relevance is . . . ?'

'So, Simon Pomeroy would know how to look after himself?' Brogan said, jumping in.

'He did then, but we're talking years ago and you've met Simon, he's clearly not very well.'

Brogan nodded. 'I understand Laura Simmons is due to arrive sometime today.'

I gave him the same long look I'd given his colleague. 'Yes, I understand she is.'

'And you'll be . . . leaving?'

I continued the stare. 'Once we've made sure Simon's OK, perhaps.'

'You know he phoned me yesterday,' he said.

Ah-ha, I wondered when we'd get to this. 'Yes.'

'You went to this Goldsmere House with him.'

'We both did,' Emma said, shifting forward on the seat so she was perched on the edge. She had definitely noticed the plummeting of the temperature between me and the two policemen.

'Why do you think Mr Pomeroy didn't choose to phone me before he went to Goldsmere House?'

'How the hell should I know?' I said.

'I think Simon was hoping there'd been some sort of terrible mistake,' Emma chipped in.

'But there hadn't?'

'No, apparently not,' Emma said.

I was getting a tad annoyed. I knew when someone was trying to play with me. 'Simon had just lost his brother only to find he'd been hiding a terrible secret from him.'

'Being?' Peters asked.

I'm surprised my mouth didn't drop open – maybe it did a bit. 'What do *you* think?' I snapped. 'Simon had been led to believe his older brother was killed almost forty years ago only to discover he'd been alive all that time and living in a mental institution. Oh, and by the way, his other brother knew all about it and hadn't told him.'

'And you hadn't any previous knowledge of this?'

'Why on earth should I? I hadn't spoken to Simon in years and I didn't know Oliver at all except to say hello to.'

'Why, then, did Simon Pomeroy ask you to come and stay at Kingsmead?'

I forced myself to stay very still and not lean back and cross my arms. It's meant to be a defensive gesture – this is how he would see it, anyway – in my case it was to stop me from punching someone's lights out.

'Everyone can do with a friend sometimes and sadly I don't think Simon has many of those any more.'

Brogan levered himself out of the chair, this time he made it to his feet. 'I'll be in touch,' he said. 'No need to show us out.'

'What about Edward Pomeroy?' I asked. 'We've been told he's a very dangerous man.'

He turned back to me with an ill-disguised sigh. 'We have it in hand. A recent photograph provided by Goldsmere House has been circulated and the local radio and television stations are asking for the public to contact us immediately, should he be spotted.'

'I don't suppose it'd be possible for us to have a copy, since neither of us have the faintest idea what Edward looks like?'

He gave an abrupt nod and glanced at the other policeman. 'See to it, will you. Now, if you'll excuse me,' and with that he stalked from the room.

His sidekick gave us a grim smile, which was more like a grimace, and they were gone.

I got up and marched over to the drinks' cabinet. 'Want a drink?'

Emma nodded, her lips pressed together in a thin line.

'VAT?'

'Yes, please,' she said, then, 'What was it with them? Why did I suddenly feel we were being treated like criminals?'

I gave her a large one, with a splash of tonic. She accepted it gratefully, but I could see she was fuming. I poured myself two fingers, then sploshed in another.

'Jed?'

I sat down next to her, clinking my glass against hers with a 'Cheers.'

'Detective Inspector Brogan made me feel really uncomfortable.'

'He was fishing.'

'What for?'

I thought about it for a moment. 'Damned if I know.'

'Do you think Laura will mind us staying on?' Emma asked.

'Two chances,' I said. 'If she chucks us out, I'm sure there'll be an inn or hotel somewhere nearby.'

She swirled the ice cubes around in her glass, staring

down at them as though they contained the answers to all the questions the universe might throw at us. 'I hate mysteries,' she eventually said, which made me laugh. 'What?'

'You *love* mysteries.' She scowled at me. 'Admit it.'

It took a few seconds before her expression gradually began to thaw and she laughed. 'You know me too well, Jed Cummings.'

'Now,' I said. 'Shall we go back upstairs and try and work out the *mystery* of what Simon's attacker was trying to find while we still have the run of the house?'

She grinned at me and swigged the last of her drink. I knocked mine back and jumped to my feet, taking her hand, and pulling her onto hers and into my arms. She gave me a peck on the cheek.

'Come on,' she said. 'We'd better get moving. Laura could arrive at any minute.'

The room was more or less as we'd left it. I stooped down to grab one of the books lying on the floor. It was an old, leather-bound novel, with gold-edged pages, by someone I'd never heard of. I dropped it on the bed with the others.

'I guess we can assume he never found what he was looking for,' I said. 'He was still in here rummaging around when I called out.'

Emma stood at the bottom of the bed and turned full circle. 'Looks to me like he's been through everywhere there is to search.'

'Hmm.' She was right, but from experience I knew if people had secrets or things they wanted to keep safe they usually found clever little places to hide them. I closed my eyes and imagined I was Oliver or Edward, it had once been his room, after all. Yes – if I were Edward where would I hide my secrets? It had been years, but I suddenly had the same surge of excitement and expectation I used to get when on a mission. I opened my eyes and smiled. If there was something to find I'd find it.

First, I had a quick look in the en suite bathroom. It was sparkling clean and smelt vaguely of bleach. Did even unoccupied rooms get regularly cleaned? From what I knew of Mrs Walters I suspected they did. I checked the low flush toilet cistern and there was nothing hidden there, and all the cabinets and drawers were empty except for cleaning products.

Back in the bedroom I searched the few drawers that hadn't already been dumped on the floor, pulling them right out and checking beneath them and inside the carcase in case something had been taped underneath or behind them. Disappointingly there was nothing – that would have been far too easy. Next, I checked all the cupboards for loose boards at the bottom or hidden compartments. When I looked up from what I was doing, Emms was sitting on the bed watching me.

'You've done this sort of thing before,' she said.

I gave a distracted grunt. 'Back in the day.'

'Can *I* do anything useful?'

To be truthful, I'd have rather done it myself; I knew what I was looking for, but it was hardly fair on Emms and everyone likes to feel they have a purpose. 'You can go through all the books,' I said. 'Flick through the pages making sure there are no underlined words, marked pages or anything hidden or unusual.'

She raised an eyebrow. 'Very James Bond-ish,' she said. I just smiled. I hadn't told Emms what I'd been or done when I was in the forces. I knew Reggie never had and I told myself by not telling her I was keeping his secrets as well as mine. I was lying even to myself. Some of the things we'd had to do were not of the sort a person could discuss with their nearest and dearest – or would want to. It could change their perception of you for ever and not in a good way.

I dragged a chair over to the wardrobe and climbed onto it to take a look on top – nothing except dust, fluff and cobwebs. I jumped down and pulled the door wide open. Two suits hung there, like the ghosts of a dead man. I ran my hands down the sleeves, checked the pockets and beneath the lapels. I felt like I was desecrating the dead. Even so I carried on, the dead sometimes did tell tales.

Disappointingly I didn't find a thing. As a last resort I would go over the suits and coats piled on the bed. My gut told me this wouldn't be where I would find what the mystery man had been seeking. If there had been something to find he would have found it. When I'd been in the job, my instincts had been what made me better than most. What they told me now was if we found what the man had been looking for, we could well be halfway there to solving a murder. Whether we would understand its significance or not was another matter.

I laid the two suits over the chair, leaving the wardrobe empty. It was huge. An antique piece and, by the rule of ugly, should be worth a fortune. It was a monstrosity. I ran my hands down the back, now and then rapping against the wood. Nothing appeared untoward.

Taking a step back I studied the size and shape, making comparisons between the inside and outside. The top and base were both ornately carved with an oak leaf and acorn pattern. The top was shaped upwards and behind it, as I'd discovered, there was nothing but bare wood. The base went down to floor level and had sunk into the carpet. I knelt to take another look inside: the bottom was flush with the door frame, meaning there was a good five inches between the bottom inner panel and the floor. This was nothing unusual I supposed and yet I felt a little hiccup of excitement inside my chest. I reached into the wardrobe, my fingers hovering above the bottom and they began to tingle. I didn't need to rap the wooden panel, I knew what it would tell me. I had found Edward's stash, whatever it might be. Now I just had to find a way of getting to it.

'Found something?' Emma asked, dropping the book she had been flicking through onto the bed to come and stand behind me.

'I think so.' I ran my fingers around the inside of the wardrobe's base. The wood didn't shift at all under pressure and I couldn't find any hidden locks or opening devices. I rocked back on my haunches to examine the carved detail. It was identical to the top. Swirls of oak leaves carved into the dark wood, with the occasional acorn thrown in for good measure. I ran my fingers over the ornate design, the tingling sensation in their tips increasing until it was almost a burn.

Emma crouched down beside me. 'Do you think there's a hidden drawer?'

'If there is, I can't see any way of opening it.'

Once again I ran my fingertips across the wood, this time very slowly, and each time my fingers ran across the carvings, in exactly the same two places, my skin began to prickle to such a degree it was like hot needles were being pressed into my skin. I knelt back studying the design. In both the places where my fingers burned there was a carved acorn.

'I think there might be some sort of mechanism,' I said, pressing each of the acorns first one at a time then both together, but nothing.

I sat back on my heels. 'It's no good. I'm sure there's something, but I can't see how to get it open.'

'Well, we can hardly take a crowbar to it.'

'Hmm.' One more time I leant forward and rested my fingertips on the wood then closed my eyes. *A little bit of help would be useful.* I wasn't really expecting a response and I definitely wasn't expecting the snarl and feeling of such intense, white-hot rage that surged through me. I rocked back so violently I almost fell.

'Easy,' Emms said, grabbing hold of my arm.

Shaken, I pulled myself onto my knees. What had that been all about? Someone was very angry indeed and I wondered who and why? Even so, despite their anger, they had told me what I wanted to know. Dragging my concentration back to the wardrobe I reached out to put my forefingers above each of the acorns and pushed down on them in a sliding motion. For a moment there was no movement and then abruptly they gave and shot downwards, there was a quiet click and a drawer sprung open a crack, partially held in by the thick carpet.

'Good God,' Emma said.

I smiled. 'I think we've found our hidden treasure.'

I carefully drew out the drawer, the pile of the carpet slowing down the process as it kept catching on the wood but, with a bit of a fiddle, eventually it opened right out. There were three things in the drawer. A large, brown-padded envelope, a plush navy jewellery case, the kind you'd keep a necklace or string of pearls in, and a Polaroid camera.

'We'd better take this lot back to our room.'

'You think?'

'Just in case someone comes creeping in here to have a nosy around. I doubt we're the only ones wondering what was worth breaking in and clobbering Simon to find.'

Emma got to her feet. 'You're probably right,' she said.

Back in our room I dropped our ill-gotten gains on the bed. Now I had the *treasure* I was a little nervous as to what I might find. Our visit so far had hardly turned out the way I'd been expecting.

Emma sat on the bed and ran her finger across the lid of the jewellery case. 'Whoever he bought this for had expensive taste.'

'Who says he bought it for someone?'

'I'd put money on it containing a gold and possibly diamond necklace or maybe even sapphire or ruby.' Her brow creased into a frown. 'Oh,' she said, jerking her hand away from the box as if burnt. 'Sugar!'

'What?' I asked. 'Are you OK?'

'You were right. Whoever he was didn't buy this for someone else. It was his and,' her expression became puzzled, 'I'm not at all sure whether he loved what's inside or loathed it.'

I laid my hand on the top of the case. A strange feeling flowed through me, one I couldn't quite place. It was like – adoration – no. No, it was more reverence and it filled me with a sense of unease.

'What do you think?' Emma asked. 'I can see from your face you felt something too.'

The vision I'd seen back at the clearing shot into my head and with it came the same rush of emotion I'd felt in Edward's room. It lasted little more than a split second and was gone, but whatever was in the case made someone very angry. I pulled over a chair and sat facing the small case lying on the bed. At the front there was a small brass clasp. I flicked it into the open position and putting a hand on either side of the lid, my unease increasing, lifted it with my thumbs and forefingers.

Emma gasped. I was somehow not as surprised as I should have been. Lying curled upon dark blue velvet was a jet-beaded silver chain, just like the one I'd seen in my vision, and surrounded by the glossy, black beads was a crucifix – an inverted crucifix.

'*This* was not what I was expecting,' Emma said.

I shook my head and reached out to touch the silver effigy with my forefinger. Once again the feeling of rage flowed through me. Rage and shock. He had been caught unawares. His betrayal had come out of the blue and he'd had no inkling of what was about to happen until it was too late.

I tucked my finger under the beads and lifted it out of the box, letting it twist and spin, until the crucifix was at eye level. It was beautiful in a terrible sort of way. The depiction of Christ in his final agony had been fashioned by a master. The delicately inscribed features of the figure were filled with unimaginable anguish and it occurred to me that they were replicated by the immense feelings the owner had experienced in his last moments.

The chain slowly stopped spinning and came to a halt. Engraved on the back of the cross was an inscription. I leant forward, squinting. I couldn't quite make out what it said.

'Pass me my glasses, could you?' I said, gesturing towards the bedside table.

Emma stretched across the bed and handed them to me. 'What is it?'

'There's some sort of inscription,' I said, fumbling one-handed with my specs. I perched them on the end of my nose and tried again. 'Oh?'

Emma scrambled off the bed to crouch beside me and, resting her hand on my knee, she too, peered at the back of the cross.

We exchanged a glance and I dropped the cross onto my palm, pushed my glasses further along my nose and looked again. Inscribed in swirling script on the back of the crucifix were the words 'Celebrant Edward Pomeroy'.

CHAPTER TEN

'I could be wrong, but I think this confirms it. Oliver and Edward were members of a cult.'

'I think you could well be right,' Emma said as I reached for the envelope.

I didn't like to think what nonsense it contained. Because this was what Satanism was – stupid, bloody nonsense and a good excuse for people who should know better to get their kit off for extramarital nooky. I was about to upend the contents onto the bed when a knock on the door made me jump and had me scrabbling to shove them, the camera and the jewellery case under the bedcovers and out of sight, while Emma hurried to the door.

'Mrs Walters?' I heard her say.

'I'm sorry to bother you, Mrs Cummings, but I thought you might like to know that Miss Laura has arrived.'

'Oh, thank you. Where is she now?'

'I've settled her in a room in the East Wing. I thought you might all like to meet for drinks at six to give you time to get to know each other before dinner.'

'That's most thoughtful of you.'

'The poor lass is probably at a bit of a loss. And of course, with Mr Simon in hospital . . .' she tailed off.

'Quite. We'll be down at six.'

'Mrs Cummings,' I heard the housekeeper say and then the pad of receding footsteps as Emma closed the door, leaning against it.

I threw back the bedcovers and retrieved our booty. 'I'm beginning to wish we'd just left these where we found them,' I grumbled.

Emms gave me one of those looks of hers she's so good at. 'Yeah, right.'

'Meaning what?'

She laughed and pushed away from the door to come back and sit on the bed. 'You accused me of loving mysteries when you're just as bad. This is all right up your street.'

'What? People getting murdered and thumped on the head?'

She pulled a face. 'No – the intrigue. You love all the delving into the unknown and seeking out the truth. Reggie was the same. You can take the man out of Military Intelligence, but you can never take the creeping around, and doing the derring-do out of the man.'

My mouth dropped open. 'You knew about that?'

She gave me one of those '*Really?*' looks. 'Even George down the pub knew. He told Jim you were in Intelligence.'

'How did he know?' There was I thinking no one had any inkling about what I'd once been, when even the local publican knew and was discussing it with his patrons.

'When a man won't talk about his military career it's either because he never really had one or he was involved in something to do with national security. As both you and Reggie served together *and* you were both so very tight-lipped it was obvious you must have been up to something covert. It doesn't take a genius to work it out.'

'Reggie said you didn't know.'

She shrugged. 'I never told him I did. He was like you, he liked to appear mysterious.' She sat down on the bed. 'Come on, then, what's in the envelope?'

Feeling ever so slightly flabbergasted I tipped the contents onto the bed. There were a further three smaller envelopes and a folded sheet of paper. 'I don't like to appear mysterious,' I muttered.

'Hmm,' she said with a smile and picked up the piece of paper, unfolding it. Her eyes jerked to mine. 'I think they're pictures of Laura.' She tapped the top of the page with a fingernail. 'Look, here's her name.' She handed the A4 sheet to me.

She was right. There were eight colour photographs of a dark-haired young woman, who I assumed was Laura, going about her daily life: walking down a street, climbing the steps into an office building, kissing a friend goodbye outside a restaurant. All everyday, normal actions.

'Someone has been keeping tabs on her by the looks of it.'

'But why would Edward?'

I turned the page over, studying it. There were two torn punch holes down the left-hand side. 'Who's to say Edward had these taken? These are professional surveillance photos and have been torn from a file.' I moved to sit next to Emma. 'What's in the envelopes?'

Emma glanced at her watch. 'We had better start to get ready for dinner.'

She was right. The envelopes would have to wait until later. I bundled them and the jewellery case together and wondered where the best place would be to hide them. In the end I pulled out the bottom drawer in my bedside cabinet, dropped in the files and replaced the drawer. The jewellery case I hid under the foot of the mattress. The camera, being the least interesting of our treasure trove, I put in the bottom of the wardrobe.

All I had left to do now was to get changed and put on a face that was a whole lot happier than I was feeling.

The photographs didn't in any way do Laura Simmons, as she was now known, justice. I could tell she would be attractive, but in real life she was more than that. The pictures hadn't captured her inner spark, which made her, for want of a better word, alluring. She was tall and a bit too skinny for my taste, but had a natural grace about her and was one of those women, a bit like Emma, who could have been wearing a plastic bin bag and would have still looked elegant. Her nose was a little long, her eyes a little too wide apart and her forehead a little too high, but when all put together she was quite captivating and I couldn't understand for the life of me why she had no boyfriend in tow.

Emma took to her immediately and before we'd finished our first drink she had teased out of her that she was presently single, unemployed and had been about to become homeless, when she had received the letter from Brandon Fredericks telling her she had been left a legacy.

'I had no idea, until I saw him this afternoon, of the enormity of it all,' she said. 'Jenny, my flatmate, said there must be property involved otherwise why make me travel all this way, but this' – she gave a vague gesture around the room – 'it's all too much to take in.'

'Had you met any of the family?' Emma asked.

She shook her head, swallowing a mouthful of wine. 'No. I didn't know I had any, other than my Auntie June and she passed away six months ago.'

'Oh, I am sorry,' Emma said.

'I still miss her like crazy, I'm just surprised she never told me about my grandfather. She always said we had no other family.'

'From what we understand there was a falling-out at some time,' Emma said, 'but you'd have to ask Simon.'

'I hope he'll be all right,' she said, her eyes glistening. 'No sooner than I find out I have family this happens.'

'He was looking forward to meeting you so much,' Emma said.

'Wasn't he a bit put out that I'd been left the family home?' she asked, glancing from Emma to me.

Emma gave her an encouraging smile. 'Not at all.'

I kept quiet. Despite what Simon had told us I had my doubts.

Laura retired to her room early pleading tiredness and we followed on not long after. To be honest, I wanted to take a look at the contents of the envelopes in Edward's stash.

When we arrived back at the room I was half-expecting them to have disappeared, but they were exactly where I'd left them, as was the jewellery case.

112

I dropped them onto the bed. 'Want to take a look?' I asked.

'Go on,' she said.

I picked up one of the unmarked brown A5 envelopes, peeled open the flap and peered inside. Polaroid photographs – who on earth used Polaroid cameras these days? I glanced towards the wardrobe, where I had put the one we'd found; Edward obviously did. He'd been locked away most of his life and it was probably his from when he'd been a child. I emptied the contents out onto the bed and immediately understood. The photos were old, about sixteen years or so, and graphic mementos of a brutally murdered couple taken at the murder scene. Laura's likeness to the murdered woman was enough for me to surmise the couple were her parents.

Emma got up and walked away. 'They're . . . they're too awful.'

I agreed, they were. I had seen more than enough death in my time. I had also seen photographs taken as evidence at crime scenes. These photographs had not been taken by a forensic team or even a professional like the pictures of Laura. These had been taken as proof of a job done. I inwardly sighed, this was getting more terrible by the minute.

I made myself study each one. William and Martine Pomeroy hadn't just been murdered, they had been ritually killed. Martine had been stripped naked and spreadeagled on the floor her wrists and ankles tied to strategically placed heavy armchairs and stabbed through the chest. Whether this was before or after her eyes and tongue had been cut out, I couldn't tell. I had an awful feeling it was probably after.

113

The photographs of William were even more harrowing. He had similarly been stripped and spreadeagled across the dining table. He had been sexually mutilated and from the blood splatter I knew he had been alive when they had done it to him. His eye sockets were a bloody mess and his mouth was stretched open in a gory, silent scream. It had been a bloodbath, a bloodbath with a message. The injuries inflicted on the couple had been carried out for a reason.

I shuffled the photos into a pile and slid them back into the envelope. This was a mess. I rubbed at the bridge of my nose. I had been wrong about the people belonging to this mysterious cult. There was more to their group activities than sex – they were truly dangerous people and Emma and I were slap bang in the middle of it all. And now so was Laura.

There was also something else: these pictures being in Edward's possession begged the question – who had ordered the murder of his brother's son and daughter-in-law?

'So what does all your Military Intelligence training tell you about this?' Emma asked.

'Apart from we should get the hell out of here?'

She moved to stand in front of me and stroked my hair back from my face. 'Like that's going to happen.'

'You should go home.'

She grimaced. 'If I'm in danger here with you, I'll be in even more danger back at home on my own if this should all get nasty.'

She was right. If they had any inkling about how much we now knew we were in deep shit. I needed to speak to Simon. He had been living here on and off about the time when William had left. If anything strange had been going on he must have realised. Perhaps he had and this had been the real reason why he'd contacted me. He was ill, he was scared, and he was all alone and he needed someone he could trust.

While Emma was in the bathroom getting ready for bed I took a seat, dropping the last two envelopes onto my knees. One was quite bulky and peeping inside I could see several more Polaroid photographs and I wasn't at all sure I had the stomach for any more of Edward's nightmarish pictures. The other was flat and it looked as though there were just a couple more sheets of paper inside.

Girding my loins, expecting to see more atrocities, I slid the photos out onto my lap. I couldn't have been more surprised. These were a different kettle of fish altogether and, if I wasn't mistaken, taken from the doorway leading into Edward's en suite bathroom.

A slender, dark-haired woman was taking a shower. Not much more than a hazy figure behind the steamy water-splashed screen, I suspected she was completely unaware she was having her photograph taken. I flicked through the others and they were more of the same, except they weren't in chronological order as the last picture had been taken before the screen had become too misted. This was the best picture of the woman. I couldn't see her face. It was angled away from the photographer, her head thrown back and her short black hair plastered to her scalp like a swimming cap, as the water pounded down onto her breasts. I pondered on who she could be before returning them to their envelope.

Inside the last one was a couple of sheets of paper, this time folded into four. Again they were torn along the left-hand edge where they had been ripped from a file. With some trepidation I unfolded them, spreading them out across my knees. It was just as well I was sitting down.

I was beginning to understand why Detective Inspector Brogan had such a rumpled and world-weary appearance. The two pages were full of pictures and once again were professional surveillance photos. These, however, didn't portray the normal, everyday life of a police officer. They had been taken with one motive in mind, to my way of thinking, blackmail.

Even though printed onto standard computer paper they were of good quality and showed the DI with a woman, and I was pretty sure it was the same one who had been photographed in the shower. Strangely enough, once again, not one of them showed her face. She was tall and slim, although shorter than Brogan. Her hair was slightly longer in these pictures and was more of a shiny black bob. The first couple were of her greeting him with a kiss not intended for family members or mere acquaintances. After those things began to get steamy, and by steamy I mean X-rated. If I had to guess I would say the photographer had somehow managed to get himself a room in an opposite building or maybe had taken the photos from a rooftop. Brogan and his lady friend hadn't bothered to close the curtains.

Each of the sheets of photos was timed and dated and I had to give it to the bloke, he was up for anything. Some of the pictures taken of him and the unknown woman in the back of his car did make me quite envious of his agility and general dexterity, though I did wonder at his naivety – his relationship with the woman had 'honey trap' written all over it. This was something else I knew a lot about. In my previous line of business we had to be aware of the signs. A compromised operative was an unreliable operative. I guessed the same could be said about police officers.

So, where had Edward purloined these photos from? Oliver perhaps? But why would *he* want a serving, fairly high-ranking policeman in his pocket? And it did beg the question – could DI Brogan be trusted?

'Anything of interest?' Emma asked as she strolled out of the bathroom brushing her hair.

'You could say so.'

'Want to share?'

I handed her the two sheets of paper and the envelope. 'I'd be interested to hear what you make of them,' I said as I made for the bathroom.

When I reappeared Emma was sitting in bed, with glasses perched on the end of her nose. Her forehead creased into a frown as she tilted one of the sheets of photographs at an angle.

'He's quite flexible for his age,' she commented.

'He's not very old.'

She looked at me over the top of her glasses. 'Hmm, I would have thought old enough to know better, but that's men for you.' She tapped the envelope. 'And this woman – she certainly gets around.'

'Doesn't she just.' I flopped down on the bed next to her. 'So, what do you think Oliver was up to? Assuming it was Oliver who had these photos of Laura taken. It certainly couldn't have been Edward, not while he was in Goldsmere.'

She shook her head. 'He was a man with a plan, that's for sure.'

I agreed. 'But what *was* the plan?'

She refolded the sheets of paper and handed them to me. 'Not sure. He had money, so it can't have been anything to do with financial gain.'

'So what is it a man like Oliver would crave other than money?'

Her eyes met mine. 'Power,' she said. 'A man who had everything would hunger for power.'

CHAPTER ELEVEN

I had a restless night. When I did manage to doze off I had anxiety-fuelled dreams, the sort that turned to smoke as soon as I woke. I couldn't remember much about them other than I was either rushing about late for somewhere I had to be or I was searching frantically for something I couldn't find. And all the while I was running or searching I could hear the whisper of chanting voices and the rhythmic thud of feet walking in time.

By the onset of morning, as the grey light of dawn crept underneath the curtains, I'd given up on trying to sleep. Of course, I immediately dropped off and didn't wake until Emma snuggled against me, nudging me into wakefulness.

I yawned, stretched and wrapped my arms around her. She laid her head on my chest, her hair silky against my chin. I smiled at the ceiling. How I'd captured this woman's heart I'd no idea. She was so out of my league it wasn't true. I had loved her from the first moment I'd seen her, the day my best mate introduced her to me as his fiancée. And yet I had been happy for him, truly happy. When he'd become sick it had hurt and when he died . . . Well, I was bereft. Emma and I were both devastated. I was her friend and we consoled each other as only best friends can. I'd never thought I would be anything else to her. I didn't dare even countenance it. But here we both were. I kissed the top of her head, her blonde hair tickling my lips.

'Come on, you lovely man,' she whispered. 'We'd better get up. Laura will be waiting and we have to phone the hospital.'

'You go first,' I said. 'I'll lay here like a gentleman of leisure while you beautify yourself.'

She pulled herself onto her elbow to look at my face. 'Hmm, perhaps *you* should go first.' She pecked me on the cheek and threw back the covers. 'I won't be long.'

'That'll be a first,' I murmured, but she was already gone.

I sprawled there feeling happy until the real world began to creep into my thoughts. Damn Simon and his psychotic bloody family. I immediately felt mean. Simon had no more control over his siblings than I did.

Any pleasure I was getting from lying in bed doing nothing evaporated and, with a huff, I hauled myself into a sitting position and groped for the dressing gown draped across the bedside chair.

I drew back the curtains and went out onto the balcony. The air was already beginning to warm and the grey mist floating above the lawn and fields would burn away by the time we'd finished breakfast. Instead of the beautiful view bringing me joy I felt deflated. Such a beautiful place, and yet so evil. No, it wasn't the place, it was the people who had lived here. Or perhaps still did. There had been many robed figures in my vision.

Unsettled I went back inside.

'Did you sleep well?' Emma asked Laura, as Maddy arrived with a fresh pot of coffee.

Laura pulled a face. 'Not really,' she said. 'Did you hear anything strange last night?'

Maddy, who had been pouring me a cup of coffee, flinched slopping hot liquid onto the table, just missing my hand.

'Careful, girl,' Mrs Walters snapped.

'Sorry, ma'am.' She tugged a cloth out of her apron pocket, dabbing at the spillage. 'I am so sorry,' she said directly to me.

'Don't worry. No harm done.'

She bobbed into what I swear was a small curtsy, then she was gone.

'I'm sorry,' Mrs Walters said as she checked the table. 'She's normally so careful.'

'It was an accident. No problem.'

'Well, if that's all?' She glanced around the table.

We all murmured our thanks and she was gone.

'What were you saying about hearing noises last night?' Emma asked.

'I heard something strange.'

'How do you mean *strange*?' I asked.

She put down her cup. 'Here's the thing – it sounded like chanting and' – she hesitated, thinking about it –

'when I went out on the balcony to listen, I thought I saw a glow over in the forest. Like maybe there was a bonfire burning.'

'Chanting?' I said, thinking of my dreams. 'Are you sure?'

'Not really. It's what it sounded like, but . . . I don't know,' she finished with a shrug.

'Maybe we should all take a ride over there,' I suggested.

'Only if you're prepared to ride Satan,' Emma said, with a laugh. She turned to Laura. 'Do you ride at all?'

'I went pony-trekking with the school as a child, but not recently.'

'Why don't you go with Laura?' Emma said. 'She could ride Angel. She's a steady mare.'

I was about to object – I mean why would a young thing like Laura want to go riding with an old duffer like me? – but before I could get the words out Laura beamed at me. 'Would you mind? I'd love to take a look around the estate.'

'Of course, I'd be glad to,' I said, feeling a bit like I'd been outmanoeuvred.

'That's settled, then,' Emma said, with a twitch of her lips and trying not to laugh. 'After we've finished breakfast, perhaps?'

'I'd better go and ask Donald to get Angel and Jericho ready for us,' I said.

'I'm sure Mrs Walters will pass on a message,' Emma said. 'She's bound to be back before we've done here.'

Emma was right, as usual, and while I made the arrangements, the girls drifted off into the hallway laughing and chatting as they went. I was glad they were getting on so well, though in the present circumstances it would make it a bit difficult to leave. With Simon gone I couldn't help feeling responsible for his grandniece.

'All sorted?' Emma asked as I joined them at the foot of the stairs.

'Yep, Mrs Walters has gone off to speak to her husband now.'

Laura started up the staircase. 'I'll see you shortly, then,' she said, glancing back at me.

I checked my watch. 'Down here in twenty minutes?'

She gave me another beaming smile and hurried off up the stairs.

I followed Emma to our room to change, me into something suitable for riding and Emma into something light and cool for sunbathing. 'While you're off gallivanting, I'm going to sit in the courtyard and make the most of the sunshine,' she told me.

I left Emma poring over several pairs of shorts and T-shirts spread out over the bed. As I strode along the corridor, Maddy came hurrying towards me, clutching a carrier bag to her chest. She made one of her peculiar little bobbing motions as I passed. When I glanced back along the hallway she was knocking on our bedroom door. None the wiser, I carried on towards the stairs to meet Laura in the entrance hall.

We heard the raised voices before we turned the corner into the stable yard. Laura gave me a perplexed look, it was obvious a full-scale row was going on. As we entered the yard a glowering young man, who I assumed to be another of the stable hands, was leading Satan out of his stall to join Jericho and Angel who were patiently waiting. The lad kept his head down, his full lips puffed into a morose pout. In the circumstances I couldn't blame him. Dan Crouchley and a red-faced Donald Walters were going head to head while Mrs Walters looked on, her forehead creased into angry lines.

'Don't you dare speak to me like that,' Donald said, and Dan burst into loud laughter.

'Or what? You'll do what?'

The stable hand coughed, giving an almost imperceptible tilt of the head towards us and three sets of eyes immediately swung our way.

Dan was the first to recover, though I think it more likely he couldn't care less if the new lady of the manor caught him and Donald fighting. His lips curled into a smile. 'Mrs Cummings not joining you?' he asked.

'Not today,' I said.

Dan laid a hand on Satan's flank. 'Mind if I tag along? I wouldn't want to disappoint the lad, he's all excited now, thinking he's going for a trot.'

Donald's face flushed a deeper scarlet. If Laura noticed, she didn't care. 'Of course not,' she said. 'That would never do.'

'I'll be getting on,' Donald said and, with a curt bob of the head to Laura and then me, stalked off towards the house with Mrs Walters in tow.

Dan watched them go, his eyes glittering with laughter and I couldn't help but wonder what the argument had been about.

'I guess you'll be wanting to take Jericho,' he said to me.

'Yes, thanks. These days I don't think my riding skills are quite good enough for Satan.'

He grinned. 'Ah, the poor lad is misunderstood, that's all, a bit like me.'

I raised an eyebrow and his grin grew wider. He turned to Laura. 'So, I'm guessing you must be the new mistress,' he said. 'I'm Dan Crouchley and if I can be of any assistance at any time, don't hesitate to call.'

'I'll be sure to remember that,' she said and by the slight flush to her cheeks I could tell she was already falling under the spell of his bad-boy good looks. I held in a sigh. Laura was a nice young woman and I didn't want a rift developing between her and the staff over Dan, however likeable he was. I haven't had an awful lot to do with servants, but one thing I did know, they were the biggest snobs in a household. Everyone had their place and they had to stick to it; mixing informally with their employers was not acceptable. Laura didn't know the rules and I doubted Dan kept to them. Maybe Emma could have a word with her, then again I supposed it really wasn't any of our business.

Dan helped Laura mount and, despite my reservations, kept his hands to himself.

'Anywhere particular you want to go?' he asked as we trotted out of the yard and onto the track leading to the fields and forest beyond.

Laura gave me a sideways glance. I took the hint. 'Er, Miss Simmons saw a fire burning in the woodland last night and we thought we'd go and take a look,' I said.

Dan frowned my way and then at Laura. 'Whereabouts?'

When she lifted her hand to point, I wasn't surprised it was in the direction of the clearing where Oliver had allegedly died.

'Could possibly be a vagrant,' he said. 'We do get the occasional drifter setting up camp.'

'I thought the security was tight,' I said.

He laughed at that. 'How do you secure a boundary this huge?' he said. 'It would take a full-time army of men.'

It was much as I'd surmised and didn't make me feel any happier. My earlier disquiet wrapped itself around me like a shroud. I doubted the fire Laura had seen would be anything to do with a vagabond.

As it happened it was very difficult to remain morose in Dan's company for long. He had the Irish gift of the gab and an irreverent sense of humour that had my spirits lifting as we ambled along, this was until we reached the woodland. Dan took us along a different track to the one Donald Walters had shown us. It was wider and more accommodating for the horses. Even so, like before, as soon as we entered the trees the oppressive atmosphere closed in around us. I soon realised it wasn't only me who noticed, even Dan's constant banter stuttered into silence.

I glanced Laura's way and saw her shiver. 'Was it somewhere in here they found my grandfather?' she asked.

'Ahead a-ways,' Dan said. 'In the direction you thought you saw a fire.'

'Why would someone bring him all the way out here to murder him?'

'Maybe he ran,' I said, remembering his frantic dash for life through the undergrowth as I had seen it in my vision, though this was something I could never tell her. I doubted she'd believe me if I did.

We carried on in silence, the only sound being the

occasional creak of a tree or the horses' puffing and snorting and the clump of their hooves upon dirt. Above us there was a rustle of leaves as they were caught in a breeze and with it came the scent of smoke and burnt wood.

Dan was slightly ahead, with us following behind. Ever since entering the forest Laura had pulled in next to me and we were so close now our knees were practically touching. If I was uneasy, she was even more so.

Dan glanced back at us. 'Can you smell that?'

I nodded. 'Smells like there *has* been a bonfire,' I said.

'Have you been here before?' Laura asked me in a whisper.

I leant towards her. 'Once with Simon and Donald Walters, and later Emma and I came on our own.'

'Is it . . . ?' She shuddered.

'There's nothing so you'd know what happened,' I reassured her. 'Just a clearing and some strands of police tape.'

The aroma of smoke was getting stronger and after about another twenty yards or so I caught a glimpse of blue and white plastic hanging in broken strands and then we were following Dan into the clearing.

'Well, I'll be damned,' I heard him mutter as he slid down from Satan. The horse stomped his huge hooves and snorted. He didn't like it here any more than we did and Jericho soon joined him in whinnying and shaking his head.

I climbed down and stroked the creature's huge muzzle. 'Good boy,' I murmured as I looked around.

There hadn't been only one bonfire. Five small ones formed a circle around the periphery of the clearing with the main fire in the middle. All except the one in the centre had burnt to blackened ashes and scorched earth. Lines had been scratched into the dirt joining each of the five outer fires. Someone had tried to scuff them out, but even a fool could see they formed a five-pointed star. I wasn't sure why I was surprised. As much as I might not believe in Satanism and the like, these people apparently did – or they were playing like they did.

'What's that?' Laura said, pointing to what remained of the fire in the centre of the clearing. 'There's something in the ashes.' She gasped. 'God! It looks like a body.'

'Stay there,' I told her.

Dan started towards it with me following. This fire had been far bigger than the others and perhaps this was why it hadn't completely burnt away. Thankfully, whatever had been burnt in the fire, it wasn't a body. Burnt flesh had a distinctive aroma and once smelt you never forgot it.

'What the f—?' Dan grabbed a partially burnt stick from the edge of the fire and poked at what appeared to be a bundle of clothing. 'Aww, this is a bit sick,' he said, lifting it out of the ashes.

'What is it?' Laura asked as she slid down off Angel.

'It's a Guy – you know like you have on Fireworks Night,' Dan said as he managed to swing it out of the pile of burnt wood and dropped it at our feet. 'Someone's gone to a lot of trouble. It's got hair and everything.'

Laura gave a sort of strangled gasp. I glanced at her. She had a hand to her mouth and the colour had slid from her face. I looked back at the effigy bewildered by her reaction.

'Ah shit,' I said as Dan, apparently completely oblivious to Laura's distress, flipped the thing over onto its back.

It was wearing a dark wavy-haired wig and a mask, probably printed from a photograph and pasted onto card. It was a woman's face: the eyes had been blanked out with splodges of dark red paint giving the impression of empty, bloody caverns. The mouth and chin were awash with the same paint and it didn't take a lot of imagination to guess what this abomination represented. What remained of the silky jade shirt it was wearing, like the face, was vaguely familiar.

Laura staggered slightly and I grabbed her by the arm to stop her falling. 'Oh God! It's me,' she said. 'It's meant to be me.'

Then I remembered the shirt. Emma had commented on it. It was the one Laura had been wearing to dinner the previous night. To give her credit Laura didn't launch into hysterics, though she did hang onto my arm, I think mainly to remain upright.

'How could they have got hold of my shirt?' she murmured as if to herself.

Dan looked her way from where he was crouched above the effigy. He'd lost his smile. 'I'd be most interested to know that too,' he said.

'Can we go back, please?' she said, her voice trembling.

'Of course,' I said and, holding her arm, walked her over to Angel. I helped her onto the horse and then, as an afterthought, pulled out my mobile and went back to the centre of the clearing.

I took a picture of the dummy, the central bonfire and then a few more of the others. Dan watched me, stony-faced. 'Just in case,' I said. He nodded. He obviously watched the same TV programmes as me.

We rode back to the house in near silence. I didn't want to say anything in front of Laura, but if I had been worried about her coming here before, now I was seriously concerned. Was she being warned off or was it a promise? I was already considering riding straight back to the clearing to have a poke around and see if I could pick up on anything after making sure she was safely inside.

Then I wasn't.

A feeling of dread washed over me in a wave, driving any other thoughts straight out of my head. 'Emma?'

'What?' Dan asked.

'It's Emma,' I said, not caring what he thought. 'She's in trouble,' and I urged Jericho forward and into a gallop.

I heard Dan call after me, but I couldn't stop. Something terrible had happened or was about to happen to Emms. I had to pray it was the latter and I'd get there in time. Jericho raced along the track, head down, ears back, maybe sensing my fear, and then I could see the courtyard at the back of the house. There was a towel lying on one of the sunbeds with Emma's book and some clothing, but no Emma.

A wave of panic swept through me and, for a split second, I was drowning. The pool. Emma was in that fucking pool.

I swerved off the track, pounding across the beautiful lawns. I didn't have time to worry about a disgruntled gardener. I pulled Jericho to a halt as we clattered into the courtyard and practically fell off him in my hurry to get inside. I ran towards the conservatory, ripping off my jacket as I went. I was vaguely aware of the sound of more hooves clattering across the paving stones and then the thud of feet behind me.

I grappled with the door to the conservatory – for a terrible few moments I thought it was locked – and then I had it open and was running towards the pool. In the sunlight the water could have been ink-black and alive. It was heaving and frothing and foaming. I hauled off my boots and, without a second thought, dived straight in.

As soon as my head entered the water I saw her: a young woman's face looming in front of mine, filling my vision. A girl of about eighteen, her long, dark hair flowing around her dead, white face like black tendrils of seaweed. She reached out to me, her eyes huge and imploring. Imploring for what? I didn't have time for her now. I swam straight through the apparition, forcing myself down and down. The dark tiles making it appear as black as night down there and then I saw a flash of white amongst the boiling water – Emma.

She was thrashing and fighting and straining to swim to the surface, but something was holding her back. The spirits of the dead obviously weren't constricted by time and space, because as I drew closer a dark shape began to become clear: the young woman, clinging onto Emma's ankles and dragging her down. No, another woman, older, her hair long and bleached almost white. I had to get to Emma. I had to get her free. Emma's movements were getting weaker and weaker. Her hands flapping ineffectually against the water.

I swam at the wraith, too afraid of what she was doing to Emma to be scared for myself. I swiped at her, my hands passing through her body as if she was smoke, but it was enough, or was it she'd had her fun? She faded away, letting Emma go, to slowly float towards the surface, arms and legs outstretched and lifeless.

'*No!*' and inside my head I heard a woman's cruel, echoing laughter.

CHAPTER TWELVE

I thrashed towards the surface and felt the water heave as someone else jumped in. When my head broke the water Dan was pulling Emma to the side of the pool. Laura grabbed her arms, holding her head above the surface as Dan hauled himself out, then Emma, and immediately started CPR.

I don't remember getting out of the pool or dropping on my knees beside her. I don't remember taking her hand. All I can remember is the despair. I might have cried, I might have prayed – I suspect I did both.

Then she convulsed and rolled onto her side heaving and throwing up what appeared to be gallons of water, certainly it looked as though there was more than she could possibly have breathed in. But she was alive, and then she was in my arms and I was holding her tight and thanking God for not taking her so soon.

* * *

Emma didn't want to see a doctor. I insisted she did. I was going to call for the paramedics, but Mrs Walters assured me it would be quicker to get the family doctor to come and see her. She was probably right; he arrived within fifteen minutes.

Doctor Bell was an elderly gentleman and every bit the old-fashioned family doctor you would expect to see in period dramas. White-haired and portly, he was dressed in a black three-piece suit and exuded a jolly bedside manner.

'I prescribe an afternoon's bed rest and a lot of TLC,' he said, with twinkling eyes and Father Christmas ruddy cheeks.

'I suspect I'll be getting plenty of both,' she said with a smile, but she sounded tired and was already slipping into sleep by the time I showed the good doctor out.

He did his best to be reassuring, but seeing my worried expression said, 'I've given her a sedative and some antibiotics to ward off any chest infection, but if she suffers any breathing difficulties or falls into unconsciousness, or you are in any way at all worried about your wife, please call me, but she should be fine after a little rest.'

I thanked him and he drove off with a friendly wave.

My first instinct was to hurry upstairs to check on her, but she'd been asleep and it was only fair I should let Donald and Sarah Walters and Dan know how she was faring. I had been truly touched by the couple's concern and as for Dan – well – he had probably saved Emma's life. Then I would find Laura. Heaven knows what she was thinking. If it wasn't for the legacy, I wouldn't be surprised if she packed her bags and ran for the hills.

The house was quiet, unnaturally so. It was almost as

though the household had gone back into mourning and I had to pause for a second or two to control the emotion welling inside me. I had thought I'd lost her. There was a moment where I really did believe I had lost her, and the image of her very still body floating upwards and away from me passed through my mind.

I made for the kitchens. Walking along the corridor I could hear the murmur of low voices. The door was ajar, so it wasn't difficult to make out what was being said. I heard my name mentioned and this was enough to make me pause outside.

'What on earth happened?' I heard Mrs Walters say.

'I have no idea, but he knew, somehow he knew,' a masculine voice said, and from the Irish lilt I was guessing it was Dan.

'Just as well. If you hadn't found the poor woman . . . ?'

'I've never liked the poolroom,' a younger, feminine voice said. 'It gives me the creeps.'

'You have too much imagination, young lady,' Donald Walters said.

There was a sniff. 'And why'd you suppose that'd be?' she said. 'This place is enough to have anyone jumping at their own shadow.'

'Now then, Maddy,' Mrs Walters said, 'I'll have none of that talk.'

'I'm only saying what we're all feeling,' the girl muttered.

As interesting as it was listening to the servants gossip, I didn't want to be found eavesdropping, so I took a few steps back and tramped along, making a bit of noise.

I popped my head around the door and all eyes were immediately upon me. 'I thought I ought to let you know the doctor's gone now and he said my wife will be as good as new in a day or so. She just has to take things easy.'

Mrs Walters bustled over to me. 'I am so relieved,' she said. 'If there's anything we can do, you've only to ask.'

I muttered my thanks and glanced at Dan. 'I didn't get the chance to say earlier, what with all that was going on, but thank you. If it hadn't been for you, I'm not sure the outcome would have been so good.'

He smiled and gave a slow shake of the head. 'I did nothing you wouldn't have.' His eyes met mine and I could see a question in them, one he didn't want to ask in front of the others.

Mrs Walters cast a disapproving look his way but made no comment other than to ask me about lunch. 'Shall I have it served at one as usual?' she asked. 'I can take a tray to Mrs Cummings.'

'Thank you. You are most kind. All of you are.' I gave everyone the best smile I could muster, muttered another 'thank you' and left them to it. I would take a trip to the stables and try and catch Dan a little later.

Lunch was a rather subdued affair, which wasn't surprising in the circumstances. I had knocked on Laura's door, but there had been no answer and when she appeared at the table, she was pale-faced and her eyes puffy. She said hardly a thing while lunch was being served and as soon as the servants had left the room I understood why.

'I couldn't find my shirt,' she said as the door closed behind Maddy. 'Someone in this house must have taken it.'

I would have liked to have been able to say they wouldn't have, but unfortunately there was no other explanation.

'I think I have to phone the police,' I said.

'But it's so awful. How can I accuse one of the staff? I've only been here five minutes.' She paused, laying down her knife and fork. 'I can't, I really can't.' Her expression became slightly panicked. 'And how about what happened to Emma? Oh God, it was all my fault.'

I frowned at her. 'How could it have been *your* fault?'

A tear overflowed and trickled down her cheek. She wiped it away with an angry swipe of her fingers. 'She mentioned the pool at breakfast and how she didn't have a costume. I said she could borrow one of mine. I got Maddy to take it to her.'

I hadn't given it a thought. Of course, Emms had told me she hadn't brought a costume – why would she? We hadn't known there'd be a pool.

'Laura, it wasn't your fault. It was . . .' I was about to say an accident, but couldn't bring myself to say the word, it would've been a lie. I certainly couldn't explain what had really so nearly happened. 'It was just unfortunate,' I finished lamely, seeing her expression.

I think she was about to enquire more, but Mrs Walters appeared by the table, giving a discreet cough to get my attention. 'I have Mr Simon on the phone for you,' she said to me.

'He's awake?' Laura asked.

The housekeeper shot her an exasperated look.

'Evidently he is,' I said, excusing myself from the table and wondering why he hadn't called my mobile, then remembered he probably wouldn't have the number.

I took the call on an extension in the office. 'Simon?'

'Jed, I need you to come and see me this afternoon. Can you get away?'

'Of course. I'm pretty sure visiting hours are at four. Do you want me to bring Laura?'

There was a sharp intake of breath. 'She came?'

'Of course she came.'

There was a shuddery exhalation. 'I was hoping she might not.'

I glanced at the calendar on my watch. 'You told me yourself, under the terms of the will she had to move in here by the end of the month. Today is the twenty-sixth.' There was a moment's silence. 'Simon?'

'I need to speak to *you*.'

'Simon—'

He interrupted before I had a chance to speak further. 'See you at four,' and he rang off.

I stood staring at the phone for a moment. Simon had sounded scared. What *had* happened the night he was attacked?

Laura was still sitting at the table when I returned to the dining room. She had pushed her plate to one side and was frowning into thin air.

'How was he?' she asked as I sank back onto my seat.

I pulled a face. 'He sounded worried,' I said. 'He wants us to go and see him. I'm wondering whether perhaps we should delay phoning the police until we've spoken to him.'

She lifted the coffee pot. I nodded and she poured me a cup and then one for herself. 'You're right. Let's talk to him first. Then we can make a decision. Did he say what happened the night he was attacked?'

'No, he was more anxious that we go and visit him this afternoon.'

'What time?' she asked over the rim of her cup before taking a sip.

'Visiting hours are at four,' I said, adding cream to my cup. 'It'll probably take us a good forty minutes to get there and parking's usually a nightmare at those places so' – I checked my watch – 'if we leave here at about ten past three?'

'It's not the ideal place to meet one's only surviving family, but I would like to see him.' She bit her lip. 'Just in case.'

I didn't ask what she meant or even try to reassure her. A dark cloud was fast settling over Kingsmead and I could sense the inevitability of another death looming ever closer. Simon and Emma had both been spared, for the moment. Next time one of us might not be so lucky.

Emma was asleep when I went back to our room. She had barely tasted her food. I removed her tray and left it outside the door so she wouldn't be disturbed if Maddy came calling for it, then sat down by the bed and watched her sleep.

For the first time, for as long as I'd known her, Emma looked vulnerable, her complexion so pallid I could see the tiny purple veins criss-crossing her eyelids and, with her short blonde hair tousled and unbrushed, she reminded me of a small sleeping child. I had to swallow back a sob. I couldn't lose her. I just couldn't.

I took her hand in mine and was shocked by how icy it felt and for a split second I thought it had all been some horrible joke and we hadn't got there in time and she was dead. I felt something warm trickle down my face and when I raised my head to wipe the tear away it was to find blue eyes looking into mine.

'Hello,' she said, her voice low and husky.

'Hi,' I said, my own not much better than a croak.

Her brow wrinkled as she studied my face. 'Jed, what's wrong?'

'I was worried about you, that's all.'

She squeezed my fingers. 'I'm fine.' I swallowed hard, wondering whether I should ask. Wondering if I dare ask. She beat me to it. 'There's something wrong with the poolroom,' she said, her voice barely more than a whisper. 'Something terrible happened there.'

'I know,' I said. 'We'll talk about it tomorrow.'

Her eyes began to flutter shut, but she struggled to keep them open. 'Look after Laura,' she said. 'None of it is her fault.'

'I know.'

She managed a small smile. 'I think I'll have a little sleep now,' she said, despite having only just woken.

I leant forward to kiss her on the forehead. 'I'm going to see Simon. I'll be back soon.'

'Hmm,' she muttered, though I wasn't sure she had heard me. I kissed her again and crept out of the room.

I had twenty minutes to spare before I was due to meet with Laura and, as Dan had made it clear he had something to say to me, I decided to search him out.

I could hear the burble of a radio floating across the yard on a waft of hay and horse manure. I followed the music into the stable block and along the stalls. Dan was in the second to last one grooming Satan's shiny black coat.

He glanced at me from what he was doing and straightened. 'How's the missus?' he asked.

'Tired,' I said.

'She'll be all right, though?'

'So the doctor says.'

He turned away, putting the brush he'd been using on Satan to one side. When he looked back at me his expression was inscrutable. 'How did you know?' he asked. I leant against the wooden wall of the stall, keeping eye contact. 'Because you did. You knew something was wrong.'

'I get feelings sometimes.'

His eyes narrowed slightly and inexplicably he laughed. 'Feelings? And what did you feel out at that place today? Did you feel anything there?'

I wondered where this was going. 'Not today – no.'

'How about when you went there with ald Walters and Mr Simon, did you feel anything then?'

'What makes you ask?'

'You did, didn't you?' His eyes crinkled at the corners and he laughed some more. 'My ald grandma was like you. She could tell if something bad had happened to one of the family hours before we got the news and if you ever lost a thing she could tell you where you'd find it. Sometimes she'd get messages from the dead. You're like her, aren't you?'

'Do you know what's going on in this house?' I asked him, ignoring the question.

His laughter died away and his expression became serious. 'No, and I intend to keep it that way. Bad things happen to people who don't mind their own business around here and I don't intend to let anything bad happen to me.'

'Is that why something *bad* happened to Simon? Is that

why something *bad* happened to Emma?' and I could hear my voice rising.

He pushed past me to take a quick look outside the stall and, seeing the coast was clear, grabbed me by the arm and drew me alongside Satan and to the back.

'I don't know about Mr Simon, but I don't think anything was meant to happen to yer good lady wife. That was sheer bad luck.'

'Was it?'

He moved in close to me. 'If you'd take my advice you'd leave Kingsmead. It's a terrible place and the people aren't much better.'

'What do you mean?'

He leant forward until his lips were practically touching my ear. 'Some men do evil things to get what they want out of life – the Pomeroys are such men. If you don't believe me, look into the family history. Violent death being the least of it.'

'Ah, there you are,' a voice said, making Dan spin around.

Maddy was standing at the entrance to the stall, a knowing smile on her lips and her eyes glittering with one of the baser emotions, if I was any judge of women and their wiles. Then she saw me, and it instantly fell away and gone was the lascivious woman to be replaced by the meek and downtrodden maid.

I raised an eyebrow in Dan's direction, and he gave me an unrepentant smile. 'Be seeing yer, Mr Cummings,' he said.

I took the hint and left, but not before muttering under my breath, so only he could hear, 'Be sure of it.'

* * *

142

It took longer than I expected to drive to the hospital. It had been a fairly quiet journey, both Laura and I being lost in thought, me thinking about my conversation with Dan, and who knows what was on Laura's mind? She certainly wasn't full of the cheer of someone about to inherit a huge fortune. The words 'it's not much good to you if you're dead', floated through my mind and I wondered if this was what she was thinking.

'Why is someone doing these things?' Laura suddenly asked.

I gave her a sideways glance. 'I don't know,' was the only answer I could give her.

'Did whoever attacked Uncle Simon mean to kill him? I mean – why would they?'

I pondered on it for a moment. 'It was probably a matter of him being in the wrong place at the wrong time. Let's hope he can shed a bit more light on it when we see him.'

She shifted in her seat so she was facing towards me. 'One of the servants must be in on it,' she said. 'Otherwise, how did someone get into the house to thump Uncle Simon? There's no other way they could have got hold of my shirt.'

I kept my eyes on the road. I had a suspicion she was right and it was an unsettling feeling, knowing the person who had served you breakfast or made your bed could possibly be working against you. 'I suggest you don't trust a soul and lock your bedroom door when you go to bed at night,' I said.

'Don't worry, I intend to.' She hesitated, still sitting slightly askew in her seat. 'You won't leave yet? I mean before Uncle Simon is allowed home?'

I flashed a quick smile her way. 'Not if you want us to stay.'

'I would very much appreciate it if you did,' she said.

It took a while to find somewhere to park and I began to wish we'd started out earlier, but by the time we entered the hospital itself it was only five past four. The place was a labyrinth of identical corridors and we went wrong twice before Laura asked for directions and we finally found ourselves on the right floor.

We started along yet another corridor, which ended with a set of double doors and a sign telling us this should be where we would find Simon's ward. It had taken us ten minutes or more to get this far.

There were only six beds, all were occupied. Only one patient had a visitor, a young chap in about his mid twenties. His eyes were open, wide and staring at the ceiling from a chalk-white face. His fear was palpable and his wife or girlfriend clung onto his hand as if her tight grip was the only thing anchoring him to this world. From the grim-faced wraiths surrounding him I sadly surmised it probably was.

The other residents were old boys, probably in their seventies and eighties. Their heads turned towards us as we walked in, eyes alight with hope, which died as soon as they saw we were strangers.

Simon's bed was in the far corner by one of the two windows overlooking more hospital buildings and a car park.

Laura's expression was anxious. I gave her an encouraging smile and guided her towards his bed. Engrossed in a copy of *The Times* spread out in front of him, he was completely oblivious to our arrival. He had never been a big man like me, but seeing him sitting there, surrounded by pillows bolstering him upright, he looked diminished and so very frail. Fine, silver hair stuck to his crown giving it the appearance of being sparser than it really was, and his pallor was bordering on jaundiced, his complexion mottled. Liver spots I hadn't noticed before, stained, vein-knotted hands that were practically skeletal.

When he eventually glanced our way, a smile creased his face and, with forced joviality, I introduced him to possibly his last living relative.

'Laura, this is your Uncle Simon. Simon, this lovely young lady is your grandniece Laura.'

His eyes regained some of their sparkle as he took hold of her offered hand. 'My dear, I am so pleased to meet you at last, and I'm only sorry I wasn't at Kingsmead to welcome you to your new home.'

I moved a seat towards the top of the bed so she could sit down close to him and pulled one to the other side for me to park myself while they made small talk.

'How are you feeling?' I asked once they'd got over the introductions.

He pulled a face and leant towards me. 'I can't wait to get out of this damned place,' he said sotto voce. 'It's like being in a room full of geriatrics.'

'Well, hopefully you'll be coming home soon,' Laura said.

'Not soon enough,' he grumbled. 'I've asked for a private room.'

The door to the ward swung open and an orderly came in pushing a trolley of water pitchers. My attention returned to Simon and it was my turn to lean in close. 'Simon, do you remember anything about what happened the other night?'

He hesitated a fraction too long before his lips pressed together in a thin line and with a flare of his nostrils he said, 'Some thieving bastard was turning over Ed's room.' He looked down at his hands. The way he was gripping the sheets so hard, bunching the material into tight ropes, made them look like turkey claws. 'I'd been downstairs looking for a book and when I came back up I heard a noise. The light was on when I opened the door and the place was a mess: books, clothes and papers strewn everywhere.' He paused, the lines on his forehead growing deeper. 'I didn't think, I just walked straight in and then – *bam!* Someone hit me on the head and everything went black.'

I looked at him long and hard. It had been a practised speech. He was lying or holding something back. On the phone he had sounded scared. 'Simon,' I said, 'you asked me to come here for a reason and it wasn't to tell me you'd been knocked on the head by a burglar.' His eyes shifted to Laura and back to me. 'Laura has a fair idea of what's going on, so you might as well spill it. She's quite possibly in more danger than you are now she's arrived at Kingsmead.'

'Has something happened?' he asked.

'Huh, you could say that,' I said.

He slumped back onto the pillows. 'Tell me,' he said, so I told him about the fires and the chanting and the effigy of Laura, only pausing when the orderly squeezed past me to change Simon's water. Then I told him about Emma's close shave and, out of everything I'd told him, I could see this shook him the most. It was almost as though all the other weird stuff was, not expected exactly, but not surprising either. I had suspected my old friend was keeping things from me, now I was darn well sure.

When I finished speaking, he was quiet for a long time and when he did start to speak he didn't look at us, but stared off into space.

'Even from a young age I knew there was something not quite right about Edward.' Laura and I shared a confused look. What had Edward to do with his assault and what had happened since? Did Simon believe it was Edward who had been ransacking his own room? Why would he? He would surely know its secrets. 'He could be terribly cruel and if he wanted something, by God he would make sure he got it. In fact, he would rather destroy a thing if he couldn't make it his own.' He went quiet for a few moments as though remembering the past. 'Ed and Ollie were always very close, but in the months before Ed . . . before Ed disappeared and I was told he was dead, there was something going on between them. They had fallen out and it was serious. Then Constance died and Ollie . . . Ollie changed. Everyone said Constance dying was an accident, but now looking back . . .' Simon raised his eyes to mine. 'Looking back and remembering little things that were said and done – I'm not so sure it was – I think it's quite possible Edward killed her.'

CHAPTER THIRTEEN

The journey back to Kingsmead wasn't much different to our earlier drive to the hospital. It was spent mainly in silence. I occasionally glanced Laura's way. She sat with her arms wrapped across her chest as though hugging herself. She was scared, so was I.

Simon wouldn't be drawn into telling us any more. He said he was tired and by God he looked it. I didn't push him as much as I wanted to and then the end of visiting hour's bell went and it was too late. As we went to leave, he told us he had a lot to think about and needed to get it all straight in his own head and I guessed he really did. Everything he'd thought about his brothers, and possibly the rest of his family, he was now beginning to realise was untrue or based on lies.

'I'll see you tomorrow,' I said.

'Yes.' He glanced towards Laura as she bent to retrieve her handbag from the floor and gave me a pointed look. 'And then *you and I* will talk.' He couldn't have made it clearer – he wanted to speak to me alone.

As we drove into the estate the back of my neck began to tingle. Apart from the women in the pool and the images I'd seen at the clearing, my friends from beyond the veil had, surprisingly, kept very much to themselves since our arrival. From the increasing pressure at the top of my spine I was under the impression this was about to change.

Laura went to her room to dress for dinner while I hurried to mine to check on Emma. I wanted to leave her alone in this place even less than I had before. From now on, if she couldn't come with me, I wasn't going anywhere.

When I entered the room, she wasn't in bed and my chest tightened in anxiety. I hurried to the bathroom, but the door was open and it was empty inside. I spun around – where on earth was she?

A soft breeze touched my face and when I glanced towards the windows the curtains were gently swaying.

'Emma?' I called.

'I'm out here.'

I crossed the room in a couple of strides and threw back the curtains. Emma was sitting on the balcony with a book and a large glass of something fresh and fruity and brimming with ice.

'I wondered where you were.'

She tilted her head to one side as I stooped down to kiss her cheek. 'I had to get up. I was sick to death of lying in bed like some damned invalid.'

'You nearly drowned.'

'But I didn't.'

I sat down at the table opposite her and took hold of her hand. 'I nearly lost you.'

She squeezed my fingers. 'I'm fine.'

I studied her face. 'Do you remember what happened?'

'I dived in, swam a couple of lengths and' – she grimaced – 'I was about to get out. The water was warm, I knew it was warm, but I suddenly felt so cold, like the heat was being leeched from my body.' She gave a small shake of her head. 'Then it was like something had wrapped itself around my ankles and it started to pull me under. I guess I must have panicked, because the harder I struggled the worse it got.' She let out a shuddery sigh. 'I know you always say the dead can't hurt us, not physically, but' – she looked at me with frightened eyes – 'I heard her. I heard her screaming at me.'

I didn't bother telling her she was wrong. I no longer thought she was. The spirit was definitely trying to harm her. 'What did she say, Emms?'

She took a sip of her drink. 'She kept screaming "He's mine – you can't have him – he's mine."' She let out a shuddery breath. 'Did you see her?'

Her hand felt cold in mine. 'There were two of them,' I told her. 'A young woman and an older one. It was the older woman who had hold of your ankles.'

She bit her lip, mulling it over for a second or two. 'I wonder who they were? And what did she mean, do you think?'

'I don't know. Maybe we should try looking into the history of this place.'

'Maybe we should,' she said, with a sigh. 'How did it go at the hospital?'

I pulled a face. 'Laura and Simon appeared to hit it off, so that's something.'

'But . . . ?'

'Simon dropped a bit of a bombshell – he says he thinks Edward might have killed Oliver's first wife.'

'Really?'

'That's what he said.'

'Are you going back to see him tomorrow?'

'I think I have to. Simon said he had some thinking to do, but he made it quite clear he wanted to speak to me alone, which could be difficult. I can hardly stop Laura from visiting him.' I paused, thinking about it. 'Anyway, this whole sorry mess has to be resolved, we can't stay for ever and I don't feel I can leave Laura here alone the way things stand.'

'I agree.'

'So,' I said, my heart sinking. 'Like it or not, we're here to stay for the foreseeable future.'

Emma had begun to flag by the time I was ready for dinner, but wouldn't hear of us eating in our room.

'I want to get to know Laura,' she said.

While I poured the drinks, the girls chattered amongst themselves. Laura was telling Emms about her flatmate, who was flying off to New Zealand, to marry a Kiwi.

'This is why I was soon to be homeless,' she explained. 'Jenny's parents owned the property and were going to sell it after she moved out. It's weird really, everything seemed to happen at once. Out of the blue Andy, Jenny's fiancé, was offered his dream job back in New Zealand, so they brought the wedding forward, then someone her parents knew made an offer on the house before it even went on the market and on the very same day my company announced job cuts due to a takeover, and mine was one of the positions that was going to go.'

'So finding out you were an heiress was like a dream come true,' Emma said.

Laura took a sip of her drink. 'It was certainly unexpected and couldn't have come at a better time. As I told you, as far as I was aware, I had no family.'

'Well, you've met Simon now, at least.'

Laura's smile slipped a bit. 'He didn't look at all well.'

'He did have a nasty smack on the head,' Emma said, 'but hopefully he'll be allowed home soon.'

'I'm looking forward to getting to know him and hearing all about the family.' Laura looked down into her glass before raising her eyes to look at me. 'So, what do we do now?' she asked.

'How do you mean?'

'Do we tell the police about the dummy?'

I rubbed at my chin. 'We should,' I said, still not sure what I thought about the detective inspector. 'They would certainly consider it a threat, or possibly a warning.'

She looked back into her drink. 'I suppose. It's all a bit of a mess, really.'

'Maybe you should have a word with Brandon Fredericks,' I said. 'It could be he can find a way of getting around you having to live here until this has all been sorted out.'

'Hmm. It is a bit of an odd condition, don't you think?

I can see why my grandfather might want me to live here for a couple of years. I suppose he was hoping I'd fall in love with the place and not decide to sell the family home, but why have I got to move in so soon? It doesn't make an awful lot of sense. I could have had commitments, a job or a holiday booked.'

'I suppose he thought with all the money you'd be inheriting you wouldn't need a job any more, and a holiday could always be rescheduled,' Emma said.

'All the same – it's a bit manipulative,' and she frowned as if this had just occurred to her – maybe it had.

Emma lasted through dinner, but when her head began to nod, I excused us and took her upstairs to bed. I did offer to return downstairs to keep Laura company, after a nudge in the ribs from Emms, but Laura said she was tired too. I wasn't surprised, an awful lot had happened throughout the day. As I turned out the light and settled down in bed, I hoped the following one would prove a little less stressful. I wasn't holding my breath.

We woke early. Emma was none the worse for her near drowning and was raring to be up and about after having a day in bed and a good night's sleep. I wasn't so lively. From the moment I'd laid my head on the crisp, white pillow and closed my eyes sleep eluded me. The spirits who had, until now, remained strangely silent decided to make themselves known. At first they were tentative, which was unusual, then they became more persistent; so much so I slipped out of bed and went to sit on the balcony rather than disturb Emma, who was sleeping peacefully. Fortunately, due to the unusually hot spring days, the temperature outside wasn't as cold as it might have been. Still, I was beginning to shiver by the time my friends had finished with me.

I had no other choice but to open my mind to them, otherwise I suspected they would go on and on all night and probably throughout the following day. One of the deceased was a distraught woman, the other a bombastic elderly man. Neither had messages for the living, all either wanted was for someone to listen.

She wept for her children, one who had been taken from her and the other who had never drawn breath. From her heavy Devonshire accent, I guessed she was a member of staff, not a family member. The man was related by marriage. Gruff and disgruntled by how his family had never loved him in life and, to his mind, had disrespected him in death, he moaned on and on. I felt sorry for her, the man not so much. He was a pompous old windbag and I suspected his family had been relieved when he'd died.

I did learn something interesting: there had been someone else who had stayed in the house who'd had the sight and, whoever this person was, she had scared them. One would think the dead no longer had anything to fear – apparently they had. This woman proved it.

They gave the impression she had been a visitor to the house rather than a permanent resident and, as the departed have no concept of time, she could have stayed in the house one hundred years ago or as recently as last month. One thing both spirits were adamant about was that *she* was one of the *Devil's* children.

The sun was creeping over the horizon by the time

they let me go and I could slide back under the covers and drift off for a couple of hours. Consequently, when Emma sprang out of bed all bright and cheerful, I wanted nothing other than to hide my head under the covers and go back to sleep.

I didn't, I had things to do, the first of which was to phone Detective Inspector Brogan. He wasn't answering his phone, so I left a message saying Laura had been threatened and for him to call me. I was probably in for a tongue-lashing for not having reported the incident earlier. I didn't much care. They hadn't made any progress on Oliver's murder and I doubted whether what he could possibly see as a sick practical joke would prove any different.

'I'm going to take your advice,' Laura said over breakfast.

'What advice was that?' Emma asked, accepting a refill of coffee from Maddy.

'Jed's suggestion I talk to Mr Fredericks to see if he can do something about changing my move-in date.'

'It's worth a try,' I said, helping myself to another slice of toast.

'Though I'm not sure where I'll go.'

'You can come and stay with us,' Emma said.

'Could I? Are you sure? You don't even know me.' Laura looked from Emma to me, her expression so grateful I couldn't have said no even had I wanted to.

'You'll always be welcome,' Emma said.

Laura's eyes filled up. 'You are both so kind.'

'You might change your mind after a few more days living under the same roof as us,' I said, making her laugh, which was good to see.

Laura excused herself as soon as we'd finished

breakfast and went off to phone Brandon. Emma and I decided to go for a hike into the village. I was finding the house oppressive and, although I doubted very much spirits talked to each other, it appeared last night's conflab had opened the floodgates. I could hear whispering and see shadows everywhere.

The weather was still unseasonably warm and as we strode along, Emma's hand in mine, I began to relax and immediately the gates closed behind us my mood grew more cheerful. We didn't talk about Simon, the house, the poolroom and certainly not the clearing where the whole nightmare had begun.

Emma told me about the book she was reading and how it was so much better than the film. I told her a bit about a trip Reggie and I had made to the country where the book was set, albeit censoring it somewhat. She didn't need to know why we'd been there, and I'd rather forget it. The country was beautiful, our reason for the visit not so much.

We took the long, scenic route following a bridle path through the fields and woods, reaching the village by midday and, once there, decided to have a light lunch in the local pub. The building was a picture postcard, white-painted, black-beamed old coach house and, judging by the number of cars already crammed into the small car park, appeared to be fairly popular. The laughter and chatter greeting us when we walked inside was enough to let us know we'd chosen well.

It was bigger inside than it looked from the car park and, with its low ceilings, wooden beams and huge open fireplace, suited us down to the ground. We grabbed a small corner table and while Emms perused the menu I got us a couple of drinks in.

I still hadn't heard from Detective Inspector Brogan, which was a surprise, but then was it? Perhaps now Oliver was gone he wanted to keep as far away from the rest of the family and Kingsmead as he could. Whatever the reason it made me uneasy.

Did he know of the existence of the photographs? And if he did . . . I would have thought he'd want them destroyed. Cynical and suspicious person that I am, this made me wonder once again about who had broken into Edward's room and what they had been looking for. Surely to God, DI Brogan . . . No – for one thing how would he have gained access without anyone knowing? And the figure I'd seen running from Edward's room was nowhere as tall as Brogan and was slight of frame. It could even have been a woman – and that set me thinking. Who exactly was his lover?

'Penny for them?' Emma asked.

I started. 'Sorry, I was miles away.'

She grinned at me. 'So I could see. Are you dreaming of the roast beef sandwich you just ordered or something far more interesting?'

My smile was sheepish. 'Actually, I was wondering why DI Brogan hasn't returned my call.'

'Hmm, it is a bit strange. I'd have thought one murder, an assault and now a threat of violence would have had him camping on the doorstep.'

'Not these days, Emms. They haven't the manpower.'

She sniffed. 'Simon Pomeroy being such a bigwig in a ministry department should have been enough to have

DI Brogan running around all over the place.'

'I never said—'

'You didn't have to. It's pretty obvious Simon is more than an office manager. Hearing him on the phone to his *assistant* was the giveaway.'

We couldn't linger over lunch as long as we would have liked. I had to be back to ferry Laura to the hospital and I was very interested in hearing what Simon had to say about the rift between Edward and Oliver, particularly given what he'd said about Oliver's first wife – and this time I wouldn't be put off.

As the gates to the estate slowly swung shut behind us my earlier feeling of oppression returned and with it a growing sense of dread. Then when we reached the brow of the hill and the downward slope to Kingsmead it turned into full-blown anxiety. Doctor Bell's old Mercedes was parked out front of the house together with another car I didn't recognise.

Emma and I exchanged a glance. 'I hope Laura's all right,' she said and we both set off down the drive at a fast stride, which was almost a jog by the time we reached the front door.

The good doctor was in the entrance hall talking to Mrs Walters and the housekeeper's expression was one of relief as we appeared through the door.

I didn't beat about the bush. 'What's happened now?' I asked.

'It's nothing to worry about,' Doctor Bell quickly said. 'Miss Simmons had a nasty fall, but she's fine. A few bumps and bruises, is all.'

'Mrs Walters, can you show me to Laura's room, please?'

Emma said and her tone was enough that the housekeeper instantly gestured for Emma to follow her, leaving me with the doctor.

'She fell, you say?' I said, looking towards the stairs, remembering the fate of Oliver's first wife.

Doctor Bell put a palm against my back. 'Walk with me,' he said and as soon as we were outside on the steps, his bedside smile disappeared to be replaced by a worried frown. 'I suggest you go and have words with the stable hand.'

'What? Dan?'

He nodded and I fell in step beside him as he carried on down the steps towards his car. 'She was out riding with him when the horse apparently got spooked and bolted. The vet's taking a look at the creature now.'

'They can't be thinking of putting her down?'

The doctor managed a small smile. 'No, not at all.' He stopped beside his car, pulling the keys from his pocket. 'Crouchley was worried about the mare. He said she wasn't herself.'

I frowned, trying to digest what he was telling me. 'If that's the case, why did he let Laura ride her?'

Doctor Bell opened his car door and leant inside to heft his bag onto the passenger seat, then straightened and moved in close to me. 'Speak to Crouchley,' he repeated. '*Alone.*'

I must have looked confused as he leant even closer. 'He couldn't say much, but he gave me the impression it wasn't an accident.' I stared at him and I knew my expression had become mean as he nodded, seeing he'd made his point. 'If Miss Simmons should experience

159

any ill effects give me a call,' he said before getting into his car and, with a flip of the hand in farewell, drove off, leaving me standing on the drive silently simmering with anger.

I immediately strode around the side of the house towards the stables. A tall, gangly, sandy-haired man in green wellies, who I assumed to be the vet, was in the yard talking to Donald Walters and Dan. 'Is this really necessary?' I heard Donald Walters say.

'Yes,' Dan said, 'it is.'

Donald rounded on him. 'I wasn't asking you.'

The vet looked embarrassed. 'She clearly isn't right, Mr Walters,' he said.

'She's scared, 'tis all.'

Dan gave a snort of disgust. 'You weren't there. You didn't see her.'

'If you'd been doing your job . . .'

Dan's fists clenched and, from the flush colouring his cheeks, there was a chance if the groundskeeper said one more word the bloke would flatten him. I hurried over to join them.

'I hear Miss Simmons took a tumble,' I said, putting myself between the two men.

'Something spooked Angel and she bolted,' Donald said, more or less repeating what the doctor had told me.

Dan crossed his arms and kept his eyes down.

'Was she on her own?'

Donald couldn't quite stop his lips curling into a sneer. 'He,' he said, jerking his head Dan's way, 'was with her.'

'Right,' I said. 'I'll have a word with *you* in a moment.'

My attention turned to the vet. 'Is Angel all right?'

'She's calmer,' he said, 'but she's not her usual self. I've taken blood for testing, just to make sure there's nothing wrong.'

I nodded. 'If you're finished, I'll walk you to your car.'

'There's no—' Donald started to say and I fixed him with a stare, which had him stuttering into silence. Satisfied he'd got the message, I walked with the vet around the side of the house to the drive. 'What are you going to test for?' I asked.

'Viruses – that sort of thing.'

'How about drugs?'

He gave me a look. 'That's what young Crouchley asked me to do.'

'And will you?'

His eyes met mine. 'Most definitely.'

I just about managed a smile. 'Thank you.'

'I'm Derek Davis, by the way,' he said, extending a hand.

'Jed Cummings.' We shook and I reached into my top pocket and pulled out one of my cards. 'If you wouldn't mind giving me a call once you have the results, I'd quite like a heads-up.'

He thought about it for maybe a second. 'Can't see why not.'

'Thanks,' I said again.

I watched him go as I gathered my thoughts before returning to the stables. As I expected, I found Donald and Dan almost at each other's throats.

'What's the problem?' I asked.

Donald's lips pressed together in a bloodless line and Dan, flushed of cheeks, glared at his boots.

I glanced at Dan. 'You and I need to have a little talk,' and to Donald I added, 'I'll deal with this.'

With one last glare at Dan, Donald bobbed his head to me and strode off towards the kitchen. I gestured with a jerk of the head towards the inside of the stable block and marched off leaving Dan to follow behind. I stopped outside Angel's stall and pulled out a packet of sugar lumps I'd purloined from the pub after lunch. I put one on my palm and held it out to her.

'There's a good girl,' I said.

She lifted her head and it didn't take an expert to see that her eyes were not quite as they should be. They had a scared and slightly wild look to them. She sniffed my hand and it took a lot of gentle words and persuasion before she eventually took the sugar between her big soft lips.

'She's not right, is she?' I said over my shoulder to where Dan was loitering. When I turned to face him, his expression was angry. 'The good doctor seemed to think you had something you might want to tell me,' I said. 'I sort of guessed you wouldn't want to say anything in front of Walters.'

His whole body relaxed, but he was still a long way from smiling. 'I think she's been given something,' he said without me asking. 'She was all right when we started off, but then Miss Laura said she was starting to act a bit skittish and before I could take a look there was a gunshot and Angel bolted. Then there was another, real close by, and she reared and Miss Laura . . . Miss Laura came off.' He stopped to take a deep breath and slowly exhale. 'For a moment . . . For a moment I thought . . . I thought she was dead.' He looked at me with pain-filled eyes.

'The doctor says she'll be fine.'

He managed a small laugh. 'Hard-headed woman that one.'

'I'd keep out of Donald Walters' way for a while, if I were you.'

He gave a sort of half-hearted nod. 'Once the police have sorted out everything here, I might move on,' he said.

I didn't say anything to dissuade him. It would be a shame, but it'd probably be for the best. He and Donald clearly couldn't stand each other and being the lower in the food chain it could be his days were numbered in his employ here anyway. Better to go with a reference than without.

I looked at my watch. 'I have to get moving,' I said. 'I was meant to be taking Miss Simmons to see her uncle, but I guess she won't be feeling like it now.' I hesitated. 'Dan, you said you heard a second gunshot.'

He grunted. 'Yeah, I did and it was close – very close.'

'Did you see anyone?'

He shook his head. 'No, but then I was chasing after L—Miss Laura and then she was on the ground and I was too concerned about her to worry about some darn fool with a gun.' He dragged his fingers through his mop of hair. 'Thing is, nobody should have been out there shooting. This is a private estate and with none of the other Pomeroys in residence there's no one here other than Walters who would be.'

'A poacher perhaps?'

'Huh, we don't stock game birds any more. Maybe a hundred or so years ago, but not recently.'

I looked him in the eyes long and hard. 'You think it was deliberate.'

He met my gaze. 'I guess we'll know once the results come back from the veterinary.'

'I guess we will,' I said as I walked away.

CHAPTER FOURTEEN

'You don't have to come with me,' I said. 'Not if you'd rather stay and keep an eye on Laura.'

Emma shrugged on a cardigan. 'She's adamant she's fine and doesn't want to be fussed over. It's bad enough Mrs Walters going into mother-hen mode without me as well.'

'She said that?'

'She didn't have to. The rolling of the eyes every time Mrs Walters left the room was enough for me to get the message.' Emma laughed. 'Anyway, it's poor Simon who's really been in the wars.'

I stood and wrapped her in my arms. 'I must admit I could do with the company, and to be honest I'd rather not leave you here alone.'

'Well then, it's settled. Did he want you to take anything in for him?'

'No, apparently Donald Walters dropped off a bag of his things when he was first taken in.'

'Perhaps we can get him something from the hospital shop while we're there.'

I dropped a kiss onto her forehead. 'Who's playing mother hen now?'

We left early and were soon flying along country roads flanked by green fields and sometimes desolate moorland or stretches of bluebell-blanketed woodlands.

'Carry on like this and you'll be able to investigate the hospital shop to your heart's content.' I should have touched wood: no sooner than the words were out of my mouth I wished I could have taken them back.

We turned into a fairly narrow country lane, which was a cut-through taking at least fifteen minutes off the journey, and practically straight away joined a queue of traffic. I stuck my head out of the window to peer past the two cars in front trying to see the problem. It wasn't very difficult. A Range Rover, which now had a crumpled front wing, had apparently skidded onto the wrong side of the road and the horsebox it was towing had come to rest, jackknifed at an angle, blocking the thoroughfare. Beyond it a white van, belching smoke, was hanging askew into a ditch. It couldn't have happened at a worse spot. It was possibly the narrowest stretch of lane, with no passing points on either side for a good hundred yards or more.

'Damn,' I said, looking back over my shoulder hoping it was possible to back up. There was no chance. Another van, the size of a small bus, had pulled in behind me, practically nudging my back bumper. I slumped down in my seat and switched off the engine. We were stuck here for the duration.

'Do you think we should see if there's anything we can do to help?' Emma asked.

Through the windscreen I could see the two drivers, red-faced and yelling at each other. 'I don't think so, Emms,' I said. 'It's probably best we stay out of it.'

A tall, horsey-looking woman in jodhpurs was apoplectic with rage and I thought at any moment she would lurch for the van driver's throat. He was a big bloke with a sneery, supercilious attitude and a limited vocabulary, which consisted of words mainly beginning with 'F'. At one point he lit a cigarette in a deliberately provocative manner and a cheer went up from the car in front when she ripped it from his fingers and ground it into the tarmac with the heel of her boot.

'What's going on?' Emma asked, leaning across me trying to see.

With a nonchalant twist of the lips, the van driver once more took out his cigarette packet and flipped the lid open. With an almost visceral snarl the woman snatched the carton from him, threw it on the ground and trampled on it.

'The beginning of World War Three I'd imagine.'

Sure enough, the van driver flipped and the yelling shot up several levels. On and on it went. Several times I thought it was coming to an end and one of the two combatants, usually the woman, would start to walk away, then the other would launch into another stream of verbal abuse more vitriolic than the last and it all kicked off again.

Then abruptly it was over. The woman gestured heavenwards with her hands and, turning her back on her adversary, strode back to her car with a face like a slapped arse, the van driver's derisive obscenities following her. With an over-the-top slam of her door, excessive revving and a bit of tricky manoeuvring, she straightened the car and horsebox and drove off with a screech of wheels, leaving the man in a flurry of pebbles and a cloud of dust. The rest of us started our vehicles and gradually filtered past him. No one had any sympathy for his plight, we had all been an involuntary audience to his posturing for nigh on twenty minutes.

The hospital car park was packed solid and there was a line of cars steadily circling searching for places. Eventually we found a bay, on the opposite side of the hospital to where we wanted to be and a five-minute hike away. My only real comfort was this time I knew where I was going. Then, when we arrived at the ward it was to find an empty, freshly made bed and no Simon. I forced down the rising tide of panic. If something had happened to him, surely the hospital would have phoned us – wouldn't they?

Emma's eyes jerked from the bed to me. 'You don't think . . . ?'

'I—'

'If you're looking for Mr Pomeroy he's been moved into a private room,' a nurse interrupted, squeezing past us. Then I remembered – he had said something about going private.

Emma visibly relaxed. 'We didn't know. Can you tell us where he is?'

While Emma obtained directions, I glanced around the ward. Three of the old boys were asleep and the fourth had his earphones plugged in and was doing a crossword. The young man across from him was still hanging on in there, his partner clinging to his hand. Maybe it was working and she was hauling him back from the brink. The shadowy figures surrounding him had faded to a translucent pale grey and their expressions had lost their grim resignation.

'We need to be on the other side of the hospital,' Emma explained as we started off on yet another trek through the maze of corridors.

The private rooms were in the newer part of the building, the paintwork fresher, the decor brighter. Looking out through the corridor windows as we hurried along, I could see the difference in location: this end of the hospital looked out over fields of yellow rapeseed and rolling green countryside. We were entering the domain of the well-heeled.

Halfway along the final corridor the doors ahead swung open and a woman strode through, walking in an exaggerated supermodel strut, giving the impression she was moving in slow motion even though she was covering ground pretty fast. She reminded me of a big cat, a jaguar perhaps. Tall and slender, she had a dark and predatory look to her. Deep red lips with eyes lined in kohl and hair cut into a shiny black bob she exuded sensuality and she knew it. She was smiling as though life was one big joke and the joke was on everyone else. As we drew almost level her eyes fleetingly met mine, her smile faltered, and I had to swallow back a small hiccup of fear. Then the moment was over, and she walked on past us, gathering speed and leaving me with an anxious tightening in my chest.

I glanced over my shoulder as she disappeared through another set of doors. 'Come on,' I said, and I began to run.

As we reached the doors an alarm went off in the passageway ahead and nurses appeared from all directions, racing towards the last room in the hallway.

I stopped, stepping to one side to get out of their way while Emma pressed her back against the wall opposite.

A flurry of activity and then, as if by magic, the corridor was empty except for remote voices and urgently shouted instructions from ahead of us.

'Jed?' Emma said, stepping towards me.

'Come on,' I said and, with some trepidation, I started towards the room at the end of the hall.

Inside, people all acting with coordinated purpose, grouped around the bed. There was an air of controlled panic as everyone went about their business and in their midst was Simon. His eyes wide, staring at the ceiling, and his mouth gaping. A nurse pulled open his pyjama jacket and a doctor stepped forward.

'Clear,' he shouted and pressed paddles to Simon's bare chest. His body jerked and then fell limp.

I felt a hand slip into mine as Emma's shoulder pressed against my arm.

'Clear.'

A nurse looked up and, seeing us hovering by the door, hurried over to gently steer us away and along the corridor to some seats. She sat us down and told us she'd get someone to come and speak to us shortly.

We sat there for a long time, Emma's hand in mine, silently waiting while Simon fought for life and, it was while we waited, my mind turned to the woman we had seen and how there was something familiar about her. She raised strange feelings inside me. I was both attracted and repelled. An overtly sexual female, she was perhaps the ultimate femme fatale.

Then I saw myself sitting in our bedroom, scanning two sheets of photographs. I hadn't seen her face in the photos, and in the Polaroids she'd been mostly a misty blur, but I was pretty sure the femme fatale was the same woman with whom DI Brogan was having a very steamy affair. I slumped back in the chair. If this was the case, who on earth could we trust? Certainly not the detective inspector.

Eventually the door at the end of the corridor opened and tired and gaunt-faced nurses began to file out. No one needed to say a word, defeat was etched into their features. The nurse who had guided us to our seats was one of the last to leave. In earnest conversation with a young doctor, she looked our way and he followed her glance. After a few more words he made straight for us and I rose to my feet.

'I am Doctor Rani. Please sit,' he said and pulled a chair over so he was sitting facing us. 'Mr Pomeroy is family?' he asked.

'I'm an old family friend,' I said.

His expression became grim. 'I am terribly sorry. I'm afraid Mr Pomeroy suffered an unexpected episode and we couldn't save him.'

'What happened?' I asked. 'Was it a heart attack?'

'I can't say at the moment. We'll carry out tests, of course. It was totally unexpected and . . .' he hesitated, 'strange.'

'Strange?' I asked.

He rubbed a hand across his face. 'He was recovering well from his head injury. A nurse had been in to see him only fifteen minutes or so before it happened to check his blood pressure and take his temperature. Everything was normal. Then' – he made a vague gesture with his hand –

'his heart just . . . stopped. She raised the alarm when she popped back in and found him.'

Emma and I shared another glance. 'What would have caused it to happen?' I asked.

He grimaced and shook his head. 'I won't know until I get the test results.'

'I can't believe it,' Emma said as we climbed into the Jag. 'I thought he was getting better.'

'So did I,' I said, feeling numb.

Doctor Rani had allowed us to go in and see Simon to say goodbye. A sheet had been drawn up to his chest, his pyjama jacket buttoned and his eyes closed. He looked healthier in death than he had in life. I had hoped for a message. Something – anything – to let me know what had happened. I had been disappointed. If Simon had something to say he was keeping it to himself.

'How on earth are we going to tell poor Laura? She was so desperate to have some family at last and now he's been snatched from her.'

I didn't know either, and unfortunately it would most likely be me who would have to give her the bad news.

'Do you think you should phone DI *I'm too important to be dealing with all this* Brogan?'

'Oh yes,' I said, 'and I have a feeling this time he might be interested enough to return my call,' and I'm sure Emma didn't miss the bitter tone of my voice.

Emma swivelled in her seat to frown at me. 'How do you mean?'

'The woman – the woman we passed in the corridor before the alarm went off – did you think she looked familiar?'

Emma faced forward staring at the windscreen, her brow furrowed in thought. 'Now you come to mention it . . . But I can't quite place her.'

'Photographs – of a certain police officer we know.'

Her eyes grew incredibly wide. 'It can't be. Oh God, this keeps getting worse and worse.'

This was true enough. It couldn't get much more than it already was. And I *was* feeling bitter. Was Simon's death natural? No – I didn't think so. I might not have still been the best of mates with him any more, but I had been once and I wanted revenge for that long-lost friend. To my way of thinking, DI Brogan was as good a place as any to start. I suspected if, as we thought, he was being blackmailed he might be very interested indeed to hear about the object of his desire having been to see Simon moments before his heart gave out – and I was convinced this is where she'd been coming from.

On the way back we passed the spot where we'd been delayed by the car accident. The white van had gone and I couldn't help but think *if* they hadn't had the accident and *if* they hadn't held us up with their bickering for twenty minutes Simon might well still be alive. Oh Simon, why did you have to be such a dick and insist on going private? Had he been in a ward with five other people it couldn't have happened, he wouldn't have been alone.

When I pulled in outside the house I found myself sinking down a lot lower than I needed to be. Emma rested her hand on my thigh and when I looked her way and saw her beautiful face I remembered what a lucky man I really was. She was right about one thing: I couldn't save the world, no one man can, but to my way of thinking I could try and get my friend justice.

Climbing the stairs to go and find Laura was hard to do. Emma held my hand and I was grateful for her being there. Telling someone a friend or family member had passed was never easy, whatever their relationship, but she needed to be told and it was only right she should be the first to know. Next it would be the staff.

It was Emma who knocked on her door. 'Laura, it's Emma and Jed. Is it all right if we come in?' I assumed she replied as Emma pushed open the door and I followed her inside.

Laura was sitting by the window and her face lit up with a smile for a split second before slipping away upon seeing our expressions.

She looked from Emma's face to mine and her bottom lip started to tremble as she began to shake her head. 'No,' she said. 'No.'

'I'm sorry,' I said.

Laura lips pressed in on themselves and she stood, wrapping her arms around her body as if she was trying to hold herself together. She turned and walked to the window to stare outside.

Emma hurried across the room to lay a hand on her shoulder, while I stood there being pretty ineffectual.

Emma looked at me and gave a nod towards the door.

I cleared my throat. 'Would you like me to speak to the staff?'

Laura gave a tiny bob of the head. 'Please.'

Emma gave another nod towards the door. This time I took the hint and left them to it. Now I had to tell the staff.

It wasn't as bad as it could have been. Simon hadn't been

174

to Kingsmead for longer than short stays for years. They were shocked of course, but there were no tears or dramas. Strangely, I would have said the overriding emotion from Mrs Walters was white-lipped anger. While the staff filed out, she and Mr Walters waited behind; the woman was practically wringing her hands.

'May we have a word?' Donald asked.

I managed a tight smile. I hoped they weren't about to hand in their notices. Laura would have plenty to contend with without having to start advertising for replacement senior staff.

'Mr Cummings, we wondered if you had any idea what Miss Laura's intentions are with regard to Kingsmead Manor?' Mrs Walters asked.

'No,' I said, 'but under the terms of the will she has to live here for at least two years.'

The couple exchanged a glance. 'We had no idea,' Mrs Walters said, and she and Donald shared a shocked and somewhat confused look, which I also found a little strange. It was as though they were expecting something else entirely.

Mrs Walters recovered first. 'Obviously if that's the case we needn't worry immediately,' she said. 'We just wondered about our positions.'

I gave them what I hoped was a reassuring smile. 'Miss Simmons will need good and trusted staff she can depend on. This is all new to her.'

'She can depend on us,' Mrs Walters said. 'Thank you, Mr Cummings.'

As soon as the door shut behind them I pulled out my mobile. Now for Detective Inspector Brogan.

I wasn't at all surprised when I was put straight through to voicemail. My message was short and sweet. 'Simon Pomeroy died this afternoon, just after being visited by an acquaintance of yours. I look forward to seeing you first thing tomorrow morning.'

Let him stick that in his pipe and smoke it.

My next phone call was to Brandon Fredericks. As Simon's legal advisor he would need to know of his client's death as soon as possible, and it occurred to me that the Pomeroys were keeping the elderly solicitor very busy at the moment.

My call was answered by a bright and chirpy young woman, who put me through right away. 'Jed, good to hear from you. I was going to pop by over the next couple of days to see how Laura was settling in.'

I cut straight to the chase. 'I'm sorry, Brandon, I have some bad news. Simon passed away this afternoon.'

There was a stunned silence at the other end of the phone. 'Simon's dead?'

'I'm afraid so.'

'Oh dear, oh dear. This is terrible news. What happened?'

I explained about the break-in, which he told me he had already heard about through the grapevine. 'You know how servants gossip,' he said.

'Emma and I went to visit him this afternoon. Laura had a nasty fall yesterday while she was out riding so she didn't come, which is probably just as well.' Then I explained what had happened when we got there, though I didn't mention the mystery woman. She was someone I wanted to keep to myself until I'd spoken to DI Brogan.

'There's something else,' I said. 'Did Simon tell you we'd been to Goldsmere House?'

There was another silence – a long one. 'Why, may I ask?' he eventually said.

'Did you know Simon's brother Edward was alive and living at Goldsmere?'

I heard him sigh. 'Yes. It was I who arranged a place for him there.'

'Shit,' I mumbled under my breath. 'Did you know Oliver took him out of their care before he died?'

There was a sharp intake of breath. 'What? No. You must be mistaken.'

'I'm afraid not,' I said.

'Then where is he now?' he asked, his voice strained.

'I have no idea.'

'This is dreadful,' he said and there was no disguising the panic in the elderly solicitor's voice. 'The man's a monster.'

I was slightly taken aback by his vehemence. 'Not when he's medicated, we were told.'

'Huh, a matter of opinion. But if he's gone missing, he won't be medicated now.' I didn't reply. 'Do the police know?'

'Yes,' I said. 'We thought a psychopath being on the loose should be brought to their attention sooner rather than later.'

'Good,' he obviously hadn't got my sarcasm. 'I'll need to see Laura at some point, she's asked me to look into something for her. In the meantime, I'll check through the family files. There are a couple of codicils to Oliver's will to do with what should happen if Simon, Edward or Laura should not outlive him by more than two years, and there are another couple of sealed documents that weren't to be opened until the beginning of next month, but in the circumstances I think now's as good a time as any. Once

I've had a look I'll arrange a meeting with Laura to discuss the implications of Simon's death.'

'I thought Laura had been left everything,' and there was another silence.

'Who told you that?'

'Simon.'

'Hmm, that isn't exactly the case, or at least it wasn't. I'll be in touch,' he said, and I was abruptly left listening to the dialling tone. Brandon was clearly a worried and flustered man.

CHAPTER FIFTEEN

'Is Laura all right?' I asked when Emma eventually joined me in the bedroom. We had eaten dinner alone, Laura choosing to take a tray in her room and Emma had been to check on her before we retired.

She flopped back against the door and grimaced. 'She'll be fine. It was a bit of a shock, that's all. If you think about it, she's been on a bit of an emotional roller coaster over the past few days. First the inheritance, then Simon's attack, the horrible effigy in the woods and then the riding accident – now Simon's dead and for all we know her demented uncle is on the loose somewhere. I'm surprised she's not a total mess, to be honest.'

She sank down on the bed next to where I lay sprawled out trying to summon the energy to get undressed. 'I forgot to ask – how did it go with the servants?'

'All right, I suppose. They were shocked, but I don't think any of them knew him particularly well so there was no weeping and wailing, thank God.'

'Hmm, not then, maybe.' Emma swivelled slightly so she was looking towards me. 'I popped down to the kitchen just now to get Laura some hot milk.'

'Hot milk?'

'I thought it would help her sleep.'

'*Really*?'

She made a huffing sound. 'Do you want to hear what I have to say or not?'

'Go on,' I said, sitting upright and plastering an attentive expression upon my face. She crossed her arms, not impressed. 'I'm listening – honest.'

She gave another huff. 'Anyway, I went to the kitchen, not expecting anyone to be down there this late and I heard voices.' She absently picked at a loose thread on the bedspread. 'When I reached the door I could hear someone crying and then I heard Sarah Walters say "I really can't take it any more". Well, I was in two minds as to whether I should go in or not. It was a bit awkward.'

'So, what did you do?'

'I could hear Donald Walters making "there, there" sort of noises, which really aren't particularly helpful when one's upset, so I poked my head around the door. As you can imagine they both straightened up pretty sharpish and Mrs W hastily dried her eyes, but the poor woman looked distraught.'

'They hadn't been particularly upset about Simon's death, more worried about their jobs, and I did try to put their minds at rest,' I said, wondering what I'd missed. They'd appeared reassured.

'Well, I asked if everything was all right, which

obviously it wasn't. I would have had to have been blind not to realise it was something serious as Mrs W was in such a state.'

'And?'

'They did the usual servant thing. "Everything's fine, Mrs Cummings. Nothing to worry about, Mrs Cummings. Is there anything we can help you with, Mrs Cummings?" Anyway, Mrs W heated some milk for me to take to Laura and I left.'

'They didn't tell you what was wrong?'

'Well, here's the thing,' Emma said, taking hold of my hand, 'Mr W came hurrying after me. He apologised for his wife's tears, which I told him wasn't really necessary and I only wished I could have been of some help. It was then he told me that they were coming up to the anniversary of their daughter's death, which was always upsetting for both of them and, with all that had been going on, Mrs W had found it a bit overwhelming.'

'That's sad. Did he say how long ago or give any details?'

Emma shook her head. 'I didn't really like to ask. He was close to tears himself, poor man.'

I squeezed her fingers. 'It must be awful to lose a child,' I said.

Emma looked down at our joined hands. 'The most awful thing in the world,' she said. 'It makes you realise some people have far worse problems than your own.'

'And ain't that the truth,' I said, thinking how poor Simon certainly didn't have to worry about anything any longer.

'You ready for bed?' she asked.

'Yeah. It's been a long day.'

She kissed me on the cheek and, with a smile that had me thinking all sorts of things I probably shouldn't in view of the day we'd had and our recent conversation, I watched her pad off to the bathroom.

I woke with a start, my heart thumping. It was pitch-black and when I peered at the bedside clock it read one-thirty. I'd been asleep only two and a half hours.

I lay back wondering what had woken me. As far as I could remember I hadn't been dreaming.

A whisper tickled my senses. No, not a whisper, a sob. Someone was crying. My body tensed as I strove to listen and then I heard it again, definitely a woman crying. Laura? No, her room was in the other wing. I held my breath listening and then I heard it again. It had the other-worldly wispy echo of someone communicating from the other side.

Exhaling I tried to relax. This wasn't anything new. It happened all the time and I was surprised I hadn't had more of it while I was in this house. I supposed I should be grateful it wasn't the grumpy old man coming back to try my patience.

I looked over at Emma. She was curled in a ball with her back to me, breathing slow and rhythmically. I slid out of bed, grabbing my dressing gown off the chair and stepping into my slippers. Tying the belt tight I slipped from the room.

The night lights along the landing had been replaced, bathing the lower part of the hallway in a muted glow, which faded to shadows cloaking the ceiling.

Padding along the darkened corridors I made my way down the stairs into the front hall and through to the back of the house, the ghostly sobs leading the way. Other than the intermittent night lights the whole house was in darkness and the passageway leading to the door to the poolroom was the darkest place of all. I stopped, staring into a corridor so black I couldn't see the end of it.

Another hiccupping sob floated through the ether, calling me to her. I was pretty sure who I would find on the other side of the door. One of the two women from the pool. Maybe their attack on Emma was only to get my attention. Or it could be realising I could see them had brought about this manifestation.

I wished I had a flashlight. I wished I had ignored her call and was upstairs spooning Emma's back. I wished I didn't have this gift – but for all the wishing in the world, I did, and I had to answer to the dead when they needed my help. It was an obligation I took seriously.

Stretching out my hands in front of me I started down the passageway. It crossed my mind I must look like the stereotypical image people had of sleepwalkers – or zombies – and, had I been smiling, the thought was enough to creep me out and wipe it from my face.

My fingers touched wood and I groped around trying to find a doorknob.

Help me!

'I'm coming, I'm coming,' I muttered, still searching for the door handle. Then my fingers found cold metal. I took it in my hand – why was I doing this? Ah, yes, my obligation to the dead. And opened the door.

The moon was bright and the room was bathed in pale light, which reflected off the water forming shimmering, rippled patterns on the furniture spread out around the poolside. The chilled, chlorine-scented air made me shiver, reminding me of early-morning dips during my teenage years spent at boarding school. I'd never given it much thought then, but swimming pools are dead eerie when it's dark, even without the presence of unhappy spirits.

I walked to the side of the pool stopping about a yard from its edge. I knew I was stupid to come to this place alone, but I wasn't a total moron.

'What do you want?' I asked.

'*Help me!*'

Was she trapped here? Tied to this world unable to cross over for some reason? It did happen, but usually because the spirit had unfinished business. Once they had passed on their message or an injustice had been put right, they usually left.

'What is it you want from *me*?'

Glancing around the pool, there was nothing other than the silhouettes of what, in my mind's eye, could have been mythical beasts lying in wait if I hadn't known them for what they were: plain old sunbeds, tables and chairs. I gave myself an inward shake; letting my imagination run away with me wasn't helpful.

I padded along the side of the pool, still keeping at least a yard from the edge, my nerves juddering and my heart thumping loud enough I could hear it. Otherwise the poolroom was in silence except for the gentle lapping of water against the midnight blue tiles.

Then another sob from somewhere near the corner of the pool. I strained my eyes to peer through the dark and there, next to the bar, a swirling mist that could have been fairy dust, if I believed in such a thing, glittered and danced and within the sparkling spiral a figure slowly began to materialise. She was trying to make herself small, curled into a ball with her arms wrapped around her legs and head down. I could see right through her, but she was of enough substance that I could tell it was one of the women from the pool – the first one, the one who had wanted something from me. I took a few steps towards her; strangely enough she acted as though she didn't know I was there.

'*Help me! Someone please help me!*'

I took a few more paces still keeping my distance from the edge of the pool. Then I heard voices coming from outside in the courtyard and the rapid thud of running feet. She huddled down even smaller, her hands covering her mouth as if to stifle a scream.

The door from the courtyard opened, but it didn't, not really. I was seeing something that had happened a long time ago. A shade of the door opened and two shadowy figures rushed inside: two men.

'*Come out, come out, wherever you are.*'

Dressed in black trousers and white shirts, with bow ties hanging loose around their necks, they spread out along the poolside still calling out, their voices thick and slurred from where they had been partying hard.

'*Come out now, you little prick tease.*'

I went to move towards them, but I couldn't, I was frozen in time and there was nothing I could do to stop the drama being played out before me.

'*She's here somewhere,*' *the slightly bulkier of the two said as he paced towards me and away from the girl. The other man stood very still, his head tilted slightly back as though he was sniffing the air.*

I couldn't make out their faces. The men were more translucent than the young woman and most of the time hardly there at all, like I was looking at a movie being projected into thin air with the poolroom forming its backdrop.

'Over there,' the second man said, pointing towards the girl.

She jumped to her feet and tried to run, but they had outflanked her; the first, bulkier man running straight through me to go around the pool, while the other went towards her from the opposite direction. He got there first, grabbing her by the waist and swinging her around to face him.

She beat against his chest with her fists, crying, 'Let me go, let me go,' as she struggled to free herself. She landed a blow to his face, his head snapping backwards. 'You little bitch,' he said, but he was laughing, enjoying himself.

I fought against the paralysis gripping me; it was no good, I was a mere spectator. I couldn't do a thing to help her – then I had to remind myself this wasn't happening now – it had already happened.

The first man, seeing the woman held captive, stopped running and strolled along the poolside to join them. He took hold of her forearms from behind. 'I'll teach you a thing or two,' he snarled into her ear. He, too, was enjoying himself in his own sick way.

'Aren't you going to wish me a happy birthday?' the second man said, still laughing as he backhanded her across the face. She cried out and would have fallen had it not been for the other man holding her so tightly. Laughing Boy balled his fist.

'No,' the first man said, pulling her back and away from his mate. 'Don't mark her face.'

'Of course not, that would never do,' he replied and he punched her in the solar plexus and she buckled with a loud groan.

'Edward! For fuck's sake!'

Edward? But how could this be? How long ago did Simon say the pool was put in? Certainly after Edward was supposed to have died, and yet here he was attending a birthday party in his honour. Ms Barnard did say Oliver used to bring Edward home for the occasional weekend, but this? I was beginning to wonder whether Edward was the only monster in the family.

'Time for fun and games, poppet,' Edward said. 'I know, let's play "how long can Suzie hold her breath?".' He jerked his head towards the pool.

She, Suzie, started to struggle again, but this time she realised she was fighting for her life. 'Please don't do this. Please.'

They dragged her to the edge of the pool and the first man forced her to her knees while Edward dropped down beside her. He grabbed her by the hair and wrenched her head back.

His face appeared clearer now, even in the dark. His expression was placid and his smile was at odds with his actions, it was kind and gentle.

He stuck out his tongue and traced the tip down the side of her cheek. 'So sweet,' he murmured. 'Like honey.' Then he shoved her forward so it was only his hand entwined in her hair stopping her from falling right in. 'Start counting, Suzie,' and he pushed her head down and under the pool's surface. The other man dropped down onto his knees beside him. 'Are you keeping count?' Edward asked.

The man laughed. 'One, two, three . . .'

Suzie began to thrash her arms and then reached back behind her head grabbing at Edward's hands trying to pull them from her hair. He responded by pushing her head even further down so she was beneath the water almost to her chest.

'Thirty-one, thirty-two . . .'

Edward shuffled closer to her body and lifted a leg over her so he was sitting astride her back. 'Shall I give her a little breather?'

'One breath.'

Edward yanked on her head and she exploded upwards coughing and spluttering. Before she could catch her breath he plunged her head back in. She struggled and thrashed and fought, but this time there was to be no relief.

'What do you think?' Edward asked.

'I'm bored now, do whatever you like.'

Edward grinned. 'All righty,' he said and, shifting forward so he was almost lying on her, put his other hand upon her head and pushed the whole top half of her body beneath the surface. Her thrashing and struggling slowed . . . and faltered . . . and stopped and he still didn't let her go, until he lifted himself off her and, with a shove, launched her into the pool. She submerged for a second or two and bobbed to the top face down.

The first man didn't even look at her. 'Come on, Ed. Let's get back to the party before anyone misses us. After all, you are the birthday boy.'

And then they were gone and very slowly the body of Suzie faded and disappeared, leaving me grieving for a woman I didn't know and who had so very nearly helped take my darling Emma from me.

I went back to bed, but I couldn't sleep. I couldn't push the brutality of Edward and the other nameless man out of my head. Every time I closed my eyes they were there.

I lay on my back staring at the ceiling, wondering about the other man, wondering about Suzie. Who were *they*? There must be some way of finding out. Emma had one of those tablet thingies and was always going onto some site or other to find answers to any questions we might have. This is where I thought we might find out about the history of the house. Perhaps she could check out Suzie. Surely there would be a record of a drowning occurring at Kingsmead.

I rolled onto my side, pulled the duvet under my chin and closed my eyes. Almost immediately I was back in the poolroom watching a replay of Suzie's murder like an old-fashioned movie. It was no good. I slipped out of bed, shrugged on the dressing gown, which was getting more use than I could have possibly imagined, and crept out of the bedroom and along the corridor to Edward's old room. If I couldn't sleep, I might as well do something useful.

Last time Emma and I had searched the room we had more or less given up when we'd found the hidden drawer. We assumed we had found what the mystery assailant was looking for. We probably had, but what if we hadn't? It was becoming more that apparent Kingsmead and the Pomeroy family had more secrets than most, so, while I had nothing better to do, I might as well see if I could find anything else worth mentioning.

Mrs Walters had tidied the room, but only in as much as she had piled the clothing neatly upon the bed and replaced the books on the shelves. I supposed at some point all the clothing would be packed off to some charity or another. I doubted Laura would be inclined to keep any of it.

I wasn't sure what I expected to find. Emma had flicked through all the books looking for hidden papers or inscriptions. I wandered over to the bookshelves. Most of the books were old and bound in cracked black leather. I ran my fingers along their spines, hoping for a psychic nudge if there was anything worth looking at, but there was nothing. I wouldn't waste my time on them. If there had been something to find I'm sure Emma would have found it.

Dispirited, I stood in the middle of the room and turned slowly around, my eyes scanning the walls, the furniture, the paintings, the—The paintings. Picture frames and the backs of paintings and photographs were always good places to hide documents or other small items. Precious coins or bonds, for instance. There were several paintings hanging on the walls in this room as well as some small picture frames containing photographs on the mantelpiece and chest of drawers.

I started with the large paintings first. They were bulky and unlikely to be disturbed by a maid while the room was being cleaned, and no one would think to look behind them unless they *were* searching for a secret hiding place.

Clearing a space on the bed I lifted the first painting from the wall and laid it face down. I was no expert on fine art, but the backing looked original as did all the fixings. I returned it to where it had come from and did the same thing with the next one. Again I found nothing and it was becoming increasingly likely that there was nothing else for me to find. Wasn't a drawer full of photographs and an inverted crucifix enough?

I moved on to the framed pictures. The majority were fairly old. There were several family portraits of serious-looking, moustached men in suits standing behind seated, sour-faced women wearing high-collared dresses and strings of pearls or black ribbon chokers. These came out of the frames quite easily and, apart from inscriptions of the dates the photographs were taken and sometimes who the sitters were, there was very little of interest to be found.

The more recent pictures were mainly in contemporary frames of polished, lacquered wood and here I did find a most interesting photograph, at least to me. It was of a very young Simon and his two older siblings. I recognised Oliver straight away as the man I'd met on several occasions while I'd been on leave. The third of the three brothers I also recognised despite never having met him. In the photo he was smiling, the same gentle smile I'd seen earlier: the monster – Edward Pomeroy.

I sat down on the bed to study the photograph. In the picture Simon could have only been about seven or eight and Oliver and Edward were little more than callow youths. I couldn't help but wonder whether Edward was already winding his way into insanity or was this before the trauma that had set him on his downward spiral into madness? Alice Barnard had intimated something had happened to him as a teenager and the smile was enough to make me think that when this picture was taken he was already not quite right.

I flipped the picture over and unclipped the backing piece of wood, flicking it out with my fingernail. I froze, chills running through me and raising goosebumps upon my arms. There was a second picture. Another picture of the three brothers. Simon looked about sixteen or seventeen – so it had possibly been taken only months before Edward's 'death'. I took a quick look at its reverse. Scrawled in blue ink across the back were the initials and figures WN 1981. I took it as 1981 being the year; I didn't know what the WN meant. Simon would have been sixteen.

I sank down onto the bed. Shit, shit, shit, shit, shit! What the fuck had Simon been playing at? He *had* clearly known about the cult; all three men were dressed in black robes. Edward and Oliver were wearing their chains of office: jet beads linked by silver from which silver inverted crucifixes hung. Simon was holding his up, his smile triumphant. If I wasn't much mistaken, he was celebrating his investiture into the fold.

CHAPTER SIXTEEN

I don't know how long I sat there staring at the photograph of the three Pomeroy boys. My head was all over the place. Everything I'd believed to be true about my friend had been blown out of the water and everything he had told me about his family had been lies. I suppose now I knew why he took what I'd told him about his brother's murder by masked killers so calmly. I was only confirming what he'd suspected.

I got to my feet. I needed to get some sleep and tomorrow – and tomorrow what? If I had any sense, Emma and I would pack our bags and go. I put the hidden photo in the pocket of my dressing gown and returned the original picture into the frame where I'd found it. I would discuss it with Emma before we went down to breakfast. It was only fair she had a choice in whether she stay or go – I didn't. I'd made Laura a promise and I intended to keep it. As Emma had said, none of this was Laura's fault.

As I left the room I glanced back over my shoulder, my eyes going straight to the picture of the three boys together. They looked so young and normal and yet I couldn't help but speculate whether even then the two older brothers were already involved in the cult, coven or whatever a group of Satanists called themselves. Oliver had been about the same age as Simon had in the second photo.

I flicked off the light and closed the door. Oh, what a wicked web the Pomeroy boys had woven about themselves.

Light was beginning to filter into the bedroom by the time exhaustion gave way to sleep. I would have slept late if it hadn't been for my mobile going off. I scrabbled to find it on the bedside table nearly knocking over my travel clock and a glass of water.

'Yep,' I said, hauling myself into a sitting position and rubbing at my eyes.

'Jed?'

'Yep. Who is this?'

'Brandon Fredericks,' a voice said, and he sounded rougher than I felt.

I glanced at the clock – it was only seven-thirty – what the hell? I was instantly awake. 'What's the matter?'

'We have to talk. Can you meet me at my office?'

'What time?'

'We open for business at ten these days, so if you could make it for nine? I'd rather we talked before my secretary and the rest of the staff get in.'

Emma was beginning to stir. She stretched and rolled over. 'Who is it?'

'Brandon,' I mouthed at her.

'Where's your office?' I asked.

'In the village, opposite the pub. You can't miss it.'

I thought for a moment. Yes, I remembered a large building opposite the Fox and Fiddle Inn, though at the time I'd paid it little attention. 'Right. We'll see you there at nine.'

'Good,' he said, then hesitated. 'Jed, don't mention you're coming to see me to anyone at Kingsmead.'

I frowned at Emma. 'What about Laura? I'd have thought you'd want her to come.'

'No, no. Just you, and Emma if you must, but definitely not Laura, not yet.'

'But . . .'

'Jed, you'll understand once we've spoken, but please believe me when I say it's best no one knows you're coming here.'

I was now completely nonplussed. 'All right,' I said. 'I'll see you later,' and once again I was speaking to the dialling tone.

'What was that all about?' Emma asked, pulling herself into a sitting position beside me.

I dropped my phone on the bedside table. 'I have no idea,' I said, 'but we're meeting Brandon at nine in his office.'

'But not Laura?'

'That's what he said. Also we're not to tell anyone where we're going.'

She raised an eyebrow. '*Laura* is his client.'

'I know, but to be perfectly honest with you, Laura being a Pomeroy might be the problem.'

She frowned at me. 'She's a lovely girl.'

'She seems to be, but I'm beginning to have a few trust

issues.' Her frown grew deeper. 'I have something to show you,' I told her, 'then you can tell me what you think.'

Emma listened to what I had to say in silence. First, I told her about what I'd seen in the poolroom and how afterwards I couldn't sleep. Then I passed her the photograph. When I eventually finished talking, she didn't speak for a full thirty seconds. When she did, she sounded as confused as I felt – and angry – like me, she was angry.

'Why did Simon ask us here? Surely he must have realised there was a possibility you'd find out, especially if you did what he wanted and managed to connect with Oliver.'

'I don't know, Emms. Maybe he really did want to know who killed Oliver. Whether it was the cult or someone else.'

'Do you really think so?'

I pulled a face. 'I don't know what to believe any more.'

Emma leant her head against my shoulder. 'Perhaps once we've spoken to Brandon things will become a little clearer.'

'I sincerely do hope so,' I said.

Laura was already at the table when we went down to breakfast. Her eyes were red-rimmed and her complexion pale. She managed a weak smile of greeting.

'How are you this morning?' Emma asked.

Laura gave a little shrug. 'OK, I guess. I still can't believe it.'

'Me neither,' I said.

'Jed,' Laura said, her expression contrite, 'I am *so* sorry. I'd only met Simon once and I throw a fit of the vapours when you were his friend and must be really feeling his loss.'

'We hadn't spoken for years,' I said, 'but I will miss him now he's gone.' I didn't add that I'd miss asking him what the fuck he'd been playing at; she didn't need to know that.

Emma gave me a sideways look, clearly guessing what was going through my mind. 'How about your aches and pains?' she quickly asked Laura.

'Not so bad,' she replied. 'In fact, I was thinking about going for a little ride this morning. You know, getting back in the saddle as soon as possible.'

'You're a braver woman than I am,' Emma said, 'but don't go on your own.'

'I won't. I'll see if Dan can ride with me.'

I inwardly grimaced, but reminded myself it was none of my business. For the moment Emma and I had other things to be worrying about and riding would keep her occupied while we slid off to see Brandon.

'Just be very careful,' Emma said.

Laura's smile was a little brighter. 'I will, I promise.'

Back in our room, Emma took a look on her iPad to see if there was any information about a drowning at Kingsmead. I wasn't surprised when she could find no mention of it.

'How about disappearances of young women from the village or visitors to the area?' I suggested.

'Ah,' she said, 'that could take some time. I'll try searching local papers, etcetera.' Emma's fingers tapped away as I shrugged on my jacket and grabbed my mobile and car keys off the bedside table.

I glanced at my watch. 'It'll have to wait until we get back.'

She dropped the tablet into her handbag and got to her feet. 'I don't know about you, but I feel a little nervous.'

Emma wasn't the only one. I didn't say, but gave her a reassuring smile. 'Let's get this over with,' I said.

By car the village was at most ten minutes away and it took almost as long to drive out of the estate as it did to get from the outer gate to the village centre.

I had been right about the building I'd noticed the day before when we'd visited the pub. Brandon's office was indeed directly opposite the Fox and Fiddle Inn.

Brandon's Merc was already ensconced in the corner of the small car park at the side of the building and I pulled the Jag in beside it. As I switched off the engine, I felt a tentative tickle at the back of my neck. Looking at the building I wasn't unduly surprised: it was old, probably Tudor like the pub across the road, judging by the white and faded black-beamed exterior.

Emma grabbed her bag from out of the footwell and hooked it over her shoulder. 'Shall we go in?' she asked.

In reply I opened the door and climbed out. The hair on the back of my neck prickled. This time, though, it was followed by a sudden blast of emotion that practically forced the air out of my lungs and I had to rest my hand on the car roof to steady myself.

Emma had started towards the building but stopped. 'Jed?' I heard her say. Realising I wasn't beside her she glanced back at me. 'Can you feel it?'

I swallowed down the fear that was in danger of choking me. 'Emms, please get back in the car and lock the door,' I said as I pushed myself away from the Jag and started towards the building. Something terrible had happened and not so long ago; I was sure of it.

She fell into step beside me. 'If something's wrong I'm coming in with you,' she said, her tone brooking no argument. My eyes met hers and she gave me a little nod. I took hold of her hand and she was by my side as we walked from the car park.

At the front of the building I stopped to peer through the leaded windows and, although it was dark inside, I could make out a reception desk and waiting area with high-backed, uncomfortable-looking chairs and a small table covered with various magazines. The front door was old, possibly as old as the building. Banded with iron, the once-black, cracked and pitted wood had faded to silvery grey. I gave it a push and it silently swung open into a darkened hallway.

Moving in front of Emma I stepped inside with her following close behind me, her hand still gripping hold of mine.

'Brandon,' I called out, my voice sounding hollow in the narrow confines of the hallway. 'Brandon.'

We carried on along the passage, the rickety floorboards creaking beneath our feet. To the left there was a door into the reception and waiting room I had seen through the window. I took a quick peek inside; it was empty. In the corridor straight ahead an open door beckoned. It was dark and gloomy and the further we went inside the darker and gloomier it became – and cold – very cold, but maybe that was an illusion. I pushed the door open with my fingertips. It took us into another reception area. There were three doors, each emblazoned with a brass plaque, I guessed inscribed with the incumbent solicitor's name. Brandon's office was through the central door.

'Brandon,' I called again and still there was silence. I reached out and took hold of the door handle. The metal was cold against my palm and my senses screamed for us to turn around and walk out of this place. 'Stay here,' I whispered, though by now you'd think I'd know better.

'You have to be bloody joking. I'm not letting you go anywhere without me.'

I turned the handle and pushed the door open and the aroma of man's mortality filled my nostrils.

'Dear God, what is that?' Emma asked with a grimace, one hand rising to cover her lower face.

'Death,' I whispered. 'It's death,' and her other hand tightened on mine.

A large, polished mahogany desk filled most of the opposite side of the room. Light streamed in through the three large, leaded windows behind it, casting diamond-shaped patterns on the desk and carpet that weren't overshadowed by the ample leather office chair facing the window.

Squeezing Emma's hand, I said, 'Stay right here.' For once she didn't argue; she didn't want to see this any more than I did.

I padded across the plush carpet, the stink of death wrapping itself around me and so thick I could taste it on my lips.

Walking around the desk, I stopped in front of the windows. Sunshine filled the large, walled garden outside. Bird feeders hung from a wrought iron stand beside a grey stone bird bath. A crow was sitting on its edge dunking a piece of bread into the water, while two blue tits jostled for position on an almost empty tube of peanuts. Bright and peaceful, a beautiful scene to look out upon to briefly escape the tribulations of the day.

I forced myself to turn and face the chair. My feet didn't want to work, I'm not sure I wanted them to.

It was as bad as I was expecting. I knew it would be, I'd seen the rope holding his right wrist to the chair's arm rest and suspected the other would be similarly tied. I wasn't wrong. The elderly solicitor would no longer look out upon the tranquil gardens. His eyes were gone and, judging by the blood soaking his chin and the front of his white shirt, so was his tongue. I made my eyes travel over his body. I had seen worse in the past and, God help me, would probably in the future. Not necessarily a once-living body sprawled out in front of me, but sometimes the visions were as terrible. The ones I'd been seeing recently certainly were.

He had been dressed for the office: white shirt, plum-coloured tie, charcoal waistcoat to match his trousers. His jacket was hung over the back of the chair. The shirt and tie were now mainly crimson, the waistcoat discoloured and slick with blood. His sleeves were rolled back, the ropes around his wrists brutally tight and stained where they had rubbed his flesh raw as he had strained against them. And his hands . . . I swiped my own across my lips. They had tortured him. Whether it had really taken mangling all eight of his fingers to find out what they wanted I would never know. I thought probably not; he wasn't a young man full of ego and pride. As a man grows older and gets closer to the end he will sacrifice pride if it means living a little longer. He probably had given them what they wanted upon the snapping of the first joint, the rest had been down to sheer cruelty – and these people *were* cruel.

I looked away. I'd seen more than enough. As if on cue my mobile began to ring. I pulled it from my pocket, fumbling to answer the call, my own fingers seemingly unable to work.

'Mr Cummings, you wanted to see me and I'm here at Kingsmead as you asked. *Where* exactly are *you*?' Detective Inspector Brogan was pissed off, I could tell.

'I'm at Brandon Fredericks' office,' I said, 'and I suggest you get here as quickly as you can.'

'I haven't time to run around the countryside searching for you.'

'He's dead.'

There was a moment's silence. 'What did you say?'

'Brandon Fredericks is dead,' I repeated.

There was a sharp intake of breath. 'I'll be straight there. Don't touch a thing.'

I didn't dignify this with a reply, ending the call with a stab of my forefinger. There was one thing I did have to do, though. I needed to take a look at the papers spread across Brandon's desk. There was a file lying open directly in front of where he'd been sitting when he was interrupted. In it was the Last Will and Testament of Oliver James Pomeroy. I took a handkerchief out of my pocket and lifted the first page.

'What are you doing?' Emma asked.

'Seeing if there is anything here that will give us a clue as to why Brandon wanted this meeting.'

It quickly became apparent there wasn't. There were no codicils and no letters when there should have been. There was a second file underneath the first. Across the top was written 'Simon Pomeroy'. It was as helpful; it contained his will and not a lot else. Surprisingly, there was no file in the name of Edward Pomeroy. I strode over to the filing cabinets in the corner. No grey metal for Brandon; fine mahogany cabinets that matched his desk.

'Jed?'

I shot her a weak smile and quickly found the drawer containing the Ps. There was one empty master folder headed 'The Pomeroy Family', but nothing for Edward and there should have been – I knew there should have been.

We went outside to wait by the front door, the fresh air smelling all the sweeter after the lingering stink in the office. Emma's complexion was unusually pasty; I doubted mine was much better.

Brogan arrived within minutes. He must have driven like a maniac. He pulled into the car park with a screech of tyres and, with a slam of his car door and the thump of hurrying footsteps, he rounded the corner, his expression grim. He was wearing a different suit, shirt and tie, even so they were as rumpled as his face. I was beginning to wonder whether he ever spent his nights in his own bed.

He gave me a hard look. 'What were you doing here?'

My eyes met his and I could see the realisation dawn that I wasn't some hick for him to mess with. 'He asked us to meet him,' I said, 'and he sounded scared.'

'Where's Miss Simmons?'

'He didn't want us to tell her we were coming. In fact, he insisted we keep it from everyone back at the house.'

He frowned at me. 'Did he say why?'

I shoved my hands into my pockets. 'No. He said it would become clear when we spoke.'

'Where is he?'

I gestured inside. 'In his office, by the window.'

'Have you touched anything?'

'Other than to open the doors – no,' I lied.

He gave an abrupt nod and marched inside. I let him go in alone. I didn't need to see it again.

'Do you want to sit in the car?' I asked Emms, as we walked back around to the car park; her pallor was beginning to worry me.

She shook her head. 'This is all turning into a nightmare,' she whispered.

I didn't disagree.

The policeman was inside the office for about ten minutes. He came out just as the first of Brandon's staff pulled into the car park. The young woman greeted us with a bright smile and a 'Can I help you?' We stood to one side and let Brogan deal with it. He told her there had been an *incident* and Brandon was dead. Surprisingly enough, he came across as kind, considerate and even provided a small, handy pack of tissues when the young woman dissolved into tears.

'I'm afraid I can't allow you inside,' he said.

'Could I at least print the solicitors' diaries off my computer?' she asked, dabbing at her eyes. 'Then I can rearrange the appointments.'

He acquiesced gracefully and took her inside. In the meantime, several other members of staff turned up, together with a police van and men in white suits, the forensic brigade.

'Maybe we *should* sit in the car,' Emma said.

It *was* getting a mite uncomfortable; the staff visibly distressed as the news was broken to them and it was clear Brandon had been loved by his mainly female members of staff.

Gradually the other cars disappeared from the car park leaving just ours, Brandon's and Brogan's. The police van was out front parked on double yellows. Brogan reappeared after about twenty minutes of our waiting.

Seeing us sitting in the Jag he marched over, his expression strained. He stooped down to talk to me through the window. 'You might as well go,' he said. 'I'll be tied up here for some time. I'll meet you back at Kingsmead at, say' – he glanced at his watch – 'two-thirty or so.'

'We'll be there,' I said. 'Do you want us to inform Miss Simmons of what's happened or do you want to tell her?'

He paused. 'Let me do it,' he said. 'I'd be interested to see her reaction.'

He gave an abrupt nod and stalked off with me frowning after him. I know *I* had trust issues with the Pomeroys, but I didn't for one minute consider Laura could be complicit in, let alone capable of, murder.

I wasn't the only one who watched him walk away wondering at his reasoning. 'So,' Emma said, 'is he one of the good guys or not?'

I wasn't sure how to answer. 'I'll reserve judgement until we've spoken about the mystery woman.'

'Hmm. I can't really see that him sleeping with this woman is grounds for blackmail.'

'It could if he's married, Emms.'

'Easier and safer to fess up to your wife rather than risk your career, I'd have thought.'

'Easier and safer not to have illicit nooky in the first place,' I said.

She laughed and leant over to kiss my cheek. 'Not everyone has your strict moral code.'

I started the car. 'Perhaps they should. It would certainly solve a few of the problems in this world.'

CHAPTER SEVENTEEN

Laura was still out riding when we got back to the house, which was good news. I didn't like that we were keeping things from her. Visiting her solicitor behind her back was bad enough, but lying to her, albeit by omission, I wasn't at all comfortable with. We went straight to our room. This way we didn't have to play-act as if everything was all right for the rest of the morning. Finding a murder victim wasn't exactly the sort of thing you kept to yourself.

'At least it won't be us having to tell her even more bad news,' Emma said.

'I suppose.'

'I wonder what it was Brandon wanted to talk to you about.'

I shook my head. 'He sounded scared, Emms.'

'Do you think he found something in the papers you said he had to read through?'

'I don't know. I mean, what could there have been that would frighten him so much? Most of it he'd have seen already.'

It was a mystery and another I didn't think I'd be getting the answer to any time soon.

Lunch was difficult. Laura had been out all morning with Dan and was full of the joys of spring. She chattered away happily. Despite her fall, she was getting more and more comfortable in the saddle.

'Dan said I was a natural,' she said, her cheeks flushed.

I gave Emms a pointed look, which she ignored. 'He seems like a nice young man,' she said, and I had to stop myself from groaning out loud.

'He's very knowledgeable about the local wildlife and Kingsmead's history.'

'Hmm,' and I almost missed it I was so wrapped up in my thoughts of how he was most likely trying to get into the new mistress of the house's knickers. 'Kingsmead's history?' I asked.

'Yes,' she said, her eyes sparkling. 'It was built in the 1700s as a country retreat for the then Lord Pomeroy. Apparently, he was into all manner of nasty stuff and wanted somewhere away from London so he could carry out his debauched practices. Story has it he was a member of the infamous Hellfire Club.'

Emma and I exchanged a glance. 'Wasn't the Hellfire Club some dubious society for upper-class devil worshippers?' Emma said.

'Huh. More like another place where they could get their kit off and act out their baser fantasies,' I muttered.

Emma ignored me. 'How come Dan knows so much about Kingsmead? I didn't think he'd worked here very long.'

Laura took a slurp of coffee, warming to her current

favourite subject – and I didn't think it was the history of Kingsmead. 'Dan has a degree in history.'

'Really?'

'Hmm, he said once he started living here he couldn't resist looking into the estate's past.'

It was true Dan had said – what had he said? Then I remembered: *Some men do evil things to get what they want out of life – the Pomeroys are such men. If you don't believe me look, into the family history. Violent death being the least of it.*

Violent death being the least of it – he'd got that much right. There had been a few of those recently. I wondered whether it was time I had a long talk with Dan Crouchley. If he already knew the history of Kingsmead it could save Emma hours searching on the Internet and would probably be more accurate than anything she could find. Once we'd dealt with DI Brogan, I'd seek Dan out.

I had just dropped my knife and fork onto the plate when Mrs Walters came hurrying in, a concerned expression clouding her face.

'Miss Simmons, the detective inspector is here and he wants to speak to you,' she said. 'I've put him in the study.'

Laura's smile all but disappeared. 'I'll be right there,' she said, getting to her feet and dropping her napkin on the table. 'I wonder what he wants.'

'Hopefully he's here to ask about what we found in the clearing,' I said.

'Possibly, though what else I can tell him I don't know.'

'You've spoken to him?' I asked in surprise.

'No, I've never met him. I saw Detective Sergeant Peters.'

'When was this?'

'Yesterday. You were out walking, when he called. It was before I went riding and got thrown.'

I wasn't surprised she'd forgotten to mention it. The day had become a little hectic. 'I suppose at least someone's taking it seriously,' I said.

'I'd better not keep the detective inspector waiting.'

'If you need us, we'll be here,' Emma said.

Laura gave us a tight smile and hurried off while Emma poured coffee for us both, giving us an excuse to stay right where we were. The DI would no doubt be wanting to speak to us soon – and if he didn't – well, I definitely wanted to talk to him about a certain dark-haired woman, who I was pretty sure had committed murder.

Maddy cleared the table and brought us a fresh pot of coffee and the third cup we requested for Brogan, not that he deserved it. Emma was a good deal kinder than I.

'If we are to talk about murder and blackmail we can at least be civilised about it,' Emma said when the girl hurried off to carry out her instructions.

Whatever he had to say to Laura didn't take long. We were still drinking our coffee when he came striding in. I gestured with a jerk of the head to a chair and the policeman slumped down opposite me.

'Coffee, Detective Inspector?' Emma asked.

'Thank you,' he said, his eyes on me. He was even more dishevelled than earlier. I suspected he'd had a bad morning, but then, hadn't we all?

'So, Brandon Fredericks asked you meet him at his office,' he said.

I pulled out my mobile and checked the log. 'He phoned me at just after seven-thirty this morning.'

'And he didn't say what it was about?'

'No, only that Emma and I should keep our visit to ourselves.'

'A bit strange, don't you think?'

I leant back in my chair and fixed him with a hard stare. 'After all that's happened over the past few days – no – not really. What I do find a little strange is that, despite my phoning to tell you Miss Simmons had been threatened, you didn't return my call. It wasn't until just now that I heard your man Peters had been here to deal with it.'

His expression was completely bemused, and I did wonder how he'd ever made it out of uniform let alone to his elevated position. 'What? Threatened? When?'

'Two days ago,' I said. 'You didn't know?'

He shook his head as he pulled out his mobile and scrolled down his messages. 'I haven't had any calls from you until yesterday.'

'Well, I did phone you,' and I passed him my mobile.

His eyes flicked from his phone to mine and back again, his expression puzzled, then he went very still, and his face could have been carved from marble. 'What was it you wanted to see me about?' he asked, his voice strained. 'You said something about an acquaintance of mine.'

I studied his face and to my way of thinking it belonged to a man who had suddenly realised he'd been played. 'I think you'd better come upstairs. I have some papers I want you to see.'

He got to his feet with an air of weary resignation. I took him into Edward's bedroom and left him there with Emma while I went to get the envelopes we'd found. I decided to

211

hold back the piece of jewellery until I had figured out how trustworthy he was – and open-minded.

When I returned to Edward's room he was by the mantelpiece, the picture of the three Pomeroy brothers in his hand. I tried to temper my suspicious nature. Could it be I was being paranoid and it was coincidental he should be examining this particular photo? I didn't believe in coincidences and decided suspicious was the way to go.

I held out the first envelope towards him. I wanted to see his expression when he saw the photographs it contained. He looked at it and then at my face. 'What is it?'

'I suggest you take a look.'

He put the photograph back on the mantelpiece and stretched out his hand, his fingers hesitating an inch from the envelope. His eyes once again went to mine.

I thrust it towards him. 'Take it.'

His Adam's apple bobbed, but he did as I said and took it in both hands. He stared at the plain front for a few seconds and then flipped it open and slid out the folded pages. His eyes widened upon seeing the first page and he looked at me with a snarl.

'Don't blame the messenger,' I said. 'We think this is one of the items whoever broke in and bashed Simon over the head was searching for.' I watched his face. 'I even considered it could have been you.'

'Me?'

I gestured with my head to the pictures in his hand.

He sank into the leather armchair by the mantelpiece, frowning at the photographs of himself with the mystery woman. He swallowed hard and a myriad of emotions played across his features in very quick succession.

'Where did you get these from?' he asked, his voice tight.

I pointed over to the wardrobe. 'There's a secret drawer.'

He wiped a hand across his face. 'Is this who you were talking about when you said you'd seen an acquaintance of mine at the hospital the day Simon Pomeroy died?'

Emma and I exchanged a brief glance. 'Yes,' I said.

His eyes fluttered shut for a moment. When he opened them again I could see his anger. 'That's why I never received your message,' he said, his lips twisting into a sneer of, I suspected, self-loathing. 'She was with me. She called me out of the blue and asked if we could meet. Of course it ended up as all our meetings ever did. She must have gone through my messages and missed calls while I was . . . While I was elsewhere. How could I have been so stupid?'

'Who is she?' I asked.

'Tanith Bloxborough,' he said and I swear he shuddered, which was an interesting reaction when saying one's lover's name. 'Oliver Pomeroy's mistress.'

Emma let out a shocked gasp. I'm glad I wasn't the only one who was stunned. 'Well,' I said, 'I can safely say I never saw that coming,' and I couldn't help but wonder about the Polaroid photos and who had taken them.

'*You* were having an affair with *Oliver's* mistress?' Emma said.

Brogan didn't look up. 'Yes,' he said. 'It's not something I'm proud of, but then again at the time he was alive and well, so there was no real reason why I shouldn't be seeing her.'

'Was Oliver blackmailing you?' Emma asked. Brogan laughed – a hollow sound. 'Hell, no. I'm not married, neither were they, so who would care? Other than Oliver Pomeroy.'

'Then why all this?' I asked. 'What did Oliver have to gain? And what would Edward have wanted with them?'

'You think this is Oliver's doing?' His expression was incredulous and then he began to really laugh.

Emma frowned at me. 'Who else?'

'Oliver wasn't the head of some government department that everyone denies exists,' Brogan said. I stared at him and his lips twisted into a wry smile.

'Are you telling me that you believe this was Simon's doing?' I asked.

His stare answered my question. 'What's in the others?'

'There are pictures of Laura, similar to those,' I gestured towards the pictures in his hand, 'in so far as they are professional surveillance photos. And some Polaroid photos of her parents.' I decided to keep the other photos of Tanith to myself.

'But why would Simon have all these photos?'

Brogan shrugged. 'He's a puppet master at the ministry; he probably couldn't help himself.'

'But what did he hope to achieve with these pictures of you?' Emma asked.

Brogan shook his head. 'I have no idea.' I wasn't sure I believed him, but he returned my sceptical stare with a defiant one of his own. 'Perhaps he was blackmailing Tanith,' he said.

'Why would he?' I asked.

'Power,' Emma said. 'We talked about this before. What is it a man who has everything craves more than anything else?'

'You're right,' Brogan said, 'and the Pomeroys were

into power more than most. From what Tanith said, Oliver Pomeroy was a control freak, but Simon,' he blew out through pursed lips, 'he was the daddy.'

I don't know why I was surprised; it was one of the reasons we'd fallen out. If something was to be done it had to be done his way.

'You said Miss Simmons had been threatened? How exactly?' Brogan asked.

'Shouldn't you have been told all this by your man Peters? He spoke to Laura yesterday.'

'Why don't *you* tell me about the threat?'

I didn't like his tone and replied through gritted teeth. 'We found an effigy in the clearing where Oliver died. It was meant to be Laura, it was wearing her clothes, and had the appearance of having had the eyes and tongue removed just like her grandfather and now Brandon. Then, the following day, she was thrown by her horse and we think it was deliberately contrived.'

'How so?'

He was beginning to irritate me in so many ways and Emma laying her hand on my arm let me know it was showing. 'She was riding Angel, a usually placid mare, and she noticed her getting a bit jumpy, then someone let off a gun close by and the horse bolted. There was a second shot and Laura was thrown.'

'Was she riding alone?'

'No, fortunately the guy who looks after the stables was riding with her.'

'Dan Crouchley?'

'Yes.'

'And did he think the horse was "a bit jumpy"?'

215

I folded my arms. 'Yes, he asked the vet to do some tests.'

'Has he had the results?'

'I shouldn't think so. I asked the vet to call me as soon as they were in.'

He raised an eyebrow. 'Taking a lot upon yourself, aren't you, Mr Cummings?'

I could feel my temperature rising and I didn't bother to hide it. 'Who else is there, Detective Inspector? Turns out the only person I thought I could trust wasn't the man I thought he was. As for the police, well, I have photographs here that prove the man in charge is quite literally sleeping with the enemy, or at least the woman who was, quite possibly, the last person to see Simon Pomeroy alive.'

Brogan flushed. 'All right,' he said. 'Point taken.'

I continued glowering at him. As far as I was concerned he was dirty – if not by choice, by association.

He climbed to his feet. 'When you hear the results of the tests could you let me know?'

'Yes,' I said, 'but before you go' – I handed him the pictures of Laura's parents – 'these were also hidden in the secret drawer.'

He sat back down and emptied the photos into his hand. His expression instantly became very grim indeed.

'These aren't crime scene photographs or even professional.'

'I know,' I said. 'We think they might have been taken by Edward Pomeroy.'

He stood. 'Can I take these?'

I was surprised he asked and gave a grudging nod.

He bundled the envelopes up. 'I'll get Walters to take me out to the clearing,' he said and, with a nod to me then Emma and a 'Mrs Cummings', he left.

I waited until the sound of his footsteps faded away. 'What do you think?'

Emma glanced at the open doorway. 'I want to trust him, but I don't think we can.'

I squeezed her hand. 'You and me both,' I murmured. 'You and me both.'

CHAPTER EIGHTEEN

When we went back downstairs it was to find Laura had gone out again. Apparently, there were several cars, which now belonged to her, and she had taken a small Fiesta, a car more often than not used by the housekeeper and cook if they ever had to pop into the village for supplies. I wondered where she'd gone and Dan's smiling face instantly popped into my head. I supposed I couldn't blame her – she needed someone closer to her own age to confide in. I only wished it wasn't Dan Crouchley.

'It's a terrible thing what's happened to Mr Fredericks,' Mrs Walters said. 'He was a lovely man.'

'Who told you?' I asked in surprise.

The housekeeper folded her hands, her expression grim. 'Maddy's sister works in the pub across the road from Mr Fredericks' office and she's a friend of the receptionist there. Nothing stays quiet for long around here,' she said. 'We probably knew downstairs before the detective chappie turned up here to tell Miss Simmons.'

'Bad news travels fast,' I said.

'Something like that,' she replied. 'Is that all, Mr Cummings?'

'I thought living in Slyford St James was a bit like being in a goldfish bowl,' Emma said as soon as the housekeeper was gone, 'but this is something else.'

'Makes you wonder how much the staff do know about what's been going on here,' I said.

She gave me a look. 'Like this cult business?'

I took her arm. 'Let's walk,' I said. Call me paranoid, but I waited until we were well away from the house and in the gardens before I carried on from where we'd left off. 'There were a lot of people involved, Emms. There must have been a whole load of visitors coming and going every time they had a . . .' I frowned – how would you describe such a thing? A meeting made it sound like a WI get-together and it definitely wasn't that. 'Every time they had a gathering,' I finished lamely.

'It's a big house, Oliver was an important man locally, having weekend parties was probably the norm,' Emma said. 'I doubt very much the servants would think anything of it.'

'With people going around in black robes, Emms?'

'They probably saved all that sort of nonsense until the servants had settled for the night.'

She had a point. 'Dan Crouchley was definitely being tight-lipped about something. He more or less admitted to knowing things he'd rather not talk about.'

'Perhaps we should get to know Mr Crouchley a little better.'

'Hmm, Laura appears to be getting to know him far more than she should.'

Emma pulled me to a halt and looked at me, studying my face. 'What's that meant to mean?'

'I'm just saying.' I hesitated. 'Maybe you should have a word with her. You know about the whole employer–employee relationship thing.'

She burst out laughing. 'My God, Jed Cummings, you're becoming quite the snob.'

'I am not,' I said, though her saying it made me question whether she was perhaps right. 'I just know what the servants in these big houses are like. Everyone has their place and they have to stick to it.'

She hooked her arm back through mine and we started off again. 'Perhaps you're right. But he is rather handsome.'

'A bad lad is what my mother would have called him.'

'And I seem to recall you telling me she thought that's what you were,' she said quietly. I could tell by her voice that she didn't mean anything by it, but she was right. My mother had despised me from the moment she realised I could see things other people couldn't. At the age of five she had thrashed me until I bled trying to get the devil out of me, then sent me away to school rather than have to see my face every day. Emma squeezed my arm. 'She was wrong, Jed. You're a good man with good intentions.'

'And maybe I should see the best in Dan Crouchley is what you're trying to say?'

'Yes, I guess I am.'

We sat down on a stone bench overlooking a square pond and water feature in the centre of the gardens. It was a peaceful spot. With only the tinkle of running water spouting from the mouths of several marble dolphins and the trilling of birdsong I could have sat there all day with the sunshine warming my face. A sudden cry of a peacock from somewhere in the distance made me think of home and I wished with all my heart we had never left it to come to this place.

A cloud passed in front of the sun, taking the heat from the air, and I got to my feet, the peace and tranquillity leeched from the spot along with the warmth. We wandered slowly back to the house in near silence. I wasn't sure what was going through Emma's head, but I guessed, like me, she was thinking of The Grange.

'How did they get hold of Laura's blouse?' Emma asked out of the blue. I hesitated mid stride. How indeed? With everything else that had been going on that snippet of information had fallen through the cracks. 'And how did Simon's mystery assailant get in?'

'Either someone from the . . .' I still wasn't sure what to call them. 'Someone from the cult must have access to the house or has a servant in their pocket.'

'And where is Edward?'

'The house is so big I guess he could be living within the same walls as us and we wouldn't know it.'

'But the servants would,' Emma said. 'Even in a house this size nothing much gets past them.'

'Except for a mysterious cult that doesn't think twice about murdering people.'

Her shoulders sagged. 'Put like that I suppose you're right.'

'Except . . .'

Emma glanced at my face and frowned. 'What?'

221

I cast the thought away. Servants might keep secrets, but they surely wouldn't be involved in some Satanic cult? That was a rich man's type of game. 'Nothing. I was letting my imagination run away with me.'

She made a humphing sound. 'In this place I'm beginning to think I wouldn't be surprised by anything.'

When we went down to dinner, we were greeted by the news that Laura would be taking a tray in her room.

'Is she unwell?' Emma asked.

Mrs Walters leant forward as though imparting a secret. 'She said she was tired, but' – she pulled a face – 'with all that's happened over the past few days the poor lass is probably feeling the strain.'

'I wouldn't be surprised,' Emma said.

When the woman had gone we ate in silence. I wasn't sure about Emma, but I was becoming increasingly uncomfortable with discussing anything of consequence at the dining table. There always appeared to be a servant hovering around and both Mrs Walters and Maddy had the ability to appear as if from nowhere. Maybe I *was* being paranoid, but I no longer trusted anyone else in the house other than Emma.

After dinner we went to sit in the living room for a while. The large sofa was comfortable and, if nothing else, the servants tended to leave us alone for the most part.

'Did you notice the detective inspector's reaction when he said his lady friend's name?' Emma said, after having a hasty glance around the room.

'Hmm, I'm not really surprised. She had a predatory look about her.'

'A black widow,' Emma said with a shudder.

'I'd been sort of thinking more of a big cat, but now you mention it she does seem like the type who would probably devour her mate and spit him out in little pieces.'

'She is very beautiful,' Emma said.

'In a dark and psychotic way.'

'How do you think she did it?'

'What?'

She tutted. 'Murder Simon, of course.'

I took a sip of my whisky and thought about it. 'We don't know for certain that she did,' I said, but it was only a half-hearted argument. I was pretty sure Emma was on the money and I would really like to know how she did it too. She'd only had about fifteen minutes according to the doctor and he said Simon's heart had simply stopped. 'Perhaps she scared him to death.'

Emma shivered. 'Don't even joke about it.'

I felt a sudden chill sweep over me too. 'I wasn't. Not really.'

'Do you mind if we go riding this morning?' Emma asked Laura over breakfast.

Laura stifled a yawn. Her complexion was pale and her eyes were underlined by dark smudges. 'No, of course not.'

'I mean if you were planning to . . .' Emma tailed off.

'No, I might go for a trot later this afternoon, but I have a couple of things I want to do this morning. I thought I'd take a proper tour of the house. You know – to see what's what and' – she grimaced – 'I guess I ought to phone the hospital to see what I have to do about arranging Uncle Simon's funeral.'

'Do you want us to deal with that?' I asked.

Laura gave me a tentative smile. 'Would you? Are you sure you don't mind?'

'No,' I said. 'Leave it to me. I'll give them a ring this afternoon. I might even pop over there. I can collect his few bits and pieces Donald Walters took in.'

'Thank you so much. I must admit I was dreading it.'

'No problem.'

Emma frowned at me over the top of her teacup. I knew the look, it was of the 'what the hell are you up to now?' variety. I smiled at her sweetly and she gave a resigned shake of the head. She knew me too well for my own good.

'What was that all about over breakfast?' she asked as soon as we were back inside our room.

'How do you mean?'

She huffed at me. 'You know very well what I mean. About you dealing with the funeral.'

'You can't really expect poor Laura to have to sort that out and, with Brandon gone, there's no one else.'

Her eyes narrowed. 'You're up to something, Jed Cummings, don't think I can't see right through you.'

I swept her into my arms and gave her a peck on the lips. 'I want to find out if the hospital has a cause of death yet.'

'And what if they haven't? Or they say it *was* natural causes?'

'Then, my sweet, I will have to do a bit more digging or lean on the goodly detective inspector to do it for me.'

'You think he will?'

'What has he got to lose? We could have made things very difficult for him and we didn't.'

'We can't trust him.'

'Maybe not, but when it comes to Oliver's death, he has no good reason not to do his job.'

'Other than Tanith Bloxborough,' Emma said, with a sniff.

'Now, her I really would like to meet.'

'Really? She would eat you for breakfast.' Emma wriggled her shoulders. 'I could well believe *she* is a Satanist.'

I kissed the end of her nose. 'Now there I tend to agree with you.'

She put her arms around my neck and pulled me in for a big kiss and my mobile started to ring.

'Typical,' I said, with a sigh. She grinned at me as I groped in my pocket for my phone. 'Yep.'

'Mr Cummings?'

'Who is this?'

'Derek, Derek Davis – the vet.'

'Oh, hello there. How are you?'

'Yeah, good thanks. I thought I should give you a call. I've had the blood results back for Angel.'

I transferred the phone to my other hand. 'And?'

'Her blood showed a large dose of something unusual, we're not sure exactly what, but it seems to be some sort of stimulant and in the levels detected it is possible it caused her hyperactivity and anxiety.'

'Could it have been administered accidently?'

There was a slight pause on the other end of the phone. 'No, in the amounts we found it would be highly unlikely.'

'Thank you,' I said.

'No problem. If you could let Dan Crouchley know I'd be grateful.'

'Sure thing.'

I finished the call and frowned into space. So, Angel had been drugged and, if I were a betting man, I'd put money on the shots being deliberately fired to spook the poor thing. But why?

'Earth to planet Jed.' Soft fingers under my chin lifted my head so she could look in my eyes. 'I take it your call was from the vet.'

'Hmm.'

'And?'

I glanced at the phone still clutched in my hand and dropped it into my pocket. 'He says Angel was drugged.'

'So was it a serious attempt on Laura's life or a warning?'

'Exactly what I was wondering.'

It was Emma's turn to stare into space. 'None of it makes any sense' she said eventually.

'No,' I said. 'It doesn't – yet. Give it time. Shall we go for that ride?'

'I would be interested to hear what Dan Crouchley can tell us about the history of Kingsmead and this lord who built the place. Maybe Satanism *is* a family tradition,' she said, and I don't think she was joking; her expression was serious enough.

The ever-present burble of a radio greeted us as we entered the stable yard, but was the only sign of life. It didn't help that as we walked across the flagstones, we were passed by the shades of two laughing children, a boy and a girl, running towards the front of the house. The girl's fair hair streamed out behind her, disappearing into mist, and her blue smock clung to her skinny legs showing white, wrinkled stockings. She was giggling. The boy, also fair and perhaps a year or two older, raced after her, the leather soles of his boots slapping the stone slabs. He wasn't quite as clear as the girl, his clothing, a white shirt and grey breeches and socks, blending into the stone walls behind him.

It was strange. Although I had always seen and heard the dead, they had been like shadows or smoky phantoms – that was until eighteen months or so ago. I had met a man who had been so close to them he would mistake the dead for living people. I hadn't had that experience and I hoped to God I never did, but the visions I'd been having recently were a new experience and the apparitions I now saw, particularly here at Kingsmead, were clearer and more tangible. It made them real and sometimes it made my heart ache for the people they had once been.

Emma paused mid stride with a little frown as they ran by, but was otherwise blissfully unaware of their presence. It was better that way. Seeing children was always worse. They didn't usually have anything to say, they were only being the children they should have been, but when they did have reason to speak, by the cringe it could sometimes be harrowing.

Angel's head appeared over the door to her stall as we entered the stable block. She whinnied softly and Emma stopped to pet her head. I carried on along the row of stalls following the music. A wheelbarrow full of steaming manure and straw sat outside Jericho's stall.

Dan was inside, still mucking out. 'Morning, Dan.'

He glanced over his shoulder. 'Good morning to yer,' he said, putting down the shovel he was using and wiping his hands on the back of his jeans. 'You be wanting to go for a ride this fine morning?'

'If it's no trouble.'

'No trouble at all. It does them good to have a good run. Ald Walters and I can only do so much.'

'Has Satan been out?'

'No, not yet.'

'Then maybe you'll join us.'

Dan stood there studying my face for a few moments. 'I'd be glad to,' he said, though his expression said otherwise.

CHAPTER NINETEEN

I took a good look at Angel before Emma mounted her. Her eyes were bright and she kept pushing her huge brow against my shoulder begging to be petted, so I guessed she was pretty calm. I knew Laura had ridden the mare since her fall, but Laura wasn't my Emma and after the incident in the poolroom I was more than a little protective. It hadn't gone unnoticed; when I looked over my shoulder Emma was smiling to herself.

'You can't be too careful,' I mumbled.

'Don't worry,' Dan said. 'I've been keeping a close eye on them and their feed.'

'Keep doing it,' I said, and his eyes narrowed.

He glanced around the yard. 'You've heard from the veterinary.'

'You were right,' I told him. 'Angel had been given some sort of drug.'

He muttered an expletive under his breath as he hauled himself up onto Satan.

I waited until we were away from the yard and had left the track to trot across open fields before I said any more. Call me suspicious, but unless they, whoever *they* were, had directional mikes they couldn't overhear us out here.

I pulled Jericho to a halt. 'OK,' I said to Dan. 'Spill it.'

He stopped beside me and sort of slumped down in the saddle. 'I don't know what you mean.'

'Don't play games with me, Dan. Three people are dead, five if you include Laura's parents. What the hell is going on?'

He exhaled slowly. 'If I knew I'd tell you, but honest to God, I don't – not really.'

'Not really?'

He dragged his fingers through his curly locks and quickly looked around. 'Let's go somewhere we can't be seen from the house,' he said, and it was then that I realised I perhaps wasn't as paranoid as I thought.

Dan took us out of the fields and onto a track that ran around the edge of the woodland. Once we had rounded an outcrop and entered another field, where we were hidden from view if anyone from the house should be watching, he drew Satan to a halt.

He started off more or less where we'd left off. 'I'm an outsider and below stairs it's a closed club where newcomers aren't welcome.'

'The servants, you mean?'

He wrinkled his nose. 'If ald Walters and his wife could get rid of me they would. Trouble is they need me. He hasn't time to deal with the livestock and the lad, Sebastien, is a bit slack in the head, if you know what I mean. So, as long as I keep my nose out of their business they put up with me.'

'It didn't sound like it the other day. You and Donald Walters were really going at it.'

'Huh,' he grunted. 'That be young Maddy's doing.'

'You should leave her alone,' I said.

He burst out laughing. 'Don't you start. I've not touched the little madam and I'm not going to, either. Too much like hard work, that one.' His shoulders sagged. 'Look, there is something going on and it's been causing ructions downstairs, but as soon as I walk in on a conversation it stops dead. I know ald Walters and his wife are deeply unhappy. When Mr Oliver died it was like a cloud had lifted off the whole place, then Mr Simon arrived and within a couple of days it all went back to the way it was before.'

'Why's that, do you think?' Emma asked.

He shook his head. 'I don't rightly know. I don't think it was Mr Simon. He never came across as too demanding and I never heard any of them moaning about him – and they would. They can moan for England, that lot.'

'This business in the forest,' I said. 'Have you noticed anything in there before?'

He gave me a strange look. 'How do you mean?' He said it as though he knew something but wasn't about to say unless I gave him some encouragement.

'Traces of any unusual activity in the clearing before Oliver's death? Or even after, I suppose?'

His expression became guarded. 'You answer me a question first. Why are you here? Now?'

I studied his face as he studied mine. There was something about him that made me think he was more than a mere stable hand. Then I remembered the university degree – if it was the truth and not a fabrication to impress his attractive employer.

'Simon and I served together in the forces. I was his friend.'

'Rumour below stairs is that you and he had a falling-out.'

I frowned. How on earth would they know that? It had been decades ago and long before any of the present servants had been employed by the Pomeroys. Or maybe not – I thought I'd recognised Donald Walters. Maybe I should ask the question.

'How would you know? I thought they didn't talk to you.'

His laugh was bitter. 'Oh, they talk all right, just not to me or about anything that matters while I'm about.'

'Except for Maddy?'

His lips quivered into a smile. 'Yeah, except Maddy, though she doesn't say much, at least about anything I'm interested in. So, getting back to *my* question – why are you here?'

Emma touched my knee. 'Jed,' she said and gave a nod towards Dan. She was usually a good judge of character and an ear below stairs would be useful. I decided to chance it.

'At one time Simon knew me about as well as a friend could. Although I never publicised the fact, he soon found out I could see and hear things other people can't.'

Dan's face broke into a grin. 'I was right – you *do* have the sight!' I didn't deny it nor did I tell him he was right. I wanted to see where this was going. 'I wondered why ald Walters was all shook up when he came back from taking you to where it happened.'

'What do you mean?' Emma asked. 'He seemed all right when he left us. In fact, he very kindly offered to come back for us.'

Dan snorted. 'Huh, probably to try and earwig on what you had to say. I saw him when he got back to the yard – all sweetness and light and quiet concern with Mr Simon until he went inside. As soon as he'd gone, ald Walters took on a face like he'd lost a fifty and found a fiver and stalked off into the kitchen.'

'Did you hear anything that was said about it below stairs?'

Satan stamped his feet, getting restless and Dan reined him around. 'Let's give these animals a bit of a run and then we can talk,' he said and, before I could stop him, took off at a gallop.

'You up to it?' I asked Emma.

'Don't you worry about me,' she laughed. 'I'll catch you up.'

As I urged Jericho on I couldn't help but grin. I had missed this. Simon, Reggie and I, when we'd stormed across the estate, we'd felt like kings.

Jericho had the wind under his tail. He pounded after his stable mate and, despite Satan's massive size and strength, Jericho was catching him. Dan must have heard us coming. He glanced over his shoulder, his hair blowing around his face, and started to laugh and I did too. Then I caught him, and I was galloping along beside him, then passing him. I was on top of the world.

I could see the edge of the field coming up and began to slow to a canter, to a trot and then stopped.

'Good lad,' I said, leaning forward to stroke Jericho's

neck. He stomped and blew air through his nose, feeling pleased with himself, I'd imagine; he'd beat his bad-lad stable mate good and proper.

Dan trotted over to stand beside us. 'He thinks he's a racer, don't you, lad,' he said, reaching over to ruffle his mane.

I could see Emma in the distance. She was cantering towards us at a more leisurely pace. I was kind of relieved. It wasn't that I didn't think she was capable: after Laura's fall I was more – shall we say – wary.

As Dan watched her coming towards us he said, 'Did you see who did it? Who murdered Mr Oliver?' His eyes didn't leave Emma.

'What if I did? No one other than Emma and Simon would believe me.'

'I think ald Walters would.' He gave me a sideways glance. 'If I were you, I'd pack your bags and take your lady wife well away from this place.'

'Why?' I asked, although I'd been thinking about it practically non-stop since Brandon's murder.

'If you saw who did it they'd probably do almost anything to make sure you kept it to yourself. Look at poor ald Fredricks. They obviously thought he knew something that could harm them.'

'They? Them? Who are you talking about, Dan?'

He met my stare. 'If you saw, you know.' And it hit me – he knew about the cult.

'Why don't you tell me what *you* know?'

His eyes returned to watching Emma. She was almost upon us. 'The Pomeroys are evil; always have been, always will be. Did you take a look at their history?'

'I was hoping you might enlighten me. I understand you've a degree in it.'

He grimaced. 'Laura?' I nodded. 'As soon as the words were out of my mouth, I knew it was a mistake. Let's hope she doesn't mention it to anyone else.'

'Would it matter?'

'It could do. Everyone here thinks I'm an uneducated Irish oik who'll do anything to earn a bit of filthy lucre before I'm off on my way again, and I'd prefer it remained that way.'

'You've been at Kingsmead a while.'

'Probably longer than's good for my health.'

'Then why don't you move on?'

Another bitter smile. 'Mr Simon was your friend – is that why you're staying? To find out what happened to him and his brother?'

'That and I promised Laura I would stay until she's settled.'

'Well, I made a promise to someone too, one *I* intend to keep, and I'll stay at this cursed place until I do.'

I was about to ask what he meant when Emma joined us. Taking in our expressions she lost her smile. 'What have I missed?'

'I have to get back,' Dan said.

'We can talk as we ride,' I said.

'You're a persistent old sod,' he said, which made me laugh despite myself.

'Oh yeah,' I said, 'and you have no idea how persistent I can be if I put my mind to it.'

We started back towards the house in a loose line, but close enough so we could talk. 'You were going to tell me about the history of the Pomeroys,' I reminded him.

He patted Satan's neck and sat back in the saddle. 'As far as I can make out it all started with Lord Francis Pomeroy. He was allegedly a member of the original Hellfire Club, but had very quickly become disillusioned. Apparently it wasn't hardcore enough for him, so he decided to build his own' – he did the quotation marks thingy with his fingers – '"country retreat" where he could get up to all sorts of things he didn't want to get back to his contemporaries in London where he was a Member of Parliament.'

'Huh,' I said. 'Doesn't seem like politicians have changed much over the centuries.'

Dan laughed. 'You're probably right, but he was into more than booze, drugs and weird sex games. He hooked up with some right strange characters and they formed an organisation he called the Order of the Blood, and wow did they go in for some unpleasant practices: devil worship, necromancy and sadomasochism being the least of it.'

Now he had my full attention. 'He was a Satanist?'

Dan pulled a face. 'Near as damn it, I suppose, but there isn't much documented. It was one of those societies where to reveal their secrets earned you an instant death sentence. All the information I found was hearsay written by one of his ancestors more than a hundred years after Francis shuffled off this mortal coil.'

'So the Order didn't carry on after he died?' Emma said.

'Well, here's the thing – the man who wrote all this was compiling a family history, like they did in times gone by. Only a few copies were published, mainly for the family and maybe a few friends, but within a few months of it being printed he was murdered.'

'And you think the publication of the book and his murder were connected?' I said and I guess I must have appeared doubtful as his expression became grim.

'Knowing what I know now – yes.' His eyes met mine. 'He was found in that there wood, where Mr Oliver died, and just like him his tongue and eyes had been cut out.'

CHAPTER TWENTY

'No,' Emma said. 'Absolutely not.'

'Emms . . .'

'Matter closed,' she said, folding her arms. 'If you're staying here so am I.'

'It's only because—'

She raised a hand. 'Enough. I will not discuss it any more.'

I sank down onto the bed. 'If something happened to you . . .'

Her frown instantly smoothed away and she came over to sit beside me and took my hand. 'Nothing is going to happen to me, you lovely man. *You* will make sure it doesn't.'

'I'm not Superman, Emms.'

'You're my Superman,' she said, stroking my cheek.

'And you're my Kryptonite.'

'I'm not sure whether to take that as a compliment or not.'

'It means if someone used you to threaten me, I'd be neutralised.'

She raised an eyebrow. 'And if that isn't spy-speak I don't know what is. What *was* it you and Reggie did?'

I took her hand in both of mine. She had long, slender fingers that always felt soft, even after an afternoon in the garden pulling up weeds from her vegetable patch. I loved her hands, I loved all of her and I didn't want to tell her something that might make her stop loving me or Reggie. She had meant the world to him as she did to me. I hoped he'd be happy for us; I think he would. Out of all of those who had passed over I wish he had spoken to me. I wish he'd given his blessing.

'Jed?'

I gave a start. I was getting maudlin. 'It's probably best you don't know.'

She took hold of my chin and turned my head so I was looking at her. 'Shall I tell you what I think?' She didn't wait for me to reply. 'I know you were in Military Intelligence. I think you and Reggie were more spies than soldiers. Not like James Bond, but probably as dangerous. And, if it came to it, I bet you could be just as dangerous now.'

'It was a long time ago, Emms.'

'Hmm. A leopard never loses his spots.'

'I think you'll find that's "changes his spots".'

She gave a dismissive flap of the hand. 'I know what *I* mean.' She took my head between her hands and leant in close. 'I know exactly what I mean,' she whispered as her lips touched mine.

We were late down for lunch. It didn't really matter as it was usually something light like a salad and we served ourselves. Dinner was the more important meal of the day and, although we didn't *dress* for dinner, we did smarten ourselves up a bit. Laura didn't appear to have started to eat and I hoped we hadn't kept her waiting.

'Sorry we're late,' I said as we took our seats.

'No problem. I've only just got off the phone to the detective inspector.'

'Really?' I said.

'He is such an old woman.'

I paused, salad server in hand. 'What makes you say that?'

She sniffed. 'He recommends I return to London until they've solved grandfather's murder and located Uncle Edward. I told him I couldn't.'

'If there's any possibility you're in danger, perhaps you should,' Emma said.

Laura's shoulders sagged. 'How can I? If I haven't moved in permanently by the end of the month—'

'Which is tomorrow,' I interrupted.

'I will forego my rights to my inheritance.'

I finished filling my plate and sat back in my chair. 'Did Brandon give you any idea at all who would be next in line?'

She shook her head. 'I presumed it would be Uncle Simon, but now, it could be anyone.' Her eyes filled with tears. 'This was all meant to be a dream come true, a new start, a new life, instead it's becoming a nightmare and I can't leave because this is all I have.'

Emma hurried around the table to put her arm around the girl's shoulders. Her eyes met mine and she was as unsure what to do or say as I was.

I dropped my napkin onto the table. I'd lost any appetite I might have had. 'I promised I'd stay for as long as you needed me to and I will,' I said.

'We will,' Emma said, giving me one of her killer looks.

'We will,' I agreed half-heartedly. 'But I can't promise to protect you from an unknown enemy.'

'Then we shall just have to find out who it is,' Emma said. 'And if anyone can it's Jed.'

'Hmm,' and something occurred to me. 'Why is it so important that Laura move into Kingsmead by the end of the month?' I said to no one in particular. 'And what was it that scared Brandon so much?'

When I looked up both women were staring at me across the table as though I was about to do something miraculous like solve world poverty. Sadly, they were going to be very disappointed.

As we wouldn't be visiting a patient we decided that, for what we needed to do, we should visit the hospital straight after lunch and hoped we might get a chance to speak to Doctor Rani. Laura said she couldn't face going there again, which was a relief. I'd be able to ask questions I couldn't had she been around.

'I'm worried about Laura,' Emma said as we started off along the drive out of the estate.

I gave her a sideways glance. 'So am I.'

'But what can we do?'

'I don't know, Emms. It's weird. I feel like I'm missing a piece of the puzzle – or more like I have the piece, but don't realise the implications of it or where it fits.'

'It was odd Brogan didn't know his sergeant had been to speak to Laura,' Emma said.

I stared through the windscreen at the winding drive ahead. At the time it had struck me as strange. 'It is a bit, but then they've probably got a lot on their plates at the moment.'

'Brogan certainly has,' she said with a sniff and I knew what she was thinking, or should I say of whom. Brogan had probably been sneaking off for illicit nooky with the predatory Ms Bloxborough when he should have been working.

A sudden thought crossed my mind. 'How did Peters know to call and see Laura if Brogan never received my message?'

Emma tapped her bottom lip with her forefinger. Over the years I'd come to recognise it as her tell that she was concentrating. Usually when she was doing a crossword or Sudoku it would be with a pencil. 'Maybe he came to see her about something else. They hadn't spoken to her before and she *was* Oliver's granddaughter and beneficiary of his will. Perhaps they had to tick one more box and he was being thorough.'

I was unconvinced. 'I would have thought Peters would have gone straight to his boss. The effigy, dressed in Laura's clothes and with a mask made from a photo of her face, would have rung all sorts of alarm bells to me, even without adding Oliver's murder into the equation.'

'Perhaps he's trying to make a name for himself. The detective inspector isn't exactly inspiring.'

I pulled to a stop in front of the gate and, while I waited for it to open, thought about Detective Inspector Brogan. He gave the impression of having been around the block a few times. And – his involvement with Ms Bloxborough aside – I didn't for one minute imagine he was stupid. His association with her was at worst ill-advised, though if what he would have us believe was true, he hadn't done anything wrong. In fact, the dates on the photographs proved their relationship had been going on for a long time before Oliver's murder.

The gate slowly opened and I drove on through. Who was this Tanith Bloxborough? And why had she picked on the DI? Was it all part of the plan? All this conjecture, with no real hard facts, was making my head ache.

'It's another beautiful day,' Emma said as we pulled out into the country lane leading to the village. 'We're having such good weather for the time of year.'

'I really should go back home and cut the grass,' I said. 'It'll be up to our armpits if I leave it much longer.'

'Tilly's brother Jude is doing it for us.'

'Huh,' I said, with a grunt. 'I hope he's making a good job of it.'

'Well, if he isn't, I'm quite sure you'll put it right when we get back. At least it *won't* be *up to our armpits*.'

I frowned at the windscreen. Jude was all right, I supposed. It was just that he was away with the fairies most of the time and didn't pay much attention to what he was doing, though I guessed there wasn't too much he could get wrong when all he had to do was sit on a lawnmower and drive back and forth across the grass for a few hours.

I took the same cut through as before, hoping we wouldn't have a repeat of our previous journey. There were still skid marks on the tarmac from where the horsebox had slithered across the road, and deep furrows in the verge where the white van had gone into the ditch, but no queue of cars. It was actually very quiet with no other traffic. Why hadn't it been like this the day Simon died? We would have arrived at the hospital twenty minutes earlier and maybe, just maybe, he would still be alive.

I felt Emma's hand on my leg and glanced her way. 'It won't bring him back,' she said.

'What won't?'

'You feeling guilty.'

'I don't,' but she was right – I did. Stupid, I know. If I had taken the other road I still wouldn't have got us there in time.

There was plenty of space to park, the rush wouldn't start until ten or fifteen minutes before visiting time. When we climbed out of the car, and I looked at the hospital towering above us, all my energy and optimism drained away.

'Come on, let's get this over with.'

Emma slipped her arm through mine. 'Do you think Doctor Rani will see us?'

My shoulders slumped. 'I doubt it. The poor bugger's probably rushed off his feet.'

She pulled me to a halt. 'Jed,' she said, looking at my face. 'Stop it.'

She didn't need to tell me what she meant. I asked anyway. 'What?'

She pursed her lips and her eyes flashed angrily. 'You know very well what. You tell me you're not Superman and then let the weight of the world fall on your shoulders.'

'I—'

'No,' she said, with that determined look I recognised. 'You will work this out. You and I, together, will work this out. And do you know why?'

'I suspect you're going to tell me.'

She ignored me. 'Because Simon was your friend. Maybe not recently, but he was once. So, Jed Cummings, you stop this feeling sorry for yourself. You have nothing to be guilty about. You might not have been able to save Simon, but now Laura needs you and you can save her.'

I took a deep breath. Emms was right. It was Laura I needed to concentrate on now. And if I could get some kind of closure for the girls in the poolroom as well, I'd be happy.

'Right,' I said, shoulders back, eyes front. 'Let's do this.' Emma squeezed my arm and we marched inside through the sliding doors.

We made straight for the private rooms, guessing this would be where they would have kept Simon's things. There wouldn't be much, only the nightclothes he'd been wearing when he'd been brought in and the bits and pieces Donald Walters had brought to keep him going. He had been wearing his Rolex and his signet ring, but otherwise no other jewellery. He wasn't that sort of bloke. Then I remembered the silver and jet-beaded chain with inverted crucifix and felt my lips curl into a grim smile. I somehow doubted he'd been wearing that at the time of his attack – then who's to say? Had I been asked whether Simon had belonged to some Satanic order I would have laughed out loud. Strangely enough I wasn't laughing now.

The nurses' station was at the end of the corridor of private rooms, directly next to where Simon had spent his last hours. A curly-haired male nurse, who I thought

I recognised from when we'd last visited, was behind the desk.

Upon seeing us he gave a welcoming smile. 'How can I help?' he asked.

'We're here to collect Simon Pomeroy's effects,' I said.

His smile immediately slipped into a gentle, sympathetic expression. 'Are you family?' he asked.

'No, close family friends,' I said. 'His grandniece is too upset to come herself,' and I gave my name.

'If you'd just give me one minute, Mr Cummings, I'll get someone to see you.' He gestured toward some chairs. 'Please take a seat,' and immediately disappeared.

Emma sat; I paced. After about two minutes she called my name and patted the seat next to her. 'For goodness' sake sit down. You're making me nervous.'

Shoving my hands in the pockets of my trousers I slumped down in the chair. 'I hate hospitals.'

'Be thankful neither of us are in need of one and are only visiting,' she said, putting her hand on my knee.

She was right. We should count our blessings. Waiting didn't help, though. As the minutes ticked by my mind began to sink down into some very dark places, so much so, when the nurse called my name Emma had to give me a nudge to bring me back to the here and now.

I hurried to the desk. 'I am sorry to have kept you. I had trouble finding Doctor Rani and there was a note on file saying he would like to have a word with you.'

It made me wonder. True – we wanted to talk to him, but why would he want to speak with us?

The nurse placed a large grey plastic bag on the desk. A printed sheet of paper was stapled to the top right-hand corner. 'If you'd just like to check the contents to the list and sign, please. A copy of the list is inside the bag for your records.'

I opened the bag. Inside was a pile of folded clothing, on the top sat the Rolex and ring beside a small wash bag and wallet. I ran my figure down the list. There was nothing of interest: shirt, trousers, underwear, pyjamas, dressing gown, slippers, wash bag plus a sublist of its contents, the watch of course, and wallet with another sublist recording two ten-pound notes, one fiver and three pounds twenty-eight in coins. A wave of emotion washed over me, it was too sad and final. It was the young man I had once known I mourned for, though I think he had faded away a long time ago.

I signed the inventory and, tearing it from the bag, handed it to the nurse. He smiled his thanks. 'Doctor Rani won't be long.'

Scrunching the top of the bag together in my fist I took it back to where Emma was sitting and slouched down beside her, dropping it on the floor between us.

It was another ten minutes before the doctor came rushing along the corridor. He had the look of a man who was racing against the clock and losing. His eyes rested on us and he hurried over.

'Mr and Mrs Cummings,' he said, grabbing a chair and pulling it over so he was sitting opposite, his knees almost touching ours. 'Thanks for waiting.'

'You wanted to see us?' I said.

He grimaced and his eyes went to his hands clasped together on his knees. When he raised them to meet mine his expression was strained. 'A police officer has been to see me and . . . I thought I should let you know.'

I frowned at him. Surely if the police were involved it would be better if he didn't speak to anyone who knew Simon?

'Thank you,' I said. This was going to be easier than I'd thought. 'So you're treating Simon's . . . Mr Pomeroy's death as suspicious?'

'No, not really. It was very sudden and totally unexpected and then, when I looked through his notes after you left, it became clear he wasn't a well man. Among other ailments, he'd been taking medication for a cardiovascular condition for some time, so it's possible his heart just gave out. But here's the thing. The detective turned up practically straight after you left,' he paused, his expression worried, 'and he knew. He knew Mr Pomeroy was dead. How could that be? Even if you had phoned him as soon as it happened, how could he get here so quickly? You didn't phone him, did you?'

'No,' I said. 'No, I didn't.'

His eyes narrowed, staring into space and he gave a little nod as though making a decision. 'He knew he was dead and the questions he asked were . . . odd.'

'How do you mean?'

He scratched his chin. 'He didn't ask how he had died or when or anything you'd expect. He asked about visitors, who Mr Pomeroy had seen over the few days he was here. I told him I couldn't say. He wasn't my patient, I only happened to be on duty when he died. Then he asked about you.'

'Me?'

He nodded emphatically. 'He asked had you seen Mr

Pomeroy on the day he died. I told him no, you had arrived after Mr Pomeroy had gone into cardiac arrest, and . . . this is going to sound weird, but he appeared . . . he appeared almost – smug.'

I glanced at Emma. She was frowning at the doctor, concentrating on what he had said and trying to make sense of it.

'Did the policeman ask to see Mr Pomeroy's personal effects?'

'No, to be honest, once he'd gone, I began to wonder whether he was a policeman at all. He flashed an ID at me when he'd arrived, but in retrospect it could have been a club card in his wallet, for all I knew.'

'What name did he give?'

'Detective Inspector Brogan.' I sucked in breath. 'You know him?'

'Oh, yes,' I said, 'and he is a policeman.'

'Ah,' Emma cleared her throat. 'Doctor Rani, could you describe him, please?'

'Oh, yes. Tall man, big man. Well dressed.'

I frowned at him. 'Well dressed, you say?'

'I'm no fashion expert, but the police must get better pay than we do in the NHS, his suit was very expens*ive*,' he said, stressing the 'ive'.

'Really?'

The doctor leant back in his chair and crossed his arms. 'Actually, he was a bit' – he wrinkled his nose – 'I don't know . . . smarmy.'

'How do you mean?' I asked.

'It was his expression. The whole time we were speaking he was smiling, a smug smile, like everything was a big joke.'

The image of Tanith Bloxborough came strutting into my head with the self-same smile as she strode through the hospital corridors like she owned the place, and it occurred to me it was becoming more and more likely the joke *was* on us.

Sighing, I leant back in the seat. 'So, Dr Rani, I suppose Mr Pomeroy having died after an assault it'll be a while before you can release the body for burial?'

I didn't think the doctor's face could get any longer, apparently I was wrong. 'No one has been in contact with you?'

I was beginning to get a sinking feeling in my gut. 'No.'

His shoulders slumped. 'Last night, before I went off duty, several men arrived. All in suits, all in black. They could have been undertakers, but' – he sucked in breath through his teeth – 'they were more like' – he hesitated – 'they were more like mercenaries. Hard-faced, no compassion. Not men used to dealing with the bereaved. They took Mr Pomeroy's body after speaking to the hospital manager.'

Emma's hand gripped my knee as I stared at the young doctor, my mind racing. 'Did they say who they were?' I asked eventually.

'Our manager said the man who spoke to her had said they were taking over the responsibility into the investigation of his death and we were not to release any information without reference to them.'

'And yet you are,' I said.

He glanced over his shoulder as if to check whether anyone was listening. 'The man said to her that if *you* should be the one asking questions you would understand.'

I closed my eyes for a moment and massaged the bridge of my nose. I did understand. Even in death Simon was doing things his way. His people in the ministry were making sure of it.

CHAPTER TWENTY-ONE

'Well, what do you make of all that?' Emma asked as I pulled out of the hospital and onto the main road.

'Simon was up to something. Though what, I'm not altogether sure.'

'And what about the so-called policeman? It certainly wasn't Detective Inspector Brogan who Doctor Rani described to us,' Emma said. 'He's one of the scruffiest people I know.'

'Someone's playing games,' I said.

'If it was Edward impersonating Brogan, why would he be interested in you? Why would he ask whether you had spoken to Simon before he died?'

I had been pondering on the same thing myself. 'When Laura and I left Simon he said he had some thinking to do and we'd talk the following day. He wanted to speak to me alone. He made that quite clear. Maybe someone was worried about what he might have told me, but never had the chance to. I should never have taken Laura to see him. If I hadn't, then maybe I'd have some idea of what the hell is going on.' We stopped at a set of traffic lights and I glanced at Emma. 'I think I have to try and contact Oliver again.'

She stared at the windscreen. 'He hasn't exactly been forthcoming so far. He shows you things, but with no explanation they're not particularly helpful.'

'It is odd,' I admitted, 'but being psychic isn't an exact science. I only get what they are willing to give me. Perhaps he doesn't want to reveal too much because if he did it would prove he isn't the hard-done-by innocent he'd have me believe.' The lights changed and I pulled away.

'He let you see he was part of the Order.'

He had and I wondered why.

The house was very quiet when we arrived back. Eerily so. Every one of our steps echoed as we crossed the entrance hall and once again it reminded me of a mausoleum.

'Where is everybody?' Emma asked as we reached the staircase.

'They're about somewhere. Probably getting dinner ready.'

She took a look at her watch. 'It's a bit early I'd have thought.'

Our room had been cleaned and the bed linen and towels changed while we'd been out. It had to be said Mrs Walters ran a tight ship. I immediately went to where I'd hidden the jewellery case and the picture of the three brothers. They were exactly where and how I'd left them. I took the picture out and flopped down on the bed.

Oliver and Edward – what had happened between

them? Had Edward killed Oliver's wife? They appeared happy enough in this photo. Oliver had his arm around Edward's shoulders. Simon was slightly in front of them, leaning forward, looking excited, holding his prize aloft. Oliver's expression was proud, while Edward was smiling that inscrutable, creepy smile. Yeah, it was creepy.

Emma dropped down on the bed beside me. 'Do you think it never stopped? Like it might have been going on for hundreds of years?'

'Hmm.' I stared at the picture, wishing I could somehow get into their heads and know how they were on that day. I flipped it over. *WN 1981.*

'What does the WN stand for, do you think?'

I slowly shook my head. 'I have no idea.' I frowned at the inscription. WN – what did it mean? Was it important? A little tickle at the top of my spine told me that perhaps it was.

'Could it be a phase of the moon or some sort of religious festival?'

'*Religious festival?*' I said, aghast at the thought. 'It isn't a religion, Emms. It's a travesty. An abomination.'

'Wow,' she said, raising her hands in mock alarm. 'When did you go all sanctimonious on me?'

I shifted uneasily. She was right – as usual. I'd always professed to have not a religious bone in my body. That religion was a man-made thing to keep the masses under control. My gift hadn't done anything to make me think otherwise. If there truly was a God shouldn't *he* be the one to help those poor souls who couldn't move on?

'Worshipping the Devil is not a religion,' I muttered.

'Well, it appears that it is, or was, to the Pomeroys, though I don't suppose Laura will be carrying on the family tradition.'

'I should bloody well hope not.' I glanced back at the picture and frowned. 'Unless . . .'

Emma studied my face. 'Unless . . . ?'

'What if she hasn't a choice?'

She sat there quietly as she thought about it. 'I wonder where Laura is now?'

I climbed to my feet. 'Where do you think?'

'Riding?'

'Most probably. Let's go down to the stables. I've been wanting to have another conversation with Dan Crouchley. He definitely knows more than he's saying.'

'Just let me slip on some comfortable shoes and I'll be with you,' she said.

We didn't see a soul on the way to the stables, which was unusual. There was normally Mrs Walters or Maddy bustling around downstairs and Mr Walters or the gardener out and about in the grounds. There wasn't even the sound of a radio coming from the stables when we entered the yard.

'Where is everybody?' Emma asked.

The stable block was empty. The lad, whose name I'd forgotten if we'd even been told it, wasn't about, nor was Donald Walters or Dan. As I walked along the centre of the block, a huge chestnut head appeared out of a stall. Jericho was apparently the only occupant.

I reached out to pet his head. 'There's a good boy,' I said, scratching his brow.

'Satan and Angel are out,' Emma said, peering into Satan's stall.

'Still think I have no reason to be worried about Laura and Dan?'

'Laura's young – she should be having fun.'

'But not with a stable hand who will likely be on his toes in a few months or so.' I hesitated. What was it he'd said?

'He's clearly not *just* a stable hand if he has a degree in history,' Emma commented.

'No, I suppose not,' I said, not really paying attention. He'd said something about staying at Kingsmead until he'd fulfilled a promise. I'd been going to ask him what he meant when we were interrupted. That's right, Emma joined us and he'd said he had to get back.

'Maybe you should take Jericho out and see if you can find them?'

'Huh-uh. There's no way I'm leaving you here alone. If we can't go together we're not going at all.'

'Then let's walk along the track. We might bump into them on their way back.'

'I suppose, if nothing else, it'll get us out of the house for a while.'

'It *is* a lovely day, so we might as well make the most of it.'

I gave Jericho's snout a good rub. 'I'll see you later,' and he replied with a snort and a stamp of his hooves, no doubt disappointed he wasn't going out for a run.

Emma tucked her arm through mine and we made for the track. The sun was warm and the air was fresh. It was so calm and peaceful it was difficult to imagine that the lawns stretched out to the side of us and the forest ahead had borne witness to the terrible last minutes of a man's life.

In the distance I could hear the rapid *click, click, click* of a woodpecker tapping on bark and melodic birdsong. Bees buzzed around us searching for nectar amongst the long grasses and other vegetation on either side of the track. A crow landed on a post ahead of us, cawing as we approached and hopping off into the field as we grew too close.

'It is very beautiful here,' Emma said.

'Not as beautiful as The Grange.'

'The Grange doesn't have its own woodland.'

I wrapped my arm around her shoulders. 'The Grange doesn't have bodies piling up in it either.'

'True,' she said, 'and let's hope it stays that way.'

I kissed her on the top of the head. 'You're not thinking of starting an unholy order of something or other?'

'You know I never wear black. It doesn't suit me.'

Two figures on horseback appeared in the distance. They were taking their time. Plodding along, deep in conversation by the look of it.

'I guess you could start a new fashion line for Satanists. Perhaps in powder blue or that crushed strawberry pink you like so much.'

She giggled and thumped my arm. 'It's not really funny.'

I shrugged. 'I'd rather we laughed than cried. Anyway, if we're being watched I want them to think we're unworried and completely unaware of how much danger we're in.'

Her smile didn't falter. 'And you believe we're in real danger?'

'Up to our bloody armpits.'

'Glad I'm not overestimating it.'

'You still won't go home?'

She rested her hand on my bicep. 'Silly man. These people sought out Laura's parents and they would seek me out too, if it suited them. At least here, with you, we're together and if there is a need to worry, we'd both know it soon enough.'

She had a point, though it didn't stop me being concerned. When exactly had our lives become so perilous? Stupid question – until eighteen months ago we were plodding along quite nicely. I had left behind danger decades before and settled into safe country life, keeping myself busy with a bit of gardening and handyman jobs and the occasional request for messages from the dead. Then a young man called Jim Hawkes came into our lives, and over a few short weeks everything changed. It wasn't his fault, he was as much a chess piece in a bigger game as the rest of us.

The only good thing that came from what followed was that I finally had the nerve to tell Emma I wanted to be more than just friends, if that was what she wanted too. Her response wasn't what I'd expected or could ever have hoped for. 'I thought you'd never ask,' she'd said.

Now there was this. A letter from an old friend and suddenly fear was creeping back into our lives just the same as it had all those months ago. But it wasn't just fear . . . I tried to tell myself it was – I was lying. With the fear came a frisson of excitement, the same fizzing in the blood I used to get as I set off on a mission. I'd forgotten how it'd felt and how much I missed it.

Laura and Dan had seen us. I'm not sure whether it was my imagination, I don't think it was, but they weren't riding so close together now and they'd quickened their pace.

Dan raised a hand in greeting and when they were a few yards away slowed to a halt.

'How did it go at the hospital?' Laura asked.

I pulled a face and decided to be a little economical with the truth. What she didn't know couldn't hurt her. 'As well as can be expected.'

'Any news on when we can start making arrangements for the funeral?'

'I left my details and they said they'd let me know,' I lied. My paranoia might be spiralling out of control, but I wasn't going to give anything away in front of Dan. He and I needed to have a conversation and I'd rather it wasn't in front of Laura and similarly I needed to have a chat with her. She was as much of the mystery as the rest of the Pomeroys.

'Nice ride?' Emma asked, deftly changing the subject.

Laura flushed slightly and she brushed the hair back from her brow, trying and failing to appear nonchalant. 'Lovely, thank you. It is a glorious day, perfect for a long ride around the grounds.'

The corners of Dan's eyes crinkled into a smile I recognised, and he looked away, making a show of petting Satan's neck. I forced my expression to remain neutral. The signals were all there. If he and Laura hadn't been up to something they really shouldn't I'd go teetotal.

A little voice inside my head told me it was none of

my business – and it'd be right – but, with Simon gone, I somehow felt responsible for her. Emma's hand slipped into mine and she squeezed my fingers. I let out a long, slow breath and forced a smile onto my face.

'We'll let you get on,' I said to Laura. 'We'll see you at dinner.'

'Yes, see you later,' she said as we stepped to one side to let them pass.

Laura went first and, when I glanced up, Dan was no longer smiling. He leant down towards me. 'I need to speak to you,' he whispered.

I nodded and, with a bob of his head in acknowledgement, he urged Satan on. Emma hooked her arm through mine, and we turned to watch them ride off down the track.

'Hmm, seems you were right about him and Laura,' Emma said.

I grunted. 'You noticed, then?'

'Have you considered he might be trying to keep her safe too?'

'By getting into her knickers?' Emma punched my arm – hard. 'Oww, that hurt.'

She ignored me. 'By keeping her away from the house.'

'Your logic escapes me,' I said. 'She was thrown from Angel while out riding with Dan. And for all we know he could be part of all this.'

'But you don't think so?' she said. She had me there. As it happened I didn't. If he were, there were certain things I'm sure he wouldn't have said to me. 'Well?'

'No, I suppose not.'

'When are you going to try and see him?'

'Before dinner, while you're beautifying yourself.'

She laughed. 'We'd better start back, then.'

'It doesn't take you *that* long.'

'Ah, but you'll have to go first!'

I scowled at her and she fluttered her eyelashes at me. 'You're probably right,' I said.

I left Emma as she was about to get into the shower. I stopped her. 'Lock the door after I leave.'

She made a huffing sound, but padded across the bedroom in her dressing gown to stand by the door. 'If I'm still in the shower when you come back, you'll have to wait.'

'In which case I'll go downstairs and have a drink.'

'Men,' she muttered as she rose up on tiptoes to give me a peck on the cheek before closing the door behind me.

I waited until I heard the click of the key in the lock and then strode off to try and find Dan.

An old Stones song blared out into the yard from the stable block a lot louder than usual. Dan was where I expected, in Satan's stall rubbing the massive beast down. He gave a nod of hello upon seeing me and carried on with what he was doing. I leant against the doorpost, so I could keep an eye out for anyone else entering the building – what I had to say didn't need witnesses. Satan's coat was a gleaming blue-black by the time he'd finished his ministrations.

Eventually he threw down the brush and gestured I should come inside. I took one more look out towards the yard and joined him.

'Something's going on,' he said, without any preamble. 'I've not seen hide nor hair of either ald Walters or his missus today and Maddy and the rest of the staff are walking around looking like the world's about to end.'

Thinking about it, I hadn't seen Mrs Walters since breakfast. We'd been late down to lunch and unusually there had been no servants hanging around, as was their habit. Maddy hadn't even appeared to clear the plates by the time we'd left the table.

'Perhaps you can sweet-talk Maddy to find out what's going on.'

He gave a grunt. 'I don't want to encourage her.'

I crossed my arms and leant back against the wall. 'Really?'

He must have noticed my expression. 'You don't know me, so don't be so quick to jump to conclusions.'

'She seemed interested in you, but now Laura's come along – a young, vulnerable woman who's just inherited a fortune – what am I supposed to think?'

'I don't need money.'

'Everyone needs money, even me.'

He pushed past me to check outside the stall, then looked back at me. His eyes narrowed to stare at me for a moment longer, as though coming to a decision. His shoulders slumped and, mind made up, he gave a jerk of the head that I should follow him and, without waiting to see if I would, strode out of the stall. Levering myself away from the wall, I patted Satan on the head and left, closing the door behind me.

Dan was already disappearing out into the yard as I hurried after him. It did cross my mind I could be wrong about Dan and he was leading me into a trap. I hoped not, for his sake. I didn't like being taken for a fool.

I caught him as he rounded the outside of the small, walled garden and immediately understood why he'd brought me here. We couldn't be seen from the house and it would be nigh on impossible to overhear what we were saying without being seen. He stalked along in silence with me by his side until we reached the furthest point from the house, where he stopped so abruptly I had taken a few more steps before I realised he was no longer beside me.

He pulled himself to his full height, his eyes almost level with mine. 'My name is Daniel Foley,' he said, any hint of his Irish drawl gone and replaced by something similar to upper-class Cambridge. I tried to hide how much he'd surprised me; I failed miserably. His lips curled into a grim smile.

'So, Daniel Foley,' I said when I'd regained my power of speech, 'what are you doing here at Kingsmead?'

His smile died away and all I could see was pain. 'Ten years ago, my sister Suzie was meant to be coming here to a party and she hasn't been seen since. According to the Pomeroys, as far as they were aware, she never arrived. I came here to find out what happened to her.' His shoulders slumped. 'Now Simon Pomeroy's dead I doubt I ever will.'

A lump formed in my throat. Suzie – they called the girl in the poolroom Suzie. I swallowed. 'Where was she last seen?'

'Her flatmate dropped her off at the station. The guy on the ticket barrier recalled seeing her getting the train to Clapham Junction. I think he was a bit sweet on her, so he remembered, and that was it.' He paused, his eyes pleading. 'I thought maybe you . . . Maybe you might be able to contact her if something did happen to her here. I know it's a long shot, but I need to know, my family needs to know.'

'What did she look like?' I asked and prayed he said she was a buxom redhead. I didn't want to have to tell him the truth. I didn't want to have to break this young man's heart.

He reached for his back pocket and pulled a wallet from his jeans. He flipped it open and offered it to me. I stretched out my hand and reluctantly took it from him. I knew in my heart what I would see. An old photograph of a pretty girl standing on a seaside promenade was slipped inside one of the credit card sleeves. Seeing Suzie like this, the family resemblance was obvious. She had the same deep blue eyes and dark curls, and for a moment I could see her face, her imploring eyes and her hair floating out behind her like seaweed.

He must have seen something in my face. 'What?' he asked.

'I'm really sorry,' I said, handing him back his wallet.

'You won't help me?' he said, but he was clutching at straws, he knew what I meant.

'She . . .' I struggled to find the words. I'd given bad news before, but nothing like this. 'She died in the poolroom,' I told him. 'She drowned.'

He stared at me, his mouth slack as all hope drained away to be replaced by despair. 'How?'

Now I had an inkling why she had called to me that night. Dan had dived into the pool to save Emma. She *wanted* me to know what had happened to her so I could tell him. 'I saw it.' I leant my back against the wall. 'She woke me a couple of nights after Emma almost drowned. She showed me what happened. Don't ask how, I've never had a vision like it before.'

He frowned at my face, struggling to take it in. 'Was ... ?' His voice broke and he looked away while he composed himself. 'Was it an accident?'

Did I tell him the truth? What purpose would it serve? Then I thought of Edward's gentle yet creepy smile as he pushed her head beneath the surface.

'No,' I said. 'Edward Pomeroy killed her. There was a second man, but I couldn't see him clearly. I think it might have been Oliver.'

He rubbed his face with the palm of his hand. 'So, it's all been for nothing,' he said. 'I can't get her justice, however much I try.' Then his face creased into a frown. 'Hang on – Edward died' – he blew out through pursed lips – 'almost forty years ago,' and I could see his hope rekindling as he questioned what I'd told him.

I felt for him, I really did, but it was kinder he knew the truth – and safer. 'Here's the thing – he didn't. As a teenager he was put away in a mental institution.'

'But everyone says he died.'

'That's what everyone was told. Even Simon thought he was dead until a few days ago.'

'So Oliver Pomeroy knew he was alive the whole time.'

'*He* knew all right. He visited him regularly and apparently used to bring him home once a month.'

'So, the staff must have been in on it,' Dan said, with an angry sneer.

'It's possible,' I said and, to my mind, it was getting likelier by the minute.

'So where is this Edward now?'

'We don't know,' I admitted.

'Jesus Christ, you're telling me this psycho's wandering around loose somewhere?'

I hesitated. 'Not somewhere – here,' I said eventually. 'The way Oliver and Brandon Fredericks both died makes me think he's somewhere around and possibly holed up here on the estate.'

'Shit,' he said. 'Shit!'

'Which means someone on the staff is helping him.'

His eyes went to mine. 'Why would they? The man's a monster.'

He had a good point. 'Perhaps they're scared.'

'I'll start poking around.'

'If you do, be very careful.' I rested my hand on his shoulder. 'I don't have to tell you how dangerous he is.'

'No,' he said. 'No, you don't.'

'Dan, I mean it. I don't want your death on my conscience too.'

He frowned at me. 'Too?'

I closed my eyes for a second. I'd given myself away. 'It's a long story,' I said.

Emma had finished in the shower by the time I returned to the room. Her expression was relieved when she pulled open the door to let me in.

'Where have you been? I've been worried.'

'I had a very long conversation with Dan, which I will tell you about later,' I whispered.

266

Her forehead creased into a frown and she was about to say something, but I put a finger to my lips, which had her raising her eyebrows and moving in close to me.

'You can't think . . . ?' she murmured into my ear.

'I don't know what to think any more.'

CHAPTER TWENTY-TWO

The following morning, while Emma was in the bathroom, my mobile unexpectedly went ping, announcing I had a message. The only person who ever texted me was Emma and she would hardly do that from the shower, unless, of course, my luck was in and it was an invite for me to join her. Ever hopeful, I crossed the room to scoop my phone off the bedside table. Disappointingly the message was from an unidentified number and was of the short, sweet and somewhat mysterious variety. *Check the passenger seat of the Jag.*

'What the f—?' I stared at the screen for a few seconds trying to figure out what the hell the message meant and who could have possibly sent it. 'Only one way to find out, I suppose,' I muttered to myself.

Knowing Emma would be at least another ten minutes or so I was tempted to slip downstairs and out to the car, but then my suspicious nature kicked in. What if the message had been sent to get me out of the way, leaving Emma alone and vulnerable? It wasn't something I was about to chance. Consequently, by the time Emma left the bathroom, wrapped in a bathrobe and rubbing her hair with a towel I was pacing the floor.

'What do you make of this?' I asked, sticking the mobile under her nose.

She pulled back a bit squinting at the screen. 'It's no good,' she said. 'You'll have to read it out.'

'It says for me to check the passenger seat of the Jag.'

'And have you?'

'Of course not.'

She continued rubbing at her hair and sank down onto the bed. 'Then perhaps you should.'

'I didn't want to leave you on your own,' I grumbled.

She stood and dropped the towel on the bed. 'I'll lock the door behind you if it makes you feel better.'

I waited until I heard the click of the lock before hurrying, car keys in hand, along the corridor, down the stairs and out of the front of the building, all without seeing a soul. I crunched my way across the gravel to the Jag, half-wondering why I was bothering. I had the keys to the car and the only other set were in the safe at home.

Even so, I wasn't surprised to find a large ivory-coloured envelope, with my name scrawled in black ink across the front, lying on the front passenger seat. I had broken into a fair few cars in my time. It wasn't particularly difficult if you knew what you were doing. Whatever was inside the envelope was fairly thick and weighty. I suspected it was a file and best inspected back in the bedroom out of the way of prying eyes.

I locked the car and started back towards the house, then stopped. The back of my head prickled ice-cold. It had been chilled for days, and I didn't need the reminder, I knew we were in danger. I swung around and returned to the car and went to the rear to open the boot. Inside, right at the back, partly hidden by raincoats, wellingtons and other paraphernalia was my old toolbox. Not one of those metal or plastic things you get these days, a good, old, solid wooden one with brass fittings. Resting the file on top of a box containing assorted car parts, the sort that were always useful to have on hand when driving an old car, I pushed the other junk out the way and made enough space to drag the toolbox to me. I took a quick glance around to make sure I wasn't being watched, but there were so many windows I could never be sure. I would just have to hope they couldn't see what I was doing.

I opened the toolbox, the top two layers extending out to leave two removable trays beneath it. Lifting them both out carefully, I laid them to one side and had another furtive look around – so far so good.

At the bottom there was a band of brass edging the box. I pressed down on the heads of the screws at either side and there was a soft click. Pushing the extending trays back together, I lifted the box leaving behind a hidden tray and the varnished mahogany case that had been concealed within it. I lay the palm of my hand on the lid – I had hoped I'd never have the need for it again, and hoped I still wouldn't, but one thing Simon, Reggie and I agreed on – always have a backup. This was mine.

With one more quick look around, I took out the case, slid it beneath the ivory envelope, so it wasn't immediately evident, and put my toolbox back together. Once reassembled, I shoved it to the back of the boot, rearranged the coats and boots around it and, with the envelope and case under my arm, hurried back into the house.

'What's that you've got there?' Emma asked, eyeing the envelope as she let me in. I had already hidden the wooden case beneath my jacket. It was something she didn't need to know about.

'I'm not sure,' I said, sitting down on the bed very carefully so as not to dislodge the case pressed between my side and my right arm.

I peeled the flap of the envelope open. Inside was a Manila file. Muttering an obscenity under my breath I slipped the file out of the envelope and onto my lap. Even in death Simon was still having things all his own way. A ministerial compliment's slip was paper-clipped to the top left-hand corner. Written in small, neat, tight letters was the message 'Forwarded under the instructions of Sir Simon Pomeroy due to his hospitalisation'. 'Sir'? When had that happened? No one had said. And again I wondered who had put the envelope in my car and whether it had been delivered in such a clandestine manner because Simon's 'people' didn't trust someone at Kingsmead? I suppose they had good reason not to, though by the looks of it the file had already been on its way before Simon had died.

Emma sank down next to me. 'Is that what I think it is?'

'Probably,' I said, not sure whether I really wanted to open this particular can of worms.

Emma gave a little shiver and pressed a kiss to my cheek. 'I'll leave you to it,' she said and hopped to her feet to go and sit at the dressing table. 'I'll finish getting ready while you read.'

As soon as she started to rummage around in her make-up bag, I slipped the case from beneath my jacket and slid it under my pillow. Another quick look her way assured me she hadn't noticed my furtive behaviour and with a sigh I slipped on my reading glasses and flipped open the file's cover. As I thought, it was a copy of the crime report for Laura's parents' murder. I ran my finger down the text. It didn't tell me anything I didn't know already – until I reached the transcript of an interview with the four-year-old Laura. The poor little thing must have been terrified.

After several questions, where it became clear she didn't remember waking in the morning and finding her parents' bodies, they asked her whether she'd heard or seen anything after going to bed for the night. She said, 'I woke up and wanted a glass of water. Mummy always leaves the hall light on, but it was dark. I got up and went to the bathroom and had a drink from the tap. I heard a noise in the hall and it scared me so I stayed in the bathroom. I waited and waited, but I didn't hear the noise again. I was still scared, but Mummy and Daddy would be cross if they found me out of bed, so I ran back to my room and jumped into bed and pulled the covers over my head. There were feathers in my bed. They got in my mouth. It was horrid, but I was too scared to get out. Then I must have fallen asleep.'

The investigating officers concluded it was going to the bathroom that had saved Laura's life. The feathers had come from the duvet. It had been slashed multiple times with a very sharp knife and either the perpetrator didn't have the stomach to check he'd killed her or didn't have time to search for Laura once he realised the bed was empty. The image of the child's room and feathers floating around me like snowflakes came to mind. Was this what Oliver was trying to tell me? That he hadn't killed Laura when he was supposed to?

Apparently, it was the postman who reported the murders. He had found a blank-faced Laura sitting on the doorstep in her pyjamas with her hands covered in blood.

I took off my glasses and massaged the bridge of my nose. Poor little kid, it didn't bear thinking about her coming downstairs in the morning to find her butchered parents. I skimmed the rest of the contents until I reached the crime scene photographs. Somehow the clinical and professional pictures of the murdered couple were worse than the ones I'd already seen.

I closed the file and shoved it back in the envelope. Had it helped? No, not really. There had been no leads, no evidence, nothing other than they thought the murders were ritualistic and possibly revenge crimes and meant as a message – but to whom they didn't know.

Oliver had of course been interviewed, but he had a cast-iron alibi; he had been holding a party attended by thirty or more people, some very influential and beyond reproach. As Edward had committed murder during his own birthday party it didn't fill me with any confidence that allegedly being surrounded by a crowd of people was any kind of alibi at all – as far as I was concerned they could all be part of this cult.

Emma swung around on her seat to find me staring into space as I mulled on the conundrum of the Pomeroy family and their very secret lives.

'Did it help?' she asked, gesturing at the file.

'Nope. Not at all. Apart from making me more depressed than I am already.'

She got up to come and sit beside me. 'I can't get my head around Simon being part of all this, but still asking for your help.'

'After he believed Edward was dead, he changed. He told me that. He began to hate Kingsmead. Said it had been like living in a mausoleum and he couldn't wait to leave.'

'Would a cult just let a person leave?'

'Maybe they didn't consider him a threat.'

'Until now,' she said.

'Until now,' I agreed.

CHAPTER TWENTY-THREE

There was a strange atmosphere over breakfast. Mrs Walters was conspicuous by her absence, although I supposed even she had the occasional day off, and Maddy appeared preoccupied and jumpy.

'So once tonight is over you will have fulfilled one of the main conditions of Oliver's will,' Emma said to Laura.

Laura took a sip of her tea and gave a relieved smile. 'Then I just have to live here for two years and it's all mine.'

'That wouldn't be much of a hardship, I'd imagine,' Emma said, reaching for a slice of toast.

Laura laughed. 'Not when I was as close to living on the streets as I had been. I have a little money that Auntie June left me, but with no job no one would give me a mortgage and with no fixed abode no one would give me a job. I was going to have to start begging nights on friends' sofas until I found something semi-permanent.'

I listened as they chatted with a sinking heart. I

doubted there was any way I could talk Laura into leaving Kingsmead, at least not without a damn good reason, backed up with proof that her life was in danger. I didn't have any proof. All I had was a cold prickling in the back of my head, and why should a young twenty-first-century woman like Laura have any reason to believe in my *sixth sense* for danger?

'We have to get Laura out of here,' I told Emma on the way back to our room.

'After tonight maybe she can come to The Grange with us for a few days.'

I gave a grunt. 'But unless DI Brogan finds Edward during that few days nothing will have changed.'

Emma bit her lip. 'I suppose not.'

'And *we* can't stay here for ever,' I said, pushing the door to our room open.

Emma sighed. 'We have to do something.'

Plonking myself down on the bed I pulled out the drawer to my bedside table to take out the picture of the three Pomeroy boys. 'I wish I knew the significance of Laura having to move in by the end of the month,' I said.

Emma sank down beside me. 'There might not be any,' Emma said. 'It could be Oliver was just giving a start date rather than it being put off again and again if Laura was reluctant to give up the life she already had.'

'I suppose.' I flipped the picture over. 'What do you think WN stands for?'

'It could mean anything.' She got up and went to get her handbag. 'I can try googling it, but I'm not sure WN will get any hits that mean anything, though.' She pulled out her tablet thingy and started tapping away. 'It's a postcode in Wigan, and a company in Toronto comes up.'

'Try WN in relation to Satanism,' I said, leaning against her to look at the screen.

She tapped in Satanism WN. A list appeared. 'Satanism, Church of Satan, Satanists . . .' She hesitated, then her hand went to her throat. 'Oh my God!'

'What?'

'I nearly missed it. Oh God, I nearly missed it.'

'What?' I repeated, putting on my glasses and peering at the screen.

She pointed. 'It says *Walpurgisnacht* as one word, but it's also known as *Walpurgis Nacht* – WN. If it hadn't noted the date . . .' She exhaled shakily. 'If it hadn't said 30th April, I would have missed it.'

'So, you were right,' I said. 'It is a festival.'

Emma's fingers danced across the screen, tapping on anything she could find of interest. '*Walpurgis Nacht* – it used to be a Christian feast day,' she said, her eyes scanning the screen, 'but is also the night when witches were meant to roam abroad. Apparently, it's celebrated on 30th April and ends on the evening of 1st May.'

'At least now we know why she had to move in by the end of the month.'

'So, you reckon it's all going to kick off tonight?'

'It would appear that way. I'm very tempted to grab Laura and run for it.'

Emma dropped the tablet on the bed next to her. 'What are we going to tell Laura? She's not going to want to just up and leave – there's too much for her to lose.'

I gave Emma a sideways glance. Her forehead was creased into a frown. She was right – Laura did have a lot to lose and her inheritance was the least of it.

'Would you risk your life for a fortune?' I asked.

'Probably not, but I'm older than Laura and have everything I could possibly need.'

'But if you were her? If you were twenty, single with nothing at all, not even family?'

Emma let out a long, slow breath. 'Then – maybe. People throughout history have risked themselves for less.' She paused for a moment. 'We don't actually know anyone means her any harm.'

'Are you willing to risk it? Simon and Brandon were killed for a reason. We'll have to try and talk her into leaving,' I said.

'Huh, good luck with that.' Emma swivelled towards me. 'What about Detective Inspector Brogan? If we told him Laura's in danger, couldn't we persuade him to provide protection if only for tonight.'

'But what about tomorrow night and the night after and the night after that? This might be an important occasion to the Order, but it's only a date on a calendar and all hogwash, anyway.'

'Not to them, I'd imagine.'

'They're deluded,' I said.

'Deluded or not, they're also dangerous.'

She was right. Two of the Pomeroy brothers and Brandon bore witness to how dangerous they could be.

'Emma,' I began, taking her hand, 'promise me you'll be careful.'

'And you promise me the same.'

'I promise,' I said.

'So do I,' she said.

I squeezed her fingers. I had a feeling it would take a good deal more than our promises to keep us safe.

We went straight downstairs to find Laura only to be told by Maddy that she had taken a car, was going shopping in Plymouth and wouldn't be back until dinner.

'Shit,' I muttered as soon as we were out of earshot.

'Now what do we do?' Emma asked.

'Wait, I suppose, and try and get her away as soon as she gets back.'

The day dragged by. The air had a hot and oppressive feel to it, like a storm was coming. It probably was, but not of the meteorological kind. Most of the staff had gone missing with only Maddy reappearing briefly to serve us lunch.

'Where's Mrs Walters today?' I asked as she started to clear the table.

'Running errands, I'd imagine,' Maddy said, after a pause long enough for me to suspect it was a lie.

'If you should see Miss Simmons, would you tell her we would like a word?' Emma said.

The girl gave a bob of the head and I had an inkling this was also a lie. I didn't trust her one little bit. Then again, I didn't trust anyone.

Having nothing better to do, we spent the afternoon walking around the gardens and they, too, were unusually quiet, without a gardener in sight. Even the stables were empty apart from the three horses who vied for our attention as though they hadn't seen a human recently.

At five we gave up and went back to our room. We would

have to speak to Laura at dinner and try and convince her to leave straight after. It wasn't ideal, but there was no other option.

'You go first,' I said. 'I'm in no rush. Anyway, I want to try phoning Brogan again.' I had called the wretched man several times throughout the day, but all my calls went straight to voicemail.

She shrugged. 'In which case I'll wash my hair.'

'We've plenty of time.'

She pressed a kiss against my cheek and made for the bathroom. I waited until the door closed before taking the mahogany case from my bedside cabinet. As soon as I touched it, icy-cold fingers pressed against the back of my head. I went very still, closed my eyes and lay my palm on the box's lid. Another chilled hand caressed my skull. It was enough to help me make a decision. If I was going to have a use for what was inside it was going to be tonight. I opened the lid, took out the contents and strode across the room to the wardrobe. I rummaged through the clothes until I found my good jacket and filled its pockets. From now on, where I went my backup was coming with me.

My next job was to phone Detective Inspector Brogan. I wasn't surprised when my message went straight to voicemail – again. The message I left was terse. 'For the umpteenth time – we think Laura Pomeroy is in danger – tonight. Call me.' I wasn't holding my breath for a speedy reply.

By the time Emma strolled out of the bathroom with a towel wrapped around her head I had hidden the now-empty box in the bottom of the wardrobe.

'My goodness,' she said upon seeing my clothes for the evening all laid out on the bed. 'Has someone kidnapped my husband and swapped him for a doppelganger?'

'Finished in there?' I asked, scooping my jacket, trousers and shirt from the bed.

She gestured towards the bathroom. 'Knock yourself out.'

'I'll endeavour not to,' I muttered and closed the door to her muffled laughter.

When I emerged, Emma was putting the final touches to her make-up. She did a double take upon seeing my reflection in the mirror. 'My, my, my, you look very smart this evening.'

'We aim to please.'

'An alien clone has definitely taken the place of my husband.'

My reflection smiled, and it crossed my mind that perhaps she was right. Tonight I was the Jed Cummings who I thought I'd left behind a long time ago. It was most strange how I had so easily slipped back into the persona. She could read the man she had married like a book, the man I was tonight was a stranger in her husband's clothing – or was he? The stranger would have given his life for Queen and country, the man I was tonight would give it without a second thought to save his wife's. All my senses were telling me this was fast becoming a possibility. Even so I was as calm as I was detached and this is the way I had to stay. It wouldn't be easy – I loved her too much to be objective – and this could be what would get us both killed.

I bent down behind her, resting my hands on her

shoulders, and planted a kiss on her neck. When I glanced at us in the mirror it was as though there was a fault in the glass. There was a slight distortion of my image, so it appeared there was a second reflection hiding behind the first. I saw my lips curl into a smile and I was sure it wasn't me smiling.

I straightened and Emma reached across her chest with her right hand to rest it on my left. 'You look beautiful tonight,' the other me said.

Her laugh was husky. 'I think I quite like this man masquerading as my husband.'

'I'm going to try and convince Laura to leave with us tonight.'

Emma looked sceptical. 'I don't think she will.'

'I have to try.'

'No luck with DI Brogan?'

I gave a grunt of disgust. 'No. If things do go pear-shaped tonight, we'll have to ring 999. If we wait for him, we'll all be dead and buried.'

Emma's expression made me wish I'd used another analogy. I patted her hand. 'It'll be all right,' I said. The nagging discomfort at the back of my head told me I was lying.

Soft music floated out of the living room to greet us at the foot of the stairs. I was expecting to find Laura in there waiting, but it was empty. Damn it. I wanted to alert her to the possibility of trouble while there weren't any servants about. I knew from the theft of her shirt at least one of them couldn't be trusted. I glanced at my watch. It was six-forty so we were a little early.

'Drink?' I asked.

'VAT, please,' Emma said.

There was fresh ice in the bucket, so the servants were about somewhere, though once again it was quieter than expected. Laura came wafting in as I handed Emma her drink. And when I say wafted it was as though she was floating on a warm cloud of happiness. She was radiant, and once again I had a moment's disquiet about the fast-forming relationship between her and Dan Crouchley, or Foley, or whatever his damn name really was.

'Laura, you look lovely,' Emma said.

She flushed pink. 'Thank you, so do you.'

Emma gave a dismissive flap of her hand. 'Have you had a good day?'

The flush took on a deeper shade. 'Great, thank you.'

'Can I get you a drink?' I asked.

'Let me do that, Mr Cummings,' Maddy said from beside my right shoulder, making me jump. At times the girl was as stealthy as a cat and I found it disconcerting and a bit creepy how she would suddenly appear from nowhere.

Laura and Emma chattered away while Maddy made a G and T for Laura. Fortunately, I had already poured mine, a large tonic. Tonight wasn't a night for heavy drinking, but anyone seeing the drink in my hand would assume I was joining Laura or Emma with my choice of beverage.

Dead on seven Mrs Walters appeared in the doorway. 'If you're all ready, dinner is about to be served.'

'Thank you, Mrs Walters,' Laura said, rising to her feet, and we followed her into the dining room.

I pushed the food about my plate. There was a slightly scented flavour to the sauce which wasn't to my taste. It had the tang of lemongrass only sweeter and even the smell made me feel a little queasy. Emma and Laura didn't have the same reservations and were munching away with unladylike enthusiasm. I dropped my cutlery onto the plate. I was anxious to speak to Laura without the servants overhearing, but irritatingly they had been in and out in a continual stream and I hadn't had the opportunity.

'Are you feeling all right?' Emma asked when she saw my barely eaten meal.

I pulled a face. 'It's a bit sweet.'

She glanced over her shoulder to see if any of the servants were lurking. 'Just eat the vegetables. We don't want the cook getting upset.'

With a sigh I speared a bit of cauliflower with my fork and munched down on it. I really wasn't hungry, though I did see her point and, feeling guilty about the staff slaving away in the kitchen only for the food to be returned uneaten, I forced down some carrots, sugar snaps and a couple of potatoes, then had to give up. 'Sorry, I'm all done in.'

'I'm having a little more of the chicken,' Laura said and spooned some onto her plate.

Emma went to pour me some wine, but I put my hand over the glass. 'Are you sure you're feeling all right?'

'I have to drive,' I said.

Emma understood immediately, but Laura glanced my way. 'Going somewhere?'

I took another furtive look around the room. 'We'll talk after dinner.'

She frowned and her aura of happiness and well-being evaporated in an instant. 'Is something wrong?' she whispered.

I gave a grim nod, but before I could speak Mrs Walters and Maddy both appeared to clear the dishes. It was bloody typical, we'd hardly seen anything of them for almost two days and now we wanted some privacy they were everywhere.

All conversation stuttered into uncomfortable silence, speaking only to thank Maddy as she offered us desserts, then coffee, until we could leave the table and adjourn to the living room without it appearing hurried. Even then they wouldn't let us be. Maddy hovered by the drinks cabinet and Mrs Walters popped in and out on imaginary errands. They were watching us. I could feel the weight of their stares.

'Why don't you leave us to it so you can get on?' Emma eventually said to Mrs Walters.

The housekeeper gave her a tight smile. 'If that's all?' she said to Laura.

'Yes, thank you, Mrs Walters,' and with a bob of the head the woman withdrew, gesturing to Maddy that she should follow.

We waited in silence until we were sure they'd gone. I leant forward in my seat. 'We need to leave – now.'

'I can't,' Laura immediately said.

'Laura, it is too dangerous to stay.'

'Why? Why is it dangerous?' she said, suddenly angry. 'You seem mighty keen for me to leave, but if I do I'll lose everything.' Her eyes narrowed. 'Or is it that you have a vested interest?'

'What?' I said and I'm sure my face flushed scarlet.

285

'Laura,' Emma quickly cut in, 'why would Jed and I have any interest in wanting you to leave other than your own well-being? Jed hadn't seen Simon for decades.'

Laura's cheekbones coloured up and the fire died in her eyes as she slumped back in her seat. 'I'm sorry. It was a terrible thing to say. You've both been so good to me.'

I could see why she might be suspicious of our motives, but it didn't stop me from being a little disgruntled. 'To cut a very long story short, from what we understand Oliver and Edward belonged to some weird sect called the Order of the Blood and tonight is one of the sect's important festivals. We think it's why you had to be moved in here before the end of April.'

'Are you saying my grandfather's death was deliberately timed so I would be here now? But why? Why would someone do that?'

I sank back in my seat, so very tired. 'We don't know all the answers, probably never will, but we do know these people don't have any respect for human life.'

Her eyes filled with tears. 'I don't understand. Why go through all this palaver?'

'I have no idea,' I said, and it was the truth. Why would Edward want to hurt her? As far as we were aware he had never even met her.

Emma yawned. 'I still don't see what the purpose of the effigy in the clearing was all about. That was more likely to make Laura run for the hills than stay.'

I shook my head. It was another conundrum. Then who would understand the workings of the mind of a maniac?

Laura's head nodded and her eyes fluttered, then she jerked upright. 'Do excuse me.'

Emma stifled another yawn. 'Don't worry about it. I must admit I feel really tired too.'

I frowned at the pair of them. We were sitting here discussing how Laura's and possibly our lives could be in danger and they were drifting off.

'Under the terms of the will, does it say you actually have to sleep here every night once you move in?' I asked.

'Er, I think so. I have to be inhabiting the house at the end of the month, then full-time for two years, other than for' – she yawned again – 'other than . . . I . . .' Her eyes fluttered again and she was gone.

'Laura?' I glanced at Emma and her eyes were closed. 'Emms?' I climbed to my feet to lean over and touch Emma's face. Her head flopped to one side and cold fingers touched the back of my neck.

'Oh, fuck,' I muttered. Emma and Laura had been drugged. But how? How come I wasn't? The chicken: it was in the sweet sauce the chicken had been bathed in.

The door swung open and Mrs Walters walked in. Behind her stood her husband, Maddy and the young stable lad who Dan had called 'a bit slack'. I wasn't so sure. He was carrying a rifle and he swung it up to point straight at me, his expression calm and calculating.

'I'm sorry, Mr Cummings,' Mrs Walters said, 'but you should never have come here.'

'Why are you doing this?' I asked, trying to think of something, anything, to stop them from doing the unthinkable.

'Because we have to,' she said, and there was a loud crack like thunder, a thud against my chest that had me reeling backwards and a feeling like I'd been kicked by one of Satan's enormous hooves. A woman's voice cried out, 'No! He said—' My knees crumpled and I fell to the ground, whacking my head on something as I went down. Everything went grey and then black and the ringing in my ears turned to silence.

CHAPTER TWENTY-FOUR

Light began to creep through my eyelids and I groaned out loud. My head was thumping and my chest was on fire, each breath hurting like shit. I rolled onto my side and groaned some more. I remembered the feeling. I had been shot once before whilst wearing a bulletproof vest. The bloody things might save your life, but you were bruised black and blue for days afterwards. Then it dawned on me: I wasn't wearing a vest today and in my befuddled state I wondered why I wasn't dead.

I slowly opened my eyes. My cheek was lying against soft, plush carpet and straight ahead of me was the foot of one of the living-room leather armchairs. They'd left me where I'd fallen. I struggled to sit, wheezing as I pulled on the arm of the chair to get myself into an upright position.

I groaned again as I slumped back against the chair. Every tiny movement sent shots of searing pain right through me. I gingerly lifted my hand to check out the damage. I was almost too scared to touch my chest. The boy had been only ten or so feet away from me; there'd be a big hole and blood, lots of blood. I pushed my hand beneath my jacket to tentatively probe the area that hurt so fucking much and touched leather. My knife, the bullet had hit the holstered blade I was carrying. The blade I had so nearly left in its box. I let out the breath I'd been holding and the pain seared my chest. It didn't matter, my injuries were survivable.

I hauled myself onto my feet by hanging onto the chair and looked around the room. Emma and Laura were nowhere to be seen. My heart gave a little hiccup.

I forced myself to move. My head hurt like fuck and I felt like I had a metal strap wrapped around my chest, which was making it hard to take anything except for small, gasping breaths. I staggered towards the door, at the same time groping for my phone in my jacket inside pocket. It hadn't been as lucky as me. It was a mangled lump of plastic and shattered shards.

'Shit.' I lifted my wrist to look at my watch and even that most simple act made my chest feel like it was about to implode. It was eleven-eighteen. The bang to my head must have been worse than I'd thought: I had been out for over three hours.

I lifted my hand to the back of my scalp. There was a lump the size of a small egg and my fingers came away wet and sticky, but I would live. I had to. Emma and Laura needed me.

I collapsed against the door frame, breathing in deep. The world about me swam for a second then slowly came back into focus. I had to figure out where they would have taken them. I was assuming the clearing in the forest, but if I was wrong it was possible they would both die. For a moment despair swelled within me like the rush of the tide, then I remembered the man I had been. The man I still was. If I was too late, I would deal with it – I would have to. There was one thing of which I *was* certain. If they did die, there would be plenty of others joining them. Edward Pomeroy and his sicko friends would wish they'd never been born. I pushed away from the door frame and made for the kitchen and the stables.

The kitchen was empty, though they'd been busy. The dinner things had been cleared away and another feast, covered with cling film and foil, was spread out over the huge kitchen table. Carafes of red wine were set on trays with large silver goblets. Being a member of the Order of the Blood was obviously thirsty work.

By the time I reached the stable yard I was walking faster and not having to stop every few feet or so. It was in darkness, only the moon and the lights from the house enabling me to see. The Land Rover wasn't about, nor the old motorbike. Neither would have been of any use to me. They were too damn noisy and the Order would hear me coming from miles away across the open countryside.

I had two options: I could walk or risk going on horseback. Walking, in my current state, would take too long. I opened the door to the stable block, groping inside for a light switch and, with a click, the building was bathed in light bright enough to make me wince and close my eyes for a second. My head swam and my legs began to tremble. I sagged against the doorway and waited until it passed. When I opened my eyes, the world tilted sideways then slowly righted itself and the terrible spinning slowed and stopped.

There was the stamp of hooves from one of the stalls and a bit of snuffling, then a loud whinny. This started the others off. I had rudely awoken the inhabitants and they were making their feelings felt.

I hurried along the stalls making calming noises as I went. Jericho pushed his head over the gate to his stall and, seeing me and recognising a friend, stretched his muzzle out demanding attention. I gently rubbed his forehead while wondering what to do. I briefly considered taking Satan. He was as black as night and would blend like a shadow into the darkness, but he didn't know me and it was possible the girls might have to take him to escape and neither of them was proficient enough to handle a stallion as huge as Satan.

'It looks like you and I are going for a midnight ride,' I whispered to Jericho.

It took me longer than I would have liked to get him saddled. Although I knew where everything was, I had to keep stopping to catch my breath, though by the time I'd finished I was breathing a lot easier than before.

Leading Jericho out of the stable, the clip-clop of his hooves overloud and echoing throughout the yard, we made our way towards the track. Once away from the house, with some difficulty I hauled myself onto his back and nudged him into a trot, hoping against hope I was right and the Order of the Blood were creatures of habit and the clearing was where they would be intending to continue their killing spree.

'Please let them be there, please let them be there,' I prayed. If not, I would never find them. And if they were – I didn't dare think about how I intended to free them. I hadn't a rifle or a shotgun. The only armoury I had in my defence was my backup; a couple of blades and a length of cheese wire. Great for close combat, but no good against men with guns.

The landscape ahead of us appeared silver in the moonlight and, as I looked out across the fields and towards the forest of trees looming skywards and into the dark, a feeling of desolation enveloped me. It was an unsettling scene straight out of the horror movies I used to watch as a kid, the stuff of nightmares – or perhaps it was my imagination working overtime knowing the type of people I was about to confront.

As I drew closer to the forest I began to doubt my judgement. It was quiet, too quiet, and the thud of Jericho's hooves upon the compacted soil of the track was loud – very loud. Then in the distance, in amongst the dense black silhouette of the woodland, I saw a glimmer of red and gold and a wisp of smoke spiralling upwards out from amidst the trees and towards the moon.

'Gotcha,' I murmured.

I urged Jericho to go a bit faster. He snorted and huffed, but did as I asked. 'Good lad,' I told him.

A puff of gentle breeze ruffled my hair and I caught a whiff of burning wood. I was getting close, and as I neared the place where the track entered the forest, I found the Land Rover parked askew across the entrance. From here I'd have to go it alone.

I slid off Jericho's back and led him past the Land Rover and off to one side. As I passed the vehicle, I laid my hand on the bonnet. It was still warm; they hadn't been here long.

I couldn't risk Jericho following me or running off somewhere, so I found a low branch and tied him loosely to it. If he got really spooked or I didn't come back he'd be able to free himself, I was sure. I was hoping it wouldn't come to that. He might be our only means of escape, unless Donald Walters had left the keys in the Land Rover, though I didn't think I'd be so lucky or him so stupid.

I gave Jericho's snout a final scratch then trudged off through the trees, trying to keep parallel to the path – difficult when I couldn't see a thing except for an orange glow in the distance. Then there was a flicker of light and the glow grew into something a whole lot brighter. They had lit some more fires and possibly torches. They must have only been ten minutes or so ahead of me. It gave me a hiccup of hope the girls were still alive and conscious. *But what about Emma?* a little voice whispered in my head, my small glimmer of hope fast turning to fear. Emma was over and above requirements. She might be lying dead back at the house, maybe even in our bedroom.

I closed my eyes and took a couple of deep breaths. I couldn't think like that. I had to think like a soldier. I had to lock my worry for Emma and Laura away in a small compartment and think like the man I used to be, the man in the mirror. When I opened my eyes, it was that man who peered out into the dark.

I started off through the trees, running in a low crouch, ignoring the raw pain in my chest. With the light ahead of me I could see more than I had before, and it meant I could move fast without the risk of putting out an eye on a low branch. I was still careful and held an arm out at an angle in front of my face, warding off any vegetation in my path.

They began to chant. It started off as a low murmur, gradually rising to more of a rousing rumble. I was close enough now that I could see shadowy figures moving around a blazing fire and after a few steps more I could see them clearly. It obviously *was* a special occasion. They had discarded the black robes the Pomeroy brothers had been wearing in the photograph for silken blood-red habits. Black leather masks obscured any features, making them faceless to their captives and to me and I wanted so much to see who these people were. I strained my eyes searching for Emma or Laura. They were nowhere in sight and I had to pray they were on the other side of the roaring bonfire where three figures stood as if presiding over their loyal subjects. All three had the silver and jet-beaded chains of office about their necks; the inverted crucifixes hanging almost to their waists.

I began to edge my way through the trees surrounding the clearing. Five small fires burned around the periphery and I could make out the star-shaped design I'd seen before scratched into the dirt forming a pentagram with the bonfire at its centre. These people were whack-jobs; they had to be to buy into this sort of idiocy. If it had been all about sex I could maybe get it, but murder? They had to be sick, that's what I told myself, that's what I had to believe.

When I reached a point halfway around the circle, I

saw Emma and Laura. Both were kneeling facing the three robed figures, their backs to the fire. They were clothed in white linen robes and, with a flash of anger, I wondered who had undressed my wife. I sucked it in – being angry now wasn't helpful. I carried on around the clearing. If I was to cut off the head of the snake, I was going to have to get behind him.

I zigzagged through the trees, ducking back when the vegetation grew thin and moving in closer when it was too thick to see. When I reached nine o'clock, the central figure being twelve, I could see the girls' faces. They must have been frightened, but Emma was glaring at her captors with a ferocity that gave the impression she would tear out their throats if given half the chance. Laura was a little red-eyed, but she had a disdainful sneer on her lips, and I doubted she would take any prisoners either. I couldn't have been prouder of them, but my heart ached and once again I had to fight to keep my fear locked in its compartment. Where there's life there's hope and so far they were alive.

Reaching inside my jacket I pulled out the blade that had saved my life. It was time it took one. I slowly moved on. I was being as quiet as I could possibly be, though I could have ridden in on Jericho and not been heard with the noise they were making.

Ahead of me something moved. I froze and sank down low. There was someone else watching from the sidelines. I slowly moved outwards and around so I'd come up behind him. The voices rose and fell and I took each step in time with their chant until I was at his back and within touching distance. I waited until the congregation let out a roar and

I pounced, my hand covering his mouth and the blade pressed against his jugular. He stiffened in my arms.

As I moved in close the aroma of hay and horse filled my nostrils. 'Dan?' I whispered.

He relaxed against me and I lowered the blade. He gave me a grim smile over his shoulder and jerked his head towards the girls.

'I knew something was up,' he whispered, 'so I thought I'd better take a look.'

'Have you a weapon?'

He reached down beside him and lifted a sawn-off shotgun. I raised my eyebrows at him and he shrugged. 'These guys don't play by the rules,' he said.

'Nor do I,' I replied and, not waiting to see if he'd follow, continued my way around the clearing heading for the area behind the three main figures.

A hand touched my shoulder. I glanced back. 'What are you going to do?'

'Cut off the head of the snake.'

He grinned, showing a white flash of teeth. 'OK,' he said.

There was another huge roar from the congregation as they circled the bonfire in a slow, steady procession like a bunch of very vocal Benedictine monks. All in all, I had counted twelve. The odds weren't inspiring, but I'd been in situations when they'd been worse.

I slipped behind the central figure. He was taller than the other two and, even covered by flowing robes, appeared stocky of frame. If I wasn't mistaken the two people flanking him were women. They were certainly slimmer, though it was difficult to tell what was beneath the red silk. It didn't matter. The man in the middle would be the first to die and, if need be, they'd be the second and third.

I took a step forward and went in for the kill. My neck gave a little tingle a split second before cold metal pressed against the back of my head. I let my hands drop to my sides.

Fuck it, I thought.

CHAPTER TWENTY-FIVE

Dan and I were frogmarched into the clearing with our hands on our heads. I had lost my blade and the cheesewire, and Dan his sawn-off. Upon seeing us, Emma tried to struggle to her feet only to be roughly hauled back by her shoulders. She wasn't about to make it easy for them. Her fist swung up and she back-swiped the man holding her smack on the nose. Blood erupted from his nasal passages and he staggered onto one knee. Another man lurched at her, grabbing her by the arms and dragging her against his chest as he snarled obscenities into her ear. She ignored him, mouthing my name as she was forced back onto her knees.

The man I had assumed to be the leader began to laugh. 'Well, well, well, you two are full of surprises,' he said, looking me up and down. 'I was told *you* were dead.'

I ignored him, my eyes on Emma. If this was the end, I wanted to die with her face engraved into my memory. She smiled at me and it was enough. This wouldn't be the end of our story. I wouldn't allow it to be.

I was nudged none too gently in the back with the barrel of a gun. 'The Celebrant is talking to you,' the man behind me said.

I gave Emma a wink and slowly turned my head towards the man who this was all about – the monster Edward Pomeroy.

The Celebrant threw back his hood. 'Simon always said you were special,' he said. 'I couldn't ever see it myself, but I have been known to be wrong.'

For a split second time stood still as something clicked inside my head and everything fell into place. How hadn't I realised? It was suddenly plainly obvious. 'Oliver,' I said. 'I wish I could say it was good to see you again, but it would be a lie.'

He laughed and very slowly, for dramatic effect, lifted his hand to his face to grip the mask and lift it off. He was smiling and it was one I recognised. Oliver was as insane as his older brother.

I stared at the man who had murdered my friend, fighting to hold back my anger. 'Why did Simon have to die? And Brandon?' I asked.

'They were both about to betray the Order and they knew the penalty,' he said, his mouth twisting into a sneer. Brandon – a member of the Order? I couldn't help it – the shock must have shown on my face and Oliver began to laugh again. 'As much as I would enjoy explaining to you why I did what I did, I have much more pressing matters to deal with.' His eyes alighted on Laura. 'A wrong must be put right,' and, with a jerk of his head, he gestured to the man holding her.

She was hauled to her feet. Next to me Dan began to struggle and, with a crack that made me wince, was hit in the side of his head with the butt of his own sawn-off shotgun. He crumpled to the ground and lay there unmoving.

'Dan!' Laura screamed and began to fight all the harder to free herself from the hands gripping her forearms. The girl fought dirty. She kicked, she bit, she gouged and against all the odds she somehow escaped from the man's grasp and threw herself across the clearing towards where Dan lay.

Emma scrambled to get up. The man behind her balled his fist. I lifted mine and drove my elbow into the solar plexus of the man behind me. I dropped down as he bent double and my second blade was out of my ankle holster and in my hand. Emma's captor's fist never landed the blow; he was too busy trying to stem the blood erupting from his chest.

I span around, punching the man behind me between the eyes as he tried to scramble to his feet, still clutching at his gut. He went down, his eyes rolling upwards as he fell to the ground. I kept moving. Dan's guard had decided I was more of a threat than Laura and was lifting the sawn-off. Too slow, much too slow. I rammed into him, driving the barrel upwards and him back. As he fell away from me, I followed him, grabbing the butt and barrel of the gun in both hands. He hung onto it for grim death. I couldn't see his expression behind the mask. I guessed it was panicked.

I pulled the gun towards me, bringing him with it, and turned slightly, putting him off balance, and then bounced onto the ball of my right foot and drove my left into his leg just below the knee. The bone broke with a loud crack, which was immediately followed by a high-pitched scream reminiscent of a distressed pig. I gave a final tug and the shotgun was mine. I kept going in one continuous movement to turn to face Oliver. I was a split second too late. He had cleared the few yards between him and Emma and whipped her into his arms, his forearm pressed across her throat and a long, thin blade pointing inwards and up below her left breast.

'Drop the gun, Cummings, or your bitch is history.'

I cocked the shotgun. 'And your brains will be splattered all over this clearing.'

The flesh below his right eye twitched, a nervous tic and a very useful indicator of an opponent's state of mind in moments of stress. At any other time I would have tried pushing his buttons to get a reaction. The knife pointing towards Emma's heart was a good enough reason not to do it.

One of his sidekicks appeared beside him and leant in to whisper in his ear. His nostrils flared and an expression of irritation crossed his face. 'Go – now,' he shouted at his followers and, after a moment of confusion, two of them hauled the man I had stabbed onto his feet between them and another two helped the guy with the shattered leg. They and the others all hurried off in different directions disappearing into the forest.

Oliver glared at me. 'This isn't over,' he said, lifting the hand with the knife and resting it below Emma's right eye. 'And if you want to see your wife alive and well ever again' – his eyes shifted to Laura – 'it would be better if you make sure this little bitch never leaves your sight.'

He began to edge backwards, pulling Emma along with him, a henchman at his side, a rifle pointed towards my chest. Emma's lips moved mouthing the words 'I love you'.

'I'll be coming for you,' I said, and she smiled. Oliver, the egotistical prick, thought I was speaking to him. Emma knew differently and she was the one who mattered.

I kept the gun aimed at his head, just in case the opportunity arose. Wishful thinking on my part, I suppose. He disappeared into the trees and was gone. His sidekick stood there a moment or two longer, the rifle now pointed at my head, giving his leader additional time to get away. I could see by the curl of his full lips that he was smirking at me, daring me to try to shoot him. At one time I probably would, but Oliver had Emma. I lowered my gun and, with a derisive laugh, he stepped back into the undergrowth and disappeared.

Laura was instantly on her knees beside Dan and then, in the distance, I heard the sound of sirens. I dropped the gun and knelt beside her.

Detective Inspector Brogan drove Laura and a groggy Dan back to the house. I went on horseback, passing the Land Rover, still parked across the track, with two policemen standing guard. I hoped I'd come across one of Oliver's henchmen on the ride back. It wasn't to be, which was probably as well. I had quite possibly killed one man. A plea of self-defence would likely get me away with it. If I killed a second man, it was doubtful it would.

By the time I'd finished putting Jericho to bed and returned to the house, Laura had changed into jeans and a T-shirt and was sitting in the living room with a white-faced Dan. Brogan sat opposite them and Peters had taken the adjacent armchair and was scribbling away in his notebook.

'Shouldn't you be in hospital?' I asked Dan as I walked in.

'I'm fine.'

'You don't look it.'

Laura stared at me. 'How about you? They told us you were dead.'

'They're going to wish I was,' I said, glaring at Brogan. 'They have my wife. What are you doing about it?'

'We have men and cars combing the area,' he said. 'Can you tell me what happened? Laura has no recollection until she came to in the back of Walters' Land Rover.'

I didn't sit. I wouldn't be able to stay still. I began to pace. 'There was something in the chicken dish we had for dinner. It was too sweet for my taste, so I didn't eat more than a mouthful.'

'I wondered how you weren't affected,' Laura said.

'So the servants were in on it?'

I know my expression turned mean. 'Up to their armpits,' I said. 'The stable hand shot me with a rifle.'

Peters looked up from his notebook. Pencil poised mid-air. 'Shot you?' his expression doubtful.

'Yes,' I snapped. 'Shot me. I'm black and blue underneath my shirt.'

He scowled at me. 'How come you aren't dead, then?'

I pulled open my jacket to show them the holster. 'I was carrying a very large knife. Fortunately for me the bullet hit it.'

'You were carrying a concealed weapon?' Peters said.

I gave him a cold stare. 'Yes, and just you try and make something of it and we might have to have a conversation about Miss Simmons' protection, or lack of it.'

'We found a lot of blood in the clearing – whose was it?' Brogan interrupted, sensing his sergeant might be about to become embroiled in an argument he wouldn't be able to win.

'Funnily enough I didn't ask his name, but he was about to harm my wife. I couldn't let it happen.'

He gave a grunt. 'Did you recognise anyone? Miss Simmons and Mr Crouchley said they were wearing masks.'

I pinched the bridge of my nose. This was taking too long. I needed to be out there looking for Emma and trying to get her away from those lunatics. 'Mr and Mrs Walters were with the stable hand who shot me. I don't know his name.' I glanced at Dan. 'It was the lad you said was a bit slack – it appears you were wrong about him.' He didn't react. 'Dan? The stable hand – what's his name?'

He blinked. 'Sebastien,' Dan said, his voice a dull monotone. 'Sebastien Berkley.'

I frowned and crouched down to look at his face. I put my fingers beneath his chin and tilted his head. 'You need to get him to hospital,' I said. 'He could be concussed.'

'So, you're a doctor now,' Peters sneered.

I stood and turned on him. 'Phone a fucking ambulance, you moron, before you end up needing medical attention too.'

'I'm OK,' Dan mumbled.

Brogan got to his feet and grabbed my arm. 'Take it easy,' he said. 'We're not the bad guys.'

'You have a mole,' I told him, still glaring at Peters. 'They knew you were coming before we heard the sirens. And whose idea was that anyway? Talk about a giveaway.'

'That was a mistake.' His eyes flashed in Peters' direction, before his attention returned to me. 'A mole? Impossible.'

'Someone phoned them, the men in masks,' Laura piped up. 'I saw one of them answer their mobile and then they whispered something to . . .' She looked at me, her eyes huge. 'Was he my grandfather? You called him Oliver.'

'Oliver Pomeroy?' Brogan asked.

'It couldn't have been,' Peters said. 'He's dead.'

I was getting mighty pissed off with his snide comments. 'And so will you be if you don't phone for an ambulance.'

'Do it,' Brogan said.

'But—'

'Now.'

The sergeant's face fell into a disgruntled glower, but he got to his feet and strode out of the room, pulling his phone from his pocket as he went.

'I'd watch him if I were you,' I said.

'He's a good officer,' Brogan said.

'*You* have a mole and *I* don't like him.'

Brogan ignored my comment and turned to Laura. 'What's this about Oliver Pomeroy?'

She shook her head, her expression thoroughly miserable. 'You'll have to ask Jed.'

Giving the impression I was the last person he wanted to talk to, he turned his attention back to me. 'Oliver Pomeroy is dead.'

'I'm afraid not. I think you'll find the body you have belongs to his brother Edward.'

'You think Oliver Pomeroy killed his own brother?'

'It's beginning to look that way.'

'But why?'

'You'd have to ask him, but from what Simon said when we last saw him, he believed Edward might have

306

killed Oliver's first wife, Constance. It wasn't long after she died that Edward was put away. Knowing what I know now it makes sense. It was Oliver who brought Edward home. It was Oliver who changed his will only days before he allegedly died. It was Oliver who in his will insisted Laura move in before the month's end.'

Brogan jerked his head towards the chair he'd recently vacated. I scowled at him, then thought 'What the hell?' and flopped down in the armchair opposite Dan and Laura. He took the matching chair. I was beginning to really worry about Dan. His usually tanned complexion was the colour of rancid milk and his eyes were sagging shut. 'Where's the ambulance?' I said.

'Peters has called for one.'

'He better have. Laura' – I noticed she was clinging onto Dan's hand – 'talk to him. Don't let him drift off.'

She swallowed and swivelled around on the couch to half-face him. 'Dan,' she said, touching his cheek. 'Dan, wake up. You have to stay awake.'

'Hmm.'

'Dan? Dan, can you hear me?'

'Brogan, he needs medical attention – now.'

The policeman heaved himself out of the chair. 'I'll go and check Peters has made the call.'

As soon as he'd left the room, I went to crouch down in front of Dan again. I rested my palm on his forehead and it was clammy to the touch.

His eyes flickered open. 'I'm OK – really.'

The door opened and Brogan came hurrying back in with a young policewoman in tow.

'Can you deal with him until the paramedics arrive?'

She gave a nod and Brogan gestured with his head that I go with him. 'WPC Sanders used to be a paramedic before she joined the force,' he said, leading me from the room.

'Where's Peters?'

He glanced around the hallway and drew me into a corner. 'I don't know,' he said.

'What?'

'He's gone. Sanders saw him walk straight out the front door after leaving us.'

'Did he make the call?'

Brogan's lips pressed together in a thin line. 'He was on the phone, but she didn't think it was to the ambulance service. I phoned them, so they are on their way.'

'If something happens to Dan . . .'

He grimaced. 'I know. It's down to me.'

I glowered at him. 'I need to find my wife.'

'We're doing all we can.'

'Are you? If your mate Peters has anything to do with it, probably nothing is being done at all.'

He stared at me for the count of three during which I could see the realisation dawn that I could possibly be right about his right-hand man.

'How long has he been your sergeant?' I asked.

'Three months,' he said automatically, his mind still churning it over. 'He was new. Transferred in. Oh shit.' He ran a hand over his face. 'You think . . . ?'

'All I know is he came and spoke to Laura and you didn't know a thing about it, someone alerted Oliver and his people to you lot being on your way and as soon as you were in the vicinity sirens and blue flashing lights announced your arrival.' I paused, remembering. 'Also, someone has been a little free and easy with police files.'

Brogan frowned at me. 'Files that were in Simon Pomeroy's possession?' and his sarcastic tone wasn't lost on me.

He was right. Simon *could* quite easily organise a mole within the police force, I would imagine. But why would he? And again I wondered what he'd been thinking when he'd asked me to get involved.

'I think Simon Pomeroy might have been playing a game,' Brogan said, reflecting my thoughts exactly. 'Perhaps he invited you here because he thought you and your wife would provide him with some kind of alibi.'

Except this *wasn't* why he invited me to Kingsmead; he'd invited me because he wanted me to find out the truth. I couldn't tell Brogan this, he would never believe me and someone in the local police force was dirty, but who? I didn't like Peters, he was an arrogant prick *and* he had disappeared, but I still had niggling doubts about Brogan. He had been sleeping with the enemy and if Simon had been having him followed it was for a reason.

CHAPTER TWENTY-SIX

We were interrupted by the ambulance arriving to take Dan away. Laura insisted on going with him and I hoped this wasn't a mistake, though better she was in a hospital full of people than at Kingsmead. Also, as guilty as it made me feel, I'd rather she was out of my hair. I couldn't protect her and search for Emma.

Brogan had his back to me and was on his mobile when I returned from seeing Laura and Dan off in the ambulance. He was talking quickly and in a low voice. It was almost as though he sensed me entering the room, as he glanced over his shoulder and, upon seeing me, said a curt goodbye and pocketed his phone.

'I hope you've sent a few officers to the hospital,' I said.

He gave me a frosty look. 'Believe it or not, my men have better things to do than babysit Miss Simmons and her boyfriend.'

'He's not her boyfriend,' I snapped.

I was rewarded by a snort of laughter. 'Yeah, right. She was clinging onto his hand like she was.'

I ignored him, mainly because, although I hated to admit it, he was probably right about the two of them. 'Someone has just made an attempt on her life.'

His shoulders slumped and he ran a hand through his unruly mop of hair. 'I've sent two men to the hospital – satisfied?'

I grunted a begrudging 'Thank you,' but I wasn't so easily placated. 'Any news on where Oliver and his people have all cluttered off to?'

'I told you, I have men combing the countryside. They can't get far.'

'Then why haven't they found any of them? They had two injured to slow them down.' I glared at him. 'They were slap bang in the middle of the estate – with nowhere to go.'

'Maybe they had other vehicles parked somewhere.'

It made sense I supposed. 'I'm going back out there,' I said.

He shook his head, raising the palm of his hand and stepping in front of me. 'No way. The forest is out of bounds for the time being. It's a crime scene.'

'They – have – my – wife!' I said, only just stopping myself from grabbing him by the collar and shouting it in his face.

'I think you need to calm down.'

I glowered at him and I could feel my face growing hot. 'Don't you dare tell me to calm down. Oliver fucking Pomeroy is as psycho as his brother and he has my wife. I need to find him.'

For a moment I thought I saw a glimmer of sympathy in his eyes. 'I—' He didn't get to finish whatever it was he was about to say as a young PC came hurrying in, his breathing ragged like he'd been running and even in the warm light of the living room his complexion had a sickly hue to it.

'Sir,' he said, licking his very pale lips, and Brogan turned away from me with a sigh.

'Constable?'

The PC glanced back into the hallway and, taking the hint, Brogan followed him outside. I watched them through the doorway. There was a hurried conversation during which Brogan glanced my way a couple of times. His face had creased into a deep frown by the time they had finished.

'Good work,' I heard him say and the constable strode off, his colour only slightly better than when he'd arrived, and my chest went tight. I'd seen the look before many times, usually when a young colleague had seen his first death, whether it had been by his own hands or another's.

Brogan stood in the hallway, his hands rammed into his pockets and his eyes on me. I wasn't sure I liked his expression, but it wasn't one of a man about to give another devastating news, at least I didn't think so. His stare was contemplative and I had the impression I was being assessed. Then it occurred to me that as much as I didn't trust him, it was very possible he felt exactly the same way about me. After all, I was a friend of the Pomeroys.

He took his hands from his pockets and slowly walked back into the room. I tried to keep my expression neutral. It was hard when all I could think of was Emma and what might be happening to her. 'We've found two bodies,' he said.

The room gave a lurch and I sucked in breath, my chest tight and my heart feeling like it was slowing to a stop. I opened my mouth, trying to speak, to say her name, but the words wouldn't come.

'The two men you injured,' he said, 'they were obviously a hindrance.'

I breathed out and my heart began to beat again.

'They'd both had their throats cut.' His lips twisted in distaste.

'Jesus.' I sank down into one of the armchairs.

'We've found how they made their escape. There's another track on the far side of the woodland. Have you any idea where they might go?'

I tried to think. 'Not that I know of. Simon has a place in Sussex, but as far as I'm aware Oliver has always lived here in Kingsmead.'

'I suppose there's no point me suggesting you go home or move into a hotel.' I just stared at him. 'I thought not. I'll leave a couple of uniforms here and' – he glanced at his watch – 'I'll be back in a few hours' time. In the meantime, you should try and get some sleep.'

'How do you expect me to sleep?' I asked. 'He's had two of his own men killed because they were slowing him down. He's not going to think twice about killing my wife if she does the same.'

'He took her for a reason.' His eyes narrowed and he stared into space before refocusing on my face. 'So, we'll have to assume he will try and contact you.'

'He won't have much luck,' I said, my shoulders sagging. 'My phone was in my breast pocket when I was shot. It's a mangled mess.'

'In which case he'll probably try phoning you here.'

'Are you mad? He'll know the place is crawling with you lot.'

He shrugged. 'Well, he'll try and contact you somehow, otherwise what's the point?'

That, unfortunately, was the problem: I didn't think there was any. If he wanted Laura, all he had to do was bide his time. Why complicate matters by involving me? Someone he would know had once been a highly trained—And that was it, this was what could keep Emma alive. He knew what I was – or had been – and he knew if he harmed her he'd better make damn sure I was dead otherwise he would be for ever looking over his shoulder, because I would find him, if it took for ever and a day I *would* find him.

After Brogan left I couldn't settle. Dawn was fast approaching and there was little point going to bed. I wouldn't sleep, my mind was running at nineteen to the dozen. I went upstairs, laid on the bed, the bed I'd shared with Emma, and my heart felt hollow. I tried closing my eyes, but it didn't help, it made it one hundred times worse.

I got up, had a long, hot shower, hoping to ease my aches and pains. The left side of my chest was a black and blue mess, but it was a small price to pay for the blade preventing the damage that could have been caused. I dressed and then began to pace. I sat down, stood and paced again. It was pointless walking back and forth in my room so, as apart from the few plod guarding the grounds, the house was empty, I decided to explore. I walked from room to room. In some I had a little tickle at the back of my neck, but no one apparently wanted to talk to me.

Simon's room was as he'd left it and I could almost imagine the door swinging open and him striding in. Funnily enough, in my head I saw him as he'd been, a rash and reckless twenty-something. And it choked me up that even then he hadn't been the man I thought, he had been involved in whatever weirdness his brothers had introduced him to.

Sitting on the edge of his bed I let my gaze wander around the room. It hadn't changed an awful lot since the last time I'd been inside it. He'd always been meticulously tidy, then we all had: him, me and Reggie. It was something engrained into us from being in the forces.

There were a couple of pictures on the mantelpiece. I got to my feet and went to take a look. I was surprised to see there was one of Simon, Reggie and me despite us all having fallen out in quite a spectacular way. It was reminiscent of the photo of the three brothers. We were all laughing, happy. I turned the picture over in my hands, unclipping it from the frame to check the back. It was inscribed with our names, a place and a date from almost thirty years ago.

I returned the photo to where it had come from. There were others, but none of the three brothers together and I found this strange. He had a thirty-year-old picture of himself with two people he was estranged from, but none of his beloved brother Edward who, until recently, he believed to be dead. Nor was there one of his other brother Oliver, who he'd told me he had relied upon so much after his family had been torn apart by the, now known to be fabricated, tragedy. Could it be the divide between Simon and Oliver had been greater than I'd been led to believe? Had Simon learnt things about both his brothers since returning from the forces that had destroyed the bond he'd had with them?

From nowhere another thought floated into my head. Why had Simon been in Edward's room that night? Having found out that Edward had been alive for all the time he'd thought him dead, had he gone there to search for an indication of his whereabouts only to find one of Oliver's people ransacking the room? If so, what were they searching for? Was it for the photographs hidden in *Edward's* room with *Edward's* medallion? In which case, how did Oliver know they existed?

If only Simon had told me what was going on. If he'd been straight with me from the very start, maybe he'd be alive and Emma would be safely here with me. I stood and slowly turned around. Was there anything in this room that might tell me what this had all been about? Starting with his bedside table I began to search. There wasn't much to find. A few odds and ends, which had probably been languishing in the drawers since I'd last visited. Some toiletries, a dish heaped with loose change, a wallet containing business cards and an out-of-date address book.

The chest of drawers didn't reveal anything other than freshly laundered underwear, shirts and socks. In the wardrobe there were several suits, jackets, silk ties and pairs of trousers. Simon didn't go in for jeans and T-shirts. Never had and now he never would. A wave of emotion washed over me. I breathed in deep. I had to hold it together.

He told me it was over.

I rocked on my feet. 'Simon?'

When Ed 'died' he told me he was done with it. The last words a sigh. *He lied.*

'Simon? Simon – talk to me.' I closed my eyes and waited, but if he had anything else to say he kept it to himself.

I thumped the mantelpiece in frustration. 'Not good enough, Simon. Not nearly good enough.' His only response was silence.

I stalked towards the door. I was angry with Simon and his psychotic family. I was scared for Emma. I was worried about Laura and, to some extent, Dan. They were all emotions that were making it hard to think clearly. When I was in 'the business' I kept my feelings in check, we all did, we had to. This was different – this was personal.

I stopped on the threshold and looked back. His desk – I hadn't been through Simon's desk and where else would there be paperwork to be found if not his writing desk?

There was only one locked drawer. The large bottom one to the right. I went through all the others first hoping, while looking, I would come across a key to the locked drawer. This would, of course, be far too easy. It didn't matter, it was antique furniture and the locks didn't take a lot of fiddling with to open if you knew what you were doing and, for my sins, I did. With the help of a couple of old paper clips and a little bit of patience I had it open in a matter of minutes. In the old days it would have been seconds – even so, I was pretty pleased with myself.

I had a few butterflies when I pulled it open. I didn't know what to expect. Surprise, surprise there were more files – and a briefcase. I took out the briefcase and laid it on the desk. I'd save the best for last.

I quickly flicked through the first couple of files. They were nothing more exciting than very old bank and credit card statements. Of course they'd be old, he didn't live at Kingsmead any longer.

Shutting the drawer I turned my attention to his briefcase. It was locked, of course. A combination lock.

Pushing back the chair, I sat the briefcase on my lap, raising my hands above the numbered wheels and closing my eyes. Breathe in, breathe out, breathe in, breathe out. I let my mind empty, lowered my fingers onto the wheels and, in my head, I saw two sets of four numbers. Zero, zero, zero, zero on the left and the same on the right. And one by one each number slowly rolled downwards one, two, three, four, stop. Then the next and the next and while this was happening I rolled my forefinger on the corresponding wheel until all eight numbers were done.

I opened my eyes and with a press of both thumbs the catches sprang open and I lifted the lid to reveal more files. I inhaled long and slow and then exhaled. The first file was on Laura and contained pages of photographs like the one we had found in Edward's room. I even found the place from where the page had been removed. It soon became evident Simon *had* lied to me. He had known her parents were dead for a long time and certainly before Oliver's faked death. I flicked through the pages, depressed by what I found. There were photographs of her friends and boyfriends, with details so intrusive I knew he must have used his position to get hold of them.

The next file was on DI Brogan and again it was clear the pictures we'd found in the envelope were originally surveillance photos taken for Simon, though there was no indication of why he had this information collated. The file on Tanith Bloxborough was a mere couple of pages plus copies of the same photographs as in Brogan's file. There was no record of where she was from or where she'd been. No passport, no driving licence, nothing. She was an enigma, and it made me wonder – had she once been in the business?

Then I came to Dan Crouchley's file and whatever I might have thought about Simon and his later career choices he was one of the best at what he did. He knew every last thing about Dan. He knew his name was Dan Foley. He knew his sister had gone missing after allegedly setting off to a party held at Kingsmead and he knew he had taken the position at the estate to get answers to his questions about his sister's disappearance. And how did he know all this? Because Dan Crouchley or, should I say Foley, was working for Simon at MI triple X and a half or whatever his department was called. Simon had spotted his potential and recruited him.

I slumped back in the chair. It was damn stupid for Simon to have this file in his possession at the house. Had Oliver found it, I would imagine Dan would be as dead as . . . as dead as Simon. But Simon thought Oliver was dead, he'd thought Edward was dead. I shivered, goosebumps pimpling my arms. Was this why Simon had been killed? Was it because Oliver had found out he and his household were under surveillance by his own brother? And suddenly Simon's words began to make a lot of sense.

He told me it was over. When Ed 'died' he told me he was done with it. He lied. Simon had known Laura's parents were dead and I'd bet my Jag that he'd known exactly how they'd died and the file containing this information had already been in his possession back at his office in Whitehall or wherever the hell he had been based. He had known they'd been ritually killed and, being as Edward was presumed dead, he put the blame squarely on Oliver's shoulders. Simon had always been fond of William and this was why he and Oliver had become estranged. Simon knew what he'd done, but couldn't prove it. Or more likely didn't want to prove it. If he had it would have opened up a can of worms I doubted his career would have survived.

Thoroughly depressed, I laid the file on top of the others and took the last one out of the briefcase. I almost laughed, but not quite. I should have known. It was a file on me. I didn't bother to read it. I knew what it would say. I dropped the files back into the briefcase and, after locking it, returned it to the drawer.

It was close to seven-thirty by the time I made my way downstairs. I wasn't hungry, but I needed to eat. I needed energy. I also needed a very strong coffee, while I thought about all I now knew and what I was going to do about it and how. My first priority would be to find Emma.

At the bottom of the stairs I caught my first whiff of fried bacon and when I crossed the hallway I saw the dining-room door ajar. I pushed the door open. The table had been laid for one and there was a steaming coffee pot and a rack of toast waiting.

'You have to be kidding me,' I murmured as I walked to my seat.

'Eggs and bacon,' Maddy said from right behind me.

I spun around and she stepped back, a flicker of fear passing across her face. 'You're serving me breakfast?'

I said, my expression must have been mean as she took another step away from me.

'Of course.'

'How did you even get back in here?' I asked. 'The place is surrounded by coppers,' which was a bit of an overstatement. I'd seen two.

She gave a dainty sniff. 'This is an old house. The aristocracy always had their own secret ways in and out for whenever the mood took them,' she said, gesturing that I sit. 'Coffee?'

I raised an eyebrow and she laughed. 'No need to fear,' she said, 'I'm not your enemy.'

'How about Mr and Mrs Walters?'

'You'll have to ask them.'

'Are they here?'

She poured me a cup of coffee. 'Eggs and bacon?'

'Why not?' I said and hoped that I wouldn't be passing out face down into my plate if I ate them.

She filled my plate and it did cross my mind that perhaps this was the condemned man's last breakfast. As long as it wasn't the food that was going to kill me, for the moment I didn't care. I was suddenly very hungry.

'Do you know where my wife is?' I asked.

Her head turned this way and that as though looking for eavesdroppers. 'She's safe – so far,' she whispered. 'It's you she's interested in,' and she bit her lip glancing around.

'She?' I asked.

She swallowed and, keeping her eyes down, said, 'I can't say. I've said too much already.'

'Do you mean Tanith?' I asked. 'Tanith Bloxborough?'

Her expression was enough to tell me I was right. Her

eyes widened and her hand jumped to her throat. 'You know about her?' she whispered.

'I've met her – or least I've seen her. She was at the hospital.'

Maddy went very still, staring me directly in the eyes as if questioning whether I was telling the truth until realisation dawned that I was. 'I wondered why—' She clamped her lips together.

'You wondered what, Maddy?'

'I have to get on,' she said.

As she went to leave, I reached out and grabbed her wrist. 'Will he come for me here?'

She gave a barely perceptible nod of the head. I held on for a second longer, then let her go. She had been trembling; she was scared of him and the mysterious Tanith. Very scared indeed.

CHAPTER TWENTY-SEVEN

I finished my breakfast alone and, when it appeared Maddy wouldn't be returning anytime soon, I left the table taking a cup of coffee with me. I ensconced myself in the study. With no one to stop me I was going to see if there was anything hidden away from which I could find out more about Oliver and the repellent Tanith Bloxborough.

Tanith Bloxborough – it was interesting the reaction people – even her lover – had when she was mentioned. In my head I relived seeing her strutting towards us along the hospital corridor, the way our eyes locked as we passed each other and how her confident smile slipped a notch. I remembered the hiccup of fear and the tightening of my chest as my sixth sense went into overdrive telling me something was wrong. Had she had a similar premonition of foreboding when her eyes met mine?

Another memory came to mind: the two spirits who had kept me awake for hours. Had it been Tanith they had both been talking about when they said there had been a guest to the house who had scared them so much – a devil's child? I had a feeling she could well be.

With these thoughts whirling around in my head I started with the paperwork on the top of the desk. As one would expect it consisted mainly of bills and general correspondence. I pushed the pile to one side and started on the drawers. Boring, boring, boring. Stationery of varying descriptions: envelopes, writing paper, pens, pencils, paper clips and the like. The contents of the deep bottom drawer looked as though it could be a little more interesting; more buff-coloured folders in bottle-green suspension files. I was wrong. How could a man such as Oliver be so dull?

He had files for everything, so many it was obsessive. Household expenses, stable costs, invoices for groceries – each had their own file and there were more. Travel documents: it appeared he had a penchant for the South of France. Cars: he had six, with a subfolder for each one containing registration documents, MOTs, insurance and running costs. Apparently, a few months ago he'd pranged his Aston Martin. I winced when I came to the total of the repair bill. He had richer blood than me. I would have expected a brand-new car for the amount he'd paid out.

I dropped the last file in its hanger and shoved the drawer shut and turned to the two others to my left. Disappointingly there was only more of the same. This left the narrow top drawer running along above the leg space. Once again there was nothing to write home about: loose change, a book of matches, a reel of black silk ribbon and some red sealing wax, but no seal and I recalled he wore a signet ring with an engraved agate at its centre, as had Simon. There were a few other bits and pieces including a packet of condoms pushed right to the back. They were in date by a good few years so a fairly recent purchase.

Disheartened by my lack of progress I pushed the drawer shut. Perhaps I should try finding his bedroom in the other wing, the one he had shared with his latest wife. I doubted I would find anything there. The reason he had kept things in Edward's bedroom was to hide them from the latest Mrs Pomeroy.

I was thinking about it when there was a knock and Mrs Walters tentatively put her head around the door. I did wonder at the cheek of the woman. She and her husband had stood there and watched me be gunned down.

She came in and pushed the door shut behind her. 'I have a message for you,' she said, coming straight to the point.

I folded my arms and stared at her, not saying a word. She crossed her own arms as though hugging herself. 'Be here at ten o'clock tonight with Miss Laura. You'll get further instructions then. Do this and your wife will be freed.' I remained silent and she shifted uncomfortably. 'If you don't,' she swallowed. 'If you don't . . .'

'If I don't?'

Her lips pressed together. 'He'll sacrifice her in Miss Laura's place.'

'Sacrifice? Why don't you say what you mean? Oliver Pomeroy will *murder* my wife.'

'I'm sorry,' she said and strangely enough I believed her.

'How exactly am I meant to get Laura here? She's at the hospital with Dan Crouchley and I somehow don't think she's going to leave him for me, particularly when she knows there are people in this household who are out to do her serious harm.'

'But you must,' she said, her voice breaking. 'If you don't . . . He means it you know. He will kill her.'

'Then you had better give him a message from me. If any harm comes to my wife, I will seek him out and, believe you me, I *will* find him and, when I do, he will wish he'd never been born.'

Her hand went to her throat. 'I'll tell him, but he thinks he's invincible.'

I laughed. 'Well, here's the thing – I don't – and if anything happens to Emma I won't rest until he's in his grave.'

'I believe you.'

'Make sure he does.'

She looked down at her feet and when she raised her eyes back to mine whispered, 'It's not only him. That woman' – she wriggled her shoulders – 'that woman is evil. I've never met anyone as wicked as her. Make sure if you go after Mr Oliver you take her down too, because if anything happens to your wife, Tanith Bloxborough will have goaded him into it.'

'Why did he kill Edward?' I asked while I had her talking.

She breathed in and out. 'It was Edward who started it. Everything that's happened, every person who's been hurt was all down to him. When they said he was dead, I thought it'd be over. I thought we'd all be free. Instead it got worse.' Her eyes filled with tears and she brushed them away with a swipe of her hand. 'Then Mr Oliver brought him back here and the real nightmare began.' She pulled her shoulders back, standing tall. 'I have to go,' and she turned to leave.

'Mrs Walters, one more thing.'

She stopped and turned back to me, a resigned expression on her face.

'Simon . . . He was part of it?' I hesitated, not knowing how to say what I wanted to.

She managed a small smile and slowly shook her head. 'He broke away. He knew it was wrong. When he was young, when he was inducted, he thought it was exciting. But it didn't take long before he started to pull away. Then he left and joined the forces and when he came back, he'd broken away from his brother's influence. He had made new friends – good friends,' she said and from the look she gave me I knew she meant me and Reggie, 'and Mr Oliver told him it was over. It was easier that way. Despite everything, he loved his little brother.'

'Then why did Oliver have him killed?' She stared at me, raising her eyebrow, her expression saying 'Work it out for yourself'. 'Tanith?' I asked. 'Tanith wanted him dead?'

'She convinced Mr Oliver. He's not the same as he once was, she's manipulated and twisted him until he's become as mad as his brother. When he turned against Edward and said he wanted him dead, I really thought it *would* be the end of it, at last.' She shook her head. 'His death was meant to free him. He was going to leave the country, assume a new identity. *She* couldn't bear the idea of someone else getting the millions he hadn't siphoned abroad.'

'But if everyone thinks he's dead . . . ?'

She shrugged. 'Brandon Fredericks knew, or he guessed. Years ago, as a young man, he'd once been part of the Order. Before it became tainted, before Tanith Bloxborough. He went away to university, and when he returned he didn't

327

want to be part of it any more. He was more use to Oliver as his legal advisor, so he told him it was over, like he had Mr Simon. He lied. It never stopped, it never even faltered. To Oliver the power he had over us all was like a drug.'

I remembered Brandon's last phone call to me. He'd been a scared and worried man. Had he realised what was going on? Had he realised Oliver was still alive and calling the shots? Oliver said Brandon was going to betray the Order – was Brandon's intention to talk to me that betrayal?

'If that's all?' Mrs Walters interrupting my pondering.

'Thank you.'

She went to leave and once again hesitated. 'There's a hidden chapel beneath the west wing. You might find what you're looking for there,' she whispered and somewhere out in the hallway a door closed, making her flinch, and before I could ask her any more she slipped from the room.

The complicated legalities and implications of the Pomeroys' deaths were completely overshadowed by this latest piece of information. Had she been hinting Emma was being held in a secret room beneath Kingsmead? I pushed back the chair. I was going to find Emma if it was the last thing I ever did.

As I walked out into the hall DI Brogan was coming in through the front door. I could do without him now, even so I doubted I could do a body swerve around a conversation whether I wanted to or not.

'Mr Cummings, a moment of your time, if you don't mind?'

'And if I do?'

He cracked what could have been a smile. 'I'm hoping you won't.'

I gestured towards the living room. If we were going to talk, we might as well do it in comfort. I slumped down in an armchair and he chose the one opposite me.

'Have you found Peters?' I asked.

He leant back in the chair studying my face. 'No,' he said. 'The strange thing is his car is still here.'

My surprise must have shown. 'You mean he never left the estate?'

His eyes stayed on mine. 'If he did, it wasn't in his vehicle.'

My fingers were stroking my beard before I realised I was doing it. I dropped my hand to my knee. 'So, what do you think? Is he one of the bad guys or is he tied up somewhere with my wife?'

'I wish I knew. That he's disappeared makes me fear the worst. If he was a mole, why would they break his cover? Surely he would be more useful to them on the inside?'

He was right. He had no reason to believe we were suspicious of him and, even if he did, he could have brazened it out. Brogan hadn't even thought about him being dirty until I raised it, and who was I to say? – I didn't trust anyone – including Brogan.

But why would they kidnap a policeman?

'Have you heard anything from Pomeroy?'

I hesitated. If he was in Tanith Bloxborough's pocket he would know anyway, and if he wasn't then maybe he could help me.

'The staff are back and Mrs Walters gave me a message from him. I am to be here tonight with Laura otherwise he will *sacrifice* Emma in her place.'

'I think I'd better have a word with Mrs Walters.'

I didn't say anything. Mrs Walters had tried to help me, Oliver could never know. If he did, I doubted her long-term well-being would be good or lengthy.

'Have you heard anything from the hospital about Dan Crouchley?' I said, changing the subject to something slightly safer.

'I went over there before coming here. He's conscious and charming all the nurses.'

'Really? I'd have thought Laura would have something to say about that.'

He stood. 'I doubt she'll ever change him.'

It was probably for the best she didn't try, and I wondered what she would make of him being one of Simon's spies. I doubted it would go down too well. Especially if she thought his interest in her wasn't necessarily for the reasons she thought. It wasn't my problem and, while she was at the hospital mopping his fevered brow, neither was she.

Brogan went off and was heading towards the kitchen when I last saw him. As soon as he was out of sight I made towards the west wing, hoping the secret passageway down to the hidden chapel wasn't impossible to find. I suppose knowing there was an entrance somewhere would help, at least I hoped it would.

I was wrong. It was of no help whatsoever. I did find a cellar, which had my hopes going through the roof, but it was full of crap and after the first few steps was so cluttered I could hardly move without climbing over discarded boxes, old bikes and various other paraphernalia. If the chapel was a regular meeting place, I couldn't see a steady stream of people in flowing robes negotiating their way through it to get to their destination.

With dust in my nose and hair and grimy hands I trudged back upstairs and tried looking elsewhere. It did occur to me that Mrs Walters might have sent me on a wild goose chase to keep me occupied, but if she had she should be nominated for an Oscar.

I was checking out some wood panelling in a corridor beneath a flight of stairs when I heard someone clear their throat behind me. I spun around. Brogan was peering at me with a puzzled expression.

'What are you doing?'

I stuffed my hands in my pockets and tried not to look guilty. 'Nothing.'

He gave a snort, with a kind of 'who do you think you're kidding?' expression.

'You wanted something?'

His shoulders slumped. 'Miss Simmons has gone missing.'

'What? How can that be? She was at the hospital.'

'Well, she isn't now, and I can only hope she's on her way back here and hasn't been snatched.'

This was not good. Not good at all. If Oliver had her, he didn't need Emma any more. Or me, for that matter.

'Did you speak to Mrs Walters?'

He shook his head. 'She's disappeared as well. The only person down in the kitchen was young Maddy.'

'The cunning old . . .' She *had* been feeding me a line. How could I have been so stupid?

I stomped past Brogan and made straight for the kitchen. Too late, Maddy had gone too. I glanced around. While I was here, I might as well find myself a couple of weapons to replace the ones I'd lost. I opened a few drawers until I came across where the cook kept her best knives. I'd lost my throwing blades, but top-quality, sharp kitchen knives could make just as good weapons if you chose wisely. I found a mid-sized stainless steel knife and laid it across my fingers. It was all about balance and weight and it would do me quite well. I laid it on the worktop and started sifting through the others. When I glanced up, Brogan was watching me with interest.

'What are you proposing to do with those?'

'Don't ask questions you won't like the answers to,' I said, laying a second knife next to the first one I'd chosen.

He leant back against the kitchen table still watching me. 'When I looked into your background it said you were an officer in Military Intelligence, but when I tried to dig deeper I couldn't really find out anything about you at all.'

I gave a noncommittal grunt and wrapped the two knives I had chosen plus one other in a tea towel to take to my room. 'These days I'm a retired gardener.'

'Hmm, all I will say is if you have to kill someone make sure it's in self-defence. I wouldn't want you to be the one in handcuffs at the end of all this.'

I tucked the purloined knives under my arm and, with a flip of my hand in farewell, left him to go to my room. I thought he might follow after me to try and dissuade me from doing something he might consider stupid. He didn't. I guessed he knew when he was fighting a losing battle.

Upstairs in my bedroom I took off my jacket and replaced my knife holster. The larger of the three kitchen knives fitted quite well and the slightly smaller one slid into the sheath around my ankle as if it was made for it. The third knife went into my jacket pocket. All three blades were lethally sharp and would cut through flesh like butter. I hoped I wouldn't have to use them; I wasn't holding my breath.

As I slipped on my jacket, I caught a glimpse of myself in the mirror. I could have been looking at a stranger. I turned away feeling – slightly strange. I'd lost weight since I'd married Emma. I was eating better and drinking less, though not necessarily by choice. For sure I wasn't the same man I'd been in the military. I was older, not particularly wiser, but over the past few months I'd lost the middle-aged flab I'd gained over the years and I didn't look like a wild man with my trimmed beard and hair, though now they were more salt than pepper and my chest hair was turning to snow.

Being with Emma had made me a better man and I wasn't about to lose her now, not after waiting so long. I took another quick glance in the mirror. I was looking . . . I was looking good and like the man Emma deserved. Now I had to do more than look like him, I had to be him. The man in the mirror smiled and the new-old me smiled back.

CHAPTER TWENTY-EIGHT

Apart from Mrs Walters, I hadn't seen any of the servants since breakfast and I'd taken it upon myself to feed the horses as I couldn't bear to think of them going without. They had been pleased to see me, but uneasy, eyes a little wild, the whites showing as they shook their heads and puffed steam from their nostrils. They knew something was wrong, the disruption to their routine was probably enough to spook them. I soothed them as best as I could, though it was hard to walk away. Hurrying back to the house I could still hear the rattle of wood as they pawed at the doors to their stalls and the clatter of their hooves as they stomped their feet in agitation.

Laura hadn't returned by seven and it became more than apparent she wouldn't be coming, not under her own steam anyway. They had her, I was sure of it, and time was running out.

I'd resorted to making my own dinner. It consisted

only of cheese, home-made bread and chutney. As good as it was, I hardly tasted it, but it had filled a hole and would keep me going as I continued my exploration of the house.

The sun was going down and I was running out of time and daylight. If they were going to make a move it would be after dark. I needed a torch and I had one in my car boot.

Outside, long shadows were creeping across the lawns and there wasn't a soul in sight. I wondered where the police presence had gone to. I hoped they were somewhere about and ready to pounce on Oliver and his motley crew should they reappear. I doubted it was going to happen. Oliver might be insane, but he had proven to be far from stupid, and this knowledge had my spirits sinking to an all-time low.

I had a moment of worry as the boot lid sprung open and I couldn't see the torch. It was too big to miss, surely to God. I shoved aside Emma's multicoloured golfing umbrella and there it was. It was a bit battered and scarred, but it still worked. I clicked it on and off to make sure the battery was good and the resultant shaft of light was bright and would cut through the dark with no trouble. I hefted the weight in my hand. It would also double as another weapon for my arsenal if need be.

I decided to finish searching the west wing. Despite my reservations about the housekeeper, a small part of me couldn't help but think she had been sincere.

Finally, I came to the poolroom. I hesitated outside. Did I really want to go back in there? As soon as I stepped through the doorway the back of my neck chilled and after a few paces a soft breeze caressed my cheek. The surface of the pool rippled and, as the breeze grew, waves began to appear and the water churned. I breathed in deep. I had a feeling things were about to get a bit weird.

I walked to the water's edge, closer than I'd rather be when I was here alone, but I could hear them calling to me. Suzie Foley hadn't been the only young woman to have died here. I could hear two voices, no three, at least three women crying out my name. I peered down into the inky depths of the pool and shivered. It was as dark as any grave. At the centre of the pool the water began to swirl, slowly at first, in lazy circles, then gradually gaining speed forming a foaming funnel and all the time the voices grew louder and louder until they were like the howl of the wind on a stormy night. I had to fight against lifting my hands to my ears it was so loud. Then with one final shriek it stopped.

I slowly opened my fists, relieving my aching knuckles from where they'd been clenched so hard, and breathed out. It was too soon to relax. The wailing might have stopped, but the whirlpool continued to funnel downwards in a frothing tube.

Jed!

Jed!

Jed!

One at a time they whispered, every call of my name reverberating in my head until it was all I could hear. Even so I couldn't drag my eyes away from the pool. Something was about to happen. I could feel it in the unnatural frigidity of the air that pulsed around me like the throb of a heartbeat. The swirling of the water began to subside, slowing until the funnel at its centre was more like a fine stream being sucked down a plughole and still they called to me.

'What do you want of me?' I said and something moved beneath the surface of the pool.

I took a step closer. Crazy I know, but I wanted—no, I needed to see. And see I did, pale flashes of something beneath the water's surface gradually gaining substance as they circled the pool. Alabaster limbs and white faces surrounded by long hair that clung to them in dark strands as they rose from the water.

The three women closed in together coming towards me and they appeared as solid as I did. They were dead, I could see they were dead, there was no doubt about it, but they could have been freshly pulled from a watery grave.

I took one step back and another. I had always maintained the dead couldn't hurt you, now I knew differently. One had almost drowned Emma.

They hovered above the water at the edge of the pool, probably not much more than a yard away and to my way of thinking it was too close, much too close. I took one more step back and sucked in my fear. If they wanted my help, I'd give it, but I wasn't about to die just yet. Emma was my priority and Laura too, if I could save her.

They stopped, all three gazing at me with opaque dead eyes, their lips tinged blue and skin like greying porcelain. The woman in the middle I recognised: Suzie, Dan Foley's sister. The woman to her left looked about the same age, though it was hard to tell – death had leeched the character from her face. Whereas Suzie's once-pretty frock had been right for the ill-fated party this young woman was wearing

337

a uniform. She had been a maid, a maid here at the house. The last of the three women was older, possibly by ten or fifteen years. My throat went dry, she had been the woman who had clung onto Emma's ankles so tightly. She was attired for a day by the pool, though she was wearing some sort of flimsy translucent kaftan that clung wetly to her body, showing the brightly coloured bikini she wore underneath and more suitable for the poolside of a posh hotel somewhere in the South of France.

I remembered Oliver had a penchant for the region and it made me wonder – was the reason he had never divorced his last wife that he had no need to? And was this why she had wanted my own wife dead? If she couldn't have Oliver neither could any other woman? From what she had screamed at Emma as she had tried to drown her it would make a sick kind of sense.

I took a deep breath. 'What is it you want from me?'

Justice, justice, justice. The whisper echoed through my mind.

'I don't—'

The maid lifted her arm and pointed towards the bar area. I frowned at her, uncomprehending. What was she trying to tell me?

They had said all they were going to. All three bowed their heads, losing substance, their bodies turning to mist, which swirled around and around as it was sucked back down into the pool until they were gone and the water's surface stilled, leaving me alone. I stood there for a second or two allowing my heart to calm a little. I was getting far too old for this kind of shit.

Turning my back on the pool I crossed to the bar, for no

other reason than it was where the three spirits appeared to want me to be. I slowly swung the torch back and forth; bottles, glasses, optics, and a cocktail shaker glinting as its beam swept over their shiny surfaces and reflected right back at me, but no clue as to what I was searching for. Frustrated, I leant over the counter pointing the flashlight downwards, looking for I don't know what, and there, behind the bar, spread out across the floor and totally out of place in the opulent surroundings, was a large coconut fibre mat. Had I seen it before I would have imagined it was to prevent slipping on the slick marble flooring while handling potentially lethal glasses and bottles. Now I wasn't so sure.

Crouching down I lifted one corner and it soon became evident there was more to it. Hidden beneath the mat a marble inlaid trapdoor filled the space between the bar and the wall. I had found my way under the house and hopefully to the underground chapel.

'Thank you, ladies,' I murmured.

Descending the stone steps into the belly of the house, the beam of the flashlight leading the way, I felt like the loneliest man on earth. The stairs led to a long, narrow, stone-clad corridor. Empty brackets for torches lined the walls just above head height and the tart, oily aroma overlying the smell of dirt and dust suggested they were put to good use. After a few yards the torch beam found a large wooden door blocking the way. If it was locked I was fucked. Just looking at it I could see it would take a battering ram to get through the thing.

Heart thumping, I grasped the iron ring handle and twisted. The gods were with me. With a loud click of the lock it opened and I stepped inside, lifting the flashlight to slowly swing it back and forth.

'Bloody hell,' I muttered.

When Mrs Walters had told me there was a secret chapel beneath the west wing, I had thought it would be a small family-sized vault for worship during times of trouble. The first Lord Pomeroy apparently didn't do anything by halves. The place was maybe not a full-sized church, but it wasn't far off it, the beam of my torch barely reaching the far end.

I doubted anyone was lying in wait in the darkness, but all the same I took my time as I walked towards the front, the softened echoes of my every step following my progress and bouncing off the walls to fill the chamber.

Something moved to my right and I spun around, the torch cutting a swathe through the dark and catching the glint of small, beady eyes, before a rodent scampered away. Rats – that's all I needed. I thought of Emma, rats never bothered her at all. 'They're more scared of me than I am of them,' she used to say, and my heart gave a little lurch. Where was she? If I didn't find her soon . . . I couldn't think that way. If I did the mission would fail before it had even begun.

Mission? What was I thinking?

The way you have to if you want to succeed. The voice in my head sounded very much like Simon, the old Simon, who Reggie and I could count on when we needed to, the voice of calm reason when we had a job to do.

I kept on walking. Apart from three rows of pews right at the back, the rest of the chapel was an open space until it reached the altar a few yards from the front. Behind it my torch caught the glimmer of black glossy curtains, patterned with gold astrological designs, covering the stone walls.

As I drew closer, I played the torch beam over the stone-hewn altar and a small stab of horror pierced my chest just above my breastbone. A swathe of rumpled red silk was piled in its centre and it looked to me as though it might be covering something – or someone.

'Jesus, Jesus,' I murmured. If there was ever a time for me to find religion it was now.

I slowly continued walking and the closer I got the more convinced I became that beneath the crimson material lay a human body. I could hear my heart beating in my ears. My windpipe felt so constricted I was finding it hard to breathe. Oliver had Laura – he didn't need Emma any more. Is this why Mrs Walters sent me here? So I could find my dead wife?

A tear trickled down my cheek and I swiped it away. I stopped about a yard from the altar. There was no deluding myself, there was a body under the covering. Darkened patches stained the material and lines of blood streamed down the grey stone forming glossy pools upon the floor.

I took one shuddery breath and then another, closing my eyes I suppose, hoping that when I opened them again the material, body and blood would be gone. It wasn't to be. I knew I was delaying the inevitable. But if I didn't lift the silk for a few more seconds, a few more minutes or maybe even a few more hours I would still have some hope. I could still believe the love of my life was alive.

I took the final couple of steps to stand looking down upon the altar. Possibly the last two steps I'd take before my life changed for ever. I reached down and took hold of the edge of the silk. It felt cool and soft between my fingertips.

'Oh, Emma.'

I took one more shuddery breath, the last one before my heart would break into a million pieces, and slowly pulled the material back.

The breath caught in my throat and I couldn't swallow as I was swamped with a myriad of emotions and – God help me – the biggest one was relief. It lasted but a moment before the whole horror of it came crashing down upon me, but I would always remember the feeling, I would remember I had felt relief that it was someone else and not my wife who had died.

Detective Sergeant Peters had died badly. Like Brandon he had been tortured before they had cut his throat to let him bleed out over the altar. They had let him keep his tongue, I guess he needed it to tell them what they wanted to know, but apparently his teeth were fair game and from the shattered stumps that remained they had taken a hammer and chisel to them. It was difficult to tell the colour of his shirt. It was a bloody mess. Once they'd run out of teeth to destroy, they'd taken the chisel to his chest, judging by the dark eruptions of gore and slim gashes in the material, smashing every one of his ribs and then collarbones.

'Jesus Christ,' I muttered, wiping my mouth with the back of my hand.

'He'll not help you, dahling,' a voice said from behind me.

I swung around and the beautiful but deadly Tanith Bloxborough smiled at me, raised her fist palm upwards slowly unclenching her fingers and, when it reached head height, puckered her ruby lips and blew. I staggered backwards as shimmering dust hit me in the face, my eyes closing not quickly enough to stop them stinging. I fell as silver sparkles erupted in my eyeballs and, as everything faded to black, she leant over me and began to laugh.

CHAPTER TWENTY-NINE

A sharp pain in my right earlobe had me struggling to open my eyes. The dwarf, who must have been sitting on my aching chest and hitting me very hard on the cranium with a pickaxe, was making it extremely difficult. My hearing felt muffled like I had cotton wool stuffed in my ears and I would have killed for a sip of water. Then I remembered Tanith bloody Bloxborough raising her hand and blowing a fine, sparkling dust into my face and it began to make sense of why I felt so awful. I'd been drugged.

Another pinch to my ear and I forced my eyelids to peel themselves from my eyeballs and open a slit. Eyes so dark they appeared to have no pupil stared into mine filling my vision, and for a couple of seconds were all I could see. I had a moment of vertigo and the world gave a lurch. She rocked back on her haunches. Tanith Bloxborough was kneeling astride my legs, her short skirt riding up to show slim, tanned thighs.

'At last. Poor dahling, I thought your heart might not have had the strength,' she said, in a cut-glass accent.

I tried to move, but my arms and legs could have been made with lead. She smiled and reached out with a long, crimson-painted nail to trace it down my exposed jugular to the collar of my shirt, then along the material and down past the open top button to the next. The reflection of gold flickering torches lit her eyes and for a split second it gave the impression of her pupils being fiery vertical slits. I gulped down my fear. I knew this woman was dangerous, but I hadn't realised how evil. It oozed from her, seemingly wrapping itself around my body and gripping me in its tight embrace.

She undid the button with a flick of her finger. Her eyes still on mine. 'You are a very interesting man and I am not quite sure what I should do with you.' Her fingernail tapped the third button and, with another flick, it was open.

I tried to speak. It was impossible. I was paralysed and the realisation caused my fear to escalate, constricting my chest and making it hard to breathe, or was that the drug? Was I to asphyxiate as my organs ceased to function while the paralysis spread throughout my body?

She undid the fourth and fifth button, her fingers moving ever downwards to linger on the material just above my belt.

'I have been told you're also a dangerous man.' Her eyes twinkled in the torchlight. 'I am a dangerous woman, but I think you know that. Perhaps we could both be dangerous together? What a team we would make.'

If I had been able to move, I'm sure I would have shuddered. The feelings she stirred in me were all of primeval dread.

She laughed and slid her hand under my shirt and now-empty holster, resting it on the left side of my chest above my heart. Her palm was warm and soft. She pressed it against my skin, hard enough that my bruised and battered flesh complained, the ache pulsing in time with my heartbeat – or was it hers?

'No, your heart is not weak. You have a strong heart. It beats with a passion.' She laughed. 'Are you a passionate man, Jed? I suspect you are. I suspect you are a very passionate man.'

Her hand slowly moved down my chest, across my stomach and back to my waist. She hooked the tip of her finger through the front of my belt and pulled. The tongue slipped out of the buckle. She pulled it back a little harder, slipping the buckle pin out of the hole holding the belt closed. I gulped as she gripped the metal and tugged, sliding the leather out of the loops around my waistband. Her eyes went back to mine. They glistened darkly in the torchlight as she ran the tip of her tongue along her bottom lip. She chuckled softly and leant back, lifting her hand and drawing my belt with it. With one final tug I felt it pull free from my trousers. With a triumphant laugh she brandished it above me, grasping the leather just below the buckle. It hung there twisting and undulating and, in my head, at least I think it was in my head, it transformed into a snake. Her hand wrapped around its neck just below its head, as it hissed and its forked tongue flicked, tasting the air, its beady black eyes glaring down at me as it opened its mouth wide, showing long, pointed fangs. Then with a snap of her wrist she dropped it to the floor and, as it fell, it became nothing more than a plain, black leather belt, with a chunky brass buckle. I managed a shuddery breath, though my chest felt like it was barely moving at all.

Her hand dropped back to my waistband and she slipped her forefinger beneath the material. 'What have we here?' Her feline smile growing upon seeing my fear. I had no way of hiding it. I was trapped, a spectator of my own fate. I could only watch as she did whatever she wanted to me.

She undid the button to my trousers and pulled out my shirt, opening it. She leant back studying my chest.

'Hmm, nice body for a man of your age.'

She leant forward again, and I heard my zip go as she slowly drew it down. As stupid as it was it crossed my mind how I was glad I had showered and changed my clothes, then I wondered what the hell I was thinking.

I swallowed and it occurred to me that maybe I was regaining some movement. This was belied by my failure to even be able to twitch my fingers.

One of hers found its way below the waistband of my boxers and her eyes went back to mine. 'So, Jed, are you the passionate man I think? Do you fill your wife's nights with lust and ardour?' Her fingers walked their way down my belly, the tips of her nails sharp against my skin, until they found what they were looking for.

I closed my eyes. I couldn't look at her. I didn't want to see her expression as she exerted her power over me, because this was what it was all about, and a hiccup of fear for Emma and Laura made me screw my eyes tight.

Her hand closed about me, squeezing hard enough to make me gasp. 'Such a shame I have no more time. But never fear – we will grow further acquainted. That is a promise.'

347

A thumb and forefinger gripped my chin very tight and her lips crushed against mine, before the tip of her tongue ran across my bottom lip.

'I will see you later,' she whispered.

I caught whiff of something spicy and my head began to spin, at first slow, then faster and faster and faster until I slipped into oblivion.

I came to with a start, my nostrils filled with the pungent, sweet perfume of incense that instantly made me want to puke.

'The old boy's awake,' a youthful male voice said.

The old boy? Little shit.

'Sit him upright.' Oliver, I recognised his voice all right.

I tried opening my eyes as someone manhandled me into a sitting position. They stung like fuck and everything was a misty blur like I was peering through rumpled polythene. I tried to raise a hand to rub my eyes and found they were bound together with a cord, which wouldn't allow me to lift them more than a few inches. My befuddled brain was having trouble working it out until I tried to move my feet and instantly felt an added pressure to my wrists. My ankles were tied and linked to my wrists by the same cord. I supposed I should have been grateful they hadn't hog-tied me. Then it occurred to me – I could move. I could actually move of my own volition.

My eyes were beginning to clear, but my head was aching like it had been used as a football, my hearing was muffled and my stomach churned worse than if I'd been on a week-long bender. I supposed it was hardly surprising. I'd been drugged – twice.

Then I could see and realised how much trouble I was in. Oliver, Tanith and the lad, Sebastien, who Dan had said was slack and then had gone and shot me, were looking down on me. My back was against a stone wall, which was most likely the only thing keeping me upright. The way I felt I would really rather lie down again.

The Boy Wonder had Dan's sawn-off pointed at my chest, his expression a little too eager for my liking. He was itching to pull the trigger and it was in my best interests that he didn't. I wondered where Emma and Laura were – even thinking of Emma in these maniacs' clutches caused an ice-cold band of anxiety to tighten around my heart.

'You really should have taken the hint and gone on home,' Oliver said. 'Now I'm afraid you and your lady wife are going to have to have an unfortunate accident.'

'Why . . .' I tried to say, but my tongue was like a flap of leather in my mouth. I had another go. I knew it was impossible to negotiate with true psychopaths, but I had to give it a try. 'Why are you doing this?'

'It's a long story and far too tedious to tell right now.'

Tanith sidled close to him, wrapping her arm around his waist. Just looking at her made me feel sick. The smile she gave me made me feel dirty. Dirty and somehow lost. 'He is about to die,' she said. 'It's only fair he should know why.'

'We haven't the time,' he said, pulling away from her, allowing me to get a view of where I was being held.

I was still in the chapel and I surmised I must be leaning against the altar. Something I had been unaware of during my time spent with Tanith. I'd literally only had eyes for her. The metallic aroma of fresh blood tainted the air and the whole area was now awash with the light from twenty or so burning torches spread out around the walls closest to the altar.

I felt like shit and if I was to be effective I needed time to clear my head. I needed to keep him talking. 'You killed your own brothers,' I said. 'You killed my friend. I want to know why.'

'Your friend?' he laughed. 'The friend you haven't spoken to for over two decades. You're as bad as him.'

He had me there, but I wasn't about to let him wrong-foot me. 'What do you mean?'

'Simon was a two-faced sneak. I let him leave. We let him leave. I told him it was over, so he'd be free, but he couldn't let it be.' His voice began to rise and his face took on a blotchy, reddened hue. 'He didn't trust his own brother. He didn't trust me.'

'Apparently his instincts were spot on,' I commented.

'You know nothing,' he snarled. Tanith's hand went to her mouth trying to hide a smile. She was laughing at him, enjoying his anger.

'Dahling, don't upset yourself so. They are dead, kaput, gone,' she said. He wrinkled his nose and she stroked his cheek. 'And in a few hours so will she be – the last of the Pomeroys.'

My already delicate stomach was beginning to feel decidedly queasy. They were both monsters. 'What has Laura ever done to you?'

Oliver stared down at me. 'Not a thing,' he said. 'She's paying for the sins of her father.'

'Your son?' I asked.

His lips curled into a bitter smile. 'Martine told him the child was his, but then she had told me it was mine –

350

it turned out that she'd lied to both of us.' He glanced at Sebastien holding the sawn-off and an expression of distaste flickered across his face.

'Go and get ready.'

'What about him?' Sebastien said, pointing the gun at my head.

'He's strung up like a turkey. Go now.' He glanced at Tanith. 'You too.'

'Can I not stay?' she asked with a pout. 'I love your stories.'

He reached out to tip her chin upwards. 'Get ready. I want you at your best tonight.'

The pout disappeared to be replaced by a slow, cat-like smile. My skin crawled. The woman oozed a dark sensuality, and Emma had been right, it was the sort reminiscent of a Black Widow right before she bit her suitor's head right off and, given half the chance, I had the feeling she had her sights set on mine. The pair of them creeped me out; even so, I used the opportunity of their being engrossed in each other to start testing the ropes binding me. From the sounds of it I didn't have much time before the ceremony was due to start.

She pressed her red lips against his cheek. 'Save a bit of him for me,' she murmured, loud enough that I could hear it. She favoured me with a lingering look and blew a kiss before walking behind the altar. Oliver stood watching me in silence until the echo of her high heels disappeared with the creak and clunk of a door opening and closing.

'I have often wondered about you,' he eventually said.

I didn't ask why – I don't think he expected me to.

He crouched down so we were face-to-face. 'Simon told me you were a very special man. A man of many,

many talents. Not only were you dangerous, you also had a gift for sniffing out danger, and on several occasions you saved him and your other friend from making disastrous, possibly life-threatening mistakes. He said it wasn't your only gift.' His eyes stared directly into mine as though trying to read my mind. 'I've come across very few real psychics, most are charlatans out for the money they can screw out of the gullible. Tanith is by far the most talented I have yet to meet out of forty years of searching – until perhaps now.' His eyes narrowed. 'Are you a true psychic, Jed Cummings, or do you just have a sixth sense for danger?' Then he laughed and, clapping his hands on his knees, straightened to loom over me. 'If you truly had a sixth sense you'd have been gone days ago, I'd have thought. Unless of course you're an idiot.'

If he was trying to make me angry he was wasting his time. I was as angry as I could possibly get without him trying to goad me. If my hands had been free they'd have been around his throat and choking the life out of him. There are many ways of killing a man with your bare hands. I know all of them and he would most definitely be a dead man if I had even the slightest opportunity. If I were to save Emma and Laura I would have to make one.

'Tell me, Jed Cummings, what restless spirits have you come across at Kingsmead?'

'I could tell you, but it'd probably take all night.'

He laughed. 'I thought as much. You're a fraud, though a round of applause for taking Simon in. Not many have ever pulled the wool over his eyes.'

'Except you,' I said. 'You apparently managed it very well.'

His good humour palled a tad, his expression growing pained. 'Sadly, not as well as I'd hoped. I'd told him it was over after Edward *died* for the first time. He believed me to begin with. Then, when he left the forces and came back to Kingsmead, he became suspicious. Things soured between us and it was a relief to us both when he went off to London and his new high-powered job. Then, of course, he heard William and his whore of a wife had died and afterwards he wouldn't let it be.

'So the Order of the Blood never ended?'

His lips twitched into a smile. 'Of course not. It was our heritage.' He glanced at his watch. 'As lovely as it is chatting to you, I have things to do and, as you aren't the man I'd been led to believe . . .'

A sharp pain in the back of my neck, as though I was being pinched by an invisible hand, had me jumping in with both feet. 'Your second wife – you never divorced her because you had no need to. It was only when you came up with the scheme of faking your own death that you realised you'd have to change your will, otherwise people would start asking questions when she couldn't be found.'

He stared at me.

'She died in the pool. I suspect it wasn't an accident.'

He opened his mouth to say something, then shut it again.

'Then there's the girl Edward murdered on the night of his birthday party, Suzie.'

'What else?' he asked, trying to hold back his excitement, but failing miserably.

'A maid. She died in the pool too. Another of Edward's indiscretions?'

He laughed out loud. 'No, no, her death wasn't down to him. Well, not directly. She committed suicide.'

'Suicide?'

'Hmm, if anyone was to blame it was William. Martine was to have been the virgin offering the year he ran off with her. Instead another girl had to take her place and Tanith can be very persuasive when the mood takes her. The girl agreed, seduced by the expectation of for ever being special and the 'chosen one', but was too young and naive to understand what it entailed. She never got over it and a few years later she drowned herself. Silly girl, she could have had the best of lives and she threw it all away over the loss of her virginity.'

I listened to him in growing horror. Was he really saying what I thought? My earlier nausea was returning together with the urge to wring his miserable neck.

'What I don't understand is how you know all this?'

I had to force myself to be civil. It was possible I could use what I knew to my advantage by causing a bit of dissention in the ranks – or driving a wedge between him and Tanith. 'The dead talk to me and there are rather a lot of them in this house.'

'But Tanith said . . .' he hesitated, frowning at me.

'What did she say? That there were no spirits here? Kingsmead is full of them,' I paused as though thinking. 'Perhaps they don't want to speak to your lady friend.' I was going to add she frightened them, but this was most likely best kept to myself. It could be better he had doubts she was the psychic he thought. Or she was lying to him.

He studied my face for a very long time. 'Hmm, I'm going to have to have a little think about you. If it weren't for you allegedly being so dangerous, it could be you'd be worth keeping around.'

I kept my expression neutral. If he thought he could use me, I might buy us some time. If not – well – I'd have to make sure I was ready for all eventualities.

'Aren't you worried the police might turn up? They were crawling all over the place earlier.'

He laughed. 'A slight exaggeration, I feel. There are two on guard outside the house,' he glanced at his Rolex, 'and they will be going off duty very shortly. When their replacements arrive they will be offered refreshments by the very capable Mrs Walters and will be out for the count until well after we've finished what we have to do. As for Detective Inspector Brogan – well, let's say he's had orders from on high, which are keeping his time occupied elsewhere.'

The door at the far end of the chapel swung open and Sebastien marched in, sawn-off tucked under his right arm. Long blood-red robes flowed around him, rippling and shining in the lamplight. A sea anemone came to mind; barmy I know, though maybe not. Once this lot got their tentacles into you, I doubt you'd ever escape them.

'Watch him,' Oliver ordered. 'But don't get carried away. I might have a use for him after all.'

The lad's arrogant smile slipped a bit. 'What good would this ald duffer be to us?'

Oliver gave him a disdainful glance. 'With age comes knowledge and experience and, in some cases wisdom, something you could do with a lot more of.'

Sebastien scowled at Oliver and then me. I was hoping Dan had been right about him and he was a little stupid and his arrogance would be his downfall. Unless, of course, he shot me or kicked me senseless first.

'I mean it, Sebastien. Just watch him and keep your distance. I've been told he was once a dangerous man to have as an adversary.'

Sebastien grunted, clearly not impressed.

'Are we clear?' The lad muttered something under his breath, but forced out a 'yes' just the same. Oliver looked down at me. 'I'll be seeing you again shortly. Don't try anything – as you know, the boy can be a little trigger-happy.'

I didn't reply. What was there to say?

With Oliver gone I turned my attention to the itchy-fingered Sebastien. It was a rather grand name for the oik and he wasn't exactly the sort I'd expect to be a member of an elite secret society. He glared down at me with cold blue eyes. I was surprised his full bottom lip wasn't trembling he was so angry, and then it came to me – the photograph of the three young brothers on the day Simon entered the fold, three pairs of the same blue eyes and the same full lips. If I wasn't very much mistaken this boy was one of Oliver's bastards – or maybe Edward's. I was getting the impression my first thoughts on Satanism were correct. It was an excuse for narcissistic people to get their kit off and have group sex when they really should know better.

He gave a sudden huff and stomped off to the right of the altar. I couldn't waste a second. I hauled my feet towards my chest making some slack between my ankles and wrists and patted down my right calf. To my total amazement they hadn't spotted my blade in its sheath.

I couldn't say the same of the one beneath my jacket or in my pocket. Tanith had taken them both before she'd started playing with me.

His footsteps stopped and there was a grating sound as though he was dragging something across the stone slabs. I had to chance I'd have enough time before he returned. I slipped the knife from my ankle sheath. He was getting closer. I had maybe a second or two. I sliced across the lower loop of rope between my ankles, leaving a few strands intact, then flipped the blade so it was facing upwards and did the same to the rope between my wrists. His lengthening shadow and the irritating scrape of wood against stone told me he was almost upon me. I slid the blade inside my sleeve. Just in time.

He shambled into view, struggling to keep the short gun squeezed beneath his arm while dragging a monstrosity of a chair, which could have come straight out of the Dark Ages, judging by its bulk and crudely carved design. He hauled it a few paces more and then dumped it down opposite me. Not too close, but close enough to be stupid. I leant back against the altar, biding my time.

He slumped into the chair, the sawn-off resting across his lap, his forearms draped along the arms of the chair. His robes had hitched up his legs showing pallid, hairy ankles and fleshy calves. At the V at the neck of his robe I caught a glimpse of a white pimply chest. He was naked beneath the crimson silk and knowing this did nothing for my temper or my anxiety. If one of them touched Emma or Laura I would cut off their bollocks.

He began to fidget. I wasn't surprised, the dark wood of the chair looked hard and uncomfortable. He shifted the sawn-off so it was resting flat across his thighs and wriggled a bit in his seat. It clearly didn't do the trick. After a couple of minutes he laid the gun on the ground by his side and got to his feet, pulling his robe down and wrapping it tight around his back with all the excess material at the front and sank into the seat again. I had hoped he'd get so bored he'd nod off, but from his performance so far, I doubted very much this was about to happen – though the sawn-off was still on the ground. I had a split second to think about it and I knew if I was to make a move it would have to be now.

I tensed my muscles in my biceps and calves and strained against the partially cut strands of the ropes binding me. They snapped immediately and I jumped to my feet and threw myself towards him in one fluid movement. My joints cried out in pain, but I couldn't afford to listen. He made a grab for the gun, but too late, much too late.

I let the knife slide down my sleeve and into my hand and went straight for his jugular. I didn't have a choice, his fingers were scrabbling for the butt of the sawn-off and I had two other lives to worry about, lives that meant more to me than his. As the blade sliced through his flesh his eyes opened wide in disbelief, any thought of grabbing the shotgun gone. His hands flew to the gaping hole in his neck as he tried to staunch the flow of his life's blood spouting in a claret stream from his throat. I pressed him back tight against the chair until the light died in his eyes, his head flopped forward onto my shoulder and his hands fell to hang limply at his sides.

When I was sure he was gone I levered myself off him, wiped my blade clean on his robe, and scooped the shotgun from the ground. Blades were good, but not much of an incentive for twelve or so maniacs to back off should the need arise. I put the knife back in its sheath. It could still be of use to me yet.

I glanced at my watch. It read a quarter to eleven and I guessed I was almost out of time.

CHAPTER THIRTY

I still had no idea where Emma or Laura were, or even if Emma was still alive. I fought back the wave of despair threatening to overwhelm me. The man I'd once been had faced worse, had fought back from worse. *He* could do this. *He* still had a chance, though there was now no likelihood of negotiation. I had killed a man who could possibly be Oliver's son and he was unlikely to forgive it.

Then who's to say what his reaction would be? He'd already arranged the deaths of his two brothers, his legitimate son and daughter-in-law and, of course, his second wife. I shivered. Who could tell what the madman would do? One thing was for sure – being a member of the Pomeroy family certainly wasn't conducive to living a long and happy life.

I left by the door Tanith had used at the front of the chapel. Had I not known it was there I wouldn't have found it. It was identical to the one at the back of the chamber, but it was hidden by the silken drapes covering the wall behind the altar.

The door opened into a darkened corridor that smelt of damp earth and mould. As it didn't very much matter whether I hid my tracks or not, I left the door behind me ajar and holding back the curtain, giving enough light to guide me to a flight of steps and a heavy wooden door that opened with the flip of an iron latch.

I stepped outside to the warmer aroma of hay and horse manure. I was in one of the stalls in the stable block, the last, empty one next to Satan's.

Creeping to the back door I opened it a crack and peered outside into the dark. One lone torch was bobbing along the track towards me at speed, leaving a comet trail of light behind it. Squinting through the darkness surrounding the stables I tried to focus on what was beneath the light. One torch didn't necessarily mean one man or woman. If Oliver was being cautious, he would send two to escort me to wherever he wanted me to be, with Sebastien following along behind with the shotgun pointed at my back.

Oliver was an arrogant dick. He had sent only one. Though it could be he had already made up his mind to dispatch me down in the chapel. Too late for that. The man was getting close now. I pulled the door closed and, laying the shotgun on the ground, took the blade from its ankle sheath, pressed my back close against the wall and waited.

The seconds ticked by and time appeared to slow. A bead of sweat tickled my back as it trickled down my spine. My heart sounded very loud in the quiet. Then, from outside, the slap of leather sandals on dirt. I grasped the knife in my fist, the blade pointing outward above my thumb ready to make a slicing motion.

The door yanked open and the man stepped inside, slowing very slightly. I silently moved in for the kill, my hand grabbing him around the forehead and pulling his head back as the blade found the soft flesh below his left ear. He didn't have time to struggle. With one slicing motion, followed by a gasp, a gurgle and a spray of blood, he slid to the floor and with a twitch or two was gone. I stooped down to wipe the knife clean on his robe and close his eyes. I thought I recognised the man, but . . . Then I remembered, he was one of the gardeners. I had seen him on the large motor mower driving back and forth cutting the lawns.

Were all the staff in on this? It appeared that perhaps they were.

I thought about dragging his body into one of the empty stalls, but there wasn't much point, by the end of the night either I'd be dead or they would. My odds of surviving until morning had improved, but by my estimation there were at least nine of them to deal with, possibly more. Mrs Walters and the young maids would most likely fold if I took out Oliver, as for the others – well, I was pretty sure Tanith would be as dangerous as any of the men, probably more so.

It was time to call the police. I didn't have a mobile any more and it would take too long to return to the house, but I was pretty sure I'd seen a phone on the wall by the entrance to the stables.

I replaced my knife in its sheath and hurried back to where I thought I'd seen a phone. It was right where I'd expected, but my relief was short-lived. The line was dead and I suspected I'd probably find the extensions inside the house would be the same. Oliver wasn't going to chance me calling for backup. I was on my own.

Returning to the back entrance, I picked up the still-burning torch and walked out of the stables and into the night – alone.

Once I was close enough for the light filtering through the trees to be sufficient to let me vaguely see my surroundings, I stubbed out the torch and carried on with only their hellish flames to guide me.

Last time there had been guards loitering amongst the trees around the periphery of the clearing. I wasn't about to make the same mistake again. I circled Oliver's play area a few yards out. If there were any guards, I couldn't see them. I moved in closer. The fires were spread out in the same configuration as before, the red and golden flames leaping and flaring unnaturally high. I was just in time to see Oliver lift a sickle-shaped blade high above his head and it swung down to a moan of delight from his followers and an eruption of blood. For a moment I couldn't breathe, then the figure who had been blocking my view moved aside to hold up a goblet dripping with the stuff. I sucked in breath. Oliver had decapitated a young goat.

His lips red and moist in the firelight, his upper face hidden by a black leather mask, Oliver took the goblet from his acolyte, handing over the sickle. A murmur of something close to rapture rippled around the congregation as he dipped his fingers into the vessel and then flicked the contents onto their glowing, upturned faces to almost orgasmic moans. I crept forward as far as I dared, and there, kneeling right at the front, were the two people I was searching for; Emma and Laura. As the blood rained down, Laura's lips twisted in disgust and she turned her head away, Emma stared straight ahead, unmoving and stony-faced, the liquid speckling her skin and staining it red.

There was a roar from the gathering and Oliver passed the empty goblet to his accomplice, who from her height, build and brazenly red lips I guessed to be the loathsome Tanith. I hoped there was a special place in hell for the pair of them, though I suspected this was what they were hoping too.

Oliver held a hand aloft and the congregation quietened. 'We are gathered here to celebrate the fertility rites of the beginning of May as our forebears did before us.' He paused and lowered his hand stretching out towards Emma and Laura. 'As you see, we have two guests and it very much depends on the actions of a third as to whether we have two more blood sacrifices this night or only one.' He opened his arms wide as if in welcome. 'So, Jed Cummings, will the blood of your lady wife be spilt or will you step inside the circle from out of the darkness?'

Tanith held the blood-smeared sickle above her head and stalked across the circle to stand behind Emma, roughly grabbing a handful of her hair to jerk her head back, exposing her bare throat.

'The choice is yours, Jed. Show yourself or your wife dies.'

Tanith was smiling, her red lips as curved as the blade hovering so close to Emma's neck. I didn't have any doubt she'd do it. I could see it in the way she stood and how she ran the pointed tip of her tongue along her lips as though she couldn't wait to taste Emma's blood. I laid the shotgun on the ground where I could find it later, should I need to, and walked into the clearing.

Oliver laughed as he beckoned Tanith to return to his side. 'I would have been disappointed had you not escaped,' he said. 'When I didn't get a call from Sebastien upon Reynard's arrival I knew you had probably done away with one, if not both, of them. I'm assuming they're both dead,' he said, his eyes on my chest. I glanced down. My shirt and jacket were dark with blood.

I didn't reply. 'Are you both OK?' I asked Emma and Laura.

Emma nodded with a half-smile. Laura's was more of a haughty grimace. Laura was definitely cut from the same cloth as Emma.

'Time for some fun, I think,' Oliver said. 'As Simon rated you so much, we're going to have a little contest.'

Tanith touched his sleeve. 'Are you sure, dahling?'

Oliver's smile turned into a snarl. 'Simon had more respect for him than he ever had for me. I'm going to prove him wrong.'

She wrapped one arm around him and, looking me up and down, tapped her bottom lip with her forefinger as if in thought. 'It would be nice to have some fun.'

'My thoughts exactly,' he said and, hugging her to him, he gave me a supercilious smirk. 'Here's the rules. I will give you a ten-minute start. If you make it off the estate without being caught by my friends here, I'll set your good lady wife free and you and I will have a little talk about *your* future; if not, she joins the lovely Laura on her journey into the hereafter and, I can tell you now, it will be quite a journey.'

There were shouts of approval from some of the other partygoers, but I noticed there were more who remained silent.

'If I escape, you set Emma and Laura free,' I said.

He snorted. 'I'm the one making the rules.'

'So you have some doubt your crazy gang can catch me without getting themselves killed.'

There was a murmur from within the ranks.

'You're not as young and fit as you used to be,' Oliver sneered. 'Like Simon, you're past your prime – an old man.'

'And yet *you're* not willing to wager Laura's life on a race between me and *them*?' The murmur turned into an angry grumble. There were only four or five who were really up for this, though I didn't doubt the others would join in if they had to. 'Sounds like a lack of confidence to me.'

I kept my hands hanging loose by my sides trying to appear relaxed. Inside my gut was churning.

'He'll never make it, dahling. Let him think he has a chance and then you can make him watch while we have some fun before I cut their throats.'

He fondled her breast through the silken robe as he stared at me, his lips tugging upwards. They were a seriously vile pair of monsters and, if nothing else, it made me all the more determined to beat them at their own sick game.

'All right, then. It's decided. You get ten minutes before I set my hellhounds upon you.' Some of the congregation began to bark and snarl as if rabid dogs. 'If you don't make it off the grounds, or should I say, *when* you don't make it off the grounds, the two ladies die.'

'And what about Mr Cummings?' Tanith asked.

He laughed. 'You, my dear, can have him to play

with for a few days, before he follows his wife into the underworld. I'm sure you can make his mental anguish dull into insignificance with your inventive talents.'

I forced myself not to shudder. I looked away. I didn't want to see her lascivious expression. The thought of spending one single moment alone with the loathsome woman was enough to raise gooseflesh on my arms.

My eyes met Emma's. She mouthed 'I love you' and I smiled at her, hoping that it wouldn't be for the last time and that she recognised my love for her in that smile. I think she did, then her lips formed the words 'good luck'. I was going to need it, but she didn't need to know it.

'Right,' Oliver said, lifting his arm so his robe flopped back to reveal a very expensive Rolex. It was totally incongruous on his naked arm and I almost laughed. The man was a total tool and mad to boot. If he was ever brought to justice, he would most likely end his days in the same psych ward where his brother had languished for all those years. 'You have ten minutes from . . . now.'

I swung around to leave the clearing the same way as I'd come in and jogged the first few steps. Oliver's cronies' chants of, 'Run piggy, run piggy, run, run, run,' ringing in my ears.

I stooped down to grab the sawn-off and then I did run. In my head a voice was screaming 'Too slow, too slow!', but I wasn't about to give up yet.

I abruptly changed direction so I was going away from the manor. I had to hope Oliver would assume I was travelling towards the house, where I had my car and possibly weapons. I had counted twelve of them including Oliver and Tanith. He would have to leave someone with Emma and Laura. One at least, so there would be ten or possibly eleven coming after me. Not many people to cover such a huge estate. Which made me wonder – why was he so confident his people would find me?

It didn't take me too long to work it out. Moving away from the fires in the clearing it was so dark I could hardly see a thing and to go too quickly was to risk putting out an eye. Not that speed was a possibility. Brambles and other vegetation clung to my clothing and tore at my skin as I forced my way through the trees.

I was beginning to despair. I must have used at least five minutes and was going nowhere fast. I took a moment to peer about me. I could still hear them chanting. I was too close, much too close. Hot fuck, I wasn't about to give up now. I took a deep breath and soft fingers traced their way across my brow followed by whispers in my head. I looked around again and glimpsed a wispy shape moving away from me, weaving in and out of the trees. I started towards it.

There was no rhyme or reason I could explain. I knew instinctively whatever it was it was there to help and, after a few steps, I could feel the difference under my feet, I had found a path.

From behind us I heard a roar. My time had just run out.

CHAPTER THIRTY-ONE

I ran along the path to the sound of whooping and jeering. I hoped it wasn't going to end the same way as it had for Edward, surrounded by a baying mob of men and women who were not much better than rabid animals.

No, I was damned if it was going to end that way. I slowed and moved off to the side of the path and waited. And as I waited I had time to think. Why disrupt his festival to hunt me? He wouldn't – not for long. He wanted me out of the way, but not dead – yet. I would wait it out. Someone would either come this way or not. If not, I would remain hidden until it all went quiet and wind my way back to the chapel. If they did – well – the hunted was just about to become the hunter.

They were still making a racket, but from the sounds of their calls I guessed they had fanned out. I noticed it was only men's voices I could hear. Tanith aside, I guessed murder and rape were mainly male-dominated pastimes.

I crouched down beside a tree and behind some vegetation, listening out for the slightest sound. Minutes ticked by. The shouting was coming mainly from the right of me and far enough away not to be worrying. Then a cold palm cupped the back of my head. Danger was apparently closing in on me. It was the snap of an ill-placed foot upon a twig that gave him away. He was coming from behind me.

Very carefully I swivelled around. I caught a glimpse of movement in the darkness. I kept my head well down hiding behind a bush. He stopped, his head turning from side to side. I strained my eyes to see. Something moved in the crowns of the trees above us making the leaves rustle and shake and his head jerked upwards. In the little light filtering down through the spreading leaves there was a glint of glass. He was wearing glasses of some description – perhaps safety glasses.

I considered how I was going to deal with him. Whatever I did it would have to be quiet. I couldn't take the chance of him crying out. The old me made the decision. Bodies were piling up and mine wasn't going to be one of them. I laid the shotgun on the ground beside me and reached for my knife.

He took a couple more steps until he was right beside me and stopped. One more step – just take one more step. He stood there and once again his head moved from side to side, but he was looking straight ahead not down. I prayed it'd stay that way and he'd take one more stride. I began to ease onto the balls of my feet getting ready to make my move and, as he took the one extra pace I needed, a shrill trill filled the air. I froze, holding back a surprised gasp, and a mobile appeared in his hand lighting up his face.

'Shit, fuck and damn it,' he muttered, his other hand wrenching the goggles onto his brow.

Goggles; he was wearing night-vision goggles. No wonder Oliver was so confident they would find me, some of his rabid dogs had the advantage of being able to see in the dark.

He rubbed at his eyes, half-blinded by the glare from his phone. 'Shit,' he said again before stabbing his finger onto the screen and pressing it against his ear. 'What?' he said with a disgruntled bark, then another indistinct voice at the other end of the phone. 'Nah. Seen hide nor hair.' He listened again. 'Huh, if that's what he wants. Twenty minutes it is.'

He jabbed his finger at the screen and, swearing under his breath, the light went out. I rose out of the dark behind him. Plastering my hand across his mouth I pulled his head back and, with a swift left to right motion, slit his throat. He struggled for a brief moment, then his hands clutched at his neck trying to stem the torrent of blood as the realisation hit him that he was bleeding out. I held him tight, my hand still over his mouth until he sagged against me and stilled. I slowly lowered him to the ground. Three nil to me.

I took the goggles from him, put them on and the world about me came alive. This was more like it. I hefted the shotgun under my arm. I had work to do and, if I was reading the situation right, I had twenty minutes to do it. Twenty minutes before they all headed back. I took a few seconds to check his pockets. There was nothing of any

371

use to me; a small ceremonial dagger and his leather mask was all.

I took one last look at him. His face looked like a bleached mask through the goggles, even so he seemed familiar. As I moved away, I wracked my brains as to who he might be. He wasn't a member of staff, that was for sure. It would no doubt come to me. For the meantime, I had more important things to worry about.

I scooted away from the track and into the forest, the goggles allowing me to see the trees and vegetation in stark black and white. I'd used this sort of equipment several times before and it didn't take long for me to slip back thirty-odd years.

Some of the people searching for me were easy to see, they had torches – mainly of the flaming variety – but several did have flashlights and if I were to get close to them I'd have to be careful, the beam of a light in the eyes when wearing night-vision goggles was not a pleasant experience as my dead friend bore witness. And it was then that it came to me – the hospital – he had been at the hospital. The orderly in Simon's ward, handing out the water jugs. What the f—? Were Oliver's people everywhere?

Shaken, I followed his rabid rabble at a distance. They had stopped their constant gung-ho calling and jeering, though I still heard the occasional shout between them and after a while the majority of them began heading towards the clearing. This was good as they had their backs to me as I stalked along behind them.

I was close enough that I could see the torches bobbing about amongst the trees as they gradually drifted towards each other until most of them converged into a line winding through the woodland.

'Listen up,' I heard a voice shout. 'We're to go straight to the chapel.'

A few stragglers moved in behind the others. As I grew closer, I could hear them grumbling as they'd missed out on their fun.

I dodged from tree to tree keeping an eye out for anyone who might have got around behind me, but to my back there were only trees. If they were heading for the chapel, I had a little longer before they were out in the open. I would have to make my move before then. I closed in on the last couple of stragglers. The one at the back was a big lumbering lump of a man. Big and beefy and the sort I'd rather was out of the way now and certainly before I followed them into the chapel.

I dropped down to take the knife from my ankle sheath and, at exactly the same moment, the guy a few yards ahead of him swung around. I froze, shielding my eyes with my hand.

'For fuck's sake, Gideon, get a move on. If you don't, you'll miss out on all the fun.'

'Huh, he said he wasn't going to kill them if y'ald man got away,' the man I assumed to be Gideon said in a voice as slow and lumbering as his gait.

'Who said anything about killing 'em? Though I suppose he will, but not until we've all had some fun,' and he made a lewd gesture with his fist in front of his groin.

My hand tightened around the hilt of my blade.

Gideon laughed. 'Now that's the kinda fun I like.'

The other man turned away to stride ahead.

'I'll catch you later,' Gideon called after him. 'I need a piss.'

The other man flipped a hand in reply and disappeared into the trees along with the glow from his torch.

Gideon stopped and lifted his robe to face a tree. I dropped the blade into my pocket, I couldn't risk him making a sound, and covered the yard or so between us as he shook himself off. I grabbed him from behind, one hand on his shoulder, the other cupping his head and with one quick, sharp jerk it was done and he sunk silently to the ground. I had raised my odds of succeeding by another few per cent. I briefly thought of ridding him of his robe and discarded it almost immediately – I hadn't the time, or the inclination. Even the idea of wearing the red robe made me feel sick.

I hurried along, weaving through the trees to catch the other man. I needed to get to him before he joined the others or realised his mate had gone missing. He was moving at a fair old lick, his torch leaving a blazing trail in the dark behind him. He and the others had bypassed the clearing and would soon be leaving the cover of the forest for the fields beyond and the track that ran alongside them to the stables. I gained speed. One more down now would be one less to worry about later.

There was a flash of light and movement directly in front of me. He was definitely in a hurry and I tried not to think about why he should be so eager to get back to Kingsmead. I was hindered by the need for stealth, but the trees ahead were thinning and I had minutes before he broke out into open countryside. I strode after him. He swerved slightly. I followed. Damn it, the trees were opening up. I pulled the blade from my pocket.

He abruptly stopped. Began to turn. I lifted the goggles and drew back my arm.

'Gideon . . .' He saw me. His eyes grew wide, his mouth opened to shout and I threw the knife. It hit him in the left side of his chest, right where his black heart should be. He gasped, looking down in incomprehension as his legs folded beneath him and he fell to the ground with a dull thud.

I waited one second. No one had seen, no one had heard. Hurrying over I dropped down beside him to retrieve my knife and wipe it on his robe. His eyes were still open and I hesitated, wondering who was behind the mask. I decided to leave it be, I didn't need to know who else Oliver and Tanith had corrupted. Inexplicably I thought of the young, floppy-haired youth who had helped with our cases on the first day we'd arrived. I hoped he wasn't one of the people who would die tonight. He had only been about sixteen or seventeen. The same age as Simon had been when he had joined the Order of the Blood, I reminded myself.

I climbed to my feet. I couldn't start feeling sorry for these people. They had Emma and Laura and would do terrible things to them if I didn't do equally terrible things first. No, there was a difference: I wouldn't enjoy doing what I had to do to save my wife and friend. I would do it because they gave me no choice. I wondered whether a court of law would see it differently and realised I didn't care. If I saved Emma and Laura they could put me away for ever as long as they were safe. As long as Emma was safe.

Waiting inside the edge of the forest I watched until

375

the line of torches had started down the track towards the house, before pocketing the goggles and following on behind at a distance. Out at the clearing I'd had room to manoeuvre, inside the chapel was going to be – difficult. I was beginning to regret my decision not to strip Gideon of his robe. It had been a clean kill. His mate's hadn't. I couldn't see any way around it. I needed a robe and the only way of getting one would be to risk taking out another of them before they reached the chapel. Difficult when they were in a fairly close group.

I needed to get closer. I had to be close enough that if an opportunity presented itself I'd be ready and waiting. I veered off the track at the next gap in the hedgerow and ran along in a low crouch keeping as close to the shrubbery as I could until I was next to the last stragglers, and again I wished I hadn't been so squeamish about taking Gideon's robe. I was a big bloke. He had been a big bloke. The last one or two in the line of people returning to the house were too short. Their robes would hang only halfway down my calves, giving me away immediately.

Then it came to me. I assumed they would enter the chapel via the stables, the closest entrance, taking them in right at the front by the altar. I would carry on across the back of the building and enter from the poolroom, where it was darker. It wasn't the best of plans, but it was all I had. I had to hope by the time I reached the poolroom I'd have come up with something better.

Crouching down by the hedge, I waited until they'd filed into the stable block, then, slipping the goggles back on, started to run. A light flared and I stopped dead as a man wandered into view, his hand cupping his lighter as he lit a cigarette. Judging by his clothing, white shirt and black or navy tie beneath a dark-coloured military-style jumper, I guessed he was one of the security personnel. The tip of his cigarette glowed white through the goggles. He pocketed the lighter and, leaning against the wall, pulled out his mobile. I waited until he was engrossed in scrolling down his messages, then, keeping to the lawn, ran past the courtyard and to the west wing and the poolroom. I'd have to hope the door was open. If not, I'd be adding breaking and entering to my list of crimes for the evening.

The rear of the house was in darkness. Even so the back of my head grew cold and all my senses screamed danger. I scanned the building, the night-vision goggles cutting through the dark so well I could clearly make out the poolside furniture through the glass of the bi-fold doors of the poolroom. My head was icy and my neck prickled like I had bad sunburn. I was more than conscious that out here in the open there was a fair chance of me being spotted should anyone look out across the lawns.

I hurried towards the edge of the patio keeping low and the closer I got to the poolroom the louder my senses screamed. I stopped to once more scan the building. The patio was empty apart from a round table and a set of matching chairs. The umbrella was down. Beyond it were two sunloungers, one with its back to me, the other . . . I peered through the gloom. A thin trail of smoke rose up above the first lounger. I started around the edge of the patio, trying to get a better view, and I saw movement. Someone inside the poolroom.

I ducked down as a door swung open and a robed figure leant outside.

'Come on, for fuck's sake,' a voice called. 'We're gonna be late.'

'All right, all right, keep your hair on. I'll only be a second.'

'You'd better be, the old man's proper riled,' and the figure disappeared inside.

I pushed the goggles onto my brow and let my eyes adjust. The silhouette of a large, hulking figure rose up from the sunbed and he wasn't exactly hurrying. The end of his cigarette glowed dark red as he took one last, long drag before he flicked it away over the edge of the patio and onto the grass. If I had my way it would be his last cigarette. This would be my only chance. I put the goggles in my pocket and waited until he started towards the poolroom door and I was on the move. I didn't have time to be stealthy. I had mere moments and whatever I did it had to be clean. No knife to the throat or through the chest for this guy.

I was as quiet as I could be considering I was running, but the thud of my feet in the near silence gave me away. He spun around before I could reach him. His hood was down, his mask was up across his brow and, instead of looking shocked or surprised, he smiled and instantly sprung onto the balls of his feet bringing his arms up in a fighter's stance. Of all the bloody luck, the man was trained in self-defence.

He should have called out, but he didn't. He wanted this. He wanted some action. He'd probably been one of the men who'd been told to escort Emma and Laura to the house and felt like he'd missed out on the fun of chasing me. I thought I recognised him – maybe I did, but from where escaped me.

'Well, well, well,' he said with a sneer. 'They didn't manage to catch you, after all.' He turned his head and spat on the ground. 'It won't make a tuppence worth of difference. We're still gonna shag your old lady and the other bitch, then cut them some before they die.'

He was trying to goad me into doing something stupid. He was an idiot. A man with something to lose is a dangerous man and, contrary to common belief, a man with a temper on him doesn't always make stupid mistakes because of it. Sometimes it makes him almost unstoppable because he becomes driven with no care for his own personal safety.

He shouldn't have alluded to Emma and what they might do to her. I saw him grinning at me through a red mist. If it wasn't for the fact I needed it to be a clean kill he would have died in a red mist of his own. As it was, all I wanted to do was get my hands around his throat and choke the life out of him.

'Come on then, old man. Come and get me.' He bounced on his feet, weaving from side to side. I wasn't sure who he was putting the show on for. There was only him and me. I took a step back. 'Scared, are yer?'

A cloud crossed the moon and I could no longer make out his features. I didn't need to. I could see where his head was. I feigned left, he took a swing at me and I caught his right arm at the wrist and above the elbow and yanked it downwards and across my rising knee. I heard his ulna snap and he let out a squeal, which was abruptly cut off as I grabbed either side of his head and twisted. With a sickening crack he immediately went limp and it was over before it had really begun. As I lowered him to the ground it occurred to me from where I'd recognised him and if I could have killed him again I would've. Last time I'd seen him he'd been standing at the side of the road being showered with pebbles and dust by an irate horsebox owner, having held me up for the vital twenty minutes that could've saved Simon's life.

He was naked beneath the robe. I left him lying beside one of the loungers where he wouldn't immediately be seen. I didn't have time to hide him away somewhere. If everything went the way I hoped it wouldn't matter and if it didn't . . . the same applied.

The robe reached my ankles. I rolled my trousers to my calves and took off my shoes and socks, exchanging them for his sandals. They were a tad big, but easily tightened by moving the buckle in a hole or two. I put on his mask and pulled the hood of the robe up over my head so, from a distance, I shouldn't be identifiable as not being him.

Carrying the sawn-off was problematic. I would have to leave it somewhere in the chapel where I could get to it should I have to. Not ideal, but the best I could do. I still had one blade and I slipped it into a deep pocket I found within the robe, to join his lighter, cigarettes and what felt like another smaller dagger. I was ready.

I hurried into the poolroom and across to the bar where the open trapdoor waited for the dead man to follow his mate and descended into the gloom to be surrounded by the otherworldly echoes of chanting filling the corridor. The ceremony had started. Chest tight and heart thumping I opened the final door and stepped through into the chapel.

CHAPTER THIRTY-TWO

The number of the congregation had inexplicably grown to twenty or more. They were gathered at the altar, illuminated by only torches and two flaming fires in wrought iron braziers, their dancing shadows appearing demonic in the flickering red light.

Fighting back despair, I lay the shotgun on one of the pews at the back, pulled the hood forward as far as it would go and padded forward, gripping my toes against the sandals to stop them slapping against the stone floor and announcing my arrival.

I slipped in line with the other masked figures. My attention went straight to Emma. She and Laura knelt, with hands tied, at either end of the now-empty altar. Someone had obviously seen fit to remove Peters' body before the festivities were to begin. Both were dishevelled and there was a dark smear across Emma's right cheek, as if I needed another reason to end Oliver's pathetic life. I breathed in deeply, it was me against a room full of fanatics and I hadn't the faintest idea how I was going to get Emma and Laura out of this goddamned, awful mess.

Oliver abruptly lifted his arms into the air and the chanting immediately stopped. 'Brethren, we gather this day to give sacrifice in worship of our dark lord and to right a wrong,' he said, to shouts of yes from a few of the assembly. He lowered his hands and gestured towards Laura. 'Today this woman will pay for the sins of her father and mother. This day her life's blood will be offered as recompense for a life lost.'

Two men stepped forward and dragged Laura to her feet. Emma struggled to get up too, but two other figures grabbed her, holding her back.

'Step forward she who has been sinned against and state your right to retribution.'

'I state my claim,' a voice I thought I recognised said. A figure stepped forward, pulling down her hood and removing her mask.

For a moment I was dumbfounded.

'Mrs Walters?' Laura said, staring at the woman in disbelief.

'Silence, whore,' Tanith shouted.

I edged a little closer to the altar.

'My daughter, Lily, took the place of Martine Pomeroy at festival and that day her spirit died. Retribution is my right,' Mrs Walters said.

Laura and Emma exchanged a bemused look. It wasn't what I'd been expecting either.

'And as your daughter suffered so shall the daughter of Martine,' Tanith shouted, raising her arms above her head, to yells of approval from some of the gathering.

'No,' Mrs Walters said, her voice quiet but firm.

The shouting stuttered and stopped to be replaced by an uncomfortable silence.

Tanith's head jerked around. 'What say you, sister?' she said, glaring at the housekeeper.

'I said no,' Mrs Walters said. 'I claim a life, nothing more.'

'No,' Tanith practically screamed. 'She has to suffer.'

'Tanith,' Oliver said, resting a hand on her shoulder. 'Our sister has made her choice as is her right.' Tanith shrugged away from him, her lips turning down into a petulant pout.

Ignoring her, Oliver reached towards Mrs Walters and handed her a dagger. The lethally honed blade shone red, reflecting the light from the flaming braziers, appearing as if already daubed in blood.

'Position her,' Oliver said to the two men holding Laura, and the crowd began to chant once more in what sounded like Latin.

Realising what the men were about to do, Laura began to struggle as they manhandled her onto the altar and tied her ankles and wrists to the iron rings at each corner of the stone slab. Emma fought against the men holding her, kicking and biting, trying to get to our friend.

'Stop it,' Tanith screamed at her and backhanded Emma across the mouth. I slipped my hand into my pocket, gripping the hilt of my blade, and began to edge my way through the throng towards the altar. How I was going to take on so many of them I had no idea, but I couldn't stand there and watch Laura and the woman I loved be slaughtered. Emma wasn't about to be stilled either, if it

384

hadn't been for the two men hauling her back she would have had Tanith's eyes.

Mrs Walters walked to one side, for a moment the blade disappeared within her robe, then she was raising the sacrificial knife high above her head. It looked different – smeared. It didn't glint and shine as it once had. She glanced down at Laura, then turned to Oliver and Tanith. 'With this blade I spill the blood of those who have wronged me,' she cried out. 'With this blade I bring an end to my pain!'

No time for subtlety, I started to really move, pushing my way through the crowd blocking my way, my head pounding in time with the rising crescendo of feet stamping and hands clapping in unison with the chanting. I didn't understand the language, but I recognised some of the names. They were calling upon Lucifer and his legion of demons. Then the chanting abruptly stopped and Mrs Walters shouted. 'This is for Lily!'

I'd left it too late. I threw myself towards the housekeeper and it was almost as though time had slowed. Mrs Walters' arm swung across her body and sliced downwards and away from the altar towards Tanith. There was a gasp from the congregation as Oliver grabbed his mistress's shoulder, yanking her backwards, but not fast enough. The blade sliced through her crimson robe and into her forearm. She staggered and, if it hadn't been for Oliver holding her, would have fallen.

'Tanith. Tanith, my dear, are you all right?' Oliver said, wrapping his arm around her waist.

'Of course I'm not, you idiot,' she screamed, shaking him off and gripping hold of her arm. Blood welled between her fingers and ran down the inside of her robe to drip onto the stone slabs in a steady patter. 'The old hag stabbed me.'

Mrs Walters smiled and almost casually raised the knife to her own throat and sliced. With blood gushing from the wound she was still smiling as her eyes closed and she sunk to the ground.

'What the fuck?' I heard someone say.

I was roughly pushed aside as someone barged past me. Pulling off his mask Donald Walters dropped to his knees beside his wife and took her lifeless hand in his.

'Why?' Oliver asked, staring down at the distraught man. 'Why would she attack Tanith?'

Walters traced his knuckles down his wife's cheek and when he looked up his pain was palpable – and his anger.

'Why do you think, Oliver? Why the hell do you think? Are you such a fucking moron you don't know?' He looked Oliver up and down and his lips curled into a sneer. 'Of course you are, you self-absorbed prick!'

There were gasps from the remaining congregation and one or two gruff grunts, possibly of agreement.

Oliver wrenched off his own mask. 'What? You dare . . .'

'Don't,' Walters said, rising to his feet. 'Don't *you* dare. Don't you dare say another word.'

'Idiots!' Tanith shrieked and I swear she stamped her foot. 'You and your stupid wife are both idiots. He's coming! Can't you feel it? Can't you feel his presence? He's coming and you . . .' She swayed slightly, her expression becoming puzzled as her legs gave way beneath her.

'Tanith?' Oliver grabbed for her.

The woman slumped against him as though losing her strength. She feebly raised a hand to her face and it came away red. 'Ollie?' she gasped, a look of incomprehension passing across her face, as blood rained in streams from her nose and tears of crimson slipped down her cheeks. 'Ollie?' she repeated and more blood seeped from between her lips. Her body stiffened as she convulsed once, and then again, arching against her lover, her spine bent into an impossibly tight curve, before flopping back in his arms, eyes wide and staring into the beyond.

'Tanith?' he whispered, confusion clouding his face. 'Tanith?' He clutched her to his chest, his bewilderment changing to anger, as he turned his head to glare down at the dead housekeeper. 'She poisoned her. The bitch poisoned Tanith.'

I glanced around me. The atmosphere in the chamber had shifted, the rabid pack was no more and a strange, confused tension radiated from the onlookers. It was like we were all balanced on the edge of a precipice.

Oliver gently lowered Tanith to the ground then stood to face his followers. 'The ceremony must be completed,' he said. 'It's what she would have wanted.'

'Are you mad?' Donald said. 'Isn't it time to end this once and for all? Edward's gone. Tanith's gone.'

An uneasy silence filled the chapel.

'Fool,' Oliver snarled and, turning his back on the groundskeeper, raised his hands into the air and threw back his head.

When he spoke again it sounded as though he was praying, but if he was it wasn't to God. Again I recognised several names, all of them unholy, those of the fallen angels. Belial, Beelzebub and Satan amongst many more. Several members of the congregation began to join in until once again the chapel rang with their voices.

I edged a little closer to the altar. I didn't need my sixth sense to tell me that we were in danger. The atmosphere tingled with anticipation. I had a very bad feeling about this.

Behind Oliver the air began to shimmer and with gasps from the gathering they as one surged past Laura, as she struggled upon the altar, towards the quivering and swirling mist rising behind her. They had given me my chance. Knife in hand, I hurried forward. Whether Emma could see the apparition too I wasn't sure, but she had clambered to her feet while her captors were otherwise occupied and was pulling at one of the ropes tying Laura to the iron rings. As I reached her there was a tremendous crash from the back of the chapel.

'On your knees! Hands on your heads,' someone yelled, and a stream of armed men poured in through the door, spreading throughout the chamber. Dressed in black body armour and full-face helmets with blacked-out visors, they had the appearance of alien invaders and I had a second of confusion when I wasn't sure of whom I should be the most scared: the red-robed Satanists or these unknown intruders with guns.

Then my feeling of disorientation cleared as I grasped who they were – Simon's men. I threw back my hood and tore off the mask. If I were to die, I would rather it wasn't by a gunshot from people supposedly meant to be saving us.

'Emma,' I said, and she swung around to face me.

'Jed, thank God,' she said, a relieved smile brightening her face.

I wanted to pull her into my arms and never let her go, but it would have to wait. I needed to get her and Laura out of this place; Oliver's and Simon's people being the least of our worries – something was happening. The atmosphere fair vibrated with a ghastly tension that reminded me of the feeling I'd had when finding the case holding Edward's inverted crucifix. I sliced through the ropes binding her wrists, then set to work on freeing Laura.

'Not them. He's one of ours,' I heard a voice shout as I helped Laura to her feet. I glanced around as a tall figure strode towards us and the two guns pointed our way were slowly lowered. 'Get them out of here.'

'Dan?' I heard Laura murmur.

Perhaps she was mistaken, either that or he didn't hear or maybe even decided to ignore her, but whatever the reason, he carried on past us.

One of the men in black gestured us towards the door, 'Sir,' while the others rushed to join their colleagues at the front. I looked over my shoulder as we were ushered towards the corridor and stairs leading to the poolroom. Most of the robed figures were on their knees. A few had lost their masks and I recognised at least one politician and a high-profile businessman amongst them. One or two were putting up a fight and I saw a rifle butt being smashed into the side of someone's head knocking him to the floor.

But it wasn't this that drew my attention. Behind the altar the air continued to shimmer, a scarlet swirling mist rising upwards, a figure taking shape. I strained my neck around as I was pushed into the corridor. A creature, a horned abomination, rose up above its captive worshippers.

It struggled to find substance, its body distorting and wavering as though tossed and turned by an unseen wind. For a split second it almost made it, losing its translucence and partly solidifying into a goat-headed travesty of a bare-chested man. It rose up on faun-like hairy legs, long, clawed fingers with talons like razors flexed and stretched, reaching out towards the oblivious military men below it.

'Dear Lord in heaven,' I muttered.

And maybe there is a God and he heard me.

A sudden gust of air came from nowhere, ruffling the hair and robes of the kneeling prisoners and causing the torches to flare. The creature blurred and twisted and, with a bellow of frustration, finally succumbed to the buffeting – and fell apart into a whirlwind of spiralling vapour that abruptly funnelled out through the cracks in the wall behind it.

I glanced around. No one else appeared to have seen or heard it, and then something else occurred to me.

'Where's Oliver?' I said, stopping dead and peering at the lines of robed figures kneeling in front of the altar. He wasn't there. I could see he wasn't there.

'This way, sir.'

'No,' I said. 'Oliver Pomeroy, their leader, he's gone.'

'If that's so, we'll find him,' the man said, his voice patient, but the grip on my arm anything but.

'Jed, come on,' Emma said. 'This isn't our battle any more.'

I hesitated a moment, straining against the man's insistent grip, then realised she was right. There were twenty or so men inside the chapel who were more than capable of dealing with Oliver and his followers.

* * *

In a daze we were escorted to the Jag and politely told to leave and that we would be 'debriefed' later in the morning.

'Did you see what I saw in the chapel?' I asked Emma as she slid into the car beside me.

She gave me a sideways frown, but didn't get the chance to reply as Laura clambered into the back seat and one of the men who had escorted us from the building slammed the door and then gave a rapid double bang on the roof to tell me to get going.

Dan's men had appeared blissfully unaware of anything strange happening. I had been so sure Oliver and his people had seen the creature from the way they had surged towards it, but had they? Was I reading something into their actions that wasn't the case? Perhaps they had been swarming towards their leader. I hoped this was so, if not . . . I didn't even want to think about it. I must have been hallucinating. I'd been drugged and stressed, I told myself, but . . . I pushed the thought aside, put my foot down and drove.

Wanting to put as much distance between us and Kingsmead as I could, I kept my foot on the throttle. Once we were on the main road home, I slowed down a tad, but didn't stop until we parked on the drive outside The Grange.

I phoned Brogan from there and it went straight to voicemail – again. I wondered if this was because he was busy at Kingsmead helping the men in black round up murderers or he was washing bloodstains out of silken robes. I decided I didn't care one way or another.

'Who were those men?' Emma asked. 'They certainly didn't look like policemen.'

'Intelligence,' I said.

'As in MI5?' Laura said.

'I think we should all try and get some sleep,' I said, not wanting to get into *that* discussion.

Emma frowned. 'Jed?' and both women looked at me expectantly.

I rubbed the bridge of my nose. 'Something like that,' I said. 'Simon's people.'

Emma stared at me for a few seconds and then, putting her arm around Laura's shoulders, went into hostess mode. 'Come on,' she said. 'Let's get you settled. We can discuss all this once we've had some sleep.' She glanced my way and I nodded. She and I did need to have a conversation, but it wasn't the sort we could have in front of Laura. Admitting to killing six people, five of them in cold blood, was going to be difficult and I didn't know what Emma would make of it.

The morning passed very slowly. I hadn't slept much, the events of the previous night and earlier that morning playing through my head again and again in angst-filled slow motion, while I tormented myself by questioning whether there was anything I could have done differently, perhaps resulting in one less death? And whether the stress of the past year and a half had finally got to me and I was now seeing monsters. By the time I gave up on sleep I was dyspeptic and out of sorts. The continual waiting for the axe to fall didn't help, and fall it would. Sometime soon there would be a knock on the door by people wanting answers to questions. Six of the dead were down to me and it was doubtful self-defence would be a good enough plea to get me out of the trouble this would bring. And, of course, there was Emma – how exactly did I tell her what I had done and, when I did, would it change the way she felt about me? It was something I would have to think on long and hard.

Emma and Laura were both pale and tired-looking and, after the initial attempts at conversation over the breakfast table, we all sank into the silence of our own thoughts.

When the ring at the door came all three of us jumped. Emma had phoned to give Tilly and Rachel the day off so, with a condemned man's leaden feet, I went to answer the door.

Through the bevelled glass panel there was the silhouette of only one shadowy figure waiting on the doorstep, which was cause to be optimistic. Dan as I'd never seen him before was waiting for me. Suited and booted he could have been another man altogether; he had definitely left his stable hand persona behind at Kingsmead.

He gave me a half-smile. 'I guessed you'd probably be here,' he said.

I pulled the door wide open and directed him towards the living room. The girls didn't need to hear any of this. 'I wasn't expecting to see *you* this morning,' I said.

He stopped in the centre of the room looking around. 'Nice place,' he commented.

'We like it.' I nodded towards a chair. 'Sit if you've a mind to.' He took a seat and I slumped in the chair opposite him. 'So, what can I do for you?'

'I'll get straight to the point,' he said. 'The powers that be have decided it would be the best for all concerned if the "occurrences"' – and he did the inverted commas thing with his fingers – 'of the last forty-eight hours never happened.'

I stared at him digesting what he'd said. 'But what about all the dead bodies piled up at Kingsmead?'

'What dead bodies?' he asked, with a smile that was bordering on a smirk. I stared at him. 'Come on, Jed, you worked for intelligence, you know how this goes.'

I did know and it was one of the reasons I'd eventually left. Doing wrong things, even if for the right reasons, had been making me someone I didn't want to be.

'I was working for *Sir* Simon Pomeroy' – he studied my expression – 'but then you probably knew that already. He was a good man, a great man who served his country well. He doesn't deserve to have his reputation tarnished by members of his family with psychological problems.'

'There were at least eight bodies that I'm aware of. And what about Oliver Pomeroy?'

'Oliver Pomeroy died weeks ago.'

'Do you have him? Do you have him in custody?'

Dan's lips pressed into a thin line. 'If you must know, Oliver Pomeroy was found dead this morning, in the grounds of Kingsmead.'

'But . . . How? Was he shot trying to escape?'

'If I said I didn't know how he died it would be the truth.' He hesitated and leant forward. Lowering his voice, he said, 'All I can say is, and this is strictly off the record, some of his injuries were a bit like his brother's. He was slashed to ribbons, although it was more like he'd been mauled than stabbed.'

'But how?' I stopped as an image of long talons sprouting from knotted, claw-like fingers flexing and stretching in the flickering torchlight floated through my head. I closed my eyes for a moment. No, it had been my imagination. It must have been. I suddenly felt very weary. 'What about Oliver's mistress? What about Mrs Walters?'

'Mrs Walters took her own life. She never got over her daughter's suicide and in the end she couldn't go on.'

'And Tanith Bloxborough?'

'Who?'

I leant back in my chair unable to comprehend how they thought they could sweep so many deaths under the carpet. 'Someone will miss the people who have died.'

He shrugged. 'Not if no one makes a fuss.' He looked me straight in the eye. 'Are you going to make a fuss, Jed?'

I opened my mouth to protest and then closed it again. I wasn't proud of what I'd done, though I'd do it again if I had to, but I didn't want to end up spending years in court trying to prove I was only protecting my wife and a young woman who was being targeted by a madman through no fault of her own.

'I guess not,' he said, and the smirk was gone. Like me, he looked tired and out of sorts. I wasn't sure he shouldn't still be in hospital. His complexion had a pallid, oily look to it.

'What about the other members of the Order of the Blood?'

'Never heard of it.' He hesitated. 'But, if I had, I'd say all the members who had wanted it to continue are gone and are very unlikely to return.' He paused again. 'What you have to understand is most of the people involved were as much victims as Sir Simon and Laura Simmons.'

'But not all,' I said, remembering the increased congregation. There had been some powerful men amongst them.

'There will be one or two members of Parliament resigning over the next week or so and the chairman of a global company stepping down from his position. The local police chief constable will also be taking a leave of absence with his resignation to follow, but at least Sir Simon's good name won't be besmirched.'

I didn't like to disillusion him where Simon was concerned. He was far from innocent, although in all fairness to him he had broken away, apparently very successfully, until Oliver had dragged him back. And why he'd done that and then killed his younger brother I guessed I'd never know. It could have been because he was snooping. Sadly, I had an inkling the most likely explanation was that a random act of kindness by the staff of Goldsmere House had quite literally signed Simon's death warrant. Had they not sent Edward Pomeroy a birthday card Simon would have been none the wiser, and after settling Laura into her new home would have left Kingsmead, leaving Laura to her fate.

Now for the million-dollar question. 'Was Brogan Oliver's mole in the police?'

Dan grinned. 'As it happens, no. Brogan is as straight as a die. The mole was far higher up the food chain.'

'But there were pictures of Brogan and Tanith together,' I said.

'I know. I took them.'

'You?' I asked in disbelief.

'For Sir Simon. It was Tanith he was interested in. She had been enticing some pretty high-profile people into the Order and Sir Simon realised it had to stop, whatever the consequences to himself. When he found out she was having an affair with a serving detective inspector it piqued his interest.' He sighed. 'Then, upon returning home after a brief visit to Kingsmead, he discovered several pages had been extracted out of his files, including photographs of Brogan and Tanith together . . . Where did you find them, by the way?'

'They were hidden in Edward's old room,' I said, my head spinning.

'Makes sense. Sir Simon thought Oliver had stolen them, but once he found out Edward was still alive, he guessed it could be him. He'd gone to Edward's room to search for them when he came across Tanith. It was Tanith who bashed him on the head.'

'He told you that?'

He pulled a face. 'Sadly no, not in person. I didn't find out until after I'd spoken to you about Suzie. He'd left a coded message with his things, as a precaution. He guessed Tanith was desperate to find the photographs and would do almost anything to get hold of them before Oliver did – as it turned out he was right.'

'But why?'

He shrugged. 'He'd split up with his wife for her, murdered for her, most probably; he would do anything for her, but he was as jealous as sin. My theory is Edward was toying with her, telling her he'd spill the beans and show Oliver the photos and that's why she convinced Oliver that Edward had to die.'

I slumped back in my seat, thinking of the photographs Edward had taken of Tanith in the shower. I thought they were more than likely the ones she didn't want getting into Oliver's hands. Edward had seduced Oliver's first wife, Tanith having an affair with Edward was something Oliver would have treated as the ultimate betrayal. I didn't bother to correct Dan. It no longer mattered. All three of them were dead. 'So this was all about sex, jealousy and revenge?'

'And money – don't forget the money. With Laura dead the estate would pass to the next in line to inherit.'

'Who was?'

He raised an eyebrow. 'Who do you think?'

I frowned at him for a moment. 'Tanith?' The look he gave me was enough.

We sat there in silence for a couple of minutes. My mind was all over the place. I couldn't believe all that had happened was down to Oliver's jealousy, Tanith's greed and their hedonistic desires and obsession with the Order of the Blood. I tried not to think of the ghastly apparition I had seen. It was down to stress – it had to have been – such things didn't exist, but the memory of the cloven hoof prints Emma had found pressed into the mud back at the clearing wouldn't go away. I told myself they proved nothing – it was what I had to believe. If not, madness beckoned.

'You will convince Emma it's for the best that this whole mess never happened?' Dan said, dragging me back to reality.

'I'll try,' I said.

He reached inside his breast pocket and drew out an envelope and placed it on the table between us. 'Sir Simon also left this. He wrote it to you while he was in hospital. He left a note saying to give it to you should anything happen to him.'

The envelope was of the same ivory, high-quality stationery as the one that had started this whole bloody thing. On the front I could see my name scrawled in Simon's familiar handwriting.

'So, is that it?'

'There will be a document for you and Emma to sign. No doubt I don't have to remind you that you've already signed the Official Secrets Act?'

I grunted my reply. The Official fucking Secrets Act. 'No, you don't have to remind me,' I said and couldn't help the bitter edge to my voice.

Dan stared at me for a very long time, I suspect only seconds, but it felt much longer, like I was in a vacuum and it wouldn't be until he had made his mind up about me that I'd be able to breathe again. 'Is Miss Simmons about?' he eventually asked, bringing air back into the room.

'Er, yes,' I said, getting to my feet. 'I'll go and get her.'

After Dan left, Laura asked for some time alone and went to sit in the garden, while Emma rustled up something for us to eat and I broke the news of what Dan had said.

'So, that's it?' she said, chopping an onion with probably more force than was necessary. 'Simon, Brandon and all those poor young women dead and everyone involved gets off scot-free?'

'Not everyone, Emms. Oliver and Tanith are dead, and they were the main instigators. Them and Edward.'

'I suppose so,' Emma said, scraping the onion from the chopping board into the pan. 'Do you think Laura will return to Kingsmead?'

I shrugged. 'It's hers now.'

'If I was her, I'm not sure if I'd ever feel safe there.'

I wrapped my arms around her as she stood at the stove

and nuzzled her neck. 'I would never let anything bad happen to you.'

She leant her head against mine and reached up to stroke my cheek. 'I know,' she said and from the tone of her voice I wondered just how much she did know – or suspect about what I'd done the previous night. She had seen the blood on my clothing, she'd heard what Oliver had said about Sebastien and his mate. Sadly, she probably knew much more than I'd have liked.

CHAPTER THIRTY-THREE

I didn't open the envelope from Simon straight away. I couldn't. My feelings towards him were too raw.

'You are going to have to read it sometime,' Emma said, after three days of the letter sitting unopened on the coffee table.

'I will when I'm ready,' I mumbled and was saved from whatever Emma was going to say in response by Laura wandering into the room.

She sat down opposite us and leant forward, hands linked together, as if in prayer. She had the look of a woman with something to say. Emma rested her hand on my knee.

'Emma, Jed . . .' she hesitated, swallowing. 'It's been lovely staying with you, it really has, but I really should return to Kingsmead now.'

'You know you can stay here as long as you want,' Emma said.

Laura bit her lip. 'I know and I could stay here for

ever, it's so peaceful, but if I don't go back now I don't think I ever will.'

I knew how she felt. 'Like getting back onto Angel after your fall,' I said.

She gave me a tiny smile. 'Yes, exactly like getting back onto Angel.'

Dan was outside the front of Kingsmead speaking to DI Brogan when we arrived there the following day. Neither looked particularly happy.

'You are here as a professional courtesy because Peters was officially one of yours,' I heard Dan say. 'Don't make me regret allowing you access.'

Brogan went to reply, but Dan abruptly turned his back on him and stalked away, leaving the policeman red-faced and fuming.

I acknowledged him as we passed, but I didn't have anything to say to him either. In fact, Emma and I couldn't talk to him about much even had we wanted to. We had both received and signed documents delivered by courier precluding us from ever speaking about what had happened at Kingsmead to anyone ever again. Emma's comment as she signed had been that she wanted nothing more than to forget all about it and who would believe us anyway.

It was weird when the front door opened. Maddy was waiting for us as if nothing had ever happened, though she was now dressed in the black dress of a housekeeper with the bunch of house keys dangling from her belt. The floppy-haired lad was hovering in the background and I was strangely relieved to see he'd made it through that night.

There were quite a few hard-faced men, in black military-style uniforms, with automatic weapons wandering around the place and not another police officer to be seen. I was greeted with unexpected deference from some of them and a couple even cracked a smile of hello.

All our belongings had been packed and sent to us, but Emma wanted to double-check our room 'just in case' and, while she took one last look around, I helped Laura take her suitcase upstairs.

'Are you absolutely sure about this?' I asked her as I dumped her bag next to the bed.

Her smile was heartbreaking. 'I have nowhere else to go,' she said.

'You can always—'

'I know. You and Emma have been so kind, but I have to do this – or at least try. If I don't – well, I'll always have regrets of what might have been.'

'If you need us, you know where we are.'

A tear overflowed onto her cheek and she pulled me into a hug. 'Thank you,' she murmured against my chest. 'Thank you so very much.'

I gave her an awkward hug back. She'd be all right. As I'd surmised, she was a little toughie.

'If you wouldn't mind, I'd quite like to go and say goodbye to the horses,' I said to Laura once we'd returned downstairs. Dan was in the hall chatting to a couple of the men in black, but from the sideways glances he was giving Laura it was obvious why he was hanging around.

'Of course,' she said, and I got the impression she would be glad to be rid of me for a few minutes so they could talk alone.

* * *

The stable yard was deserted, with not even the Land Rover or motorbike anywhere to be seen or a radio playing in the background. I thought this would mean I'd be alone in the stable block, but when I went inside Donald Walters was mucking out Satan's stall.

He looked my way upon hearing me enter and leant the shovel he'd been using against the wheelbarrow.

'Morning,' he said.

I couldn't help but feel sorry for the man. His face was pale and drawn, his eyes bloodshot and swollen. 'Should you really be working?' I asked.

He managed a grimace of a smile. 'Best I keep busy and these beasts are good company.'

I stopped by Jericho's stall to scratch his head and make a bit of a fuss of him. I'd miss the lad and hoped Emms and I might get the occasional invite to visit so I'd have the chance to see him again.

'I'm sorry for your loss,' I said.

Another grimace. 'I lost my wife fifteen odd years ago when Lily died. She never got over it, not really.'

'And she held Tanith responsible?'

He nodded. 'Neither of us blamed young William and Martine for running off together. Who would? We'd have run off too, if we'd had half the chance, were going to when we'd saved enough, but then that woman . . .' He sucked in a breath and shook his head. 'Cruel bitch she was. Insisted the ceremony go ahead and as Lily was the right age . . .' His eyes filled with tears. 'Tanith talked her into it. Made it sound like an honour and that she'd for ever be special. Lily said she'd do it. She didn't realise, didn't understand and I couldn't stop her.

I couldn't save my little girl. I was too weak. Weak and scared.' He swiped at his eyes. 'Then Mr Oliver found William and Martine and . . . you know. Oliver wanted the child, little Miss Laura, dead as well, but although Mr Edward said he'd done it, we found out later she was still alive. It wasn't 'til a few years ago that we found out why. She was Edward's child.'

'Edward's? But Oliver thought she was his granddaughter.'

Walters laughed out loud. 'No, he thought she was his daughter. They were all as bad as each other, dipping their wicks where they weren't wanted. That's why they ran. Martine was a nice girl, but too pretty for her own good.'

Then I remembered what Oliver had said about Martine. It hadn't clicked at the time. She had told William and Oliver that the child was theirs, when she wasn't either's. 'Shit,' I muttered.

'When Tanith fucking Bloxborough found out she was still alive she wouldn't let it rest. She wanted her dead and Oliver would give her anything.'

'But wasn't he married?'

Walters looked at me as though I was simple. 'Tanith was always there. Always. Oliver only married again to get her attention, but she didn't care. Then Tanith crooked her little finger and the wife disappeared. He said she walked out' – he gave a bitter smile – 'but we guessed she'd gone somewhere she'd not be coming back from.'

As he was in the mood for talking, I thought I'd try asking some of the questions that had been bothering me.

'The effigy on the bonfire and the gunshots causing Angel to bolt – who was that down to?'

He folded his arms. 'Sarah couldn't bear to see yet another young woman destroyed by the Pomeroys. We hoped the burnt effigy would do it. The morning after the ceremony I went back and stuck it on the fire and I intended for Dan to go to the clearing so it'd be found, but he was being difficult. As it turned out he ended up there anyway with you and Miss Laura. When this didn't have the desired effect of getting her to leave, Sarah gave Angel some herbs to make her jumpy and I fired the shotgun.'

'Laura could have been killed.'

'Better that than what Oliver and Tanith had in store for her.'

I supposed he was right, but they'd taken a big chance with her life. I let it go. The man had just lost his wife and, when all was said and done, Laura was alive and well and hopefully out of danger.

I had one more question. 'Did Edward kill Oliver's first wife?' I asked. 'Is that why they put him away?'

Walters slowly shook his head. 'That's what Oliver would have had everyone believe and yes, it was why the Pomeroys had their eldest son locked away, but Constance's death wasn't down to Edward.' His eyes crinkled at the corners as though he was remembering. 'Sarah was in the hall when it happened. She saw it all. The thing you have to understand about Edward is that he was like a spoilt child. If he wanted something, he had to have it. Sadly for Oliver, Edward wanted Constance. The day she died she foolishly told Oliver that the child she was carrying wasn't his. Oliver was incandescent. They fought and he deliberately pushed her and she fell. Sarah slipped away, terrified at what she'd witnessed and too scared to tell a soul but me. If she had,

406

her and I would have been long gone, and I don't mean to pastures new – Oliver would have seen us dead.'

In retrospect I wished I'd never asked. Simon's elder brothers were both psychopaths, and in my opinion their no longer being in this world was a blessing to everyone who remained.

I patted Jericho's head and fed him a lump of sugar. 'Will Laura be safe here now?' I asked.

He picked up the shovel. 'Yes. There's no one here that'll harm her. In fact, most of us will for ever bless the day she came. Here starts a new era. One without the Order of the Blood hanging over us like an axe waiting to fall.'

I met Emma on the way back to the house. 'I've just seen Donald Walters,' I told her.

'How's he holding up?'

'Too early to say, but we had a long talk about Edward, Oliver and Tanith.'

She shivered. 'Tell me about it when we get home,' she said, linking her arm through mine. 'I think I've had enough of them to be getting on with.'

When we got back to The Grange, I took Simon's letter out to the conservatory with a large glass of malt. When I finished reading it, I slumped back in the chair to look out onto the garden and listen to the peacocks' mournful cries. They didn't help my melancholy state of mind. The letter had mostly been an apology.

He confirmed much of what Dan had told me and assumed, if I was reading the letter, he was dead and we hadn't had the chance to speak as he'd intended. He said he was sorry for involving me and then leaving me to pick up the pieces. He was also sorry if he had put Emma and me in danger, but when he'd written to me, he had believed Oliver was dead and had genuinely only wanted my help to find out who had murdered him. When he realised he wasn't, he hoped I'd help him protect Laura as he had, unbeknownst to her, for years.

It was he who, upon hearing of William's and Martine's deaths, had arranged for Laura to be whisked away and put into the care of June Simmons, one of his former operatives and fully trained in protection duties. He'd had Laura's name changed to Simmons and hoped he had done enough to keep her safe. He didn't straight out say he knew who had killed his nephew and his wife, he didn't have to. His actions spoke louder than any words.

He then told me how a young man called Dan Foley had approached him, aggressively demanding his help in finding out what had happened to his sister. Simon was so impressed by Dan he had recruited him on the understanding that if he worked for his department he would, when the time was right, have him inserted into the staff at Kingsmead as part of an ongoing investigation into corruption in high places, sexual abuse and murder. His brief was to report back on untoward activities in the household and any high-profile visitors. While he was there if he could get any leads on his sister's disappearance, then all well and good. And, as I read, it became quite clear that, despite what I might think about Simon's use or misuse of his power, he had been investigating the Order of the Blood and his own family for a very long time, to try and put a stop to an obscene cult, which had many influential people within its ranks.

The catalyst that finally put the wheels in motion for its ultimate demise came when June Simmons died leaving Laura alone and unprotected. Simon immediately arranged for the disappearance of a member of staff at Kingsmead and for Dan, by this time a seasoned and senior operative, to apply for the resultant position. He then had another of his team, a serving police officer, Sam Peters, promoted to detective sergeant and transferred to the local force.

When Simon heard of Oliver's alleged death in such horrific circumstances, he thought it at last signalled the end of the Order. His relief was short-lived. Upon learning of the contents of his brother's will, alarm bells began to ring and he immediately dropped everything to return to Kingsmead; that he had been diagnosed with a debilitating heart condition bolstered his resolve to rip out the disease infecting his family home – the Order of the Blood. Then, of course, the birthday card arrived and, after speaking to Alice Barnard at Goldsmere, Simon had guessed what Oliver had done and how he was more than likely still alive. Simon had identified what he thought had been Oliver's body and explained how it wouldn't have been difficult for Oliver to convince him, and the world, it was his remains that had been found in the clearing. Edward and he were of a similar build, they both wore a signet ring bearing the family crest and they both had the same tattoo on their left shoulder. The clincher of course was that he thought Edward had died forty years ago. Simon realised there must have been a reason for Oliver to go to so much trouble and, knowing what he did about Laura's parents' deaths, he was sure Laura's life *was* in real danger too.

All this was relayed in Simon's typical dispassionate way until he spoke of Laura. *I will not let my beautiful grandniece join her parents. Protect her for me if you can.* And his final message to me: *Jed, I know I haven't always been the friend I should have been or the man you wanted me to be. All I can say to you is you have always been, and always will be, my greatest friend. Never has there been a man I have respected more than I have respected you, and by coming to my aid, despite the way we parted and when you had no reason or need to, has proved to me that never has the old adage of blood being thicker than water been more untrue. As usual you put a friend's needs before your own. With my sincere thanks for being my friend when I needed you most. Your old 'mate', Simon.*

His words set me to remembering how we had parted all those years ago. Reggie had warned me. 'All that matters to Simon is the endgame,' he'd said. 'The people who could possibly die are just collateral damage.'

I'd argued Simon knew what he was doing and we hadn't had any casualties. Reggie had grunted. 'Not yet,' was his reply.

Almost two years later, when what Reggie had said was inevitable happened, Simon's and my friendship came to an abrupt end.

We had been keeping tabs on a possible terrorist cell and had managed to infiltrate the group. We were almost ready to move in and I had argued for a young, female undercover operative to be extracted. It had been getting too dangerous and we had all of the intel we needed. Simon had disagreed. Just two days later her communications

410

stopped. I went against Simon's orders and took a team in to raid the place. We were too late – much too late. She had died terribly – torture and rape being the least of it. Her presence had been there waiting for me. She asked what had taken us so long. I didn't know how to reply other than to tell her I was sorry. She slowly faded away, but her bewildered expression of betrayal stayed with me for a very long time afterwards.

I had been beyond angry. She was one of ours and she was dead. When we got back, I'd stormed into Simon's office and said quite a few things I probably shouldn't have, my tirade ending with me shouting at him that I was resigning and him shouting back, 'Good', it would save him sacking me.

The last time I'd seen him was when I'd handed my letter of resignation to his secretary. His door was open and he was on the phone inside his office, laughing and joking with some high-ranking caller, I imagined. I saw his eyes alight on me and the letter I was handing her. His nostrils flared and a flicker of anger crossed his face before he turned his back on me, and that was the bit that hurt. We had been friends and he'd shown how little he thought of me with that one gesture – or so I thought. I walked out of the building and never went back.

I reached into my pocket and pulled out the photograph of him, Reggie and me. The one I'd purloined from his bedroom. The picture he'd kept for all those years, while any of his two brothers he had not.

Emma found me watching the sun go down with an empty glass and eyes full of tears. She didn't ask – just went and brought the bottle and poured us both a large one.

'To Simon,' she said, clinking her glass against mine and raising it to the photograph perched on the table.

As if in reply a lone peacock's cry floated across the garden, as the first drops of rain for over two weeks pattered against the conservatory roof.

I gazed down at the faces of the three young men in the photograph. Happy and laughing, we'd been at the beginning of our lives. Reggie had his arm around my shoulders, I was grinning at Simon, pulling back as he reached out as though to ruffle my hair. Me and my best buds in the world.

'To Simon,' I said, raising my glass, 'and friendship,' and I'm not sure whether it was wishful thinking, but I thought I heard a voice whisper, '*Cheers.*'

ACKNOWLEDGEMENTS

I have often heard it said that being a writer is a lonely profession. Funnily enough I have never found this to be the case. I am, by nature, an introverted person and actually quite shy, but since becoming a published writer I have met a tremendous number of people, some of whom I can now call friends. Being a writer is being part of a community and a very welcoming one it is too. So firstly I would like to say thank you to all my fellow writers who, whether online or in person, have been supportive in my endeavours. You know who you are.

I would also like to thank my lovely agent, Heather Adams of the HMA Literary Agency. I have learnt a lot from her, and I couldn't wish for a nicer person to work with on my novels.

I would also like to thank the team at Allison & Busby, in particular Susie Dunlop, Lesley Crooks and my wonderful, and very patient, editor, Kelly Smith.

And finally I really should thank the person who has to put up with me on a day-to-day basis, my husband, and best of friends, Howard. He has no real idea of what I do or why I do it, and yet he is always there to support me and give me a confidence boost should I need one. He also makes a mean cup of coffee! Cheers m'dear.

S. M. HARDY grew up in south London and worked in banking for many years. She has now given up the day job to allegedly spend more time with her husband; he, however, has noticed that an awful lot more writing appears to be going on. She currently lives in Devon.

smhardy.co.uk   @SueTingey